The Crevasse

by

Amy Craig

The Crevasse

Contact Information: info@thewildrosepress.com

Cover Art by *Diana Carlile*

The Wild Rose Press, Inc.
PO Box 708
Adams Basin, NY 14410-0708
Visit us at www.thewildrosepress.com

Publishing History
First Edition, 2023
Trade Paperback ISBN 978-1-5092-4976-3
Digital ISBN 978-1-5092-4977-0

Published in the United States of America

"I'm glad you wrote down my number."

"I memorized it," he said.

She stopped buckling her seatbelt. "You did?"

"How long did we work together, Vivi?"

"At least a year." She secured the belt and juggled the folders in her tote. "That feels like a lifetime ago."

"And before that, you were with Johann. I kept an eye on you."

She wondered if Damon still saw her as an obligation.

He cleared his throat. "Mama Clarke's hosting a low-key welcome home party this afternoon. You should come."

"It's Friday. I have meetings." Her faint excuse sounded like a new hire's response to onboarding documents. What was the point of having millions of dollars and running her own company if her meeting schedule ruled her life? She started the car and waited for the vehicle to connect to her phone. "I might be late, but I'll be there as soon as possible."

"Really?" he asked.

"Why do you sound so shocked? Aren't we friends?" She held her breath, waiting for his reply. She missed their easy camaraderie, and the withdrawal left her feeling uncertain.

"Of course, we're friends. It's us against Silvia."

"Um"—she cleared her throat—"Silvia and I are friends now, too."

"It's a trap," he said. "You know she sleeps with one eye open."

"She's picking you up from jail!" His deep, booming laugh chased away her inhibitions. No matter what had happened in jail, Damon had returned.

Praise for Amy Craig

"Amy Craig has a way of drawing you into cozy, small-town worlds full of friendly people where romance blossoms."

~Pamela Jonas

~*~

"I just recently discovered Amy Craig and I can't seem to get enough of her writing."

~C Biby

~*~

"This is the first book (THE PENINSULA) I've read by Amy Craig, but I'll be looking out for more. I really enjoyed her writing style."

~Long and Short Reviews

~*~

"THE PENINSULA was a great romantic suspense. The story moves along fairly quickly, with plenty of twists along the way. It isn't immediately obvious who's behind the death, and I appreciate how well Craig weaves the suspense into the story and keeps you guessing."

~Liliyana Shadowlyn

Acknowledgments

Writing novels outside your direct experience is a risk, and I appreciate the members of Writers for Diversity. The members of the Facebook group are committed to helping authors create diverse worlds and characters through education and awareness. By no means does the group "endorse" my novel, but when I had questions and needed a safe place for hard questions and respectful dialogue, I appreciated the aid they rendered. I hope I can contribute to their ongoing dialogue. I would also like to take this opportunity to thank Leanne Morgena, Senior Editor at The Wild Rose Press, for training me to be a better writer.

Chapter One

Being the CEO of Hoat Analytics made Vivian a ridiculous amount of money, but she remembered her Central Valley roots. Before she amassed millions of dollars, she toiled over takeout containers, wrecked her posture at a desk, and ran errands for a rich, handsome asshole. Leaving the California Central Valley took nerves, but her Palo Alto gambles paid off, and data analytics made her a wealthy woman. Some days, the meetings never stopped, and her feet ached from wearing high heels, but she came so far that she refused to look back.

A knock sounded on her office door.

She looked up from her files and pushed back from her desk.

Michael, her company's first employee, stuck his head into the office.

She appreciated his work performance, but she struggled to understand his aesthetic. His premature-white topknot contrasted with an ironic blue blazer. If she had to guess, his navy-and-white-striped sweater came from a local thrift shop. *I don't understand why he dresses like an off-Broadway shipwrecked sailor.* Picking up her coffee cup, she sipped the cold brew and tilted her head. "What's up?"

"The Steadman contract is raking me over the coals." Michael slipped inside the door and leaned against the glass wall separating her office from the hallway. Crossing his arms over his chest, he kicked out one loafer-clad foot. No socks.

She remembered the day she hired him and the leap of faith he took joining her start-up company. Her employees were more than personnel numbers, but each hire felt like a step closer to accomplishing financial freedom. One—Michael Williams. Two—Valentina Harding. Three—Isaac Martin. She knew the list by heart, but her photographic memory scared people. Putting her coffee back on a coaster, she crossed her arms on the desk. "The Steadman Group is suing us for a breach of contract."

"They keep bringing up a verbal agreement," he said. "They want to own all the resulting intellectual property we developed while working on their projects."

"Of course, they want to claim it." She pushed her chair back from the desk and stood. The Steadman Group developed a mobile-centric carbon management platform that enabled small-scale farms to improve their efficiency and sustainability, but the firm depended on Hoat Analytics to feed data into their system.

Although she regularly worked offsite and discussed business over meals, she took meticulous notes. If she offered Steadman's CEO a slice of IP, she would remember the offer. Looking toward the hive of agile workers performing data analytics beyond her office, she knew she had to retain their innovations.

When she came onsite, office hijinks amused her, but her staff capitalized on her presence and brought her petty problems. Taking initiative produced better results. She pulled dead leaves off a ficus tree and made a small pile on the windowsill. "If Steadman's CEO wants our data analysis, he has to respect our trade secrets. Any process improvements belong to us."

Michael clicked a pen. "That's what I told their project manager."

"Good." She wondered how aggressively to prune the tree. Cutting away too much character led to streamlined processes, but she needed more than mid-level performance. She swept the pile of leaves into a hand and trusted Michael's ability to grow into his role. "Don't bend. If they keep pushing, call our IP attorney and let him go to war on our behalf."

Michael wrinkled his nose. "He's expensive."

She let the stiff, brown leaves flutter into her office trashcan. *I built my firm into a nimble, Silicon Valley resource. People come to me for business intelligence and big data analytics. If they think I'm a pushover, they haven't done their research.* Dusting clean her hands, she shrugged off Michael's apprehension. "We can afford his fees. If we make exceptions for the Steadman Group, or anyone else, we'll fail." She tilted her head. "We don't fail."

"No, we don't." Grinning, Michael turned and walked toward the office door.

Assuring herself she wasn't the worst boss in the world, she hummed the intro to *South Pacific* and waited for Michael to raise any remaining issues.

Silvia barged into the office. "Here you are! Why aren't you home? Have you eaten?"

Vivian wondered how her friend passed security, but she tabled that issue for another time. Instead of kicking the diminutive, sixty-year-old woman and her tight, black bun out of the office, Vivian worked her jaw and enjoyed an overdose of Silvia's old-school perfume. The sweet, light citrusy scent was perfect for weekend adventures and reminded her of the softness behind Silvia's focused gaze and furrowed brow. After witnessing Johann's marriage to Hadley, Silvia, his housekeeper, promoted herself to his executive assistant and started a lifestyle blog that raked in copious advertising profits. When Silvia wanted something, nothing stood in her way.

Michael pantomimed calling security.

Vivian ignored his offer. He knew Silvia as well as he knew the downstairs barista.

Michael sighed.

Kissing Vivian's cheek, Silvia turned, crossed her arms over her chest, and jerked her head toward Michael. "Why's Captain Millennial here? Does he need you to tie his shoes?"

"I can hear you." Michael rubbed his eyebrows and sighed. "I'll tackle the Steadman contract and follow up on the team chat for any support needs."

"Perfect," Vivian said. "Thanks."

Saluting, he backed out of the office.

Silvia perched on the desk's edge and crossed her arms. "You usually work from home. I braved downtown parking to find you."

"Noted." Gathering up her belongings, Vivian replayed the meetings that pulled her into the office. The firm's problems wore down her reserves, but she genuinely liked her employees and their quirky habits. As the company grew, business demands created distance, and she missed the long nights that helped launch the start-up. One day, she would find the balance between friendship and authority. In the meantime, she let Silvia boss her around like a domineering grandma because she missed having older relatives in her life. She closed her leather tote and hung it over her shoulder. "You know I can't run a company from a bungalow."

"You could have fooled me." Silvia reapplied her lipstick in a pocket mirror. "Based on my observations, you rarely leave home."

Vivian shrugged off the reproach and looked out the window. Spring's longer days gave her time to work, return to the bungalow, and walk Precious before putting in more hours in front of a computer. "What was so urgent you needed to find me?"

"I have news." Silvia dropped her lipstick into her purse and rubbed her palms. "Good news!"

Setting down her tote, Vivian tilted her head. She could use good news.

"Damon Clarke's getting out of jail!"

Vivian clapped her hands and wrapped Silvia in a hug. "That's great news!" She missed Damon's easy smile. No matter the circumstances, he carried himself with pride and an enviable amount of self-confidence. While she and Damon worked for Johann, she suppressed her interest—despite being fascinated by Damon's energy and defined muscles— and focused on laying the groundwork for Hoat Analytics.

When she watched Damon go to jail for reselling stolen goods, she tried to help him, but he pushed aside her efforts. Respecting his choices, she gave him space, but on his birthday, she had caved and called him. His terse responses seemed at odds with the jocular, handsome man she knew. Deflated, she set down the

5

phone and had stared out the window at the sparkling Pacific Ocean. She might be a decade older than him, but success in her thirties might have sucked too much joy and spontaneity from her life. *He'll make it through his incarceration, but I worry about his heart. Can he see the ocean?*

"We should throw him a welcome home party," Silvia said.

Vivian remembered the last time she reached out to Damon and straightened. She smoothed her dress and tamped down her enthusiasm for his homecoming. He had a family and friends who loved him. Her affection for him and Silvia's enthusiasm for throwing parties shouldn't dominate his homecoming. "I don't think that's a good idea."

Silvia frowned.

Picking up her tote, Vivian beckoned Silvia out of the office. "Let Damon make the first move. When he wants to see us, he'll let us know."

"Of course, he wants to see us!"

Vivian had her doubts. Maybe she should have done more to help him legitimize his charity schemes. If she'd pushed harder, would he have given up his side gig and focused on a nine-to-five job? She was so focused on her dreams she worried she failed her friend. Burying her doubts, she adopted her confident smile, waved goodbye to staffers, and made her way to the elevator.

Silvia hustled to keep up.

Vivian slowed her pace to accommodate the shorter woman's stride.

The elevator chimed.

Stepping inside, Vivian held the door.

Silvia waited until the doors closed. "I'm picking him up from jail."

The confession unleashed a dam of disappointment, and Vivian let Damon's rejection wash over her. Mama Clarke, his mother, ran a convenience store and rarely drove more than a mile from her house. If Silvia had been Damon's second choice, Vivian had to respect his decision. Instead of letting Silvia's admission fell her, she pulled out her phone and focused on business. "Give him my regards. Whatever he needs, we'll make sure he has it." She looked up. "Right?"

Silvia deepened her frown. "Whatever he needs?"

Stepping free of the office building, Vivian took a deep breath and watched evening settle over Palo Alto. A light mist encouraged sweatshirts, warm drinks, and lingering conversations, but she rubbed her arms. This town ate ambitious people, and she refused to get distracted and be the next course. "I don't want to overstep my bounds."

"That's the problem with you, Vivian. You're laced tighter than a nun's corset." Shaking her head, Silvia muttered in Spanish and left Vivian standing alone on the sidewalk.

Do nuns wear corsets? Self-conscious, Vivian unlocked her electric car, settled into the driver's seat, and turned on a pop music stream. In the car, nobody cared whether her deodorant failed halfway through the afternoon or her firm made quarterly profits. Silvia was right. She was high-strung, but people depended on her, and she had too much to lose.

She followed the glowing streetlights through the city's leafy shadows. Mid-rise buildings gave way to orderly residential blocks, green lawns, and subdued wealth. Anywhere in the country, she could afford a mansion, but she treasured her Palo Alto bungalow.

Parking in her home's driveway, she examined the tidy, white house. Landscape lighting flooded the lawn. Upward-pointing lights illuminated oaks and created shadows on the walls, but the lights gave her a sense of security. A swaying porch swing gave her an excuse to enjoy afternoon breezes.

Before she sprang for the property, she rented it and savored the house's grace and serenity. When tree branches brushed the structure's leaded glass windows, she recalled almond trees groaning in the wind on her family's farm. She had come a long way from her childhood bedroom. Her pastel coverlet and desktop computer remained in the old farmhouse, but her agricultural roots tethered her past like the ropes on a hot-air balloon, and she wondered where she would be in five years. *Were the years of drudgery at a global consulting firm worth the loss of developing a community? Am I enjoying my life, or am I working too hard?*

Using a key fob to open the bungalow's front door, she slipped off her turquoise heels. A blown glass dish waited on the foyer table. She dropped her keys in the dish and placed her tote on a lower shelf. Hearing Precious bark from the kitchen, she quickened her step. "I'm home!"

The rescued Welsh Springer Spaniel spent most of her day sleeping beneath backyard trees. A dog walker checked on her at midday and crated her before the afternoon heat intensified. At thirteen years old, an ashen mask muted the animal's bold red-and-white markings, but Precious could hear a pin drop. She belonged to the bungalow's former owners, but when their health deteriorated, they asked if Precious could come home.

Vivian crouched until she could make eye contact with her pet. "Did you miss me?"

The geriatric dog wrinkled her nose and shoved her white snout against the grate.

Opening the crate, she scratched the old girl's chin. "I'm sorry I'm late."

Precious licked her face. Her strong eye twitched.

"I know, you forgive me." The dog's whiskers tickled her skin, and she pulled back. Taking care of a pet had terrified her, but she had learned to appreciate the dog's simple affection. The dog walker sent text messages with updates, and Precious had a good day. She stepped back and swept her arm toward the room. "Your kingdom awaits."

Precious ambled out of the crate and stretched.

Vivian reached for the white ceramic jar sitting on a honed marble countertop. Uncapping the jar, she offered Precious a treat and scratched her pet's ears. The dog's soft fur soothed away some of her stress.

Taking the treat without nipping Vivian's fingers, Precious settled onto a sheepskin rug near the computer and buried her muzzle in the white wool.

I wish I could wind down that easily. Vivian opened the refrigerator. Shelves held prepared meals from Metabolic Minds. The compostable trays hid exotic, vegetable-laden entrees. Sparkling water, white wine, and bottles of green juice occupied a lower shelf, but nothing looked good. *I want cheese and crackers. Why don't I ever buy the indulgences?*

She eyed a can of whipped cream and a jar of stuffed olives waiting in the door compartment. The ingredients were for Irish Coffees and martinis, but she struggled to remember the last time she invited someone over for drinks. Instead of making herself a festive cocktail, she pulled a quinoa salad from the shelf. *After work tomorrow, I'll pick up a pizza.* Remembering her schedule, she shook a small carton of vinaigrette dressing and bumped pizza to late-night delivery. *Precious will be thrilled to help me eat it.*

Precious thumped her tail against the sheepskin rug.

A glass of wine eased the day's tension from Vivian's shoulders and added a modicum of flavor to her quinoa entree. Picking up her heels, she walked down the hall to the extra bedroom she used as a closet. Shelves lined the far wall. She placed her heels in spot fifty-two, stripped off her sleeveless suit-dress, and hung up the garment. The cotton pajama pants and loose shirt she slipped on felt like a breeze against her skin. Adding a pair of soft leather moccasins, she felt at peace.

Precious padded into the room.

"Oh, no, my lovely. You and your silky, red coat stay out of this room."

Sneezing, Precious pawed at her nose.

She looped a finger through Precious's collar and led her back to the living room. White slipcovers protected oversized couches from indelible marks and silky dog fur. The remaining pieces in the room tended toward weathered wood and cool leather. *I should invest in art.*

Precious sneezed again.

"April and allergies go together." She considered giving Precious an antihistamine, but the veterinarian warned her to save the medicine for a last resort. "Maybe you should stay inside tomorrow."

Yawning, Precious settled onto the sheepskin and closed her eyes.

She closed the drapes and dimmed the house lighting. When she bought the house, she considered Johann's recommended security company, but Precious and high-visibility lighting made her feel secure. With Damon returning to town, the last few years of ambition and achievement seemed like a stress-fueled dream. *Had she made the right decisions?*

Replaying her romantic relationship with Johann felt like a waste of time. They looked good on paper, but the passion fizzled. In a few days, Damon would return to town, and she would do everything she could to help him find his groove outside jail. She turned to her sleek, new computer. At her touch, the screen brightened.

She focused on the part of her life where she created success. Data patterns and permutations filled her screens with colorful swirls and stark slashes. *I turned data into art.* She tapped the keyboard, and the rhythmic clicks sounded like a white noise machine.

Precious snored.

Following the dog's cue, she tabled her esoteric questions and focused on the problem simmering in her subconscious. *Data can't lie.* After buying the bungalow, monitoring local real estate market became a hobby, but a recent data anomaly piqued her interest.

Anna Claire, a local businesswoman who founded and ran a payment processing application, took ownership of a multi-million dollar estate, held it for sixty days, and sold the property to a holding company.

Vivian suspected the holding company belonged to the home's original owner, and as she dug, she found more suspect real estate transactions associated with Anna Claire. *With ScanCharge in Anna Claire's pocket, laundering money should be a piece of cake, so why is she playing shell games with foreign investors? She has billions.*

Vivian rubbed the back of her neck. The transaction histories made zero sense. By the time she turned off the computer, she listened to the neighborhood slumbering in darkness. Yawning, she let Precious into the backyard and watched her amble into the artificial brightness. She rubbed her arms against the evening fog and scanned the yard.

Precious sniffed the base of a tree.

Crickets chirped.

In the front of the house, glass shattered.

Vivian started and registered the wail of the house alarm.

Precious howled and charged toward the disturbance.

Dropping to the hardwood floor, Vivian caught the old dog and held her close. As her heart raced, a car peeled out, and she wondered whether the alarm or the dog scared off the vandal. Closing her eyes, she took measured breaths. "Okay. You stay out here. Slicing your paws on cut glass is the last thing I need."

Straining against the hold, Precious whined.

"Outside." Vivian shouldered the dog into the backyard and made her way through the bungalow. Broken window glass littered the front room. Each fragment reflected the security lights meant to reinforce her safety. Bending, she picked up a plastic bag filled with limestone gravel and a lawn service advertisement. The weighty projectile shattered a window, but the entrepreneur had fled.

Her cell phone rang.

"This is Vivian Hoat."

"This is Active Security. Do you have the passcode?" the caller asked.

She closed her eyes and took a deep breath. "Almonds."

"We detected an alarm."

"Someone throwing out advertisements hit a window." She wiped her hair out of her face. "A stupid mistake."

"Are you sure?"

She thought of the hardscrabble years she worked her way through an MBA, the tears of frustration she shed, and the unspoken fear she would fail. More than once, she had a lucky break, and everyone deserved the chance to recover from a stupid mistake. "Everything is fine."

"Have a good night, Ms. Hoat."

Ending the call, Vivian let Precious inside, held the dog's collar, and bolted the kitchen door. She could rationalize the mistake, but completing tasks soothed her nerves. Drawing a deep breath, she made a second phone call. "Hello, this is Vivian Hoat. When the office opens, please send someone to board up a broken window. I need a replacement, and I'll pay for priority service. Thank you."

"Of course," the night operator said.

Precious scratched at the back door.

"Too much action, old girl?" Vivian asked.

Dropping her paw, Precious sniffed the air.

"A careless mistake. The window company will take care of it." She left the exterior lights at full brightness and led Precious down the long hallway. A locked bedroom door and an aging canine would be her security detail. Unless the Steadman Group had gone rogue, she had zero enemies.

Precious huffed and dropped into her spot in the bedroom corner.

Pulling back the covers, Vivian shed her slippers, claimed her bed, and listened. Feeling the bed shake, she bolted upright.

Precious rooted through the bunched covers and found her hand.

"Only for tonight." She yawned and scratched the dog's ears. "You're supposed to sleep on the floor."

****

Snoozing her alarm for the third time, Vivian rolled over and wondered why the broken window left her feeling so on edge. *I didn't get a wink of sleep, but being the boss has its benefits.*

Precious licked her face.

She pulled up the duvet. "This is my bed." The duvet muffled her words, and she yawned. "You have to go out, don't you?"

Precious barked.

Throwing back the covers, she exhaled and swung her feet to the cold, hardwood floors. Her slippers sat where she left them, and the house remained quiet. Sliding her feet into the soft loafers, she led Precious to the backyard and leaned against the doorframe while cool, fog-tinged air swirled around the landscaping and

14

urged her inside. *Sleep deprivation is a form of torture.* Rubbing her arms, she yawned.

Precious returned to the back steps.

Readmitting Precious to the house, Vivian confined her to the crate and made her way to the white-tiled bathroom. A ring of cobalt-blue tiles anchored chest-high wainscoting. Framed 1930s movie posters rode the tile ring like glamorous stars cruising the Amalfi Coast. Every morning, Fred Astaire and his coifed dance partners smiled while she fixed her blonde hair, slipped into a day dress, and applied bright lipstick.

The posters echoed the house's age, but *Swing Time* was her grandmother's favorite movie. The woman's blatant longing for black-and-white Hollywood amused her, but the actresses looked like they knew the secret to success. *Imagine how long they spent in wardrobe and makeup.*

Turning on the curling iron, she transferred her life to the 1930s. *It wouldn't have worked. Those women danced backwards and in high heels, but how many of them could query a database? Ginger Rogers' character said, "I've got enough nerve to do anything!" but how did she choose her films? What would she do today?* Pulling a strand of hair forward, she added dry shampoo and closed her eyes against the iron's heat. *What if Hoat Analytics wasn't the right choice?*

She chose a white dress with red polka dots, considered her shoe collection, and added red leather sandals with an audacious gold clasp. Lined and piped with gold, the kid sandals made her feel glamorous and unique. *Who else wears this kind of shoe in Palo Alto?* She smiled and set down the curling iron. *Probably the university's swing club's members.*

Grabbing her keys, she let Precious lead her around the block.

An elderly neighbor whistled from her front porch. She waved.

Precious stuck her nose into a grassy cluster.

When the dog completed her business, Vivian returned to the house and confined her to the crate to keep her safe.

Whimpering, Precious laid down her head.

"I'm not sure I picked up all the broken glass. A break from the pollen will be good for you, and the repair company won't have to weather your inquisition." She scratched the dog's ear through the grate and thought about how much of her life she spent worrying about adverse outcomes. Controlling a computer, she was relentless. Comporting herself in public? Her knees shook, but she persevered to reach her goal. "Settle down, and I'll be home for lunch."

Hearing her phone ring, she dug the device from her purse. She considered letting the unknown number go to voice mail, but the window company might have opened earlier than she expected. On her way out the door, she picked up her tote. "Hello?"

"Vivi!"

The pleasure of hearing Damon's voice stole her breath. She pretended she could stay removed, but hearing his voice provided a rush, and she swallowed to steady her voice. "Damon! New number?"

"You know me," he said, "I like to keep things fresh."

Laughing, she closed the front door and walked toward her vehicle. Her heels wobbled, but she slid behind the car's wheel and pulled shut the door. "I'm glad you wrote down my number."

"I memorized it," he said.

She stopped buckling her seatbelt. "You did?"

"How long did we work together, Vivi?"

"At least a year." She secured the belt and juggled the folders in her tote. "That feels like a lifetime ago."

"And before that, you were with Johann. I kept an eye on you."

She wondered if Damon still saw her as an obligation.

He cleared his throat. "Mama Clarke's hosting a low-key welcome home party this afternoon. You should come."

"It's Friday. I have meetings." Her faint excuse sounded like a new hire's response to onboarding documents. What was the point of having millions of dollars and running her own company if her meeting schedule ruled her life? She started the car and waited for the vehicle to connect to her phone. "I might be late, but I'll be there as soon as possible."

"Really?" he asked.

"Why do you sound so shocked? Aren't we friends?" She held her breath, waiting for his reply. She missed their easy camaraderie, and the withdrawal left her feeling uncertain.

"Of course, we're friends. It's us against Silvia."

"Um"—she cleared her throat—"Silvia and I are friends now, too."

"It's a trap," he said. "You know she sleeps with one eye open."

"She's picking you up from jail!" His deep, booming laugh chased away her inhibitions. No matter what had happened in jail, Damon had returned.

He recited Mama Clarke's address on Annapolis Street.

She scribbled the address on a folder. "I'll be there."

"See ya." He ended the call.

She watched the dashboard screen blink and fade to black. Damon's new phone number lingered like an intriguing afterimage. Putting the car in Drive, she depressed the pedal and listened to the motor's purring response. Hoat Analytics was a success, Precious loved her, and she had a ridiculous number of shoes. The little girl from the Central Valley grew up, and despite life's little setbacks, she could weather the storms.

Chapter Two

At three o'clock, Vivian passed over a concrete bridge spanning San Francisquito Creek. Trash and an abandoned shopping cart littered the dry creek's sides. At the depression's bottom, an overgrown tangle of trees, bushes, and vines filled the gully where water should flow to the bay.

Since moving to Palo Alto, she learned the creek marked the boundary between East Palo Alto and Palo Alto. Long-time community members remembered EPA's notoriously high murder rate, but economic investment led to plummeting crime and new opportunities. Real estate along the creek bed existed in a perpetual war between the families who felt priced from the neighborhood and young professionals eager to advance gentrification. She checked her car's side mirror. *It's the same everywhere, isn't it?*

Learning about local neighborhoods helped her understand real estate fluctuations. As she passed a big-box shopping mall, she thought about the high school and that residential neighborhood once occupying the site. *The city relocated thousands of people to build that commercial center. The metro council needed the revenue, and EPA residents needed the jobs, but was losing the community worth it?*

She slowed for a red light and spotted the convenience store owned by Damon's mother. Tapping the steering wheel, she wondered why she never went inside. *I always dropped him off and went back to my life. If I had visited, would he have taken my calls?*

The light changed. Small businesses and local restaurants gave way to residential blocks.

She made a right turn and realized she no longer needed navigation.

Parked cars lined both sides of Annapolis Street. Laughing people milled outside a light-blue house. Despite the bare dirt and the weedy remnants of a front lawn, partygoers clustered behind a white-painted, iron fence. They sipped drinks and laughed in small groups, as if they were old friends. Retracted garage doors revealed more people inside the house and an unobstructed view of a crowded backyard.

I thought this was a small gathering of friends. Parking her car at the end of the busy block, she climbed from the vehicle, grabbed a bottle of wine from the passenger seat, and smoothed her skirt. Clicking the lock button, she secured the car but recognized the action and paused. *I would lock the doors wherever I parked it, wouldn't I?*

She dropped her keys into her pocket and considered the guests milling in the front yard. The crowd looked like they came from a diverse mix of communities. She might have overdressed for the party, but other than her retro sundress, she saw no reason she should stand out. Walking up the sidewalk, she waved at the people who made eye contact. *Why do I feel so conspicuous? My best friend in the Central Valley lived in a rundown neighborhood just like this one.*

A woman in a hot-pink dress stood from a folding lawn chair. Black hair swept over one eye. False eyelashes and thick liner framed the other eye and made her makeup pop against her dark skin. Hoop earrings and shiny lip gloss flashed in the sunlight, but her pursed lips fell short of a smile. Pushing aside her bangs, she scratched the edge of her lips and stared.

Vivian held up a bottle of wine. The woman's long, pink nails were the same shade of pink as her dress, but she doubted the woman wanted to exchange fashion tips. "I'm looking for Damon."

The woman narrowed her gaze. "He's in the back."

She swallowed. "Great."

"How you know him?"

"We used to work together," she said.

The woman raised an eyebrow. "Go through the house."

Relieved to skip the small talk, Vivian walked toward the front door.

"He's been busy all day," the woman said. "People missed him."

Vivian raised a hand to acknowledge the comment, but Damon invited her to the party. If he were too busy to see her, then she would drop off the bottle of wine and return home.

Inside the house, tile floors, textured walls, and a brick fireplace looked like the 1970s ranch houses she remembered. Guests stood or perched on the arms of oversized microfiber couches. In the kitchen, food dishes covered laminate countertops. A woman rooted through a drawer and held up a plastic serving spoon. A few people glanced at Vivian, but they returned to their conversations.

Vivian glanced at the tile floors. Mama Clarke's gleaming, ceramic floors reflected the sunlight streaming through a pair of French doors. *A developer would love to sweep through this house with cans of paint and engineered flooring.* She shook her head at the implications for Damon's family and followed the line of footprints leading toward the backyard.

Stepping through the French doors, she blinked past the sunlight and stood on a concrete patio. Music played through a set of speakers wired to the house. As she adjusted her gaze, she focused on the scraggily trees and retro steel swing set anchoring the fence line. Folding white tables and metal chairs filled the intermediate yard, but the crowd near the patio played cornhole and pickleball.

A pickleball player lunged for the ball, kicking up dust.

"Vivi!"

Turning, she saw Damon walking toward her with his arms outstretched. He wore a hunter-green polo shirt, jeans, and a smartwatch with a white strap. Sunlight burnished his pockmarked, ebony skin, but his welcoming smile shone bright. She held up the bottle of wine like an offering.

He wrapped his arms around her and enveloped her in a hug.

Closing her eyes, she leaned against his sunbaked warmth and savored his familiar smell. Coconut, ginger, and mandarin softened the edges of his strength. He felt stronger and happier than the last time she saw him. Thrilled to find him in good health, she pulled free before self-consciousness wiped the smile off her face.

He lifted her from the patio and swung her in a circle.

"All right, all right, that's enough!" She pushed

against his chest, felt her feet touch the patio, and met his gaze. In her heels, she matched his height. Two years of age and wisdom had filled out his features and his shoulders. *What did they feed this man in prison?* She lifted the bottle of wine and searched for familiar ground. "I brought bubbles."

Taking the bottle from her grasp, he held it in the sunlight, read the label, and whistled. "Fancy."

"Not really." She cleared her throat. "I thought you might want to celebrate."

"I do." He handed the bottle to a passing teenager. The kid wore black cargo pants, and his fabric belt kept a black T-shirt tucked into the pants' waistband. "Ricky, go put this on top of the refrigerator. It better be there at the end of the night."

The teenager held the bottleneck between two fingers and carried the vessel an arm's length from his body. "Who'd steal this shit?"

She remembered fast cars and teen heartthrobs impressing her teenage self, but her grandmother's old movies gave her a taste for glamour. If she'd grown up in EPA, she wondered if she would view the Brut Champagne as an adult treat or a fussy inefficiency. "I guess he wasn't impressed."

Damon laughed. "He'd swipe it in a heartbeat."

She smoothed her dress and wondered how to respond.

"Have you missed me?" he asked.

She dropped her hand. "Hardly. You're never gone long enough to miss."

At the old joke, he winked.

Except this time, he was gone too long. Absently rubbing her arm, she considered whether his return warranted more than a smile. Her body responded to his touch, but their friendship was too complicated for a one-night stand. "So, how are you?" she asked. "Really?"

He flung wide his arms. "Free!"

His booming voice made her smile, but she glanced at the people standing nearby. Several stared back, their narrowed gazes caught between curiosity and suspicion. Clearing her throat, she focused on Damon. His ability to live in the moment always charmed her, but it rarely put her in the spotlight. *I wouldn't say felony grand theft agrees with him, but I'm glad he's done with that part of his life.* She blinked. *Isn't he?* Uncertainty clouded her ability to find her balance.

"Silvia said you wouldn't come," he said.

She looked away. "You called her for a ride. I never received a call."

He wrapped an arm around her and dropped his head. "I missed you, but I didn't want you to see that part of my life. I didn't want to think about how much I was missing. Would you replay your darkest days?"

Indecision and uncertainty stole her sleep, but Damon lived on fast-paced extremes. She ducked from his arm and looked for a place to sit. Like her worries, dust and small pieces of gravel could creep through her sandals and irritate her soles. The woman wearing hot-pink was right. Other people at the party missed Damon, too. "Go enjoy your party. I'll grab a chair."

Looking at a pair of teenagers, he jerked his head.

They groaned but surrendered their chairs.

She claimed a chair and crossed her legs at the ankle. "Thanks, but don't worry about me." Remembering the pink woman's warning, she waved him off. "It's good to see you, but I don't want to take you from your party."

"It's fine." He dropped into the opposing chair. "I didn't think you'd come."

"Do I need to block Silvia?" she asked.

He laughed and spread his knees. "Vivi, you've been busy. Hoat Analytics made the papers."

She ignored the nickname. He had a way of doing what he wanted. After dealing with frenetic entrepreneurs and laid-back tech hippies, his good-natured, upbeat personality felt refreshing, but learning he followed her company's progress alienated her from their past friendship. "A few feel-good stories about a small business."

He raised his eyebrows.

"Every business owner watches the bottom line, but Hoat Analytics helps customers understand traffic and sales spikes. We look for trends and optimal outcomes."

Slouching until his shoulders rested against the frame, he folded his hands in his lap.

She sat straighter. "The quantity of available data can overwhelm people. We offer the right tools, the right metrics, and the right applications to understand small business data." Her throat felt dry. "I don't need to bore you with the details."

"And the Outcomes Foundation?" he cocked his head. "What's that? A side gig with a friend?"

She thought of Johann's wife. Hadley started the Outcomes Foundation to advance her research into the pain-relieving property of cannabidiol derivatives. "In the grand scheme of things, the foundation's research on CBD *is* small scale. My firm helps expedite the research, but we can't compete against market giants. Hadley will have to lead the next innovation from the lab."

He laughed. "So many buzzwords. You sound good."

Realizing she slipped into business mode, she cleared her throat. "Thanks."

"Like a chief executive officer."

She adjusted her skirt. "I am a CEO."

He smiled. "When I left, you were an aspiring CEO."

Closing her eyes, she leaned back and wondered if their lives diverged too far to resume their friendship. She told Silvia she would make sure he had everything he needed, but she wanted to be more than a resource. Upbeat, hip-hop music swirled around her. The lawn games pitched laughter against thwacks and grunts. She gripped the chair arms and took a deep breath. "I should go."

"Don't."

She opened her eyes and stared. His cologne made her think of the Virgin Islands, but nothing about this conversation felt easy. He was nearly ten years younger. Of course, their lives had diverged.

Leaning forward, he braced his arms on his knees. "I'm proud of you."

Her cheeks warmed, and she bit her inner cheek. "Thank you."

"When I saw Hoat Analytics make the paper, I bragged to the other guys in prison. Hey, that's Vivi's company. I know her! If she can build an empire, I can, too."

She opened her mouth to encourage him.

The woman in the pink mini-dress put a hand on Damon's shoulder.

Silhouetted against the sun, her figure looked like an hourglass. Vivian focused on the woman's nails. They rested against Damon's shirt, her thumb stroking his collarbone. *We might all be animals at heart, but I can't mistake her claws.*

"Your mama's looking for you," the woman said.

He scanned the crowd. "Tell her I'll come over in a second. Vivi's never met her."

"Vivi?" The woman perched on the arm of Damon's chair and draped an arm over his shoulders, but she stared down Vivian. "That's a cutesy name."

Vivian tilted her head and narrowed her gaze. "I love a good nickname. What does Damon call you?"

"Doll."

She swallowed a laugh. "How authentic."

Damon snorted.

She met his gaze. *What else was I supposed to say?*

Winking, he stood and dislodged the woman's claim. "Shani grew up on this block. She's loved long-legged, doe-eyed dolls since she was a kid. What'd you have, like fifty of them lined up on your windowsill?"

"Not quite," Shani said.

"We used to find her dolls all over the neighborhood. Her dog would get ahold of one, bolt from the yard, and bury it under a flower bush. Looked like Halloween, with one brown plastic arm sticking up from the dirt."

"That's terrible," Vivian said.

Shani stroked Damon's arm. "He always brought the dolls back."

"What else would I do with them?" He rolled his

27

shoulders.

Frowning, Shani turned from him and arched her eyebrows.

Vivian held up her palms.

"They're probably collector's items now." Damon cracked his knuckles. "You could make a buck or two."

Except for the dog's teeth marks. Hoping to make friends rather than enemies, Vivian shrugged. "Why would she sell them? One day, they'll probably be a hit with her kids. I had Christie, the main doll's friend. She looked the best in the wedding gowns."

Shani grinned. "That she did."

The music changed to a thumping, gangsta rap artist from the mid-1990s.

"You want me to open that bottle of wine?" Damon asked.

"No, you enjoy it." Vivian jostled the keys in her dress pocket. "I should go."

"Stay. I'll get you lemonade punch." Pivoting, he shouted someone's name and walked into the house.

Unwilling to leave without saying goodbye, she smiled at Shani.

"He's mine." Shani stepped forward.

"Excuse me?"

"Those dolls he dug up?" Shani arched an eyebrow. "The dog didn't bury them. I did. I've known Damon since we were eight years old, and we'll be together when we're eighty. Don't think you can waltz in here and change that fact. You need a fix of Jungle Fever? Go somewhere else, Jane."

"It's Vivian."

Shani rolled her eyes and turned on her sky-high heels.

She watched Shani saunter across the patio and step onto the bare dirt. A damp cloth could wipe the dust from Shani's shoes, but nothing could erase her attitude. *Point taken, Doll. You want the man, but why haven't I heard your name?*

Silvia rounded the house corner, carrying two bags of ice. Pink lipstick picked up the embroidered colors on her traditional, floral blouse. Wrinkles fanned the skin near her eyes, but she wore long shorts and chic sandals. Dumping the bags of ice in the cooler, she turned and waved.

Vivian crossed her arms. "Why did you tell Damon I wouldn't come?"

"Why do you have a stick up your ass?" Silvia patted her cheek. "How long have you been here?"

Arguing with Silvia was like arguing with a brick wall. The woman never budged. Vivian relaxed her shoulders and appreciated the chance to connect with old friends. "A few minutes."

"Damon'll be glad to see you."

"I saw him. He looks"—she searched for a word to describe the mix of friendship, surprise, and pleasure she felt when he wrapped her in a hug—"good."

Silvia fluffed her silver-streaked, black hair. "Good?"

"Maybe prison gave him a fresh start. He can put everything behind him and move forward."

"Nobody puts their life behind them," Silvia said. "You take the good with the bad, and you move on."

She frowned. "Surely he learned a lesson."

Silvia tilted her head. "Don't get caught?"

Damon returned carrying two drinks. He squeezed Silvia in a side hug. "Both my ladies? I'm a lucky man."

Silvia swatted his arm and took a cup.

Accepting the other drink, Vivian drank deeply. Vodka's harsh bite burned her throat. "It's spiked!"

"It's a party." Laughing, he bumped her shoulder and walked away.

She eyed the cup. "I should have asked for bottled water."

"Too much trash." Silvia licked her lips. "Not too bad. Rosemary would help."

Silvia had an herb for every occasion.

The back door opened. Johann and Hadley walked onto the patio.

For a man she once called a lover, Vivian had little interest in seeing his cropped black hair or piercing blue eyes. Instead, she shaded her gaze and scanned Hadley's loose sundress for signs of a bump. "Hadley looks good. You'd never know she's pregnant with twins."

"Give her a few more weeks," Silvia said. "The babies will be here before too long."

She volunteered to host Hadley's baby shower, but she wondered if Silvia had new information. "The doctor said everything looks fine. Hadley's picking out names."

"Between her research and the Outcomes Foundation, she's under a lot of stress. It's not enough to know how to ride—you must also know how to fall," Silvia said. "Motherhood's going to hit her hard."

She stopped examining Hadley's face for signs of stress. Her wavy brown hair and golden highlights looked perfect. Shading her gaze, she focused on Silvia. "Do you know something I don't?"

Silvia sipped her drink. "No, but I like to wait on these things. Naming babies before they're born is bad luck. Wait to see what the Lord gives you before you give it a name."

Vivian cocked her head and looked at Johann and his wife. Her friends were like erratic, inexplicable data anomalies. If they would settle into predefined roles, she would know what to expect. Life should be like the movies with a beginning, a middle, and an end. Guiding customers toward achievements was her job, but if her friends kept throwing her curve balls, she wouldn't be able to spot the path forward.

"You beat us!" Hadley released Johann's arm and waved. She tucked a length of hair behind her ears and walked across the patio. "I thought we would get here earlier."

Vivian accepted Hadley's hug and presented her cheek for Johann's polite kiss. "I wasn't sure I would make it."

"Oh, Damon would have been so disappointed." Hadley released Silvia from a hug. "He loves getting you riled up."

"Is that why he ghosted me?" Vivian rubbed her arms.

The trio exchanged glances.

Silvia dumped the remnants of her drink into Vivian's cup.

Taking the hint, Vivian knew she had to get over the past. She took a long, hard sip.

"Remember when he called you Vivi? Or Bibi?" Hadley tapped her chin. "Or was it Babs?"

Vivian ran her tongue along her teeth. The drink went down too easy. "It wasn't Babs." She hiccupped.

Silvia snorted.

Hadley shrugged and peered into Vivian's cup. "What are you drinking?"

"Hard lemonade. If Damon tells you it's punch, he's lying."

Hadley exhaled. "I'm so tired of seltzer water."

"Boss!" Damon's voice rang through the crowded yard. Walking up to Johann, he shook the man's hand.

Johann pulled him into a hug and slapped his back. "You've grown. Are you sure you don't need a job? You could stand around and glare at the press on my behalf."

Laughing, Damon shook his head. "No way, man. I have my own game. I socked away my savings in an online account, and I'm turning legit, or something like it. I won't have enough time to keep your ass out of trouble."

"Don't worry." Hadley stroked Johann's arm. "That's my job."

Vivian averted her gaze from the intimacy and sipped her drink. *Rosemary would be an interesting touch. Silvia should open a restaurant.* She tried another sip and wondered how much alcohol the drink contained. *Grapefruit would also work.*

"We're not here to talk business," Damon said. "We're here to celebrate. I'm a free man!"

Hearing his playful exuberance, she smiled over the empty cup's rim.

Johann checked his phone. "Indeed."

Hadley rubbed her stomach. "Did you learn your lesson?"

Damon winked. "Don't get caught."

Does Damon mean it? Wait, how many glasses of

lemonade has he had? No wonder he picked me up and hugged me. Why didn't he hug Hadley? He probably knows about the babies. She blinked away the bright sunlight. *Men can be so ridiculous.*

"All right, who's coming to meet Mama Clarke?" Damon asked. "She knows the dirt on everyone else at this party. You four"—Swinging his finger, he encompassed the group—"are fresh meat."

Vivian grinned and relaxed into the afternoon. She already faced down Shani. How much trouble could Damon's mother be? "Sure, why not?"

"That's my girl, Vivi." He swung an arm around her shoulders. "Remember, her bark is worse than her bite. I survived eighteen years under her rule. You have to last eighteen seconds."

The smell of coconut intensified her lemonade buzz. Stumbling, she gripped his arm for balance. "Sorry, I can't move as fast in heels. Are you going to keep living with your mom?"

"Details." He waited until she regained her balance and shortened his stride.

Letting him guide her through the crowd, she assumed Johann, Hadley, and Silvia followed in their wake. *What am I, the sacrificial lamb?* She spied an older woman sitting in a lawn chair. Arms crossed, the woman presided over the dusty yard like a border agent wearing a maxi dress. Her sleek, silver-tinged hair and gold jewelry reflected the sunlight, but she stared like she had a take-no-prisoners attitude.

Vivian straightened her shoulders.

"Boy, did you invite every damn person on your contact list?" the woman asked.

Damon released her and jerked his chin over his

shoulder. "You know Johann, and Hadley came by the store."

"I know who they are," the woman said.

Reaching around Vivian, he pulled forward Silvia. "Silvia put together the black bean salad you like."

The older woman softened her gaze. Looking at Silvia, she dipped her chin. "Amazing."

Silvia beamed.

Vivian waited for her nuanced introduction.

He urged her forward. "This is Vivian."

That's it? Where's my endorsement? She was so far out of her element she wondered how she would get back to her easy, sterile office. Thrusting out a hand, she tried a smile. "Nice to meet you."

The woman narrowed her gaze.

She dropped the hand. "Great party."

Standing, Ms. Clarke let crumbs fall from her lap. "How do you know Damon?"

"I was Johann's executive assistant," she said. "I worked with your son."

She pursed her lips. "You came to East Palo Alto for a coworker?"

Considering the question, she shook her head and realized she could craft her own introduction. "No, he's my friend. High-stress situations build relationships. We've had our share of fun, but keeping Johann out of trouble forged our friendship."

Johann coughed.

"My boy doesn't need more stress"—Mama Clarke inclined her chin—"or fun."

She wished she had another drink to sip.

Damon cupped his chin in a hand and watched the show.

"He needs to buckle down and take care of business," Mama Clarke said.

Vivian nodded. *I couldn't agree more.*

Mama Clarke softened her gaze. "I've missed him at the store."

Vivian frowned and considered whether Damon wanted to return to running the convenience store. The thought of him schlepping cardboard boxes felt wrong, but why wouldn't he support his mother's store? He said he socked away his cash. Maybe EPA was enough for him. Knowing the Central Valley had never been enough for her, she smiled at Mama Clarke. "We've all missed him."

The admission bolstered her confidence. Defying the woman's stare, she inched closer to Damon. She might want to pull him up, and Mama Clarke might want to pull him home, but he could make his decision. "Thank you for opening your home for this celebration."

"I had one son." Mama Clarke crossed her arms. "My home is always open."

"C'mon." Damon squeezed her shoulders. "Lay off Vivi. She's here to have a good time."

Mam Clarke raised her eyebrows. "That's why I'm worried."

Shani walked up and handed Ms. Clarke a plate of food. "You need anything else, Mama Clarke?"

"Pull up a chair, Shani. Tell me what's been happening at the salon. Damon, fetch her a chair."

"Yes, Mama," he said.

Vivian made eye contact.

He shrugged.

Mama Clarke was his family. What else could he

do? Feeling like an outsider, she turned toward her former coworkers. Their presence mimicked the pleasure and familiarity of close family, but they were busy building their own families. She had a dog and a career. For most of her life, she thought the career would be enough, but she had doubts.

She scanned the partygoers and wondered about the people she could meet. Shani had warned off her attention, and Mrs. Clarke had tolerated her presence. Would Damon's neighbors care about her opinions or her professional achievements? Heading for the drink dispenser, she anticipated the warm flush a drink would send coursing through her limbs. Before she reached for the spigot, she admitted she had a reason to smile. Damon cared. Whether he cared for her or needed something from her remained to be seen, but the lemonade punch would wash away her insecurities.

Chapter Three

"What are you doing?" Damon waved at a new arrival to the boisterous, backyard yard.

Vivian shook her phone. "Waiting to download a ride-sharing app."

"I'm not an expert, but shaking devices rarely speeds up download speeds."

Looking up from the screen, she saw the laughter in his gaze. Effervescent goodwill carried her through his eclectic homecoming party, but evening air set in, and Shani's watchful presence lingered. Damon's presence had everything to do with her decision to linger past the time Johann, Hadley, and Silvia departed. Now that he stood beside her, she had no idea what to do. "Instead of selling stolen phones, you could have spent your time"—she hiccupped—"improving them."

"True." He tugged the phone from her hand, dropped it in his pocket, and swung his arm around her shoulder. "C'mon, Vivi. I'll drive you home."

Relaxing against his warmth, she made a noncommittal sound, thought better of acquiescing, and pulled back. "You can't leave your party."

"Party's over. Might meet a few friends downtown. I can walk from your house."

"What will your mom say?" She kicked a discarded cup.

He laughed. "Mama Clarke's asleep."

She rolled her eyes. "Good. I don't think she likes me."

"She didn't kick you out," He opened a fenced gate.

"What a threshold for success." She looked for a path through the poorly lit side yard. "Nobody likes me. Silvia said I need to make more friends. My employees respect me." She stumbled and rolled her ankle. "Ouch!"

He swung her into his arms.

The smell of ginger and coconuts enveloped her senses, and she compartmentalized the pain radiating through her ankle. She nuzzled his neck. Beneath the bright scent, she smelled sweat, dirt, and sunshine. "You smell good."

Laughing, he adjusted his hold. "Damn, you're a mess."

She fished the car keys from her pocket and leaned her head against his shoulder. "I know, but don't tell anyone."

"Your secret's safe with me."

Closing her eyes, she listened to his heartbeat. *Is it?*

He lowered her into the passenger seat.

Snuggling into the leather seat, she slept. Feeling Damon slow the car, she blinked away her grogginess. Heat blasted from the vents and cradled her in a cozy glow. Yawning, she straightened and confirmed her neighborhood.

"Vivi, your house might be visible from space," he said.

She frowned and looked at the stars. "Huh?"

"Your neighbors can probably do crossword puzzles at night."

"Hardly. They're too busy watching television." Catching onto the joke, she wrinkled her nose and scratched her side. Her lips felt sticky, and she wondered why her mouth felt so dry. *How much lemonade did I drink?*

Pulling the car into the driveway, he put the vehicle in Park and glanced over.

She took a deep breath and focused on his observation. She could deal with her self-doubts and poor decision-making skills at a later time. "The lights are security measures."

"Why?"

"Why what?"

"Why'd you light up the house?" he asked. "Why's the front window boarded up? What's frightening you?"

She looked at the small, single-story bungalow from his perspective. Facts informed every decision she made about the house, but its classic lines and afternoon breezes captured her heart. How could she explain how safe she felt within its walls? "Someone tossing out advertisements shattered the window. The lights are"—she rubbed a hand over her face—"for peace of mind. I like visibility. Facts."

He laughed. "You scared of the dark?"

"No, but the verandas creak. The trees groan." She crossed her arms. "I'm a light sleeper."

"You *are* scared." He whistled. "The Great Vivi has a weakness."

"I liked you better when I was drunk."

He turned off the motor. "No doubt."

Opening the passenger door, she stepped out. Her ankle protested, and she exhaled. "I should have stayed home."

He walked around the car and handed her the keys. "But you would have missed the party."

Would I have missed you? She put weight on her ankle and winced. *No heels for a week.*

He crouched and lifted her into his arms.

She dropped the keys. They jangled against the concrete drive.

Without flinching, he squatted and picked up the keys.

Settling in for the ride, she exhaled. "I thought the whole prison-gym-rat thing was a Hollywood trope."

"People in prison have nothing but time." He walked up the front path. "Exercise and education gave me shit to do. Without activities, I would have lost my mind."

"You should keep working out." She yawned. "It looks good on you."

"Distracts you from my skin, huh?"

Raising her hand, she traced the pockmarks.

He flinched and looked away.

She dropped her hand. "Sorry, I didn't know they bothered you."

"They don't, most days," he said.

"But today?"

He adjusted her weight and climbed the stairs. "Too many people looking at me."

"You were an excellent host." She shifted the keys she held and wondered how much of the party was a performance. She understood standing at the front of the room and delivering results, but she appreciated buffers and predictable reactions. Damon navigated a flood of attention. "You can put me down."

Meeting her gaze, he raised an eyebrow and lowered her feet to the floor.

Gripping his arm, she mourned the loss of his heat but shifted the keys she held until she found the right fob. Passing the small piece of plastic across the sensor, she unlocked the door. "Precious! I'm home!"

The Welshie raised her head from the slipcovered couch. Nose in the air, she sniffed and filled the house with a long, mournful howl.

Damon stepped back. "When did you get a dog?"

"Last year. She's not supposed to be on the couch." Holding tight to him, she raised her voice so he could hear her over Precious's howls. "And she's usually not this loud. Help me get her situated? If she knocks me over, I might not be able to catch myself."

"Shit." He edged forward.

Leaning on him, she tugged on Precious's collar. "The dog walker usually crates her."

Precious refused to budge.

"C'mon, girl. I'm too tired for this," she said.

Precious stopped howling and cocked her head.

"Good girl." She tugged the animal from the couch and flopped down in the warm spot.

Damon cleared his throat. "I'm headed out."

The howling resumed, and Precious raced toward him. She skittered across the wooden floors on sharp nails.

"Precious. Heel!" Vivian gripped the couch arm and pulled herself upright. Lunging for her pet, she lost her footing and landed hard. The wooden floor slammed against her cheek and knocked the wind from her chest. Moaning, she felt tears welling in her eyes and knew she never should have left the house.

Strong hands lifted her from the floor. "You okay?"

Precious danced around Damon, barking and nipping at the air but never making contact.

He ignored the animal and raised her chin.

"I'm sorry about the dog," she said.

"I get it. She doesn't like Black people."

"She's old." Rubbing her face, she wondered if the fall would leave a bruise. "The handyman came by to board up the broken window. Maybe she's on edge. She can't see very well."

He sank onto the couch with her in his arms. "She can see well enough."

Precious growled.

He cleared his throat. "Quiet!"

Eyes wide, Precious sank to her belly on the floor.

Vivian opened one eye and stared at her pet. "Now you're obedient?"

Precious rolled onto her back.

"Oh, come on. He won't hurt you." She patted the couch next to her and Damon.

Taking a wide angle, Precious approached the couch, sniffed Damon's shoes, and claimed the farthest corner. She dropped her head and stared at Damon.

Vivian yawned. "See, she likes you."

He laughed and deposited her between him and Precious. "If that's liking me, I'd hate see her bad side."

She stroked Precious's long, silky fur. "I always wanted a dog, but we couldn't spare the extra money."

"Me, too."

Exhaling, she tucked her legs to the side and

rubbed her ankle. "Everything costs money."

He stretched an arm along the couch's back. "True, but not everything's worth the price."

She felt him toying with her hair and wondered if she should act on her interest. They were always friendly rivals, nipping and dancing around each other while they did Johann's bidding, but then he went to prison. Incarceration cost him years of freedom, and she wondered if his schemes were worth the price. At least their friendship remained intact.

"When did you buy this house?" he asked.

"Right after you went to prison."

He tensed and looked into the kitchen. "It looks like you dumped a gallon of white paint on everything."

She considered the house from his perspective, but the crisp, clean aesthetic soothed her. "I paid a decorator a lot of money to channel a calm, comfy, coastal beach house vibe."

"It doesn't look like you."

Straightening, she met his gaze. "What does that mean?"

"Coastal grandma isn't your vibe, Vivian." He dropped her hair and pulled her back into position. "You need bright colors, but right now, you also need to sleep."

Lethargy weighted her limbs. Tomorrow, she would worry about next steps, but right now, she could savor this easy, weightless moment. "So now I'm Vivian?"

He swallowed. "The name suits you. So polished and pristine."

"Like the house," she said.

"Not like the house."

She turned her head. "Why do you keep calling me Vivi?"

He slouched on the couch and leaned back his head. "I could know a Vivi."

She closed her eyes. "Same person."

"Are they?"

She replayed his absence. She should have tried harder. He downplayed a phone call, but would he have refused to see her? She wet her lips and thought about him lying awake at night in a cold cell. He was so much stronger than she. She opened her eyes and looked at his handsome profile. "I am afraid of the dark."

Opening his eyes, he turned his head. "Why?"

"Too many movies," she said. "When I was a kid, I stayed up late, watching them with my grandfather. The scary ones stayed with me. Hang out with me awhile? It's too early to meet up with your friends."

He glanced at Precious. "Your guard dog might bite me."

Precious licked her lips.

"You might jump me," he added.

She imagined summoning the energy and grinned. Their friendship mattered, but when she made eye contact, her heart rate jumped. Having him on her turf offered her the upper hand. She tilted her head. "Would that be so bad?"

He closed his eyes. "Ask me again when you're sober."

"I'm sober!"

He smiled. "Two years is a long time to wait, Vivi. I can wait another day."

She shifted, put her head on his muscled thigh, and tucked her throbbing ankle beneath Precious's silky fur.

"You're happy to be out of jail."

"Truth."

"And you had fun at your party."

He stroked her shoulder.

His thumb traced her collarbone and lulled her with easy comfort. "Anyone would."

"Is that what you think?" he asked.

She closed her eyes. "Wouldn't you?"

"Vivi, when I make you come, you'll scream my name."

Bolting upright, she stared. His arrogance and his whispered statement kindled the heat between her legs, but caution tempered her response. His scene wrapped around her, but the gulf between their experiences stretched so wide she feared drowning. Bracing herself on one arm, she considered her response. "You're messing with me."

Heavy, dark eyes stared back. "I'm not."

She shifted her weight and grazed his cheek with a hand. "You promise?"

Turning, he kissed her palm and resettled her on his lap. "I promise."

Eyes closed, she shifted her hips, heard him groan, and searched for the energy to do more than indulge in his warm, intriguing embrace.

****

Yawning, Vivian opened her eyes to sunlight streaming through her bedroom window. The light felt too bright. She squinted, tucked her chin, and pieced together memories from the prior day. She remembered pieces of Damon's party. *I need acetaminophen and a strong cup of coffee.* Throwing back the duvet, she put her foot on the floor and winced. "Let's get moving,

Precious."

Silence answered her.

"Precious?" She looked to the dog's corner and frowned. *Shit. I hope I didn't leave her locked up in the kitchen all night.* After popping a couple of tablets, she kept one hand on the wall and hobbled down the hallway. Biting her lip, she hoped the combination of drugs and caffeine revived her senses.

The boarded-up window cast a deep shadow over the living room, but Precious raised her head and peered over the couch's back.

"Bad dog." Her half-hearted reprimand felt like too much effort. "Next thing I know, you'll want whipped cream and a pillow." Yawning, she slapped her thigh. "Come on, my lovely. You probably need to pee."

Precious cocked her head.

"Fine." She walked toward the couch, intent on pulling the entitled Welshie to the floor and reestablishing her dominance. Drawing closer, she realized Precious occupied a slim margin of couch cushion. Damon occupied the rest. His hunter-green polo rode up his chest, revealing tight skin and defined muscles. Boxer briefs peeped from the top of his jeans. Instead of freaking out, she admired the view and reconstructed her memories. *He drove me home. He didn't know about Precious. Did I ruin his party? Did I ask him to stay?* She swallowed. "Damon?"

He rolled on his side.

She regretted losing sight of his abs. "Damon?" She raised her voice, hoping to wake him but fearing what would happen when she did. Her ankle was the part of her body that ached, but she touched her lips and wondered what it would take to make them sore.

"Damon!"

He bolted into a sitting position. "Vivi!"

Stumbling backward, she gripped a chair. "Too loud?"

Rubbing his face, he flopped back to the couch. "What the hell?"

"Seriously?" she asked. "What the hell are you doing here?"

"Fuck if I know. Keeping you from face planting in the driveway?"

She snorted.

Precious slid off the couch and ambled toward the back door.

Replaying the party, she followed the dog and hoped the cool morning jogged her punch-soaked memory. After releasing Precious to the backyard, she turned and found Damon standing in the doorway with his arms braced above his head. Prison honed his physique, but he needed larger clothes. Until he indulged in that shopping spree, she would enjoy the view. "I'm sorry for shouting. That's a terrible way to wake up."

"You have coffee?" he asked.

She bit her lips and forced herself to meet his gaze. "Yes."

"Do you know how to make it?"

She frowned. "Yes."

"Forgiven, but for the love of God, Vivi, make the damn coffee."

She leaned against the kitchen counter and crossed her arms. If one of her employees talked to her like Damon did, she would make a note in their personnel file. "This is my house."

"Yeah," he said, "but I'm the one who slept on the couch."

Memories of settling into his arms warmed her cheeks, and she recognized the shift in their relationship. Alternative sleeping arrangements might have satisfied an itch, but they would have complicated everything. She focused on the coffeepot and dialed a strong cup. "Eight ounces?"

Walking to her side, he eyed the machine. "Is this a test?"

She grinned and reached for a coffee cup. "No, but I prefer a minimum of six."

He laughed and bumped her hip. "Nice jammies."

Looking down, she saw her nipples straining beneath a loose shirt and crossed her arms. "Thanks for driving me home."

He opened the refrigerator and withdrew a carton of half-and-half. "You're welcome."

Releasing one arm, she pressed the machine's start button.

The device sputtered to life, and steam seeped from the edges.

"Not to be rude, but why are you still here?"

Placing the cream on the counter, he leaned against the counter. "You fell asleep in my lap."

"So?" she asked.

"So, every time I moved a limb, your guard dog growled."

Swiveling her head, she reconciled her aged dog with a fierce protector. "Precious?"

"Do you have two?"

She walked to the back door and found her dog calmly sitting on the top step and looking as pretty as a picture. She opened the back door.

Precious raised her white muzzle, walked past her, and sat by her bowl.

"You ready for breakfast?" She leaned down to open the cabinet. Blood rushed to her head, and she winced. "How much did I drink?"

"I thought you had one or two."

"Must have been more." She rubbed her eyes. "Silvia kept me topped up."

"It's always the quiet ones."

Gritting her teeth, she scooped the dog food and vowed to buy quieter bowls. When the clatter subsided, she straightened and eyed Damon. "Thank you for taking care of me."

He walked toward her. "What's the last thing you remember?"

She frowned. "Your mom doesn't like me."

Laughing, he hooked an arm around her waist and drew her close.

Instead of resisting, she closed her eyes and wondered how two thin, cotton shirts could transmit so much heat. Her nipples strained, and she abandoned her pretenses. *I'm ridiculous. Silvia was right. I need to get out of the house.*

"I missed you, Vivi," he said.

How could anyone miss me?

Dropping his head, he grazed her lips.

The brush of warmth and his coffee-scented caress pulled her into the moment and anchored her senses. In the span of twenty-four hours, she went from missing him to lusting after him, and a hangover failed to temper her body's eager response to his kiss. She turned her head to the side before she jumped him and wrapped her legs around his waist. "I missed you, too."

His lips followed the curve of her cheek, settling in the hollow beneath her ear. "I thought about you every single night." He gripped her hips. "And here you are, mostly sober."

"Damon"—she pulled back from whispered heat of his breath—"we can't do this."

"Why not?"

His challenge hung in the air. She calmed her quickened breaths and weighed his question. *Why not? Why can't I drag this man back to my bed and spend the rest of my weekend having the time of my life?* She frowned. "Because…"

"Did you miss me?" he asked.

"We're friends. Of course, I missed you!"

He tightened his hold. "I want you to be more than a friend, Vivi. Every time you touched me at the party, I wanted to kick out everyone and convince you I was more than a scrawny kid."

"I touched you?"

He laughed. "Maybe you didn't notice, but you always had your hands on me. As long as we worked together, you were like a cardboard cutout I could never claim. But two years is a long time to spend reevaluating priorities." He kissed her jawline. "Tell me you want to be more than friends."

She wanted to strip him naked, but she turned her head. "I haven't brushed my teeth."

"I don't care about your damn breath." He claimed her lips, tugging free her bottom lip and tightening his embrace.

She yielded, lost in the surprise and pleasure of finding him in her home. Had she thought of him this way? She had. Had she acted on it? She moaned. Hoat Analytics consumed years of her life, but satisfaction eluded her. The man in her kitchen was kissing her before the coffee finished brewing. His lips felt strong and confident. His kiss teased her lips until she wanted to yield. The intensity of the heat echoing through her body stunned her. If he wanted to get naked, she would meet him halfway.

The coffee machine sputtered.

It's Damon. I can't ghost him and move on. I said I would get him anything he needed, not use him for my pleasure. Pulling free, she braced her arms against his chest and exhaled. "We can't."

He frowned and took a step back. "Why not?"

She scanned the room and struggled to organize her arguments. Precious sat in the corner wagging her tail. "I have to take Precious to the vet."

He turned her chin. "Bullshit."

Looking away, she extracted herself from his embrace, reached for the fresh cup of coffee, and shoved the porcelain toward his chest.

Gripping the cup with two hands, he stared.

"You're lonely." Grasping at straws, she tidied the kitchen counter.

He put the cup of coffee on the honed countertop. "I'm not."

I am. And horny. And confused. "Damon, what would…"

"Don't bring up Johann."

She stopped and looked up. "Johann?"

He rubbed his temples. "What were you going to say?"

"What about Shani?" She straightened a bowl of

51

apples and risked a glance.

"What about her?" He frowned. "Shani and I were never together."

Thankful she wouldn't have to confront the hot-pink wonder for Damon's attention, she crossed her arms and faced Damon's observation. "Don't hold my past against me. This isn't the 1950s."

He poured cream into his coffee, the skin of his knuckles lighter where he gripped the handle. "And if we were together, it'd be over. I'm not standing in your kitchen because I want to spend time with Shani."

"Why are you here?" She dialed another cup of coffee. Swiss dials and sputtering steam offered little refuge, but she could press buttons until she had her wits.

"I wanted to see you home, and then you tripped, and your dog lunged for my jugular."

She snorted.

"I debated whether to stay or to go."

"Stay." The gurgling coffee maker drowned her whisper and bought her time. *I can't use him for pleasure and change my mind the next day.* She turned and sipped the bitter espresso she concocted. "We both have work."

He laughed. "You mean you have work." Straightening, he drained the coffee cup and set it on the countertop. "Two years ago, I finally got a little something together. It's a mess."

"Something? You had three somethings, Damon. I'm surprised you found time to sleep. Your problem wasn't lack of employment, it was lack of principals."

He stared. "What does that mean?"

"It means you ran odd jobs for Johann, worked at

52

the Greek restaurant, and sold stolen goods from your mom's convenience store. Any of those gigs could have turned into a career"—she sipped her coffee—"well, except the one that landed you in prison."

He slapped the table. "I did it for the kids! Someone has to look out for them."

"The kids! The kids! The kids!" She dropped her coffee mug into the sink. Clattering porcelain echoed in the kitchen. Bracing her arms on the counter's edge, she wished she chose a quieter way to make her point. Her head ached, and winning the argument would alienate Damon. *He's trying to give the kids a leg up in the world, but he's sacrificing himself to do it.* She took a deep breath and looked up. "It's a terrible deal, Damon. You can't jeopardize your life for their lives. I don't care how many of them look at you with hero worship in their eyes. You need to take care of yourself before you can take care of them." She turned and pointed a finger at his chest. "And that means staying out of jail."

He narrowed his gaze.

She dropped her finger. "You need to look after yourself."

He spread his arms. "What do I need, besides you?"

Surrounded by material possessions and the hallmarks of a successful start-up, she compared her luxuries to his realities. He spent two years in jail for selling stolen goods, but he funneled the profits into his neighborhood and lived a simple life with Mama Clarke. She swallowed and reconsidered her arguments.

Turning, he picked up a throw pillow and tossed it on the couch. "I need food, a few changes of clothes, and a place to hang my hat. Should I go shuck boxes at the big box store for minimum wage? Fantastic. Then I can hand the government half my paycheck and count myself lucky I have a television set. What a life!"

"You'd be an excellent teacher." Her suggestion sounded weaker than gas station coffee.

Clapping together his hands, he laced his fingers and stretched his arms in front of his chest. "No college degree."

She rolled her eyes. "How ironic. If only someone kept you out of trouble."

He unlaced his fingers and stepped forward. "Vivi…"

She held up a hand. "You'd be an excellent teacher, Damon. Growing student enrollment keeps many districts in a perpetual hiring mode. You could start a degree program and ask for a credential waiver."

He rolled his eyes and picked up a second pillow. "I'm sure my criminal record would float my application to the top of the pile."

"Don't let history weight down your ambitions."

He rubbed his face. "What would I teach?"

"Civics? Economics?" She narrowed her gaze. "You socked away your profits and multiplied the cash to help kids. How'd you do it?"

Rubbing a hand over his face, he dropped to the couch. "Everybody loves a cocky Black server. I picked up stock tips from the restaurant customers."

Picking up Precious's chew toy, she straightened. "You eavesdropped?"

He dropped the hand and grinned. "You're the one who told me to diversify."

She rubbed her forehead. "I meant divest. I meant give up the surplus military equipment and unlocked cell phones. I meant get your butt on the right side of the law."

"Aw, now you sound like Mama Clarke."

"Good." She dropped her hand. "At least, you know I'm looking out for you." Walking into the living room, she folded herself in a ball onto the couch's corner. *Why does this spot have to smell like coconuts?* Grabbing a pillow, she wrapped her arms around the bulk and stared at the wood floors.

He leaned toward her and tugged on her ankle. "Hey, are you okay?"

"Too much sugar and too much alcohol." She muttered into the fabric. *Did the acetaminophen ease the ache in my head, or was it his kiss?*

"Do you want juice or something?"

She raised her head. "I need time to get my bearings. This tension between us? I like you." She swallowed. "I want you, but when the novelty wears off, I don't want to lose our friendship."

"Novelty?" He released his hold on her ankle.

She missed the warmth of his touch, but she heard the hurt in his voice. *If one kiss hurts him, what happens after more?* Clearing her throat, she channeled her boss voice. "I'm worried about you. Our lives went in different directions, but I want to help you."

He tugged on her leg. "We're not that far apart."

Stubborn man. Uncurling, she straightened her legs and draped them over his lap. The weight of his hands felt good. She might be a decade older, but he'd more than grown up. *Maybe our friendship can survive an affair.*

"In fact, we were friends," he said.

She smiled. "We are friends."

"As a friend, I'm telling you that your skin looks like cold oatmeal. I can't tease you in this condition."

Tease? Five minutes ago, I thought you wanted to fuck. She raised a hand to her cheek. "Thanks, I think."

"We had good times, Vivi. Remember when you fussed over me and played nurse?"

"You fell off a boat." She leaned forward and traced the scar near his left eye. Faint ridges marked the line where stiches held his skin tight enough to heal.

"Well, strictly speaking, the boat exploded." He covered her hand. "I didn't fall off anything."

Rolling her eyes, she pulled free her hand. "Your ego hasn't mellowed."

He exhaled. "A few pounds heavier, but I'm still the same man."

"What happened to the idealistic guy who bounded out of bed and chugged an energy drink to drive to Tahoe?"

Toying with the string on her pajama pants, he smiled. "You're right. Maybe I've mellowed. I can wait until we can do this right." He made eye contact. "Somehow, you're always right."

"Can I get that in writing?" She wet her lips and smiled.

He dropped the fabric and looked out the front window. "Last night's party felt good." He massaged her calf. "You feel good, but I need to decide how to reclaim my life. The night before they arrested me, I overheard a local tech CEO schmoozing an Indian guy. She pitched him hard on ScanCoin."

"I've never heard of it," she said.

He toyed with a fingernail. "It's a new cryptocurrency."

She shook her head. Person-to-person digital currencies operated without central authority or banks. Legitimate systems recorded transactions in a blockchain, which showed the transaction history for each coin and proved ownership. In theory, users could send instant payments to anyone in the world, but she never heard of ScanCoin. As the coffee kicked in, she dredged industry news from her memory. "That was two years ago. Did it go bust?"

"No. The value went up." He looked at the ceiling. "Way up."

Sitting up, she released the pillow and stared. Her photographic memory had failed her. Supply and demand, market competition, and exchange activity drove the price of cryptocurrencies. They never went up without making the news. "How can something I've never heard about be way up?"

"The founder reserved early investment opportunities for high net-worth individuals. When I worked at the Greek Restaurant, I overhead her give out the passcode to the investment portal." He smiled. "If Anna Claire is wining and dining investors, she should limit herself to one glass of wine."

"Stop! Anna Claire?" Digging her palms into her temples, she replayed the last forty-eight hours of her life. Coincidences were a joke, but cognitive biases were real. She worked hard to stay aware of her biases and test her methodologies, but cultural and personal experiences could effectively blind a person. Had she known about Damon's interest and blocked out the information? Without her analytical skills, she was a nobody.

Finding nothing to connect her real estate inquiries

with Damon's crypto investment, she wet her lips and focused on the handsome man in her home. He defied her expectations and piqued her interest. Data might seem objective, but humans analyzed it. Until she could get a handle on her life, she couldn't trust herself, but she could trust him. "Tell me everything."

Chapter Four

Damon cocked his head. "I'm talking about the chick who did the ScanCharge app."

"I know who she is!" Vivian scrambled to her knees. "Damon, how much did you invest in ScamCoin?"

"ScanCoin," he said.

She grabbed his shirt. "How much?"

"Eight hundred thousand."

She released the fabric and leaned her head on his shoulder. "Damon, something's off with that woman." She took a deep breath. "It could all be gone."

"Hold up." He tipped up her chin and narrowed his gaze. "What do you know?"

"Nothing, but two years is a long time in the tech world. Why haven't I heard of ScanCoin? How much do you think you have?"

"My investment's worth three million."

She surveyed the airy living room and everything it represented. She had that kind of liquidity, but relinquishing it required more than a sob story. If a woman with billions of dollars enticed Damon to invest in her schemes, she owed him restitution. Any other solution rubbed Vivian the wrong way. Scrambling from the couch, she stood and winced. "We have to get back your money." Hobbling across the hardwood floors, she powered up her computer. "Can you withdraw the investment? Sell your shares or bits or coins."

"Tokens," he said.

She waved off the correction. "Whatever."

Standing, he wrapped an arm around her waist.

His touch stilled her nervous energy. Turning from the computer, she braced her hands against his chest and took a deep breath. "Ok, this isn't an insurmountable problem. There are laws against fraud and making false claims." She swallowed. "I have a lawyer on retainer. We should make a list of action items."

"I don't need one of your fancy lists. I set a goal, and I work toward it, hell or high water."

"What if you're up a creek without a paddle?" She brushed an errant throw pillow feather off Damon's shoulder and wondered how much of his life would soon unravel. "What if this success kept you going in prison, and it's not there?"

"You kept me going." He shifted her closer and traced her spine. "I don't need your help, but you look like you're the person who's about to collapse."

Leaning into his embrace, she looked up and saw the steadiness in his gaze. Of course, he needed help. If he refused her assistance, he could talk to Johann. Despite Mama Clarke's steely gaze, the woman probably had limited knowledge of emergent investments, and Silvia might come out with guns blazing. If he refused to admit her needed help, the two years in prison might have been a complete waste of time.

"You weren't the only thing I studied in prison," he said.

She swallowed.

"ScanCoin isn't public knowledge yet, but the investor rolls are growing. The names on the marquee read like a who's who in Silicon Valley. You'd recognize the finance groups. I have no doubt the shareholders behind limited liability companies have money to burn, but high net-worth individuals made investments, too."

"Maybe you should teach finance and investing."

He laughed. "The trick to gambling is to know when to walk away. I'm already planning to withdraw the money and expand the scholarship program for neighborhood kids. If it calms your skittishness, I'll set up a nonprofit. With enough resources, I can go legit."

Skittishness? Aware of the choices she made in the preceding decade, she pulled free. *I danced through the tech world in high heels, but every stumble set me back ten paces.* She smoothed a hand over her hair and vowed to relinquish the fight. "Why are you so committed to neighborhood kids? Most people look out for themselves."

He rubbed his hands over his face. "To thrive as a neighborhood, EPA needs more than money. We don't have Fruitvale or the International Corridor." He looked at the boarded-up window like he could see another world. "I'm building my neighborhood's future, one kid at a time. When those men and women come home from college, they'll start the businesses that will keep the community alive. Some of them might be your employees."

She blew her hair out of her eyes. Beneath the jokes and self-confidence, he had a beautiful heart. "So, you don't want me to donate to the nonprofit?"

Amy Craig

He turned and grabbed her hip. "I want things from you, but not your money."

Raising a hand and drawn to the intensity in his gaze, she stroked his cheek. When she felt shut out, she downgraded their friendship to a business relationship. Her body betrayed her and tempted her with something more, but until Damon said the words, she feared revealing her interest and her vulnerability.

He leaned into her touch.

"I was right, you have a poet's heart," she said.

He laughed. "By poet, do you mean the guy on the corner with the tangled beard and the cardboard sign?"

"No!"

"Good." Turning his face, he kissed her palm and hooked his grip around her waist. "At the end of the week, ScanCoin's hosting a black-tie gala to celebrate early investors. After the event, Anna Claire will open an exchange to convert appreciated tokens into American dollars."

She frowned. "The demand must be high."

"People have been asking what I did with my money. I won't give them the information to access the investment portal, but the attention feels good. Helping my community."

"If you believe in ScanCoin, why won't you let them invest?"

"Because I can start over. I can hustle until my mind or my body falls apart. People on my block?" He shook his head. "They can't afford to lose what they put together."

She considered his altruisms and remembered the way the party guests swirled around him. Mama Clarke might have organized the party, but he was the star of the show. She managed conceited individuals on a daily basis, and the hint of ego underpinning Damon's heroics humanized his efforts, but she wouldn't let his motivations blindside her. "I think you like playing superhero."

"Doesn't everyone like a dash of celebrity?"

When she let success go to her head, she made mistakes, and she lay awake at night replaying her failure reel. Stepping back from Damon, she leaned on the desk chair for support. Precious curled on the sheepskin was proof that life's simple pleasures could be worthwhile. Damon deserved success, but squaring up his motivations would help him achieve it. "Some people like serenity and the reward of a long day's work."

"Are these people content, or do they have a choice?" he asked.

"Everyone has choices." Making eye contact, she swallowed the line. She chose to leave her simple life in the Central Valley, and he knew it. Her million-dollar bungalow, high-tech car, and catered life abounded with conveniences. She could preach simplicity, but she had to live it for her sermon to ring true. As much as she hated bland quinoa, she ate the stuff because it was good for her. Damon was too close for a one-night stand and too unpredictable to fit into her neat, ordered world. "You should go."

He sat on the couch and put on his shoes. "Come to the gala."

"I don't want to interrupt your flow." She rubbed her arms. "Go network with other investors."

"What if I want to network with you?" He looked up.

She turned away from the warmth in his expression. Complicating his life was the last thing she should do. "I have nothing to wear."

He laughed and resumed tying his shoe. "Vivi, that's a lie. You have a room full of clothes, and this is Silicon Valley. You could show up in jeans, and nobody would care."

The man had a point. She cleared her throat and regrouped. "And then?"

He bridged his hands over his stomach and leaned back. "And then I'll listen to your schemes for gainful employment."

She tilted her head and glimpsed a future where Damon stood at her side and recounted his schemes at laughter-tinged cocktail parties. If attending the gala and keeping him from her bed bolstered their chances of success, she could put together an outfit appropriate for shaking down a billionaire. "Deal."

"Deal?"

She sat in her desk chair and adopted the professional smile that let her analyze without showing her cards. *One week will give me time to figure out what Anna Claire's doing, if she left breadcrumbs, and if I can help Damon.* Kicking out her legs, she glanced at her swollen ankle and looked away before she lost her nerve. "I think the currency's a scam, but one week won't make a difference. For the chance to see you in a tux, I'm willing to dress up."

He shook his head. "I'm not wearing a tux."

Her smile wavered. "That's disappointing."

He raised an eyebrow. "I'll still dance with you."

She stopped thinking about Anna Claire and tilted her heard. "They have live music?"

"If they don't have music, I'll sing to you beneath the stars."

She had no doubt he would do it, but the implications shook her foundations. The jocular, mischievous man she knew had grown into a self-confident poet, and she needed to keep her wits about her. "I've never heard you sing."

Walking toward the front door, he paused and looked over his shoulder. "You don't know everything about me."

His promise stirred the butterflies in her stomach. *Or is that nausea?* "Let me give you a ride home."

Shaking his head, he raised a hand and left.

The door shuddered in his wake.

Precious woofed.

"He means well." She touched her lips and replayed the morning. Two years ago, she posted his bail and watched him walk away. *How many times has he disappeared into a crowd, content to work behind the scenes to make something happen? If ScanCoin is a bust, he won't let me help him.*

Jumping on the couch, Precious scratched the slipcover, shifted the fabric, and made a nest.

"Where do you sleep when I'm not home?" she asked.

Precious wagged her tail.

"Instead of going for walks, do you and the dog walker loaf on the couch?"

Yawning, Precious dropped her head on her paws.

She leaned over the couch back and scratched the animal's ear. "I could do with a little couch surfing, too, but work never stops." Eying the front door, she imagined how the day would have unfolded if Damon stayed. His abs and his kiss were as tantalizing as brewed coffee, but then she learned about ScanCoin. *How did a two-year absence turn friendly affection into wanton lust? I have to figure out what I'm doing before things go any farther.* She shook her head and pulled up a command line. *A low-key welcome home party. Did he plan to upend my world?*

****

That afternoon, Vivian hobbled from the bungalow, climbed in her car, and drove to the property Anna Claire might have used to launder money. The ranch house looked modern, but her research traced the house's roots to 1937. Built by an architect known for imbuing small homes with a spacious feeling, the modest house had escaped the frenzied bulldozers of the first dot-com boom. *I hope the person who modernized the house left behind a shred of character.*

Based on listing photos, the four-bedroom house needed additional updates, but fickle market conditions put the address in the gray zone between a starter home and a teardown. She pegged the house's value at close to two million dollars.

Anna Claire sold it for six million.

"This isn't her home," she said to herself as she rolled down a window, "and she's not a contractor. Why did she hold title? Why would a holding company hand over that much cash?"

Chirping birds answered her whispered question.

Pursing her lips, she considered knocking on a neighbor's door to drum up gossip. Real estate prices in the neighborhood crept toward eight thousand dollars per square foot. *It's a nice address, but Anna Claire's a power player, and she owns a gated estate in Atherton.*

She's a female tech CEO. Why would she get her hands dirty with this transaction? I doubt she drew up plans for an outdoor living room, sent the plans to her contractor, and balked at the price.

Thinking of Damon's ScanCoin investment, she swallowed and adjusted her perspective. *How many opportunities can eight hundred thousand dollars fund? What about three million?*

****

By two o'clock, Vivian's head hurt, and she was no closer to untangling Anna Claire's real estate transactions, rumors of ScanCoin, or her interest in Damon.

Precious wagged her tail from the bungalow kitchen.

"No, you can't have any brie," Vivian said. "It's bad for your pancreas."

Precious dropped to her belly, legs splayed. Her long, red-and-white coat draped the hardwood floor.

"Maybe Silvia will slip you a bite. She's coming for a late lunch, and I'll pretend not to notice when she drops half her food on the floor."

Precious covered her strong eye with her paw and wagged her tail.

The doorbell rang.

Barking, Precious charged the door.

She grabbed her pet's collar and checked the video feed. For a second, she hoped Precious's animated greeting signaled Damon, but Silvia stood on the mat. Her friend's severe black bun looked imposing, but she wore pink lipstick and carried a paper bag in her arms. *I'm in luck. Red lipstick signals disapproval.* Opening the door, she smiled. "You're early."

Silvia walked right into the house. "I'd rather be five minutes early than five minutes late."

Rolling her eyes, she released Precious.

The Welshie sniffed Silvia's black sandals and retreated.

Silvia glanced at the dog and unpacked the paper bag on the kitchen counter. "My niece made you food."

"She didn't have to do that." Vivian bit her lip. Silvia's nieces lived on a legacy *ejido* in Guanajuato. After Silvia promoted herself to Johann's executive assistant, she invited her oldest niece to move stateside and fill the role of Johann's housekeeper.

"Ceviche." Silvia unpacked a container and placed it on the countertop. "Chili Lime Shrimp. Salmon patties."

Maybe Silvia's verdict on me is still out. She opened the refrigerator. "Really, I have plenty of food."

Silvia shook her head. "You've lost weight."

"Most people consider that a compliment."

Silvia cocked her head. "Not in my hometown."

She picked up a pristine wedge of plastic-wrapped cheese. "I bought brie and crackers."

Precious lifted her head.

Silvia crossed her arms. "I went gluten-free."

Exhaling, she reached toward a pullout pantry. "I have rice crackers." A spider crawled across the shelf. She slammed a hand over her mouth and shut the door. "Ceviche sounds delicious."

"What happened after the party?" Silvia asked.

Turning, she swallowed. "Nothing."

Silvia pulled open the silverware drawer. *"Ustedes fueron como agua para chocolate."* Selecting a knife, she held it up to the light and sliced open the avocado

68

she held in her hand. "That's not what I saw. You two looked good together."

Vivian knew exactly who Silvia meant, but letting Silvia dissect her feelings for Damon felt too risky. "Who?"

Silvia knocked the knife into the avocado pit. Withdrawing the blade, she waved the knife and the pit in the air. "Don't even try, *mija*. I'm talking about you and Damon."

She put two plates on the table and cleared her throat. "We're friends. Did Johann ask him to return to work?"

Silvia shook her head and tossed the pit in the compost bin. "I've heard nothing."

"Maybe he'll get a teaching certification and work directly with the neighborhood kids." She smiled at the thought of Damon standing in front of a smart board explaining supply and demand. Who knew what he would teach those kids? "I wish him the best."

Silvia put the cutting board in the sink. "Don't we all."

Frowning, Vivian pulled out a chair and sat at the kitchen table's corner. Damon's invitation to the gala felt too loaded for idle gossip. As Johann's new personal assistant, Silvia ran his life with Machiavellian mastery. *I prefer to run mine on my terms, and Damon does, too.*

Silvia joined her at the table.

They sat elbow-to-elbow, gossiping about neighbors, Silicon Valley rumors, and downtown's newest ivy-covered restaurant. "The menu looks decadent," she said. "I'm looking forward to trying it."

Silvia raised an eyebrow. "When?"

"When I"—she dabbed her napkin against her lips—"have a girls' night out."

"You need a date."

She cleared her throat. "That's not true. I need to spend time with my friends."

Silvia raised an eyebrow.

Leaning back in her chair, she lifted her chin. "Hadley and I are friends."

"*Ustedes se cogieron al mismo hombre.*"

What? Narrowing her gaze, she recognized an insult when she heard one, but she refused to cave and admit her nonexistent Spanish skills. "I'm happy with my life. I donate to charities. Hoat Analytics has a very low attrition rate."

Silvia raised her eyebrows. "Your employees don't count as friends."

She sighed and poked a piece of shrimp with her fork. Beyond her first three employees, she managed ten technicians, a human resources specialist, and a personal assistant. Thinking of her time with Johann, she smiled. *Well, maybe my assistant manages me.* "I've been busy."

Her protest sounded as weak as the vinaigrette in her refrigerator. She thought she despised seafood, but the tart bite of ceviche refreshed her palate. *Maybe I should pay more attention to Silvia's advice, too.* "I'll call a few people for dinner. You should come."

Silvia's threw back her head and laughed. Thumping her chest, she shook her head. "I don't think so."

"Why not?" Vivian asked.

Silvia narrowed her gaze and tapped the table. "I have a better idea. Get laid."

The woman drew out the last word and left zero doubt about who Vivian should romance. Sighing, she stared at the computer equipment tucked out of sight. "It's not that easy."

"Yes, Ms. Hoat."

Turning her head, she appraised her houseguest. Silvia's tight-lipped smile and averted gaze channeled 1950s subservience, but the woman's shrewd mind and organizational skills outclassed that role. "Don't pull that act on me. Hoat Analytics makes me gobs of money. It's like winning the lottery. Ten million dollars and people think you can quit your job. Fifty million and you hear every sob story in town." She pointed her finger. "You and I predate the money."

Silvia cocked her head. "Did you make fifty million dollars?"

Standing, she carried her plate to the sink and favored her uninjured foot. "I'd prefer not to discuss my compensation."

Precious yipped.

She looked over her shoulder. "Silvia, please don't feed Precious from the table."

Two sets of doe eyes stared back.

Shaking her head, she braced her hands on the counter and stared out the kitchen window. "My last date was a nightmare. He spent the entire night grilling me about the company."

"Go incognito." Silvia pulled open the dishwasher and loaded her plate. "Call yourself Sally."

She turned. "I doubt that would work. People spend more time researching their dates than they spend enjoying their conversation. I'm not comfortable setting up a fake life to hide my assets. What if my date falls for Freewheeling Sally instead of Analytical Vivian?" She thought of Damon. *I don't have to hide with him.*

Silvia braced her hands on her lower back and stretched. "You're not always analytical."

"I might as well call the matchmaker who advertises in the inflight magazines." She ran hot water over the cutting board. "Dating isn't a priority."

Silvia pushed her out of the way. "Trust the people who know you best."

Made redundant in her own kitchen, she sighed. "Do you have someone in mind?"

"Not particularly, but I've met a few interesting characters. The world is strange."

Tell me about it.

Silvia walked to the table and picked up the napkins. "Ask Hadley to set you up with someone. She's an excellent judge of character."

Catching Silvia's grin, she snorted. "Is that so?"

"She pegged you from the start. She said you were possessive."

Chewing the inside of her lip, she composed a response that might keep her out of hot water. "What gave that impression?"

Silvia set the napkins on the counter. "After breaking up with Johann, you stayed by his side. That kind of loyalty says something about a person."

She shrugged. "He offered me a good job."

Folding a paper bag, Silvia placed it in the recycling bin. "Most women would cut their losses and stop taking his calls. You stick by people."

I want them to stick by me. Opening the back door for Precious, she replayed the year she spent making Johann's travel arrangements and booking his appointments. Her interest in his affection waned, but her appreciation for his lifestyle remained. Damon's friendship meant more than a well-stocked wine closet. She reframed their relationship in the Central Valley and knew she would have gone to the same backyard party and felt the same way, but she needed personal achievements before she had anything to give. "I'm an only child. Letting go of people I know and trust is hard."

"So date someone you already know and trust." Silvia opened her purse and reapplied her lipstick. "You'll have already heard their sob stories, and they'll have already heard yours."

She cataloged her MBA classmates, coworkers at the management consulting firm, and peers in the world of data analytics. "I'll keep an eye out for someone." *Someone who thinks spending equal amounts of money on shoes and technology upgrades is cute.*

Silvia paused and made eye contact. "I thought you'd already found him."

Swallowing, she tilted her head and thought of Damon. *Have I?*

Silvia drummed her nails on the table. "So, I'm thinking of hosting a little party next Saturday. You will come."

Shaking her head, Vivian decided to lay her cards on the table. "I kind of have a pseudo-date."

Silvia jerked up her chin. "What?"

Vivian rubbed her head to dampen the bark of Silvia' question. "It's Damon."

"You'll need a dress."

She frowned. "I have fifty."

"None of your corporate sheaths," Silvia said. "Get

your purse. We're going shopping."

Laughing, she accompanied Silvia to the boutique district. All the downtown women's clothing stores went by whimsical, vaguely botanical names. When she wanted to find special, chic clothing, Currant & Sheen had her back. *Or was it Cassis and Shine?*

Silvia adjusted her glasses and sorted through racks of cocktail dresses. "I'm glad you're giving him a chance. You and Damon are good together. You always have each other's backs."

Vivian wanted to give him a chance, but she also wanted to reclaim his investment. Until she untangled her desires, she had no business romanticizing the gala. She looked at the shop owner. "Isn't that what friends do?"

The woman's shoulder length hair looked straight from a salon blowout, and her unassuming makeup guaranteed she faded into the background. She held up a simple, black dress and raised her eyebrows.

Vivian subtly shook her head.

The owner returned the dress to the rack.

Moving to a different rack, Silvia continued her quest. "I remember when Johann's boat exploded. You brought towels for Damon and that Gary kid, but you held back."

She thought of the scar above Damon's eyebrow. The old wound felt smooth to the touch. *Friends don't caress other friends' faces.* Clearing her throat, she debated what kind of dress she needed for a pseudo-date at a pseudo black-tie gala. "I'm sure you had everything under control."

Silvia raised her eyebrow. "Are you?"

Grinning, she pulled out a beaded ensemble. "Fine.

Maybe you needed my help."

"Damon did." Silvia looked at the beaded dress and shook her head. "My point is, the minute you saw Damon sway, you ran to help. Blood dripped from his chin and splattered on your shoes. *On your shoes!*"

"I loved those shoes." She sighed and handed the beaded dress to the shop owner for consideration. Contemplating the racks of clothes, she headed toward colorful, spring hues and wondered if Silvia had rehearsed her messaging. *I should let her manage my employees.*

Silvia joined her at the rack. "Damon's perfect."

Half listening, the whispered comment caught her off-guard. She turned and frowned. "How can you say he's perfect? We've always been friends, and sometimes that friendship wasn't enough."

"Always means nothing. I've always been a *Mexicana.*" Silvia folded her arms across her chest. "Now I'm running a rich man's empire and reviewing ad rates for my social media accounts."

She wondered whether Silvia would give her pointers about advertising Hoat Analytics. The older woman evolved in the last two years, and if she could do it, other people could, too. She cleared her throat. "I'm surprised you have to advertise."

"People change." Silvia narrowed her gaze. "Give Damon a chance to sweep you off your feet."

Looking at Silvia's pristine lipstick, she grinned. "You're a busybody."

"Probably so." Laughing, Silvia held up a strapless red dress. "What do you think?"

The dress would show off her shoulders, but she doubted Damon would like the full skirt. *When did I start dressing for men?* Her stomach rumbled, and she eyed the beaded dress waiting in the fitting room. The sleek and refined dress had a hemline that would display her legs and the tall sandals on the opposite side of the room. "Buy that one for yourself," she said to Silvia. "Get yourself a date."

The woman caressed the fabric. "This is a younger woman's dress."

"Silvia, you're not that old…"

"Don't say it!"

Rolling her eyes, Vivian pulled back the curtain to the dressing room and stepped inside. She slipped into the dress she picked out and felt the smooth lining glide across her skin. Pulling up the zipper, she met her reflection in the mirror. *I've come a long way from the almond farm.* Grateful for Silvia's encouragement, she hung up the dress and checked the time. After dress shopping, Silvia would drop her at home, and she could take a conference call from her couch. Work would give her an excuse to stop thinking about Damon and Anna Claire, but she would come back to the tingling sensation at the base of her neck. Where there's smoke, there's fire, but she had no idea whether the last few days would save her or burn her life to the ground.

Chapter Five

"I could have picked you up." Vivian adjusted her phone to avoid the beaded tassel earring she bought with Silvia last week. Music spilled from the three-story museum building, but clear cell phone reception and improvements in background noise reduction made the call crystal clear. If only Golden Gate Park provided closer parking.

"Where's the fun in letting you pick me up?" Damon asked over the phone. "Without an audience, we might have skipped the party and chilled?"

"It's not too late," she said.

He laughed.

If only he knew how close she came to taking him up on his offer. Hung over from the backyard party, she considered one-night stands and unscratched itches, but every time she indulged the idea, she let practical obstacles sway her. After a week of strait-laced business meetings and encouraging friends, her interest simmered, and she wanted something more substantial than a fling. If nothing else, she would help Damon get to the bottom of ScanCoin or compile enough evidence to engage the police's interest. She focused on her phone call and the evening. A lucky parking spot put her at the steps of the museum, and attendees flowed toward the museum doors. "Where are you?"

"You look amazing," he said.

She spun and scanned the crowd. "Damon?"

"Turn to your left."

Hearing the smile behind his command, she ended the call, turned, and caught sight of his confident swagger. Feeling her stomach drop at the sight of him, she grinned. He wore light slacks and a crisp button-up shirt. His confident grin shone through the San Francisco fog. This time, she recognized the combination of desire and nerves warming her cheeks. *I spent the entire week wondering if the party was a fluke.* She waved. *I'm glad it wasn't.*

A woman tilted her head toward Damon and stepped away from her group. The woman's lime-green dress had a plunging neckline that revealed the swell of perky, surgically enhanced breasts.

Vivian increased her pace.

He walked right past the woman and held his arms wide open.

The movement strained the fabric of his shirt, adding tension to the small white buttons shielding his chest. *I hope one pops.* She walked into his embrace half hoping he would pick her up and embarrass the hell out of her.

"You feel amazing, too," he said.

"What? This old thing?" The beaded cocktail dress skimmed her hips. She loved the length and the way it put her legs on full display.

Kissing her cheek, he lingered near her ear. "It's brand new, isn't it?"

She laughed and wondered if she left on a tag. Guessing he could spot the confidence a new dress gave her, she preened and welcomed him into the moment. "It's been a long time since I went out on a date."

He straightened. "A date, huh? You're not here to mock my investment?"

"I can't find any police reports or insurance claims citing ScanCoin." *The shadows beneath my makeup proved I tried.* She scanned the crowd posing for selfies on the museum steps. The after-hours guests ran the gauntlet from silver-haired senior citizens to wide-eyed tourists clutching guidebooks. True to the invitation, gala attendees wore black tie and evening gowns, but a contingent sported jeans and black T-shirts.

If people wear the same outfit every day to avoid decision fatigue, they should pick a more interesting outfit. Her dress's silk lining shifted against her smooth skin. *Nice clothes feed my creativity.*

The T-shirt contingent moved toward the museum's front door and handed over their identification cards. Their furtive gazes dared the security guards to question their presence.

Checking the list, the security team admitted them to the party.

Why don't I recognize anyone here?

Whistling, Damon took her hand. "Let's party."

ScanCoin's logo shone on the three-story building's exterior. Beyond a set of metal detectors, fuchsia lights pulsed with the music, and a spotlight illuminated a mid-size *Tyrannosaurus rex*. "I haven't been here in ages." She squeezed his hand. "I'll give Anna Claire the benefit of the doubt. She dropped money on the party planners. Rexy looks like he's about to dance."

"It's not real," he said.

Frowning, she stared at the dinosaur.

"The skeleton's not real," he said. "It's a cast."

"How do you know?" Tilting her head, she examined the lobby's centerpiece. The song changed, and the strobe-light pattern paused. Removed from the flashing beat, the bones looked too neat to be fossil specimens. *Damn, he's right.*

"School field trips." He squeezed her hand. "But, you can't have a science museum without a dinosaur."

She swiveled her head to catch glimpses of the exhibits. "What else is fake? Do they have animatronic fish?"

He chewed his lip. "You look so disappointed."

She squeezed his hand. "They overhauled the museum in 2010. Surely, they could have found something in their collection to take center stage that was *real*." Hoat Analytics focused on big data, but she appreciated the scale and reach of neighborhood institutions. The museum hosted a citizen science event on six continents. An online community confirmed species identifications and awarded prizes. In return, user data helped scientists detect patterns. *Instead of a cast, maybe they should have chosen a gallery.* "I mean, I would have even sponsored it. This is the Bay Area. We thrive on authenticity."

"Yeah, but authenticity's expensive." He released her hand and fished his identification from his wallet. Handing the card to the security team, he cleared his throat and placed a hand on her back. "Damon Clarke. Vivian Hoat is my plus one."

She recognized the pressure on her back from her time with Johann and grinned. More than once, she used the gesture to guide people where she wanted them to go. *Did I try that trick on Damon, too?* She smiled. *What other bad habits rubbed off?*

The guard returned Damon's card. "Please proceed to Melinda."

Replacing his identification card, Damon glanced over and smiled.

She returned the expression and tried not to notice the cool air where she missed his touch. "How do you always look so confident?"

He laughed. "Nobody knows what they're doing, Vivi. Everyone's doing their best."

Missing a step, she considered the ramifications.

Melinda held a clipboard and beckoned. "While visiting the museum, ScanCoin invites you to enjoy an exclusive VIP experience. To the left of the aquarium, you'll find a reserved VIP area and an open bar for early investors."

As she talked, her blonde ponytail bobbed.

Vivian thought of Shani's doll collection.

"Docents wearing light-up lanyards are available for behind-the-scenes tours of the gem and mineral collection." Melinda handed each of them a lanyard.

Damon slipped the lanyard over his head. "The gem collection?"

Melinda tilted her head. "Which exhibit would you like to explore? I can make it happen."

Vivian rolled her eyes and draped her lanyard over her purse. *I'm not about to mess up my outfit with this blinking piece of junk.* "Do you have a schedule for the evening?"

"Sure!" Melinda pulled a sheet of paper from her clipboard and presented it.

Scanning the printout, Vivian realized she and Damon had more than an hour until Anna Claire delivered her opening remarks. She handed the paper back to the perky attendant. "We'll keep ourselves busy."

Melinda's shoulders relaxed. "Excellent."

"So, about this open bar…" Damon said.

Vivian laughed and shook her head. "I learned my lesson. No more fruity drinks."

"You'd rather have a glass of wine."

She felt strangely pleased he knew her habits. At first, he was Johann's jovial security force and a friendly face in shifting crowds. After she ended her relationship with Johann and worked as his executive assistant, she counted Damon a continuing part of her life. He drove, scouted venues, or ran odd jobs. *When did I start depending on him? When did we start working as a team?* She smoothed her dress. "A glass of wine would be nice."

Scanning the crowded foyer, he jerked his chin toward the section marked for VIP attendees.

She eyed a couple taking a photograph in front of the imitation fossil. "I don't understand. I thought the party was for early investors in ScanCoin." She frowned. "Some of these people don't live in the Bay Area."

"You can tell who has money from a glance?" He wrinkled his forehead and looked from guest to guest. "They all look entitled."

"People with money don't get excited about party decorations."

He laughed. "I don't know, Vivi. The invitation said what it said."

Looking over her shoulder, she watched the security team direct guests toward Melinda or toward the wide foyer. "There are two lists."

"Did we make the right one?"

She frowned. The museum's dry, air-conditioned interior raised the hairs on her skin. "I don't know."

"Let's find the open bar and enjoy Anna Claire's hospitality." He ran his thumb beneath his collar. "The sooner I grab a drink, the more at ease I'll be. This crowd makes my skin itch."

Grabbing his hand, she squeezed. "You look good, Damon. Better than anyone I see."

He smiled. "Well, let's see if I can hang with the big guns."

A security guard stood at the entrance to the VIP area, but he let them pass without comment and kept his gaze on the crowd.

Damon walked to the bar. "Anyone could walk into this joint."

She twirled her lanyard. "Anyone with a credit card and a box of LEDs. It's a cheap gimmick, but it works."

He frowned and rubbed the lanyard between his fingers.

Diminishing his achievement was the last thing on her list. Approaching the bar, she debated whether a cocktail was a good idea. Drops of water speckled the black tablecloth around stainless steel containers. Brown bottles of beer and green bottles of wine soaked in the ice baths. Beyond the bartender, hidden lights illuminated rows of liquor.

"What will you have?" the bartender asked.

"Red wine," Damon said. "And water."

"You're not having anything to drink?" she asked. "What happened to being at ease?"

"I just need something to hold." He looked over. "You look disappointed."

She remembered his promise. "I thought we might dance."

"I don't need alcohol to dance with you."

Laughing, she accepted a glass of wine from the bartender. "No, but if I fall flat on my face, alcohol might help erase your memory. I'm not a great dancer, and my ankle's still sore."

He eyed her shoes. "I won't let you fall." Turning to the bartender, he pointed toward a local beer. "I changed my mind. Hook me up."

The bartender handed him the beer and a small white napkin.

"Vivian Hoat!" a man said.

Turning, she blinked and focused on the man speaking. He wore a three-piece suit and a plaid pocket square, but she had a strong desire to throw her wine in the man's gleaming face. *Did he get a face lift?* She gritted her teeth. "Hello, Boulder."

Damon's hand anchored the small of her back.

"I thought that might be you." He leaned in and kissed her cheek. "What a charming dress. Who's your friend?"

Wiping her cheek on her dress seemed like an insult to the dress. She cleared her throat. "Damon, this is Boulder MacIntyre."

Boulder offered a hand. "Of the Clan MacIntyre."

Shaking the man's hand, Damon smiled. "You're far from home."

"Oh, my family has lived in California since the gold rush. Yours?"

"Couldn't say." Damon's thumb stroked her back. "How do you know Vivian?"

"Boulder was a senior vice president at the global

management consulting firm where I worked before I took Johann's job." She drew in a breath and smiled. "Boulder retired while I was still there." *Human Resources pushed him out the door, and it was the happiest day of my life.*

"I remember your first day in the office," Boulder said. "You were fresh out of your Ivy League MBA program. Did you hang your diploma on your wall?"

"Not that I recall," she said.

Boulder winked. "Who knew you could accomplish so much!"

"I did." She straightened and debated bringing up the intern who reported Boulder's sexual advances and prematurely ended his career. The intern had accepted a full-time offer, earned a promotion, and landed a multinational client for the consulting firm. Vivian couldn't be more proud, but she wanted her accomplishments to be the thing people remembered most about the woman.

"And you have a little project," Boulder said.

"Hoat Analytics helps our customers understand their livelihoods. We offer the right tools, the right metrics, and the right applications to understand small business data."

"What a great elevator speech." He patted his chest. "Gets you right here, ya know?"

She narrowed her gaze. "Funny, most people think with their heads. How much profit did your firm clear this year?"

Boulder cleared his throat.

"What did you used to tell me over lunch? Your clan hailed from western Scotland. I'm surprised you didn't retire there, Boulder. You always spoke of the landscape in such glowing terms."

He removed his pocket square and blotted his forehead. "Well, I'm not done yet! Maybe ScanCoin will make me as rich as a laird."

She picked at her fingernail and looked up. "I doubt it."

Jerking back his chin, he stared.

She smiled. "It's so nice to see you. I hope ScanCoin gives you everything you deserve."

Withdrawing a business card, he presented it. "You call me if you need help growing your company. I heard about the Steadman contract you're negotiating. If you're going to win against those jerks, you need to fight dirty. I know a few tricks I'd be willing to share. Call it mentoring."

Damon shifted.

She considered tearing the anachronistic card into confetti, but she abhorred litter, and the conversation left a sour taste in her mouth. Refusing to give the man any openings, she slipped the card in her purse and vowed to recycle it. "Thanks for the tip."

He glanced at Damon. "It's so modern of you to bring your employee to these functions."

"Damon isn't my employee," she said. "He's my friend."

Raising his eyebrows, Boulder shrugged. "My mistake."

She tilted her head and waited.

Looking away, Boulder waved at someone in the crowd. "If you'll excuse me."

"With pleasure." She turned to Damon. "Sorry about that"—she cleared her throat—"interruption."

"I've never seen you act rude to someone." He sipped his beer and toasted her. "I used to have so much fun getting a rise from the unflappable Vivian Hoat. Maybe I should have pushed you harder."

"I'm not unflappable," she said.

He sipped his beer. "And I have other ideas to flush your cheeks."

Savoring the innuendo, she sighed and took deep breaths. Compartmentalizing her life was the key to success. No matter how much she accomplished, she had to work harder than people like Boulder. "That nasty old man is pretentious and handsy."

Damon narrowed his gaze. "I can still punch him."

She shook her head. "He's not worth losing your temper over. You're better than brute violence. Forget him."

He worked his jaw.

She linked her arm through his arm. "So about this dancing."

Taking a deep breath, he turned his back on Boulder's retreat. "Are you sure you don't want to see the gems exhibit? Melinda seemed very helpful."

"Melinda was a ditz." She pulled him toward the museum's center atrium. "Let's find the action."

During normal business hours, rows of chairs and a podium occupied the space, but nearly a hundred people matched the pulsing beat and kept their drinks from splashing on the floor. A stage loomed over the atrium, and a DJ controlled the mix.

"Maybe we should finish these drinks before we go out there." She filled her mouth with the rich red wine, and the familiar cabernet taste soothed her nerves. She wanted Damon, but the repercussions had yet to settle into a pattern she understood. *It's one thing to surrender to his touch. It's another thing to match him step-for-step without embarrassing myself or him. I have to stop throwing up roadblocks and choose.* "Maybe they'll play a slow song."

The beat changed, and a pop goddess's anthem filled the air space.

Downing her wine, she set her glass on a tall table and grabbed Damon's hand. "Now or never."

He abandoned his beer, wrapped one arm around her waist, pulled her close, and moved his hips to the music.

No matter the beat, his gaze stayed true. Lost in his arms and the music, she surrendered and regretted not dancing with him the first day she met him. *Every woman should dance with a man before sleeping with him.* Public scrutiny kept her from kissing him on the dance floor, but she considered making a move and testing his reaction.

The music changed.

She felt his hold shift and blinked off her trance. His enthusiastic greeting warmed her heart, and the heat of his kiss surprised her, but how had she enjoyed dancing? The combination of public exposure and sustained contact usually turned her into a wallflower. She pulled away. *What if I make a fool out of myself? I might break a shoe?*

"Not so fast, Vivi." He pulled her closer. "Where are you going?"

She scanned the room's perimeter. An exit sign blinked in the corner. "My feet get tangled up."

"We'll look strange doing the box step," he said.

Charmed, she draped an arm over his shoulder. "The box step?"

"Gym class." He shifted his hips. "We also spent a

week learning line dances."

She laughed and tempered her urge to flee. "I can't see you riding a tractor."

"But you see me teaching economics?" He shifted her to the right.

His erection pressed against her thigh, and her throat went dry. The off-center contact made it easier to follow his lead, but it raised the stakes. Looking over his shoulder, she watched a couple grinding and wondered if she could release her inhibitions.

The couple dropped their hips, and the woman rolled her back over her partner's arm, fanning her breasts to the crowd.

Vivian shifted back to center. Her pulse raced, and as much as she wanted to close the deal with Damon, the thought of losing everything she had sent her into a panic. She scanned the backlit exhibits, the tipsy crowd, and the servers hurrying between tightly packed tables. Between the beats, the bass throbbed, and the volume pushed partygoers closer to talk. She circled back to the grinding couple, fascinated by their rhythm and the ways they stayed focused on each other.

Damon glanced over his shoulder. "You picking up tips?"

Caught staring, she rolled her hips against his side and exaggerated the move. "I learned from the best."

He flared his nostrils and pulled her flush against his body.

His confidence and his presence overpowered her inhibitions. She ground against his heat. "I'm feeling inspired."

He stopped dancing on a dime.

Losing her balance, she grabbed his arm.

"We can leave right now," he said.

Swatting his chest, she shook her head. "No! This is your party."

He raised an eyebrow. "Screw the party."

I'd rather screw you. She fingered a button on his shirt. "ScanCoin? Remember?"

He grabbed her hand and led her back to the tall table. "Everyone in the room knows why they're here." Adjusting his collar, he rolled his head. "People have too much riding on tonight to forget the stakes."

She looked at the crowd and searched for a familiar face. *This party isn't catering to high net-worth individuals and the who's who of Silicon Valley. These people look like doctors and law students gambling their tuition.* "I didn't think it would be this big."

He raised his eyebrows.

Flipping a hand toward the party, she picked up her drink and grinned. "The party, Damon."

"Vivi." He leaned close. "The moment you and Johann ended, I should have said something, but I worried you would laugh in my face."

She thought about the months she spent organizing Johann's life. *He set me aside like a lamp.* After she broke up with him, she let Hoat Analytics consume her time, but she heard the sincerity in Damon's voice. "I wasn't ready."

"Neither was I."

"And then, you weren't there." Staring at the tablecloth, she wondered if Damon's confinement unleashed a rash side. *I worried about ghosting him, but I don't want to be the trophy fuck. I don't want to feel set aside once again. What if he slakes his thirst and moves on?* Shaking her head, she scanned the room's perimeter. A green exit sign shone from the corner. "I'm going to the bathroom."

"We just arrived," he said.

She downed the remainder of her wine and shrugged. Bolting before he could challenge her, she turned her shoulder and pushed through the crowd.

A server carrying a tray of empty glasses stepped out of her way and lost his balance. The tray wobbled in his hand, and a half-full, plastic wine glass hit the polished concrete floor. "Shit, sorry!"

Swallowing a chastisement, she exhaled and looked at the red wine splattered across her legs. *At least, he missed my shoes.*

The server jerked a hand toward a black, fabric curtain suspended from a metal frame. "The bathroom's over there!"

Frowning, she considered her options. The exit sign beckoned. The lobby offered bright lights and perky Melinda. Damon could carry her from the room and make her scream, but what happened next? Biting her lip, she strode toward the black curtain, pushed it aside, and headed for the bathroom. In the deserted hallway, she straightened her shoulders and lifted her chin. *No more stalling. I need five minutes to make a calculated decision.*

Pushing open the bathroom's swinging door, she walked toward the vanity and stopped in her tracks.

Anna Claire stood at the sink.

The notoriously decisive businesswoman glanced up and continued powdering her nose. She wore a belted midi dress and towering heels. Overhead lights highlighted her loose, glossy, black curls and flawless, light brown skin.

Anna Claire opened a tube of lipstick. "This bathroom is private."

She crossed her arms. "Says who?"

Making eye contact in the mirror, Anna Claire lowered the lipstick. "Do you know who I am?"

Tapping her chin, she looked at the ceiling tiles and brainstormed a pithy response. Finding her war chest empty, she swallowed. *On the ride home, I'll come up with a million good comebacks.* Instead, she met Anna Claire's gaze and smiled. "It's Anna, right? I recognize you from local cover stories. You must have a good publicist."

Turning from the vanity, Anna Claire straightened.

Her height and heels gave her six inches, and Vivian wished she wore taller heels.

"I prefer Anna Claire."

"Oh, my gosh! Right!" She covered her gaping mouth. "You're the woman pitching ScamCoin."

"ScanCoin."

Vivian tilted her head. "I know what you call it."

Rolling her eyes, Anna Claire dropped her makeup in her purse and strode toward the door.

Unwilling to let the CEO escape without hearing her piece, she reached out, caught the woman's arm, and held fast. No matter what she decided to do about Damon, she wanted him to recoup his money and continue his life without feeling cheated by Anna Claire, the system, or anyone who might have betrayed him.

Anna Claire narrowed her gaze. "Take your hands off me."

She complied, but she shifted and blocked the exit. "I don't own any of your shares or bits or coins."

"Tokens," Anna Claire said.

"I don't care what you call them. They're worthless, aren't they?"

Anna Claire worked her jaw.

"All your guests think you're about to open an exchange so they can convert their tokens into dollars." She tilted her head. "What's going to happen tonight? Website error? Are you going to take the mic and offer everyone a last chance to invest?"

"You're not an investor?" Anna Claire leaned close. "A wannabe millionaire?"

She shook her head. "I've already made my millions."

Anne Claire straightened. "Then why do you care?"

She tilted her head and thought of Damon and the eager investors waiting for Anna Claire to make her celebratory speech. "When did this crap begin? Two years ago? Three? You wined and dined Silicon Valley power players for initial investments? Some took the bait, but not enough. The people out there? They're not VIPs flush with cash from IPOs." She jerked her chin toward the music pulsing beyond the door. "Do you have any idea how many lives you'll upend?"

"You're wrong." Anna Claire crossed her arms over her chest.

"At best, it's a pyramid scheme." The accusation felt too simplistic, but straightforward explanations made the most sense. "At worst, you're laundering money. I've seen the real estate transactions tied to your name. You hold properties for a heartbeat, and then you sell to foreign investors for twice what they're worth."

Anna Claire blinked. "I didn't catch your name."

She smiled. "Vivian Hoat of Hoat Analytics."

"I've heard of you."

"Good. You'll keep hearing of me until I expose what you're doing." She stepped to the side and cleared a path for egress. "The next time you're on a magazine cover, I doubt the story will praise you."

Anna Claire walked past her, her heels clicking on the hard floor, and reached for the door handle.

"Wait." Empathy softened her approach, and she cleared her throat. Whatever Anna Claire had done, she had a compulsion. "I remember when you made the cover of the *Valley Investor*. 'Young, Indian woman founds and retains control of emerging payment processing application.' Your story made quite the headline."

Anna Claire looked over her shoulder. "Don't believe everything you read."

"Is that how you'll start your speech?" she asked.

"I did my research, Vivian Hoat." Anna Claire looked away. "Everyone in the museum had the chance to do the same. ScanCoin's Phase One investors passed screening requirements. Some sought out me." She shook her hair over her shoulder. "ScanCoin isn't the first cryptocurrency, and it won't be the last."

"Copying a successful idea doesn't make yours real."

Anna Claire turned. "Green is never an attractive color." She glanced at Vivian's legs. "You might want to get cleaned up before you embarrass yourself."

"Excellent advice. I'd hate to start a rumor."

Tilting her head, Anna Claire opened her mouth and then turned and gripped the door handle.

"That's the problem with such a folksy

community," she said. "People talk." *Or, in Damon's case, eavesdrop.* "I'm betting secondary markets for ScanCoin already exist. You have no way of knowing who ultimately holds your"—she smiled—"tokens."

"I have the name of every person in this building. Security has a list."

"What about guests? Anonymous donors?" She tapped her chin. "Did you know I would be here?"

Anna Claire turned the door handle. "I've considered throwing you out."

"Oh, that's the problem. You don't know who I came with." She dropped her voice. "You'd hate to alienate your biggest investors."

Looking over her shoulder, Anna Claire frowned.

The music died, and an amplified voice welcomed guests to the gala.

"That's your cue," she said. "I hope you've practiced your remarks."

Anna Claire adjusted the belt cinching her dress. "Would you like to take the microphone? I could use an opening act."

She thought of Damon standing at the tall table and waiting for her to emerge. Instead of confronting Anna Claire, she wanted to spend the remainder of the night dancing with him and slipping a hand beneath his shirt to tease his warm skin. To build something substantial, she had to take a risk. Instead of running into his arms, she closed her eyes and summoned the last of her courage. "You have to tell the crowd the truth, Anna Claire. If you don't, someone will."

The door swung closed.

Chapter Six

No longer considering an exit, Vivian retraced her steps to Damon's side to report on her discovery. Sidling up to him, she leaned in close and let his scent envelop her. No longer picking up notes of sweat, dirt, and sunshine, she focused on the allure of ginger and coconuts. For a night, she could escape in his arms.

He wrapped an arm around her waist. "I thought you'd bolted."

His touch claimed her focus, but excitement tamped down her desire. To help him, she had to think about more than her desires. "Guess who I saw in the bathroom?"

"The president."

She swatted his arm. "Anna Claire!"

Attendees swelled into the room and filled the floor in front of a stage.

"I'm not surprised." He shifted his grip around her waist. "After all, it's her show."

"Is it?"

On the stage, the man wearing a microphone sipped water and nodded toward the audio engineers. "Ladies and gentlemen, welcome to the ScanCoin gala!"

The crowd clapped and cheered.

"Despite market swings, blockchain projects and cryptocurrency influencers continue to bolster new investments. Technologists, investors, policymakers, and visionaries have entered the crypto space, leading to endorsement and regulation. No longer content to fuel start-ups, today's leaders recognize the power of mass adoption and thoughtful integration into traditional infrastructure. Anna Claire's pioneering payment processing application revolutionized the way we do business, and you're a part of it."

"Anna Claire wasn't the first app on the market," she said.

Damon glanced over. "She added value."

"To herself." Rolling her eyes, she stared at the VIP section and wondered if she could snag another glass of wine. *Never mind. I don't need liquid courage.* Biting the inside of her cheek, she smiled for Damon's benefit. "I hope I'm wrong."

"Why?"

She scanned the attendees, their eager faces tilted toward the stage. In profile, their bright eyes, hawkish noses, and pressed lips gave off a mix of optimism and nerves. "Because you all want her to be right." Narrowing her gaze, she stared at the stage. "Because legitimacy matters."

Damon withdrew his arm from her waist.

What did I say?

"This year will be an exciting year for mass blockchain adoption, but I'm preaching to the choir." The announcer laughed. "You all recognized the future. You recognized how easy-to-use mobile apps, crypto credit cards, and a crypto exchange would revolutionize personal finance. You also recognized Anna Claire as a leader in the industry. Without further ado, we welcome ScanCoin's creator and chief executive officer, Anna

Claire."

Applause filled the room.

She squinted, waiting to see Anna Claire emerge from the black curtains, mount the stairs, and prove her wrong. She toyed with a tassel earring and counted to twenty. "Come on. They're waiting for you."

"Must be cutting a fresh deal," the announcer said.

A few audience members cheered.

She closed her eyes. "Prove me wrong."

The murmuring crowd drowned her whisper.

"After Anna Claire's remarks, she will open an exchange to convert appreciated tokens into American dollars. I hope you're all feeling bullish and planning to hold your tokens, but those of you with weak knees can use the mobile app, or the kiosks set up in the museum's lobby, to access the exchange."

Turning, Vivian watched the back half of the crowd shift.

Investors turned toward the lobby, spilling their drinks and bumping shoulders with the attendees who remained fixed on the stage.

"She's not coming out." Damon loosened his collar.

Grabbing his free hand, she threaded her fingers through his grip.

"What did you say to her?" he asked.

"I called ScanCoin a pyramid scheme." She stared at his hand. *Is he strong enough to hear the truth? I don't have facts. I have intuition.* "And"—she swallowed—"I told her ScanCoin could ruin a lot of lives."

"Damn, Vivi. No wonder she lost her nerve." Extracting his hand, he rubbed his face.

"Her nerve?" She straightened. "Leaders don't get nervous when they're pitching a room full of investors. They don't get nervous when they're gambling with retirement accounts and personal savings. They state the facts."

He exhaled.

"What are the facts? Anna Claire used her reputation to pitch a digital investment. Where is she?"

The woman wearing the lime-green dress cupped her elbow. Her long, black eyelash extensions fluttered in the artificial lights. "What do you know?"

Recoiling from the unexpected contact, Vivian freed her arm and moved closer to Damon. "Nothing. My friend and I wagered on the outcome of the evening. We're as clueless as you."

Damon rubbed his forehead. "Some of us went all in."

The woman stared, shook her head, and marched toward the lobby.

"Ladies and gentlemen," the announcer said, "please give us a moment to resolve this confusion. Anna Claire will be with you in a moment."

Damon pulled his phone from his pocket and opened the ScanCoin app. "The app is still running."

She peered at the glowing screen. "Is the exchange open?"

He shook his head and pocketed his phone. "Let's move."

Planting her feet, she second-guessed the intensity of her reaction. "Anna Claire might show up."

Placing a hand at the small of her back, he pushed her toward the glowing exit sign. "It doesn't matter whether she's in the building or not." He looked over her shoulder. "The crowd's about to give up on her, and I don't want you here."

Following his gaze, she saw the woman in green lunge toward a man in a tuxedo.

Another man grabbed the woman around the waist, limiting her reach.

Feeling overextended could unleash a person's inner beast. Vivian swallowed. "Whether she gives a speech or not, the outcome's the same."

Damon tugged her beyond the atrium's cloying intensity. "I'm poor."

She stopped walking and grabbed his arm. "Damon, that doesn't matter."

"It matters to the kids." Shaking his head, he grabbed her hand and pulled her forward. "Let's go."

His ambitions tugged at her heartstrings, and she struggled to find a way to support his ambitions. "You'll find another way to help the kids."

A bottle shattered.

"Vivi." He cleared his throat. "Move!"

She looked over her shoulder. A table toppled to the floor, the loud bang followed by shouts and accusations. "All right, let's go."

Reaching the exit, he opened the door and urged her through the opening.

She inhaled the summer evening's cool humidity. The soft, pungent smell of eucalyptus blended with the sharp tang of mowed grass. High-wattage lighting illuminated a small parking lot filled with service vehicles and wooden pallets. Sirens wailed, and a fleet of park security vehicles rounded the corner. "Where are we?"

"At the edge of the park," he said.

She frowned. "My car's parked on the street."

"Why didn't you park in the garage?"

She flexed her ankle. "I found a closer spot."

He rolled his shoulders. "You got lucky."

Well, that was my plan for the night. Fishing her phone from her purse, she pulled up the map application and showed him the pin marking her car. "The spot's not too far from here." She smiled. "I wouldn't have walked far in these heels."

He scanned her legs and admired her shoes. "They look good on you. Any shoes would. You have fantastic legs."

"Do I?" Her question felt so empty, she swung her hands. "I'm sorry about the party. It went south, fast."

He took her hand and walked toward her parking spot. "I don't want to talk about the party right now. I need fresh air."

"Claustrophobic?"

He nodded.

"I get nervous in front of a crowd." She fell into step beside him and thought of the times she saw him challenge Silvia's stern demeanor or pilot a boat, gleefully crossing wakes. *"Subdued" was never a word I would use to describe him. What other unintended consequences did prison have?* She unlocked the rental vehicle and wondered if she should let him drive, but he had a lot on his mind.

In fog-shrouded silence, the rows of Victorian houses, upscale bodegas, and stark gas stations surrounding the park looked menacing. She drove through the city, navigating urban blocks until the freeway carried them past San Mateo.

"You were right," he said.

Letting her arms collapse, she exhaled and glanced over. "Maybe."

He shifted in the passenger seat. "You don't have to be smug."

Smug? She focused on the road and heard him recline the seat, but she refused to look. "I can't win."

"It's not your problem, Vivi." He sighed. "Don't worry about it."

"I want to help."

"Why?" he asked.

"We're friends."

He laughed. "Fucking perfect. I don't need a friend."

"We all need friends." She lowered her voice to a whisper. "Maybe more."

Silent, he stared out the window.

She drove home, wondering if he slept, but she doubted his mind rested. *What would I do in his situation? Go to the police? Fight back?* Downtown Palo Alto rolled into quiet suburban blocks. Pulling up in front of her bungalow, she powered down the vehicle and cleared her throat. "A jury would indict Anna Claire for fraud and making false claims. If the people in the museum band together, you might not have to fight her alone. Every lawyer in town would be interested in representing that kind of class action lawsuit."

"Don't bring up lawyers." Straightening in the seat, he rubbed his face. "I'll handle it."

"How?" she asked.

He opened the door and climbed from the vehicle.

Instead of walking to the front door, she watched him shove his hands in his pockets and turn toward the sidewalk. She climbed out. "Where are you going?"

He stilled. "Right, you've had a dry streak. My bad."

Crossing her arms on top of the vehicle's cold, metal roof, she tilted her head and counted to ten. "I'm tired of watching you walk away, Damon. When are you going to fight for yourself?"

Turning, he stared. "Find another charity case, Vivi. I don't need a rescue."

"Of course, you need someone to rescue you. It's called life. It's called having friends." Straightening, she walked around the vehicle. "Silvia called me out for spending too much time alone. I'm calling you out for trying to go it alone."

"This isn't a chain letter."

She bit her lip, refusing to laugh. "When Johann and I broke up, who do you think kicked me in the butt?"

He crossed his arms. "Silvia."

That was too easy. She cleared her throat. "Silvia told me to swallow my pride and take the job as Johann's executive assistant."

"Cute. You two can life-coach the rest of the world." Shaking his head, he left her driveway.

"Damon!" Refusing to let him walk away without speaking her mind, she half-ran after him and grabbed his arm.

Instead of jerking away, he stiffened and exhaled.

Watching his shoulders rise and fall, she counted to ten. *Growing up, who helped Damon?* Dropping a hand, she swallowed and pared down her emotions. She wanted Damon, and he wanted her. Without ScanCoin, his vulnerability, or her reserves, nothing held them apart. "Why did you invite me to your welcome home party?"

He made eye contact. "I invited everyone."

Rejection and disappointment crushed her need to connect. "Fine." Turning, she headed toward the house.

"Vivi…" Her name escaped his lips in a sigh. "I missed you."

She kept walking. "I get it. I was a p-pinup. I was a distraction to keep you occupied."

"Where do you come up with these words?" He closed the distance and spun her. "That's not right."

For once, she managed to keep her balance. Closing her eyes, she gritted her teeth and blocked the sweet smell of his cologne. If the night had gone well, his scent would have marked her pillow, and the starched white shirt he wore would have littered her floor. Instead, she searched for a way to preserve her dignity and end the teetering feeling that held her on edge.

"I'm tired"—he exhaled—"of scraping together solutions. I don't want to waste my life fighting Anna Claire. I thought I had enough money to step out of the shadows, but I'm back to square one. That's heavy. I need time to think about what happens next." Brushing a hand along her cheek, he smiled. "This thing between us can wait a few weeks. I don't want to screw it up."

His soft promise unmoored her frustration. She told her employees to strip down their analysis until they understood the raw data. Behind her doubts and hesitations, she wanted Damon. Stilling his hand, she turned and kissed his knuckles. "I've always rooted for you. You're sentimental, but don't paint your life as a tragedy."

The Crevasse

"This isn't your problem." He brushed his thumb along her lip. "Let it go."

"Let me distract you." She pulled his hand to her breast. His quick exhalation was a reason to smile, but she arched into the heat of his palm, her nipple rubbing against her dress' silk lining. Grasping his shirt, she claimed his lips and deepened the kiss. Bridging the void her words failed to conquer, she moaned and pressed her body against him.

His hand tightened on her breast, and he shifted her until he controlled the kiss. Pulling back, he rested his forehead against hers. "On the sidewalk? Your neighbors might enjoy the show."

She smiled. "They're probably glued to their windows."

Raising his head, he scanned the street and looked back. "The last time I left your house, my balls hurt so much I couldn't walk straight. You're dangerous."

She reached down and cupped his erection. The thrill of finding him full and heavy echoed in her core. "You're not going to have that problem."

He cleared his throat. "When did you change your mind?"

Shrugging, she met his gaze. "We're both adults, and you can deal with the fallout. So can I."

"Oh, is that all?" Bending, he scooped her into his arms. "You planning to use me, ignore my calls, and tell yourself I made my choice?"

"No." She bit her lip and smiled. "I mean, I would send flowers."

Laughing, he ascended the steps and adjusted her in his arms. "Where's your key?"

Precious barked from the kitchen.

She fished the fob from her purse and pointed toward the keyless lock.

Lowering her, he waited until the door clicked open.

"It's me!" She wiggled until he set her down. Discarding her heels, she padded into the kitchen, opened the crate, and scratched Precious's chin. "You're on your own tonight, old girl. The couch is yours." Turning, she met Damon's gaze.

He waited in the living room, one step past the doorframe.

"Nice shirt," she said. "Take it off."

Grinning, he closed the front door, crossed his arms, and pulled the shirt over his head. "I love it when you're bossy."

"Do you?" she asked. "I excel at it."

He walked forward, slipping a hand around her waist. "Used to drive me crazy watching you size up Johann's appointments and put them in their places. You never let the assholes faze you."

"You faze me." She ran her fingers up his chest, lingering between hard muscles. "If I'd known what you looked like shirtless, I would have cleared my schedule earlier and done something about it."

"I needed time to catch up." He dropped his head and kissed her neck. "People change."

Turning to grant him better access, she closed her eyes and searched for the right response. *Which one of us changed?*

He unzipped her dress and peeled the heavy, lined fabric from her shoulders.

"We can talk about it later," she said.

Drawing back, he grinned. "Impatient?"

106

She held his shoulders for balance and stepped from the dress. "Dry spell."

"I can't say that I'm sorry." He scanned her lacy, beige underwear and swallowed. "You'd better do the honors."

Looking down, she eyed the small blue bow between her breasts. A second bow sat above the keyhole opening covering her ass. The company's advertisements urged women to control their destiny. *I should have kept on my heels.* Looking at him, she grinned. "You won't break me." Turning, she walked down the hallway.

"Damn, Vivi."

His sigh intensified her grin. She sashayed toward the bed, intending to sprawl on the duvet and beckon him. Instead, she felt him loop a muscled forearm around her waist and draw her close. His cock pressed against her thigh, thick, rigid, and achingly close to where she needed it. *I should buy shares in this lingerie company.*

"You know you look good." He dropped his head and kissed her neck, a hand sliding between her legs to cup her heat. "And you're wet."

"For you. For this." She swallowed. "Damon."

Turning her in his arms, he claimed her mouth. "You were worth everything."

Was I? She closed her eyes and let the pleasure of his touch override her thoughts. Her success depended on shielding her emotions and teasing reason from data. *If I'd looked up from my computer sooner, would I be happier?* He rubbed her clit, and her consciousness flicked. *I have one life. I've spent it solving problems and maintaining control, but this?* She shuddered. *I*

107

understand why people make irrational decisions.

As his lips skimmed her collarbone, he murmured praises against her skin. His mouth tugged on her nipples, and his hands roamed, clutching her ass.

She shifted, impatient to feel his body skin against skin. "Take off your pants. I'll do the rest."

"The rest?" He released her and raised his eyebrows.

Stepping back, she unhooked her bra and waited for his reaction.

He wet his lips and hooked a finger in the waistband of her panties. "Come here."

Tensing, she waited for him to rip the lace.

His finger dipped and swiped along her abdomen's smooth skin. "I've imagined seeing you like this so many times."

She shivered and closed her eyes.

"Don't bail on me, Vivi. You'll always regret it."

Any other time, the arrogance in his voice would have raised her hackles, but she shifted, yielding to her desire to believe him. *I want more than deference. I want him to deliver.*

His finger dipped, tantalizingly close to where she needed his attention.

She gripped his forearm. "Touch me, dammit."

He grinned, cupping her wetness and sliding his finger between her folds.

"Yes." Waiting for his heated touch seemed like the biggest mistake she'd ever made.

Pulling up his hand, he trailed his thumb against her clit.

The pressure was strong enough to promise how the night would end. "More." Her panted response brought warmth to her cheeks, but she rocked into his hand, needing more of his touch.

Withdrawing his hand, he cupped her ass and hauled her against his length.

Finding her mouth level with his lips, she angled her head and claimed his lips.

He tore free and squeezed her ass. "Fuck."

"I thought we were clear on that objective."

Lifting her higher, he laved her nipple. "I thought I'd get to take my time with you."

"Wrong." Leaning forward, she bit his earlobe.

Laughing, he walked toward the bed and dropped her on her ass. "So that's how you want to play?"

Looking up from her elbows, she raised an eyebrow. "I didn't buy this underwear so I could admire myself in the mirror."

Hooking a thumb through the side of the panties, he tugged down one side. "They're new?"

She lifted her hips. "They are."

He grinned, pulled the lace from her legs, and tucked it in his back pocket. Releasing her gaze, he focused on her body and grinned.

Heat radiated from her core, and she let her knees fall, baring her sex to his hungry stare. Beginning at her collarbone, she traced the contours of her body, knowing his gaze followed every dip and curve. She dropped a hand to the thin strip of curls above her clit and stroked the soft hair.

Shaking his head, he braced a knee on the bed and pulled her hand above her head. "Not so fast."

"What if I want fast?" she asked.

He drew a sharp breath.

Pulling together her legs, she arched her hips and

pushed him toward the edge, curious as hell when he would fall on her temptation and take her where she wanted to go.

He settled against her, pinning her with the weight of his body. "You smell like apples and roses."

"Great." She blinked, trying to maintain focus. Her body ached, demanding pleasure.

"Then I get up close to you, and I think I smell cedar, like redwoods on a dry, summer day."

She tested the range of her hips, but his weight pinned her. "Must be the sex."

He laughed, pulling her other hand above her head and restraining both hands. He trailed a hand along her curves, pausing at each dip and swell to taste and caress.

The pleasure built, but she glared, sure new underwear and an open invitation should have gotten her over these awkward, naked moments. Nerves and desire swirled without a clear path to resolution. "Damon, I don't think I could be any clearer…"

He looked up and made eye contact. "Shut up, Vivi."

She gasped.

"Can you stay still?"

Swallowing, she nodded.

Releasing her, he stripped off his pants and straightened, legs braced, thighs corded with muscles. The contours of his chest tapered to a lean waist, and a thin line of hair ran from his bellybutton to his jutting cock. The thud of his pocketknife sounded like a muffled gong. "You look good, Damon."

He bent down, retrieved a condom from his pants, and tossed it onto the bed.

She smiled. "And you came prepared."

Straddling her, he dragged his cock along her skin, shifting his weight to the side.

Instead of covering her, he slid his hands beneath her arms, lifted her shoulders, and then her waist. When he reached her hips, she arched, sure he would drop his mouth and taste her.

He backed off the bed, skimming her thighs and teasing her calves.

Every inch of her skin tingled.

He grasped her ankles and pulled her ass to the edge.

She reached for him.

Shaking his head, he ripped open the foil packet. "I told myself I wouldn't rush."

Biting her lip, she waited, feeling her nerves settle in the heavy heat of anticipation. He spread her legs and stroked her entrance, his thumb circling her clit, adding pressure where she needed it most. Closing her eyes, she lifted her hips and savored his touch. Going slow had advantages.

He cupped her ass with one hand. Pushing a thumb past her entrance, he slid her juices across her folds. "Is sex going to ruin our friendship?"

She opened her eyes and met his gaze. "Do you care?"

Angling his hips, he rested his cock against her entrance. "Yes."

She felt the heat and pressure of him, encased in latex, and knew she wanted more. "We're adults." She circled her hips and watched him close his eyes in pleasure. "I won't let sex ruin anything."

Grasping her hips with two hands, he stilled her

movements and made eye contact. "Do you care?"

She swallowed, craving his touch and the heady pressure of feeling him inside her. "Yes."

"Then we're equals." Leveraging his grip, he pushed into her body, stretching her wide.

She closed her eyes, pivoting from his grasp and searching for the rhythm she needed. His skin slapped against her skin and her moans rose, matching his grunts. He carried her weight, and she dropped her arms, hands tangling in the duvet cover, lost to the pressure building in her core.

"You feel amazing."

Moaning, she blinked and searched for a clever response. If she had known what she was missing, she would have channeled a black-and-white villain and staged a jail break. He filled her completely, kept her steady, and proved as generous a lover as he was a friend. "Yes!"

He angled her hips, one hand shifting to rub her clit.

The rhythm of his thrusts was as steady and powerful as the muscles cording his thighs. She arched her back and worried she had failed to keep up her end of the bargain. "I'm about…" The warning died on her lips. Dropping her head, she let the shattering orgasm commandeer her system. Her world narrowed to a bolt of pleasure before it exploded into shivers racing across her skin and a heart ready to burst. "Damon!"

He yelled, tightening his grasp and pumping his hips.

Riding the aftershocks of her pleasure, she watched his face tighten and release, eyes pressed tight as he surrendered. As his rhythm slowed, his hips continued to move against her, and she absorbed the yearning reverberations. *Again.*

Withdrawing, he lowered her to the bed.

She placed a hand on his chest.

Taking his weight on one elbow, he stretched beside her and rolled to his back. "Give me a minute."

She smiled. "Stay the night."

He turned his head and stared.

"Or not." She toed the duvet out of the way and closed her eyes. Lace and availability carried her through their first encounter, but she would pay attention and learn what pleased him. In his arms, she could let herself go, and she was almost sure he would catch her.

His hand settled across her abdomen.

The warm and comforting gesture quieted her thoughts.

"Vivi."

The nickname ended on a sigh. Smiling, she savored the moment. "I'm a big fan of morning sex." She felt his hand flex and release, spanning her abdomen. After several deep breaths, she turned her head and watched his lashes flutter. "Damon?"

Propping herself on one elbow, she dislodged his hand.

It dropped to the sheet.

So much for pillow talk. Tracing the scar above his eye, she settled beside him and watched his chest rise. Running Hoat Analytics tested her discipline, but millions accumulated, and she walked a tightrope to make it happen. To her customers, she was competent and polished. To her employees, she was open-minded and understanding. Neither party saw her steps falter, but Damon asked nothing from her. His easy breathing left him at peace by her side. Convicted, uneducated, and unemployed, he sprawled across her sheets and occupied more than half of the available space, but she fell against the pillow with a smile. Risking their friendship for the pleasure of coming apart in his arms had been worth the chance of losing him, but she would find a way to hold it all together.

Chapter Seven

"Vivi."

Recognizing the deep timbre of Damon's voice, Vivian smiled in her bed.

In the middle of the night, his warmth and weight had pulled her from her dreams. The streetlight shining through the window assured her she had hours to rest, but, she scooted to the bed's edge and pulled the sheet to her chest.

He reached out and snagged her leg, his thumb kneading her calf muscles. "Come back to sleep."

The landscape lighting highlighted his profile. She dropped the sheet and tilted her head. Pleasure had buoyed her ambition, but the evening air chilled her skin.

Opening his eyes, he made eye contact. "Unless you want to be up."

She shook her head, crawled across the bed, and accepted the weight of his arm around her waist. "I have work tomorrow."

"You always work." He closed his eyes. "Tonight, you rest."

Worried she would spend the rest of the night teetering between desire and confusion, she complied and took deep, steadying breaths. For the remainder of the night, she could savor the feel of Damon at her side and the rough tickle of his chest against her cheek.

Morning light filtered through the window.

"Your dog's staring," Damon said.

She yawned. *I've never slept that well in my life.* "Go away, Precious."

"That didn't work."

She laughed, raised her head, and found Precious's white snout resting on the sheets.

The dog's soft, fluttering lashes hovered above her cloudy eyes. Her whiskers twitched, and her ashen jowls pooled on the bed. One ear, tinged with youthful red, sat folded over itself and revealed soft pink skin.

"Are you hungry?" she asked.

Precious whined.

"Do you need to go outside?"

Precious cocked her head.

I wasn't trying to insult you. Sighing, she sat and stretched.

Damon turned his back on the dog and traced the swell of her breast.

His touch made her smile. Memories of the night replayed like a favorite movie she wanted to watch repeatedly. She frowned. *What happens after the credits roll?*

Precious jumped onto the bed, curling into the warm spot left by Damon's weight. Her tail thumped.

She pulled her hands to her hips and frowned. "Off the bed."

The dog whimpered.

She climbed to her knees. "I'm serious."

Damon flopped onto his back. "So much for morning sex."

Turning, she stared. "You remember me saying that?"

He smiled. "Barely."

Precious barked.

Exhaling, she buried her face in the animal's fur. "You're ridiculous." Conscious of her nakedness, she debated reaching for a robe or curling into Damon's side and laying her head on his chest. Despite the nighttime intimacy, sunlight and a smelly, geriatric dog made the morning too homey for her nerves. The furnace pumped heat through floorboard grates, and its soft rumble mingled with chattering squirrels and chirping birds. She focused on calming breaths. *Who leaves first?*

Damon climbed from the bed. "Bathroom?"

"Down the hall." She rubbed her temples, relieved he had decided.

Turning, he picked up his boxers and made his way toward the bathroom.

She watched his back muscles shift and considered recording round two. *What would it be like to watch him watching me?* She cleared her throat. "Do you want coffee?"

"Yeah."

His voice echoed down the hallway.

She found her robe, belted it tight, donned her slippers, and shuffled into the kitchen.

Precious followed at her heels.

Opening the back door, she stood to the side and released the animal to wreck havoc on urban wildlife. "The squirrels are fair game."

"What's up with the old movie posters?" Damon asked.

She turned and found him standing in the doorway, arms crossed above his boxer briefs.

"My grandma loved old black-and-white films," she said.

He raised an eyebrow.

"*Swing Time* was her favorite movie. Fred Astaire's character falls for his dance instructor while he's trying to make twenty-five thousand dollars and woo another woman."

He straightened. "Is that all it takes?"

She frowned.

Rubbing his hands over his face, he exhaled. "Sorry. I'm not awake yet."

Giving him space, she fixed two cups of coffee and set his cup on the kitchen table. Selecting a corner of the room where she could see the house and the yard, she sipped her coffee and considered whether to flee, drag him back to bed, or address Anna Claire's no-show at the gala. Relaying history required fewer decisions. "My mom was a single mother. I spent a lot of time with my grandma and grandpa."

He picked up the coffee cup, opened the refrigerator, and added oat milk creamer. A small sip led to a wince, but he pulled out a chair and stretched his legs. "Must have been nice."

"Nice?" she asked.

"Mama Clarke didn't have anyone to help. When I aged out of neighborhood daycares, she kept me at the store."

She liked hearing more about his past and how it shaped him. "How old were you?"

He shrugged. "I dunno. Eight? Ten? I was old enough to look after myself."

"Were you?"

He made eye contact. "I'm here, aren't I?"

Clearing her throat, she looked out the window at the swaying oak trees. "For me, movies filled the time. Even though my mom and grandparents loved me, I think they found me tiring."

"All kids are tiring," he said, "but they're worth the effort."

She sipped her coffee. "Nobody in my family knew how to talk about emotions. All the adults in the movies wanted kids to be seen and not heard."

"Where'd you grow up, Vivi?" He wrinkled his nose. "Victorian England?"

She shrugged. "Central Valley."

"That must have been hard." He stood. "Most kids I knew went to the skate park or the basketball court."

Watching him step closer, she stiffened, unwilling to expose her doubts. *Why didn't my family enjoy their lives instead of enjoying a film about someone else?* "Sometimes I think the Internet raised me."

Frowning, he stopped in the room's center. "Say what?"

She laughed at his exaggerated response. Friendship bridged the awkward morning following great sex. "Library books and chat rooms were my friends."

He filled his coffee cup. "I had a neighborhood crew."

"And Shani," she said.

He scratched his ear. "And Shani."

"I didn't have anyone my age, but I learned a lot about computers. I learned how to do my homework in a spreadsheet, search the library catalog with Boolean operators, and poke at the code behind the chat rooms. When the most popular Internet dial-up service launched a new software version in 1998, the company consumed global CD production. They dominated the market for weeks." She worked her jaw. "My classmates thought I was a nerd."

"Is that what you wanted to do when you grew up? Dominate the market?"

She shook her head. "I want to feel validated."

Pulling out a chair, he sat and shifted his weight until his long legs stretched out in front of him. "I made shoebox cars and used those CDs for wheels."

She grinned. "By the time the service provider released its chat service to non-subscribers, my online friends meant more to me than the kids in my school. Web nerds were the people who taught me to think beyond DSL and cable modems. They taught me to think big."

His brow furrowed. "They were probably slimy, old men."

"Probably, but their encouragement worked, and nobody sent me dick pics." She peered into her coffee cup and took a deep breath. "What are you going to do for a new gig?"

"Vivi, we went over this last night." He stood and walked toward the kitchen corner. "We can be friends, but I still don't want you to manage or save my ass."

She looked up. "It's a nice ass."

"It's still poor." Stroking her cheek, he sighed. "I didn't find my purpose in the Internet's secret garden. I hustled neighborhood kids and collected change with buckets and bogus signs for football uniforms. If Mama Clarke knew what I was up to, she would have beaten my ass."

"She didn't know?"

"As long as I showed up at dusk, helped unload trucks, and kept my school absences to a minimum, she kept her questions to herself."

"You should have attended college." She shook her head. "You should have had a chance."

He dropped his hand. "Mama Clarke tore up the Free Application for Federal Student Aid application and told me college debt wasn't worth the risk. She said I probably wouldn't finish my degree, and I could work at a convenience store with or without a diploma."

"You shouldn't have listened."

Crossing the kitchen, he put his mug in the sink. "And you shouldn't have kept to the shadows, befriended old perverts, and ignored the real world." Bracing his hands on the counter's edge, he stared out the window. "We listened to our parents until we were old enough to know better." He exhaled. "Now we're grown, and everything's going to work out fine."

She was so accustomed to his jocular banter that she found his uncertainty endearing and reassuring. Crossing the room, she laid a hand on his back.

He tensed.

"Damon, fine isn't enough…"

Her phone rang. Biting her lip, she considered letting the call go to voice mail.

"Take it," he said.

Wondering if he needed space, she walked to the living room and picked up her phone. Michael's name flashed on the screen. "What is it?"

"The Steadman lawyer convened a meeting, but you're not here, and our lawyer's running late. He said something about discovery and document control."

"That was ballsy." She tapped her fingers on the

table where she'd left her phone. "Does he know he's not running my company?"

Michael laughed. "Having you here would be helpful. I can't read this guy."

She turned and met Damon's gaze.

He shrugged.

I don't know him well enough to read that shrug? Okay, do my work? Okay, I'm leaving? Ok, this affair is over? She swallowed and focused on Michael. "Is the request urgent?"

"I mean, nobody showed up with cardboard boxes to cart away our stuff."

She frowned. "Our *stuff* resides on servers."

"Right." Michael laughed. "You know what I mean. I can keep him busy in the conference room for a few hours, but it would be great if you were here."

His laugh sounded hollow and nervous. She imagined him keeping corporate wolves at bay and knew she couldn't leave him defenseless. "Okay, I'll be there as soon as possible."

"Thank you." Michael cleared his throat. "He wants any emails that predate the contract with the hospital."

"Of course he does." Turning, she tapped her computer's keyboard. "All of them?"

"All of them," he said.

"Perhaps he'd like my firstborn, too." Ending the call, she searched her mailbox. If she could find a few benign threads, she could forward them to Michael and keep the Steadman lawyer busy until she arrived.

Damon pulled up a chair from the kitchen table. "Work?"

"Yep." Hitting the arrow key, she paged through

old correspondence. *Work-life balance is a joke.*

He pulled up a chair and lifted her feet into his lap. "You don't look happy."

Glancing away from the screen, she smiled. "When I woke up, I was happy."

He rubbed the insole of her foot. "But?"

Blinking, she balanced the search results and her reaction to his touch. Most of the time, she hated people leaning over her shoulder or asking her to multi-task. But Damon? She gravitated toward his touch. When his thumb pressed into her soft instep, she sighed and released the mouse. "That feels amazing."

His eyebrows rose. "How amazing?"

She remembered a bunch of celebrities admitting their fondness for toe sucking, but she chalked up the trend to bandwagon publicity, salacious gossip, and the public's love of shock and awe. "Amazing enough that I'm glad I had a pedicure last week." Turning back to the computer screen, she checked her query's progress. "However, I have to go into the office."

"All those shoes," he said. "I spent a lot of time wondering if you had a foot fetish."

She snorted. "Hardly. They're like works of art." She smiled. "They make me feel like a work of art."

He increased the pressure. "So, no foot worship."

"I have no idea what that means."

He laughed. "My sweet, vanilla Vivi."

Blinking, she tilted her head. "Is this a Black-and-white-thing?"

His laughter filled the room.

Frowning, she turned back to the computer. "Let me tackle this request, and then we'll take Precious for a walk and talk."

"How long?" he asked.

She narrowed the search terms. "Not too long. She tires easily."

Picking up the pressure, he rubbed her heel. "I'm not talking about the dog."

"Hmm." Old emails triggered memories and lists of follow-up items. *I wanted to revisit our early analysis and see how much we got right.* She shook off the impulse. *I need to focus on forwarding the informal agreements my lawyer needs to keep Steadman's lawyers at bay.*

"So, I'm on standby while you work?" Damon asked.

She blinked. "What?"

"Vivi, I've been sitting here for twenty minutes. Can you give me an idea how long this stuff will take?"

"Why?" she asked. "Do you have somewhere to go?"

Swiveling her away from the computer, he raised her foot to his mouth and wrapped his lips around her toe. Eyebrows raised, he watched her, licking and teasing every digit.

She felt every delicious stroke and labored breath. As much as she yearned to succumb to the pleasure of his teasing caress, she should respond to her waiting employees. "Damon, I'm busy."

He rubbed her heel, maintaining eye contact while he circled his tongue.

"Maybe I'm not *that* busy." She relaxed her shoulders, giving him the power to set the pace. *If he wants to suck my toes, so be it. I won't stop him.* She grinned. Every kneading stroke of Damon's hand and heat-tinged swipe of his tongue triggered nerve endings about which she rarely thought. *I would have gone down on him for a foot massage.* She watched her toe disappear into his mouth and shuddered at the added eroticism. The unexpected pleasure and the intense concentration in his gaze heightened her response to his touch.

He released her foot into his palm. "If you don't like this game, I'll stop."

Scrambling to the chair's edge, she leaned forward. "You're a tease."

He leaned back. "Worried I'll steal your title?"

She climbed into his lap and straddled him. "I'm not a tease." Rocking her hips against his erection, she let the heat and pressure build in her core. "I can't spend all day and all night in bed, even if I want to stay there with you."

Grasping her hips, he stilled her momentum. "Trust me, I can be fast."

She tilted her head. "And then what?"

"I can move so slowly you'll scream."

She arched an eyebrow. "In frustration?"

He grinned. "In release, until your muscles ache."

Dropping her head to his shoulder, she inhaled. "Don't make promises you can't keep."

Tilting up her chin, he smiled. "What makes you think I can't keep them?"

"We've never spent this much time alone," she said. "I can describe you to a reporter, but what do I tell a friend? Do you leave dirty dishes in the sink? Towels on the floor?" She stroked his cheek. "What do you smell like after you shave?"

Stilling her hand, he kissed her palm. "I bet you're terrible at one-night stands."

"You'd be the first." Scooting away from his heat, she sighed. "I thought I would be married by twenty-five."

He frowned. "That's too young. I'm twenty-five."

She knew his age, but she wondered how he crammed so many experiences into so few years. Looking out the window, she examined her life's trajectory. "All those hours I spent working in front of the computer shaped me. I learned to work alone and knew the responsibility stopped at my door." Meeting his gaze, she gripped his bicep and un-straddled his lap. "Maybe I'm no good with relationships."

He cocked his head. "You have employees."

She fixed her hair. "They take my directives. I don't want to give you directives"—she smiled—"unless we're in bed."

He grabbed her hand. "Listen. You haven't found the right partner, yet."

The intensity of his gaze unnerved her. "Is that what you want to be? A partner?"

Raising his eyebrows, he released her. "Do I have that choice?"

She matched his expression. "Do I?"

He dropped her hand and stood.

Retreating to her computer, she pressed the Enter key. "Give me the space I need to work. We'll take this thing between us one step at a time." She jerked her chin toward the couch. "You can hang out as long as you want. Grab a laptop and look through the job listings."

He paced near the window. "Vivi, don't handle me."

The frustration in his voice cracked her focus.

Standing, she walked across the room, wrapped an arm around his waist, and laid her cheek against his back. "I'm not trying to push you in any given direction." Feeling him exhale, she dropped a hand to the line of hair disappearing beneath his boxer briefs. "I'm used to living alone, and I need a little time, but I want you here."

"You're playing dirty." Turning in her arms, he held her hips and stared. "What *are* you doing?"

Smiling, she stroked his length. "You started it. You wanted me to stop working."

"I wanted to know how long you expected me to wait."

She gripped him. "Friends with benefits shouldn't have to wait."

He closed his eyes and moaned. "Can we be friends?"

Pulling free a hand, she raised an eyebrow. "Which is it, Damon? Friend or fuck? Idle observer or complicit assistant? I can make Anna Claire shake in her boots." She swallowed. "Or at least answer a few questions from the police department. Is that what you want me to do?"

He rolled his eyes. "I can't call up the police and admit I had ten times more proceeds than they thought. Well, guys, that prison sentence wasn't long enough. Help me recoup my cash, and I'll consider doing another five years time. Fuck." He shook his head. "I don't want you to get involved in this mess."

"What mess?"

"The mess that's my life! What if Anna Claire's not deceptive, but dangerous?"

"I'm not fragile." She walked her fingers up his

127

chest. "And I'm already involved. I'm almost positive the woman's laundering money through real estate transactions."

He narrowed his gaze and grabbed her hand. "How do you know that?"

"Data irregularities." Freeing a hand, she pulled back to meet his gaze. "Real estate transactions move along trend lines. Dollars per square foot. Zip codes. Transactions might lag for flips and remodels, but the sales data jumps from one curve to the next. I built a program to monitor that sales data. Anna Claire's transactions didn't fit the model."

He exhaled. "But you don't have any skin in the game."

She grinned and figured Michael would forgive her. "Speaking of skin..."

"No," he said.

She frowned. "No?"

Moving away from the window, he cleared his throat. "Vivi, should I spend the day wondering if you're going to call me? Our dynamics are so whack that unless you commit a little, this thing between us can't go anywhere. You have a million dollars in the bank..."

She bit her lip and decided not to discuss the sum of her assets.

"...and I'm unemployed and broke."

Moving to his side, she stroked his upper arm. "I'm interested in *you*. If ScanCoin were legit, you'd still be broke. The money's for the kids."

He rolled his eyes. "Let me amend my statement. I'm broke and stupid."

Sighing, she dropped her arm. "You're not stupid.

Weathering tough times on your own is difficult. I went full speed ahead on Hoat Analytics, and what has it given me?"

He spread wide his arms, encompassing the bungalow.

"I mean, yeah, that part worked, but let's talk about feelings."

"Let's not," he said.

She laughed.

"Your gamble seems to be paying out fine. Me, on the other hand?" He shook his head. "Until I find my footing, we should table sex."

She recoiled and marveled at how quickly the pleasure of Damon's touch had slipped through her hands. "What does that mean?"

"Exactly what it sounds like it means. You want to work together to unravel ScanCoin? Great, then we're coworkers. I look forward to working with you."

She cleared her throat, ready to mount a counter argument and fight for her pleasure, but he offered her what she thought she had wanted. Now, she wanted to build a relationship *and* enjoy ground-shaking sex. Weighing her options, she grinned and doubled her lingerie order. *He'd turn down a job, a business introduction, or any type of professional help I could give him. At least if I solve this riddle, I can help him, and I'll get another shot at screaming his name.* "Fine."

He raised an eyebrow. "Fine?"

Turning her back, she headed for the hallway.

"Where are you going?" he asked.

"To get dressed for work." She paused and looked over her shoulder. "When I'm done for the day, I'm going to lie around naked and find something entertaining. Care to join me?"

He groaned, and his dick tented his boxers. "C'mon, Vivi. That's not playing by the rules."

Smiling, she let her hips sway. "We're adults, Damon. Who said anything about playing by the rules?"

****

By the time Vivian arrived at the office, her team had drained their coffee cups and worn through the visiting legal team's tolerance. She bypassed the conference room, set down her leather tote, and tucked her red-soled heels beneath the desk chair. Before she took charge of the situation, she wondered how much time she spent on business management. *I'm better at the analytics.* Instead of dwelling on her company's internal structure, she texted Michael and asked him to step from the conference room.

Rising from a black, leather chair, he let himself into her office and ran a hand through his loose, white hair. A hint of lavender showed through the long layers.

He kept the sides undercut, but she never saw his topknot loose. "It's purple."

Rolling his eyes, he sighed. "Like the shadows beneath my eyes."

"I like it," she said.

He cocked his head. "Really?

She nodded.

Shoulders relaxed, he pointed his thumb toward the conference room. "Does he know we have plenty of work?"

She shook her head. "Terry's trying to make sure his company has the upper hand. It's his job."

"But we don't need their business!"

Placing a hand on his arm, she tried tugging him into motion. "We'll get back to the good stuff."

He stared at her hand. "You're touching me."

Retracting her hand and shoving it in the pocket of her black pants, she tilted her head. "I'm so sorry."

"No, it's fine. You just, uh, never touch anyone."

Shifting her stance, she frowned and replayed her interactions with her employees. She maintained emotional distance from her direct reports, but she wondered when that distance turned into a cold approach. "That's not true, I touch"—*Damon.* She cleared her throat—"my friends, but I didn't mean to cross that line with you."

"It's cool. You surprised me, is all. We can be friends."

She laughed. "Are you angling for a free lunch?"

"No!" He widened his gaze and dropped his voice. "Yes."

"You earned it." She adjusted the backing on her earring. "By the way, I really do like the purple."

"Uh, nice shoes."

She snorted. "Don't overdo it. Tell the rest of the staff I'll be there in five minutes."

From the opposite side of the glass wall, Valentina and Isaac exchanged looks.

She squared her shoulders. "All right, let's give Steadman's overstepping lawyer the boot."

"I'm so glad you're here," Michael said.

She snorted and breezed into the conference room. "Thank you so much for this discovery session." Walking up to the whiteboard, she dropped her phone on the table and tapped a handwritten notice of attorney-client privilege. "I have our lawyer on speakerphone, and we have items to discuss. Between us, you know we're in the clear on this case. If your client thinks we had a verbal agreement, he misconstrued a conversation, and you failed to get it in writing." She jerked her head toward the door. "Surf's up."

The Steadman lawyer picked up his phone. "You're not in charge of my time."

She crossed her arms. "But this is my office building, and you're not making me money."

Rolling his eyes, he slipped his phone into his back pocket. "After the first-year associates comb through the material you produced, I'll let you know what else we need."

"Talk to my lawyer, not my staff." She sat on the table's edge. Watching him salute the receptionist, she felt bad about giving him the boot, but she sensed the exhaustion in the room. Her employees spent most days glued to screens, but when administrative tasks loomed, their creativity and analytical skills suffered under the load. "Valentina, order lunch for everyone who came in today."

Valentina widened her gaze. "Everyone?"

"Pick something healthy so we don't have to charge the rest of the day to overhead." Vivian swung her foot and wondered how long the Steadman lawyer would have intimidated her staff. If kicking him out of the office made her a bitch, she would play the role. Few people, like Damon, saw through it.

Valentina waved her phone. "On it."

Isaac pursed his lips. "Should we expect more late mornings from you?"

She raised her eyebrows. "Which one of us puts in

more hours?"

He tipped his head.

"Which one of us started the company?"

Michael cleared his throat.

Okay, too much. She chewed the inside of her cheek. *I don't need more friends, but I do need more time.* Watching Valentina scroll, she wondered if the woman's high billability was legitimate, or she accomplished more in less time. *If I challenge her, can she do more?* She stared at the clusters of techs and business analysts working through tasks beyond the glass walls. "I'm over the horizontal org structure."

Valentina looked up from her phone.

"Seniority gives the three of you natural leadership, but your project skills and technical expertise deserve formal recognition. I'm instituting a soft buffer between grunt analytical work and high-level planning. Find your sweet spot and write-up the job description you want. We'll negotiate on salary."

Isaac let his mouth gape.

Profit-sharing no longer felt like an idealistic dream. She depended on her employees, and she wanted them to understand their worth and benefit from their achievements. "So, yes, you should expect to see less of me."

"And if we don't come to an agreement?" Isaac asked.

"At will employment." She softened her tone. "But I hope you'll stay."

He nodded.

"Also, I want an internship program," she said.

Valentina's phone clattered on the table. "No way, not me."

Thinking about the teenagers she met at Damon's party, she realized her Central Valley years and their EPA years had a lot in common. *None of us knew who we were and who we wanted to be. I chose formality and an Ivy League education. Some people don't have those choices.* She looked at Michael. "I had someone else in mind. Send a note to the area high schools and ask for nominations. Nothing fancy, but target the kids who understand hardware but might not see the potential of what they can do with it."

"Are you terminal?" Isaac leaned forward. "You can tell me."

She laughed and ran her hand through her hair. "We're in the black. It's time we gave back." Her phone rang. "Hello."

"How fast can you get to San Mateo?" Damon asked.

She frowned and wondered why he called. "Twenty minutes."

"I decided to fast-track our professional agenda."

Our agenda or our plans for lingerie? She smiled. "Is that so?"

"ScanCoin's website lists a physical address."

She looked at the flex space housing Hoat Analytics and wondered how Anna Claire's corporate office compared to her space. "How charmingly retro. I'll meet you there." Ending the call, she realized all three employees stared. "What?"

Michael grinned. "Leaving so soon?"

She shrugged. "Give my lunch to the receptionist." Picking up her purse from her office, she grinned at the change of plans. *I told Damon I needed space, but as soon as I left the house, I wanted to go back.*

The elevator doors opened, and she blinked in the sunlight. *After we reclaim his cash, I'll deal with the fallout from work and spend the afternoon in bed with Damon.* Beaming, she stepped onto the sidewalk. *How long can one confrontation take?*

Chapter Eight

Vivian unlocked her car and reached for the door handle. A strong breeze blew off the bay, and clear, sunny skies warmed the car and her skin.

"Wait!"

She turned.

Michael ran from the office building and skidded to a stop on the leafy sidewalk. He threw his arms around her and hugged her tight. "Just, thank you. For bailing us out of the Steadman quagmire. For giving the three of us a chance."

"Thank you for giving Hoat Analytics a chance." She took a deep breath and wondered if she would now have to hug her employees when she entered the room. Change required time, and she required air to breathe. "Also, this is too much PDA."

Jerking back, he dropped his hands. "I'm so sorry. I don't know what came over me."

Tucking her hair behind her ear, she smiled at his mortified expression. Together, they would find a balance. "It's fine. You, Valentina, and Isaac will do a good job. I'm not going anywhere, but you need the authority to boot people from the office, take risks, and own rewards."

He shuffled his worn, leather loafer along the rough sidewalk. "And if we screw up?"

She shrugged. "I'll pick up the pieces." Replaying

the last five years, she reconsidered her answer and how much she had to lose. "But don't get sloppy!"

Cracking a smile, he nodded, stole a second hug, and backed away.

Dropping into the car's driver's seat, she rolled down the window and waved.

One hand shoved deep in his wool, trouser pockets, Michael waved back.

As she pulled away from the curb, she heard tires squeal and looked in the rearview mirror.

A white sedan switched lanes, hopped the curb, and clipped Michael before peeling off.

Thrown off balance, he fell backward and slammed his head on the sidewalk.

She threw the car into Park and ran toward him. Blood seeped from his mouth, and his wild, purple-tinged hair spread around him like a halo. Her pulse skyrocketed, and she dropped to her knees. "Michael!"

Spectators dialed emergency services.

She checked his pulse and kept anyone from touching him. "Hey, buddy. You're going to have a wicked headache. Just stay with me, okay? Can you hear me? Can you blink?"

Skin pale, he reached for his head and managed a blink.

Exhaling, she squeezed his hand and waited for first responders. Within an hour, she oversaw Michael's medical transport, provided a police statement, and texted Damon about the delay.

"And you're sure it was an accident?" The motorcycle officer adjusted her black sunglasses. Sunlight glinted off her badge and her holstered gun.

Vivian leaned against her car. "We run a data

analytics firm. Our clients write terse emails. They don't order hit and runs."

"There have been no other threats?"

She considered the broken bungalow window, her encounter with Anna Claire, and Michael's injuries. Analytical by nature, she looked for patterns in discrete data. No matter how she weighed the probabilities and made connections between the disparate events, she struggled to understand how three occurrences pointed toward a threat. Considering her data set, she weighed which event might be an outlier, but she needed more information. "I haven't received any threats. Michael hasn't reported any threats. If you find connections, I want to be the first to know about it. I refused to put my employees in danger."

The officer nodded.

Rubbing her arms, she exhaled and looked up at the offices for Hoat Analytics. Silhouettes peered through the windows. The free lunch had arrived, but the incident had shaken up her staff. Heading upstairs, she flashed the lights on the work floor. "Everyone, power down and head home for the afternoon. As soon as I have an update on Michael, I'll let you know."

Whisperers intensified as she turned and left the office. For years, the team celebrated technical successes, but she struggled to gauge their reaction to a threat. Hearing her heels echo in the hallway, she continued walking. Without answers, she could provide her team little comfort, but she could give them rest.

****

"Are you sure this is the right place?" Twenty minutes after leaving her office, Vivian shifted in the driver's seat. Across the street, grime coated a warehouse's windows. Black pants felt too crisp for this kind of adventure, and she had yet to receive an update on Michael, but Damon deserved her time, too. He offered to call off the outing, but she decided to take her own advice and spend the afternoon away from her computer and wait to see if distance brought the facts into focus.

Damon peered through the windshield. "This address came from the website."

She analyzed the building housing ScanCoin's San Mateo office. The structure looked like a cross between a grocery store and a garment factory. Workers unloaded cardboard boxes from semi-tractor-trailers and ferried the boxes into dark, nondescript openings. A cluster of people smoked cigarettes on their breaks and checked their phones. Their blue jeans and T-shirts looked dingy, and she wondered if they accumulated that much debris in a day or repeatedly wore their clothes without washing them.

A short, bearded man spit into a disposable cup and tossed the cup toward an overflowing trashcan. Missing his mark, he shrugged and left the cup on the ground. Viscous brown liquid oozed onto the stained concrete.

She shuddered. "Anna Claire could have rented flashy office space in the city."

"Why pay San Francisco rent when you only need servers and call center staff?" Damon asked.

She frowned and hoped the building's interior was cleaner than its exterior. Servers needed a clean environment, and lackluster housekeeping often led to equipment failures. "You can rent those services in a professional environment, too."

He glanced over. "Maybe the inside is industrial

chic."

"Chic?" She shook her head and climbed from the car. "The only thing chic about this place is the tax write-offs. Ten-to-one, we find a dead rat before we find exposed ventilation, hidden LEDS, and bike racks."

He opened the door, stood, and stretched on the other side of the car. "What did you say?"

She smiled. "I said, 'I hope they have a receptionist'."

He laughed. "I doubt it."

"Me, too." Walking around the car, she linked their arms and tried to focus on the outing. "I've been thinking about the terms of our"—to dislodge a piece of gum, she stopped and rubbed the toe of her shoe against the cement—"deal. Coworkers sleep together all the time."

"How many employees do you have?"

"Fifteen," she said.

He raised his eyebrows. "And how many of them sleep together?"

She frowned, thinking of Michael's promptness and Valentina's willingness to meet the delivery driver who brought lunch. *Would they be a good match? How many of my employees have seen each other naked? Never mind, I don't want to know the answer.* She shuddered and wondered if Michael's close peers needed more than an afternoon to calm their nerves. "Numbers aren't important."

Damon laughed and tugged her into motion. "I'm not buying that answer."

"How are you going to convince Anna Claire to see you?" she asked. "The woman certainly won't greet me."

"I have three strategies," he said. "Ask her, surprise her, and trick her."

Quickening her stride to match his step, she stared at the building. "Which strategy is first?"

"Ask politely."

She made a noncommittal noise. "Polite people don't invite their investors to a gala and leave them dumbfounded." She glanced over. "You should have called to set up an appointment."

"I prefer the element of surprise." He squared his shoulders. "She'd better have a damn good excuse for failing to open the exchange."

The hint of anger stopped her, and she planted her feet. "You're right, polite won't work, but without an appointment, we'll never get face time. *The last time Anna Claire and I shared a bit of girl talk, the toilets heard our testimony, and she skipped her big ScanCoin presentation. If she hates confrontations, we have to get close.* She tapped her chin. "We need a compelling story. Maybe our car broke down, and we need to use the bathroom."

He shook his head. "You've watched too many movies."

"That's probably true." She glanced at the loitering workers. "What about playing good cop, bad cop?"

He laughed. "You could be my reclusive wife."

She shuddered and held up her left hand. "Bare." Watching him rub the small scar over his eyebrow, she cleared her throat. "Plus, I would have no reason to accompany you on a business trip."

"Reporters?" he asked.

Shaking her head, she focused on the loading dock.

"It's a shared space. What if we're press members covering labor relations?"

"Relations with who?" he asked.

She tilted her head. "Unions?"

"If we wanted to pull that shit, we should have done research and printed fake press credentials."

"You're right." They had stalled too long, and she felt conspicuous standing outside the building. Her stomach rumbled, and she wondered how much time they had left before the dock workers changed shifts. "Let's get inside and wing it."

He moved his jaw from side to side. "If we impersonate reporters, Anna Claire's public relations team might permit an interview."

"I wouldn't know where to start," she said.

"China is on the cusp of launching a digital version of the Yuan. We'll play up her fear of competition."

She whistled. "Nice. I should have offered you a job."

He glanced over. "Before or after you jumped me?"

Smiling, she stepped toward him. "The jumping was mutual."

He grinned and stepped toward her, but he pulled himself back.

Registering the conflict in his gaze, she smoothed her shirt and sighed. "Do we actually need to see Anna Claire? We can find a way to withdraw your investment. Scare her, pocket the eight hundred thousand, and stop for the day. We can celebrate by going back to my place and picking up where we left off."

"What if ScanCoin's legit? What if I'm sitting on

142

millions?" he asked.

What if the only thing he's sitting on is his good-looking ass? She stared at the building. "How many cryptocurrencies can exist? What are the odds Anna Claire's company beats out all those other companies?"

"She runs ScanCharge. Maybe her currency's more efficient."

Rolling her eyes, she tugged him into motion. "At bilking people of their money?"

"At utilizing the smart grid."

"You want to think the best of her," she said. "Is it because she's a minority?"

"No, and I doubt she wants to be your ethnic best friend, so skip the race card."

"Hey." She put her hands on her hips. "I can be fun."

He stopped and spun her around. "I think you're fun."

She heard the implication and swallowed. Few people shared his opinion. "Okay, we'll stick to the reporter script. What suite are they in?"

"1A."

"Of course." Dropping her hand, she approached the building.

A man whistled. "Hey, good lookin'."

Keeping her gaze straight, she ignored the whistle and the compliment.

"What? You too good for us? Got you some Black dick? Once you go Black, you never go back?"

She stiffened, ready to release a tirade about women's rights, racial inequality, and mutual respect.

Damon put a hand on the small of her back and urged her forward. "Don't be obnoxious."

Frowning, she judged his protective response against her right to assert herself.

"Ignore the man," he said.

"I'd rather tear into him." She ground out the words, but every part of her body ached to confront the whistler. *I wouldn't say those things to a friend or a stranger. Who warms my bed is none of their business.* She glanced at Damon. *Or who stubbornly refuses to share it.* "Cryptocurrency is the wave of the future."

He bumped her ass. "Good girl."

"Woman," she muttered the correction, but she could care less if he caught the subtlety of her word choice. He respected her achievements. *That other man? I'd like to kick him with my shoe's pointy end.* She imagined the catcaller hopping on one foot. *Maybe I have watched too many movies.*

Closer to the building, the smell of garbage and motor oil overpowered any odors from the milling workers. A small sign listed ScanCoin as the occupant of suite 1A. The names of the other companies meant nothing.

Damon reached for the door handle and pulled.

Remarkably, the door opened. Fluorescent lights illuminated a long hallway. Dry air-conditioning and the bitter, residual smell of cleaning products made her wrinkle her nose. "I guess we're going in."

"Don't look so shocked."

"Shocked?" she asked. "This is my game face."

He laughed. "You wouldn't last a day in EPA."

The jibe soothed her nerves. Remembering his party and the self-consciousness that drove her to drink, she exhaled. *What if he's right? What if I can't hang in the real world?* Straightening her shoulders, she followed him into the building.

His shoulders thrown back, he pulled suite 1A's door handle. "It's locked."

His first knock sounded polite. His second knock rattled the glass.

Slamming his fist against the door, he cursed and dropped his forehead to the opaque glass. "I'm a fucking idiot."

She laid a hand on his back, rubbing circles to ease the tension and her inability to alleviate it. "You're not. You're holding someone accountable for what they promised. I do it every day. It's a hallmark of business."

He flexed his fingers, palm splayed against the glass. "Do I look like a businessman?"

Checking the suite label, she found a piece of paper taped to the wall. "ScanCoin's office renovation will be complete in two weeks. We're sorry we missed you." She dropped the paper. "I bet."

Lifting the paper, he read the text and tossed the paper to the floor.

"Maybe the construction workers are installing the bike racks," she said.

He pulled his phone from his pocket and dialed the office number. "Nothing." Rubbing his temples, he closed his eyes. "Fucking nothing."

"Did you try the social media channels? We can send a direct message."

"I want to talk to a person," he said, "not a bot."

She recalled Anna Claire's jaded gaze in the bathroom mirror. "There might not be a difference."

Straightening, he stared at the door. "Maybe they're reorganizing." He looked over. "Am I naïve?"

"Optimistic might be a better term. I wish I knew how to fix this mess, Damon. I'm good at data and poking around where I don't belong." She eyed the remaining glass doors lining the hallway. Walking the length of the hallway to check the legitimacy of other offices, she saw people at work, but none made eye contact. "Let's get lunch and regroup. After Michael's accident, my emotions are maxed out."

"Where should I take you? The taco truck?"

She smiled. "Is that what you want to eat?"

He shook his head. "It's about all I can afford."

Biting her lip, she wondered what combination of feminine wiles and fluttering eyelashes would enable her to enjoy a meal with aluminum foil wrappers. She swallowed. "Silvia keeps pushing me to try something new."

"I assume you don't mean smoked ribs."

"What about lamb chops?" she asked.

He kicked the door to 1A and turned his back on ScanCoin's office. "You pick this meal, but the next one's on me."

Replaying Michael's accident, she looked over her shoulder and scanned the hallway for threats. Finding it empty, she exhaled. She would willingly pay for every lunch to keep the people she valued safe from harm.

****

Vivian found a restaurant by the bay with outdoor seating and an expansive menu. Left Coast Fish House promised to deliver high-quality, sustainable seafood with a Pacific twist. Badges from the local aquarium's Seafood Watch and Smart Catch programs proclaimed that even if the food bombed, she and Damon could feel good eating it. *On a day like today, feeling good might be the thing that matters.*

Given the rare, sunny afternoon, patrons occupied patio seats.

Gulls flew overhead, and she looked away from the restaurant's entrance to gauge Damon's opinion. "Does this look good?"

He shrugged.

After leaving the ScanCoin's San Mateo office, he remained quiet, and she used the silence to check on Michael's recovery. His family had arrived. She relinquished her primary involvement and told his family to contact her if they had any problems.

Taking his silence for agreement, she walked past the iron railing framing the patio and waited by the host's stand. A rock kept a stack of menus from blowing away in the wind.

When no host appeared, they sat themselves at a painted blue metal table. A sunshade stretched over half the patio and provided shade.

A server walked up to the table. Acne peppered his forehead, and a lock of hair blew over one eye. Tucking the hair behind his ear, he shifted and looked at his smart watch. "I'm Samuel. What can I get you?"

So much for making eye contact and repeating the specials. Determined to expand her palate, she scanned the paper menu for a dish most people loved. *Fried fish. Baked fish. Grilled fish. What is fish, like a conduit for seasonings?* She smiled at the twenty-something server. "I'll have the Dungeness crab cake salad."

He looked at Damon. "And you?"

"What's the fresh catch?"

The server yawned. "Panko-crusted and oven-fried Rockfish."

Damon cocked his head.

Samuel shrugged. "Some people call it Rock Cod."

"Is it good?"

Scratching the side of his nose, the server shrugged. "It's fried white fish. How could it not be good?"

Damon laughed and put down the menu. "All right, man. Let's do it."

Samuel picked up the paper menus, walked away, and threw the papers in the recycling bin.

"So what do you want to do next?" Vivian asked.

He tapped his foot against the concrete patio. "Eat."

"I meant about Anna Claire." She sipped her water. "Have you considered contacting other ScanCoin investors?"

"Short of staking out the firm's offices, posing as a construction crew, or changing my name to billionaire investor, I don't know what we can do to get her attention." He drummed his fingers on the table. "I need to see her face to get a read on the situation."

Withdrawing her phone, she downloaded the ScanCoin app and invested a modest amount of money. "The website's still generating tokens."

"What?" He grabbed the phone, glanced at the screen, and dropped it to the table. "Why did you give her any more money?"

She shrugged. His flash of anger meant more than his bad manners. He turned the tables on her by denying her more hookups, but she worried about his laconic demeanor. The man she knew bubbled with energy. Since he returned, he was a changed man, but she hoped he changed for the better. "What if you're right about the currency? I'll be rich."

"Richer."

Beneath the table, she slipped off a shoe and rubbed her foot along his calf. "Maybe you need a backrub."

He raised an eyebrow.

She needed a better currency. Pulling back, she slipped her foot back into her shoe. "What? You said no sex, but you never mentioned flirting. Everyone flirts."

He cocked his head toward the restaurant. "Should I go chat up the hottie at the bar?"

Turning, she looked inside the building. A woman sporting long braids stirred sugar into her tea and leaned close to a whiskered man. The woman's black-and-white *adinkra* blouse outshone the man's polyester track suit, but Vivian stared at the suit's stale, gray fabric and wondered why it seemed familiar. *Is it retro or new wave?*

Slowly turning his head, the man made eye contact.

Caught gawking, she swallowed and focused on Damon. "Why? Trying to add to your underwear collection?"

"So far, the collection extends to one pair of overpriced panties," he said.

At the memory, wetness pooled between her thighs, and she smiled. "I could help you expand the catalog."

"I plan to take you up on that offer, but no more ScanCoin. Save your cash for lace."

Glancing at her phone, she shifted against the hard seat and watched the value of her tokens rise. "I'm not the only person investing today."

"No, but you might be one of the few people who

knows better."

A harried busser delivered the food.

She picked up a fork and pulled out a lump of crabmeat. The sweet meat and savory fried breadcrumbs had an interesting, savory texture, but her surly lunch companion made the day worthwhile. *It's a beautiful day. Work's under control, and Damon's here.*

"Shit." Damon spat his food into his napkin. "This fish is horrible!"

She frowned and lowered her fork. "What?"

Standing, he gestured to the server.

The man frowned and approached the table. "Is something wrong?"

"What did the kitchen do, dredge the fillet in salt?"

"Ugh." Samuel stammered. "Do you want to send it back?"

Damon closed his eyes and inhaled. "Maybe I should go back to prison."

The server backed up.

She set down her fork. *I hate making a scene.* Taking a deep breath, she let Damon handle the encounter and toyed with her water glass.

"I can get you the owner," the server said.

"That would be good." Damon's shoulders rose and fell. Opening his eyes, he looked her. "I'm sorry."

His frustration with the day had boiled over, and the steeliness of his response told her how much he struggled to get his emotions under control. She had seen him rub people the wrong way, but his caffeine-fueled antics and ribbing remarks had played on his audience's expectations and turned tension into laughs. She bit her lip and waited for him to settle.

He rubbed a hand over his face and dropped into his chair.

The owner came through an unmarked door and approached the table. He wore wide pants and a matching tunic with large, gold buttons that made the outfit look like a cheap costume. Glancing at Samuel, who cowered near the bar, he approached Damon. "I'm Chef Caesar. Is there a problem?"

Damon put his napkin on the table. "There are many problems. Nobody greeted us at the door. We sat ourselves and waited for ten minutes before someone dropped off two glasses of water." He glanced at the damp tablecloth where the glasses sat. "I would have left at that point, but this is our second date."

She offered a clipped wave.

"The server spent more time looking at his watch than explaining the menu." Damon nudged his lunch plate toward the owner. "And the fish is terrible."

"A bad batch, I'm sure."

"Or careless oversight. Why are you hanging out in the building instead of supervising the patio?"

Sweat beaded on Caesar's forehead. "I was in the office. We're having issues with our suppliers."

Damon leaned back in his chair and crossed his arms. "You need a manager."

"We used to have one." Caesar scanned the crowd. "I'll comp your lunch and have the kitchen send out another dish."

"Don't bother." Damon tossed his napkin on the table.

Straightening, Caesar bit his lip. "You're going to leave a critical review."

Damon shook his head. "No, man, but I know how

Amy Craig

to fix this place. I used to work at Georgios's Greek Restaurant in downtown Palo Alto. I can whip this shit into shape within the week." He jerked his thumb toward the twenty-something server. "Starting with your boy over there."

Vivian remembered to keep her mouth closed. *I don't care if this ploy works or not. It's hot.* She bit back a smile.

"How are your crab cakes?" Caesar asked.

"Good." She looked up and made eye contact. "I mean, a side of lemon would be nice."

Damon tapped the table. "See! That's the attention to detail you need. Otherwise, when a chain restaurant stamps their menu with sustainability logos and undercuts your prices"—he scanned the patio crowd—"your customers will bail."

Caesar stepped back. "When can you start?"

"Tomorrow." Damon crossed his arms over his chest. "Thirty-three dollars an hour. Give me two weeks to show you what I can do."

Jamming his hands in his pockets, Caesar scanned the patio. The wind whipped his graying hair into his eyes.

Vivian imagined seeing the patio through his eyes. Straw wrappers littered the concrete floor, dishes overflowed a bus station, and a seagull pecked at an abandoned plate of food.

"Come by at eight to fill out paperwork," Caesar said.

Damon offered him a hand. "Done."

She watched Chef Caesar walk away and met Damon's gaze. "Impressive."

"Thank you," he said.

152

Damon maintained a stoic impression. She tried not to giggle.

Samuel hurried over and delivered a new plate of steaming rockfish. He hovered near the table, too far away to touch and too close for private conversation.

Taking a bite, Damon held up a hand for a high five.

The server slapped it and scampered off.

She picked up her fork. "You didn't mention your conviction. Will that bite you?"

"I have about forty-eight hours to impress the owner before he gets the results of a background check. I know you value honestly, Vivi, but I didn't lie." He raised another bit of fish, swallowed the bite, and winked. "I omitted a fact."

She sipped her water and considered how often she withheld information during critical negotiations. An hour ago, she would have pretended to be a reporter to see Anna Claire, but she thought she understood the stakes. "It's not like you were selling guns." She swallowed. "Were you?"

"No." Leaning against the chair's back, he stared. "But what I did two years ago doesn't matter. People extrapolate and jump to the worst conclusions." He exhaled. "A criminal record might keep me out of schools or a white-collar job, but restaurant staff members are flexible. I'll impress the owner on day one."

She put down her fork. "For thirty-three dollars an hour."

"It's an honest wage," he said.

Pursing her lips, she exhaled. "I would have paid you more."

"To do what?"

She toyed with the silverware. "Customer service." Glancing up, she searched for his reaction and saw disbelief. "Do you think you're worth less?"

Shaking his head, he picked up his fork and stared at his plate. "You wouldn't hire a kid with a high school degree and a criminal record to represent your company."

Thinking of her nascent internship program, she conceded the point and knew the kids would have to demonstrate technical credibility and problem-solving skills. "I know you. You're good with people."

His gaze remained fixed. "Only in EPA or Johann's world."

"Isn't it the same world?" she asked.

He shook his head and ate a bite of fish.

Crossing her arms and leaning back, she battled the urge to kick him under the table. "One in three adults has a criminal record, but rehabilitation certificates matter. If an applicant has good references and a solid performance record, I'm going to hire that applicant. When they were younger, some of my employees committed misdemeanors or substance-related felonies."

"That's cute." He sipped his drink. "Did one of your techies get a DUI in college?"

She cocked her foot beneath the table and considered kicking him.

He rested his chin in his palm and rubbed his eyebrow. "Possession of stolen goods sounds a lot like grand larceny. Nobody trusts a thief." He sighed and looked at the bay. "And they shouldn't. I have to work ten times harder to get over my mistakes."

Placing her napkin on the table, she stood. "You don't have to work harder with me. I want to swing by the office and make sure my employees locked up after Michael's accident, but I think we should spend the afternoon unraveling ScanCoin. Getting a solid answer from Anna Claire is the only way you can move on."

"How?" He looked up. "My plan didn't work out."

Flipping open her sunglasses, she slid them in place. "Anna Claire's not running a mechanic's shop, so the business's physical address hardly matters. If everything's in the cloud, we'll go to her house and surprise her where she least expects a confrontation."

"Her house?" He let his mouth gape. "Are you insane?"

"Hardly." *Sometimes I feel like I might lose my grip on my life, but spending time with him feels good. If I'm lucky, we'll spend the evening in bed.* She cleared her throat. "I prefer audacious and nosy. A few months ago, a gossipy news article about Atherton real estate deals mentioned a 'young, payment processing tycoon'. I'm pretty sure I know where she lives."

"What am I going to say?" he asked.

"The same thing you would have said if you found her at the office." She opened her wallet. "Only Anna Claire knows the truth about your investment." Placing a twenty-dollar tip on the table, she turned toward the street and held her breath. *Will he follow or did he lose his nerve in prison?* Hearing chair legs scrape against concrete, she exhaled. *He still has hope.*

On the way to the office, she listened to her voice mails and dictated internal responses. The emails requiring longer, thoughtful replies could wait until she returned to her computer. Spending the day with

Damon felt good, but a pile of work would accumulate. "Siri, tell Valentina…"

"I don't understand half of what you're saying," Damon said.

Keeping one hand on the wheel, she rubbed her throat. "Do you want to understand it?"

"What's a Sequoia Server?"

She laughed.

"Why are you laughing at me?"

"I'm not, but I doubt big tech wants you to rebrand their money-maker."

"Vivi, the only thing I know about that company is how to use the spelling feature."

"Well, you're ahead of half my employees. Never take a picture of our whiteboards. In my opinion, word processing ruined spelling bees and penmanship, including my own."

"Are you sure it wasn't the chat rooms?"

She smiled and glanced over. "They didn't help." Slowing the car for a crosswalk, she cleared her throat. "The server I mentioned is a proprietary relational database management system. SQL is a standard programming language, but big tech's implementation added a set of proprietary constructs. The company wasn't the first to market, but it was big enough to get attention and traction."

"Like ScanCoin."

Shaking her head, she turned at the corner. "For twenty years, big tech's server worked exclusively in their environment, and the company raked in the cash. A few years ago, they lost market share and let it run on other operating systems."

"Is this your version of talking dirty?"

Laughing, she thought of his lips wrapped around her toe. *I'm open to new ideas.* "You know more about digital currencies than I do, but I don't think it gets you hot and bothered."

He sighed. "Look where it got me."

Reaching across the center console, she laid a hand on his leg. "Damon, we might reclaim your money."

"And we might not."

She squeezed his muscled thigh. "You'll find a way to get through this mess. I believe in you."

Adding his hand's weight to hers, he squeezed. "Thanks. That means something, Vivi."

She pulled into a parking spot outside the fair-trade coffee shop on the building's first floor. Scanning the sidewalk, she looked for blood and remnants of the hit-and-run investigation. Strangers walked past the building without looking up, but she would struggle to see the entrance without replaying the assault on Michael's life. She cleared her throat and focused on the future.

"How long will you be?" Damon asked.

She glanced at the second-story windows. "It shouldn't take long. You can come up or grab a coffee and wait downstairs. Maybe fifteen minutes."

"I'll come up," he said.

"Really?" She made eye contact.

He tucked his chin. "Unless you don't want me to visit."

Holding up a hand to stop further objections, she cleared her throat. "No! Come see what I do. You might change your mind about the PR job."

He rubbed his jaw. "I doubt it."

She tilted her head and examined the offer from his

position. PR jobs required a certain skill set, but Damon's easy charm and quick intelligence made him a natural choice. "You're not an interruption."

"What am I?" He dropped his hand from his face.

She moved to touch him, but she sighed and opened the driver's door to give him space. "I don't know. More than a friend? Maybe now's not the best time to answer that question."

Shaking his head, he climbed from the car and walked toward the coffee shop.

"The building has a separate entrance for office guests." She reached into the car to grab her purse and straightened. "Just follow me."

He waved her off. "I changed my mind. I'll order a coffee."

Watching his broad shoulders disappear into the shop, she sighed and wondered if she should push him or let him set the pace. Lost in his arms, she reveled in his control, but this was her side of town. Pulling her lipstick from her purse, she used the car's window reflection to check her appearance. *Deflection never works. Damon said he likes to keep things fresh. Well, the night after the gala felt like a breath of fresh air, but how do we get back to that first, unencumbered rush?*

Chapter Nine

Tucked away at the end of a quiet cul-de-sac, Anna Claire's slate-gray home hid behind a screen of mature, native oaks. From satellite imagery, Vivian knew the grounds boasted grassy lawns, a swimming pool, and a cabana, but she doubted she and Damon would find the ScanCoin entrepreneur sitting poolside. "Her trees are beautiful."

Damon scratched his head. "Her trees?"

"This lot! It looked green on the imagery, but I had no idea how pretty the trees would be."

"I didn't know you were so into trees," he said.

She picked up a palm frond from the sidewalk. Blown by the wind, the leaf had escaped Anna Claire's walled garden and landed on the sidewalk like a piece of large confetti. "The city was named for its trees. *El Palo Alto* is the eleven-hundred-year-old coast redwood by the park creek."

"Then why aren't there more redwoods in town?"

She dropped the frond. "Without flowing water, the city is too far inland and too dry to support redwoods. It's a delicate balancing act. When people moved to California, they planted the trees they knew. Decades later, those trees are dying. Liquidambar is the beautiful street tree we admire in the fall." She rubbed her foot over the dry frond. "This one's native to tropical islands. We should plant local species."

"At least they didn't name the city *carajo grande.*"

She turned. "What does that mean?"

"The big fuck."

Laughing, she tucked her hair behind her ear. "Outside of food, I know zero Spanish."

"Silvia didn't teach you anything?"

She brushed her hands. "No, did she teach you?"

He laughed. "All the curse words."

She frowned. "It took her a long time to warm up. Maybe I'm hard to like."

Pulling her close, he kissed her lips.

The brief, sweet gesture stole her words, and she touched her lips. "What happened to tabling sex?"

He pulled back. "I like you and your quirky knowledge."

"Good to know"—smiling, she cleared her throat— "but after you stayed the night, liking me was kind of obvious. Are you ready to end your dry spell? We can totally skip this outing and head back to the bungalow."

He cocked his head. "You don't let your dates sleep over?"

"What dates?" *The gap between you and Johann was as long as your prison sentence.* Clearing her throat, she looked at the bright green fresh growth on Anna Claire's oak trees. "I would never leave this lot, but I'm surprised she hasn't thinned out the non-native species."

He stared at the canopy. "Maybe they give good shade."

She shook her head.

"Maybe she works from home."

She shrugged. "Well, she has about sixty-three hundred square feet back there, so she can take her pick of desk locations. According to public records, the house had five bedrooms and five-and-a-half baths."

He whistled.

"She laid down fifteen million for her slice of paradise. Who knows what the house looks like now?"

"We're about to find out," he said.

"Good cop, bad cop?" she asked.

He shook his head. "Document courier."

"The security team will never let you past the gate." She glanced at her electric vehicle. "Don't we need like a truck or something?"

"We're not delivering toilet paper, Vivi."

She rolled her eyes. "We're not delivering anything."

"This was your idea."

This was your investment strategy. If you'd asked me for advice, I would have suggested an exchange-traded fund. EFTs are timid, but they spread out risk. She batted her eyelashes and smiled. "Lead the way."

He picked up a manila folder from her backseat. "Let's do this."

Admiring him cross the street, she cleared her throat. *I'd believe he's a document courier. His ass looks like he spends all day delivering packages.* She stifled a laugh and watched him consider the control panel in front of the security gate. *He can pack my box any time he likes.* Making a mental note to order brown shirts for role-play, she crossed her arms, leaned against the car, and looked innocuous.

Pressing a button on the control panel, Damon shifted from one foot to another.

She waited a minute and slid into the driver's seat. *Nobody's home. Well, we tried. Back to bed.* She schooled her expression to avoid looking like a horny, maniacal woman sitting alone in a car.

After five minutes, he returned holding the folder and climbed into the passenger seat.

"No luck—"

"I have an idea." He tossed the folder into the footwell.

"Does it involve a lingerie set with a garter belt?"

He cleared his throat and glanced at her breasts. "No, but thanks for that mental image."

Tilting her head, she wondered how far to tempt him. Recovering his investment should be a priority, but she knew a surefire way to burn off stress, and she preferred his assistance. "It's red."

He picked up the manila folder, laid it over his lap, and secured the seatbelt. "Nobody answered the intercom, but I heard trucks idling on the property. Let's go back to Mama Clarke's house and pick up a drone. At least, we'll know if Anna Claire's there or not."

"Isn't that illegal?" She checked the vehicle's side mirrors.

He shrugged. "Keeping track of civil ordinances can be difficult."

Narrowing her gaze, she set aside her plans to seduce him. "Is the drone stolen?"

He checked the side-view mirror. "Nope. Let's go."

She put the car in drive and checked the rearview mirror. The street looked deserted. For a moment, she considered putting the car on autopilot so she and Damon could continue the conversation without the distraction of speed limits and brake lights. *I hate giving up control.* Instead, she cleared her voice. "Is it stolen?"

"Not to my knowledge," he said.

Hearing the evasion in his response, she removed her foot from the accelerator.

The car came to a sudden stop.

"This thing drives like a golf cart," he said.

"Don't be fooled." Clenching her teeth, she swallowed. "This *thing* goes from zero to sixty miles per hour in two seconds flat."

He whistled and settled lower in the seat.

"Did asking about the drone offend you?" She chose her words. "I don't want to get caught up in old grievances."

Shaking his head, he made eye contact. "I traded services for the drone. A photographer wanted to install cameras on the outside of his studio. Someone kept stealing his packages. I gave him a bundle of cameras, and he gave me the drone. It worked fine for him, but he wanted to upgrade to a model that could sense obstacles, avoid them, and hold its position in the wind. Do you feel better?"

Sheepish is more like it. Her cheeks warmed. "Yeah."

"All right, hit the pedal."

She hesitated. "Do you know how to fly the drone?"

He rolled his eyes. "It's easier than a video game."

She turned the car around in front of Anna Claire's gate. "Plug your address into the navigation system."

Tapping the screen, he paused. "Should I save it as a favorite?"

I don't know. Are we going to spend a lot of time at

163

Mama Clarke's house? She cleared her throat. "So, where did you fly the drone?"

"You mean, before I landed my ass in jail?"

She nodded.

"The high school field. Open spaces. Some neighborhood kids borrowed it for a middle school project." He exhaled. "Well, that was two years ago. Now, those kids are in high school."

"Tell me about them." The prompt felt safer than discussing his prison time.

Staring out the window, he talked about the teenagers and their documentary project.

Instead of joy, she heard grief and regret. *Can he reclaim that time?*

She pulled up to the light-blue house on Annapolis Street. Beyond the white-painted iron fence, the bare dirt and weedy remnants of a front lawn remained unchanged, but a pot of begonias sat on the concrete steps. "I didn't take your mom for a big gardener."

"Shani brought over those flowers," he said.

She frowned. "Is pink her signature color?"

"Seems that way." Opening the door, he paused and looked over. "You coming in?"

"I'll sit tight and"—she picked up her phone—"answer emails."

"Chicken," he said.

She forced a smile, but she felt self-conscious in front of the humble house. *I don't bake brownies. I don't garden.* The begonias shifted in the breeze, seeming to taunt her. *I spend my days analyzing data and contracts.* She swallowed. *Has he seen how many shoes I own?*

Damon returned with a leather backpack and the

drone. Setting both objects on the backseat, he climbed into the car and buckled his seat belt.

Folded up, the drone looked innocuous and manageable, but the backpack worried her. She pulled away from the curb and eased forward. "What's in the bag?"

"Mostly batteries. Drones eat them up. You might get thirty minutes of fly time before you have to swap your gear."

She swallowed and pressed the accelerator. "I hope they're rechargeable."

He laughed. "They are."

"Was your mom home?"

He looked out the window. "Nope."

Reaching over, she rested a hand on his thigh. "Maybe I should have come inside."

"Maybe you should have thought about that ten minutes ago."

She slammed the brake. "You offering?"

The sudden deceleration threw him forward. Bracing his palms against the dashboard, he turned and shook his head. "You're ridiculous."

"The whole toe thing?" She grinned. "I've been thinking about it all day. I'm wearing red."

He shook his head. "Not until we unravel ScanCoin."

She sighed, impressed by his resistance, but not impressed enough to give up hope. "Too bad. The day was looking up."

****

Parking in front of Anna Claire's home, Vivian wondered if the security company monitoring the property had already run her license plates. "So, you're

165

going to fly the drone, snap video, and we're out of here?"

"If you download the app, I can live stream the footage to your phone."

A whiskered man wearing a tracksuit walked a dog down the sidewalk, looped the cul-de-sac, and headed straight for her vehicle.

"Damon, that's the guy from the restaurant." She ducked, pretending to rummage in the foot well.

"What guy?" he asked.

"The one in the polyester track suit. Get down here."

He laughed. "Vivi, that man's walking a dog. He's probably a neighbor."

Peering through the window, she watched the man stop at the end of the street.

The dog lifted his leg and peed on Anna Claire's wall.

With a gentle tug, he directed the animal to turn and walk back up the street.

"What are the coincidences?" she asked.

Damon frowned. "Are you sure it was the same man?"

"Maybe." She swallowed. "No."

"C'mon, give me your phone so we can find out if Anna Claire's home. I've been thinking about red lingerie since we left Mama Clarke's house."

"And then what?" She raised her eyebrows and handed him her phone, wetting her lips in anticipation of his response.

"I'll scale the wall."

Abandoning the power of red lingerie, she considered the wall. "Watching you climb that wall would be kind of hot." She imagined him striding across the grounds and calling Anna Claire's name. *Would the tech executive take one look at his bulked-up physique and run for the safety of her house? She doesn't know he's a softie at heart.*

Damon shook his head and tapped the touch screen. "I was joking."

Rolling her eyes, she climbed from the vehicle, leaned against the frame, and let him do his thing.

After unfolding the drone, he snapped in a fresh battery and turned on the power. Each rotor spun, and the drone hovered.

As the drone rose, its whirring sound diminished. "Impressive."

"That's what she said."

Laughing, she wondered if the time she spent with him would always be a mix of surprises and laughter.

He handed over her phone.

"Why didn't you put the app on your phone?" she asked.

"Figured you had a big, fancy data plan."

"There's a joke in there somewhere."

He laughed. "Tell me when you find it."

The drone rose in the air, passed the wall surrounding Anna Claire's house, and skimmed over the oak trees. The app on her phone displayed the property like the real estate photos she spent so much time stalking. "You were right," she said. "I count at least three trucks."

"Big ones or small ones?"

She peered at the phone. "Like box trucks. What are they doing?"

Holding the controller, he kept his gaze on the

drone. "You tell me."

"She must be remodeling. They're loading a bunch of crates into trucks. I can't tell if the crates contain household goods or deliveries. Oh, cute, she has a dog. Wait. Two dogs."

Raising their heads, the dogs sighted the drone and unleashed a racket of barks and howls.

The man walking the dog on the street pulled his animal away from the melee.

She rubbed her ear. *Precious never makes this much noise.* "Well, if Anna Claire's home, she knows something's up. See if you can get the drone to the back of the house. I want to see the pool."

"Are you enjoying this?" he asked.

Standing at the street's end left her feeling trapped and vulnerable, but Damon's presence tempered her fight-or-flight response. With him at her side, she felt less alone, but without his influence, she also doubted she would have gotten herself into this situation. She enjoyed spending time with him, but she could think of other activities with better risk-reward ratios. Then again, when had she ever flown a drone? "I should get my real estate license so I can poke around empty houses in real time."

"What would you do with Hoat Analytics?"

The drone dropped in altitude, and the video feed lapsed.

"Damon! Be careful."

He snorted.

"I don't know," she said. "I was mainly kidding. Start another company?"

"You don't enjoy running the one you have."

"I do, but I miss the action." Making a

168

noncommittal noise, she zoomed in on the feed. "Damon, the pool's almost green. She's not remodeling." Raising her gaze from the phone, she saw him exhale and close his eyes. Resignation weighed down his shoulders, and she wanted to comfort him. "She's leaving."

He nodded and flicked a thumb control.

The drone turned back toward the street.

No longer interested in spying on the pool, she touched his arm. "She probably left after the gala."

His shoulders slumped. "Yeah."

With everyone's money. "Come back to my place."

He navigated the drone through the dense oak trees.

She decided to look on the bright side. "If Anna Claire's gone, we're no longer coworkers. We can do dirty things. I can help you forget all about ScanCoin."

He rubbed his chin. "What kind of dirty things?"

"I'll straddle you," she said.

He shrugged.

She narrowed her gaze. "I'll straddle you on the couch, lock your hands on my hips, and bend backward until my head is by your feet, and my feet are by your ears." She could almost feel his hands gripping her hips. Her lace underwear caught the moisture pooling between her legs. "You can fuck me that way, Damon. My body will be wet and completely exposed. As you slide in and out of me, you'll see everything."

"Shit!"

"I know." She licked her lips. "I've wanted to try that move for ages."

"I'll fuck you sideways."

She grinned, ready to take him up on the offer.

169

He pointed toward the trees. "But right now, we have a problem."

Hearing the frustration in his voice, she pouted, but she saw his drone lodged in a tree branch near the wall. Instead of panicking, she grinned at the thought of distracting him with sex. "Did I do that?"

"The battery died," he said. "I guess they go bad."

She exhaled. "The battery died."

"That's what I said."

Faced with his practical explanation, she reevaluated her priorities in life. *I should be at the hospital with Michael. Cocktails on the terrace with the rest of my employees. In bed with Damon.* Out of her element, she rubbed the chill from her arms. "A stroke of bad luck."

He handed her the remote control. "I'll go get it."

"How?"

He tightened his belt. "I'll climb the wall, shimmy along the branch, and snag it."

The thought of him shimmying along anything made her laugh. *The man weighs over two hundred pounds.* "Good luck. Say hi to the Rottweilers."

He widened his gaze. "Rottweilers."

"Two of them." She picked at her nail cuticle. "Spiked collars."

"What a bitch," he said.

"Hey!"

"I meant Anna Claire." Shaking his head, he tossed the remote control into the back of the car and sighed. "I guess I'm down one drone."

The resignation in his voice worried her. *How many knocks can a man take before he's down?* "The dogs can't climb trees. Plus, you like Precious."

"I also like keeping my ass intact."

She tapped a shoe. If he left the drone in the tree, someone would eventually find the gizmo and link it to him. *I doubt Atherton's finest will believe Damon's a flight hobbyist. I don't care what he says about civil ordinances. He has a record. Three strikes and you're out.* She tucked her hair behind her ear. "I'll go get it."

He laughed. "Vivi, you're wearing heels."

"Well, I'll take them off. Give me a boost over the wall and I'll"—she raised her eyebrows—"shimmy along the branch."

"Is that right?" He crossed his arms.

Pride straightened her spine. "Do you want your drone back or not?"

"I don't need you to rescue me," he said. "Stay put."

"I'm not rescuing you. I'm rescuing your drone." Determined to accomplish her boast, she claimed his lips and let her emotions guide the kiss. Defiant, she wrapped an arm around his neck and held him close, determined to convey her frustration and the night they spent in bed. Breaking free before she embarrassed herself, she stepped back and lifted her chin. "Give me a boost?"

He stared, and the muscles in his jaw tightened.

"Damon?"

He put his hands on his hips. "I don't want you to do this, Vivi. It's not safe."

She rolled her eyes. "Fine, then you do it."

Shaking his head, he walked across the street and reached for the top of the wall. His fingers gripped the rough stucco.

The dogs barked from the shaded yard.

171

He closed his eyes, exhaled, and pulled down his arms.

To keep from laughing, she bit her lip. "Nice doggies."

Sweat shone on his forehead. "I doubt they heard you."

Pushing her way to the wall, she slipped off her heels and eyed the drone. From the top of the wall, the device sat out of reach but close enough to tempt her into action. "Get down on one knee."

He raised an eyebrow. "It's a little early for that move."

A month ago, she wondered if she would ever hear from him. No matter how well their bodies fit, their worlds remained apart, and running her business had to come before her pleasure. This adventure thrilled her, but the wisp of danger kept her from delving into his remark. She hip checked him.

Complying with her instructions, he dropped to the sidewalk. "Hurry, so we can get out of here."

"What's the difference between losing a basketball over the fence and losing a drone?"

He scanned the cul-de-sac. "Fifteen million dollars of residential clout."

Stepping up, she pushed against his thigh muscles, clambered to his shoulders, and used both hands to reach for the top of the wall. A hand at her back steadied her. She pushed up on her palms, sat on the top of the wall, and grinned. The drone rested above a large oak branch. Its black, motionless rotors absorbed the sunlight. "I can get it."

Scratching at the wall, the dogs barked and whined.

"Go dig up a flower bed." She stood and wobbled.

Arms wide for balance, she bit her lip and reached for the tree. Her fingers brushed the leaves, but the gap between the tree and the wall looked too wide for an easy transfer. *How much money does a drone cost?* She considered her bare feet and the streaks of dust marking her pants. *More or less than a visit to the emergency room?*

Focusing on the tree, she stretched her fingers until she grasped a branch, shifted her weight, and jumped to the large oak. Making contact, she held onto the shaking limb, laughed, and felt the adrenaline pumping through her system. "This might be as much fun as sex."

"Vivi?" Damon asked from the sidewalk.

"Almost have it!" Loosening her grip on the branch, she crawled toward the drone, snagged the body, and retreated to her landing spot.

Beneath her, the larger Rottweiler spun in circles.

"Can I toss it over the wall?" she asked.

"Yes!"

"Here it comes!" Unable to see where he stood, she pitched the drone over the wall and hoped his quick reflexes compensated for the inaccuracy of her toss. *One more jump and I'll have a story to tell.* She bent her knees, knowing if she grasped the wall's top, she could pull up to sitting. The wind shook the oak leaves. Closing her eyes, she tested the tree's resiliency.

Near the trunk, the branch splintered, and the crack sounded like a resounding gunshot. Wobbling in the air, she flailed her arms and searched for an anchor.

No longer stationary, the branch listed toward the ground.

She lost her balance, tumbling through lower

branches until she landed on the hard ground. Anna Claire's grass did little to soften the blow, and her tailbone ached. Any minute, the dogs would attack, and she would have much bigger problems. She remained perfectly still. *I am so screwed.*

The dogs stopped barking.

Turning her head, she risked a glance.

The Rottweiler sitting beside her licked her face.

"Good doggie," she whispered the endearment.

"Vivian?" Damon asked.

His voice sounded far away. "I'm fine," she said. "Give me a minute."

"I'm coming to get you."

She looked at the dog's warm chocolate eyes. "Don't bother."

"What?" he asked. "Hang tight."

She imagined him standing on the other side of the wall, eyebrows furrowed and muscles tensed for action. Unwilling to move her arms or legs, in case she did more damage than she thought, she turned her head and searched for the second dog. Finding the beast on its belly near the wall, she smiled. "All bark and no bite?"

Pushing up to her elbows, she scanned the grounds. Leaf fall littered the grass, and weeds sprouted near tree trunks. *My gardener would have a field day with this mess.* Looking toward the house, she saw a pot-bellied security guard approaching, and she closed her eyes. *I should have known retrieving the drone wouldn't be this easy.* Getting to her feet, she winced at her soreness and brushed the dirt from her pants.

"You're trespassing." The guard raised a radio to his mouth.

"Oh, Anna Claire and I are old friends." She

pointed to the lazy dog. "See! The dogs love me."

He eyed the Rottweiler. "We'll see what Anna Claire has to say about your claim. In the meantime, I'm calling the police."

Afraid to get any closer, she shrugged. "Why waste everyone's time?"

"Lady, this is my job."

Damon threw a leg over the stucco wall.

Looking up, the guard patted his belt, but he came up empty. "You come over the wall, and I'll have you arrested."

Hearing panic in the guard's voice, she stepped between the men. "Nobody's coming over the wall." Meeting Damon's gaze, she raised her voice. "Nobody's coming over the wall."

He rolled his eyes and dropped to the leaf-strewn ground. "Are you hurt?"

The guard backed away and radioed for help.

Ignoring the pot-bellied guard and his radio arsenal, she hobbled toward Damon. "What are you doing?" Her question came out like a hiss. Clearing her throat, she softened her tone. "I could have talked myself out of this mess."

"This mess is going to end in the back of a patrol car." He cupped her elbow. "Lean on me."

She pulled free her arm. "Why? So the mall cop has a reason to tackle us?"

Biting back laughter, he shook his head. "So he knows you're not fair game."

"Fair game for what?" Damon's protectiveness intrigued her, but independence gave her the confidence to launch Hoat Analytics and define how she lived her life. When did she need a hovering protector?

He narrowed his gaze and stared at the guard. "Whatever mall-cop fantasies keep him sane in this job."

"There's nothing wrong with a job well done."

Glancing at the dogs, he raised his eyebrows. "Sure. I bet he trained the security patrol, too."

She turned to the guard and raised her voice. "I'm so sorry about this confusion." Years of black-and-white movies taught her politeness and confidence, and analytical presentations taught her arrogance, but she doubted the security guard prized those attributes. She batted her eyelashes and extended a hand. "Can I lean on you while we walk to the house?"

He recoiled. "Lady, don't touch me. I don't know what the hell is going on, but I want you both to keep your distance." He pointed toward a small accessory building. "We'll use the grounds phone to call the police. Walk in front of me. Both of you."

"Or what?" Damon asked.

She elbowed him and smiled at the guard. "Go get Anna Claire from the house. She'll explain everything. We really are friends. I saw her at the ScanCoin gala."

He waved a hand, urging her to move. "She left earlier today."

Planting her feet, she pouted. "Permanently?"

The guard braced his hands on his hips and stared. "How the hell would I know?"

I'm wondering if you know anything. Wouldn't a motion detector and a monitoring contract be cheaper than paying your salary? Peering through the trees, she saw a driver pull down the loading door on an idling truck. "I guess we're too late."

Damon placed a hand at the small of her back. "It's

fine."

The guard cleared his throat. "C'mon, you'll have plenty of time to chitchat at the police station!"

The dogs raised their heads and fell into line. One head-butted her dangling hand.

They must smell Precious. Exhaling, she peered through the trees and considered how to extract Damon from the consequences of her fall. *Stubborn man. Getting him out of this mess will be a lot harder than I thought.* She stumbled on a root.

The nearest dog whined and nosed her thigh.

Damon shifted his hand, cupping her elbow. "Do you want me to carry you?"

Shaking her head, she put one foot in front of the other and winced. "I can do it on my own."

"But you don't have to," he said.

How much time before his lesson sank in?

Chapter Ten

Vivian wiped her sweaty palms on her clothes. Beyond the Atherton police station's two-story, Mission façade, a modern, antiseptic bureaucracy housed the city's police force. Yellow light fixtures punctuated the tiled ceiling, and small cameras blinked in the corners.

Lieutenant Anthony Jayne's black hair matched his uniform shirt. He wore too much hair gel, and his shoes looked fresh from the box, but he wore the badge. Sitting on the edge of a polished, wooden desk, he crossed his arms. "We're classifying you two as suspicious people who we caught trespassing."

Vivian glanced at Damon and swallowed. *I shouldn't have gone out on that limb.*

Leaning back in the station chair, Damon raised an eyebrow.

Let me guess, trespassing is child's play. Did you have a juvenile record? Clearing her throat, she tamed her frustrated pettiness and focused on Lieutenant Jayne. "Shouldn't you be on the streets catching criminals?"

The police officer smiled. "The men and women of the Atherton Police Department spend more time dealing with missing bicycles than armed intruders."

She struggled to her feet and winced. "We weren't

The Crevasse

armed!"

The lieutenant stood and held up his hand. "I appreciate that fact. If either of you carried a gun, we wouldn't be having this polite conversation." Picking up a sheath of papers lying on the desk, he looked at Damon. "Although, I wouldn't put anything past Johann's friends."

"Don't look at me." Damon laid his hand on his chest. "She's the expert shot."

"Really?" Lieutenant Jayne looked over. "Who knew you had so many skills?"

She tilted her head. "My grandfather taught me, but I only shoot for target practice." Shifting her weight, she smiled. "I heard the new Palo Alto police station has quite the gun range. Perhaps I could have a tour?"

The lieutenant cocked his head. "Funny. Most suspects want to minimize their time in police custody."

"Funny isn't the right word." Acquiring a criminal record seemed more likely by the second. She sighed and drummed her nails on the desk. "What's the penalty for being a suspicious person?"

"For you?" He tapped his chin.

She nodded, hoping her professional reputation would come into play.

Dropping his hand, he shrugged. "A few months in jail."

Her stomach sank, and fainting seemed like a reasonable reaction. Who would run Hoat Analytics? Michael was in the hospital, and the remaining leads would fight without clear delineation. "There has to be…"

Damon snorted. "All right, Lieutenant Jayne. Book us, or let us go." He uncrossed his ankles, stood, and

179

stretched. "Watching Vivi squirm is fun, but I have other ways to accomplish that task."

Heat flooded her cheeks. Her professional success depended on business etiquette, but Damon cracked jokes about getting her off. As soon as the lieutenant left for a moment, she would ask Damon to let her handle the precarious situation. Risking a glance, she caught his smile and wondered if his experience with law enforcement gave him the upper hand.

He winked.

Lieutenant Jayne cleared his throat. "'No person shall operate any model aircraft to which is attached any device capable of receiving, recording and-or transmitting visual images or sound, including but not limited to any still or video camera.'" Lieutenant Jayne stopped reading from the papers and looked at Damon. "The city passed the ordinance several years ago."

Damon shrugged. "I was busy."

"But it was your drone." Lieutenant Jayne tossed the papers on the desk.

One paper drifted to the floor, and neither he nor Damon bent to retrieve it. They stared at each other, and silence filled the room. Stepping between the men before testosterone caused more harm than terse statements, she picked up the paper and focused on the officer. "We're not suspicious or interested in criminal mischief. We're trying to find Anna Claire."

"Why?" Lieutenant Jayne asked.

She sat on the desk's edge. "She took something that belongs to Damon. I want to help him get it back."

He crossed his arms. "File a police report."

Batting her eyes seemed like overkill, especially with Damon in the room. *I'll never hear the end of it.*

She dropped the tone of her voice. "The men and women on this force have better things to do than mitigate neighborly disputes."

Lieutenant Jayne snorted. "You'd be surprised."

Closing her eyes, she inhaled, counted to ten, and met the man's gaze. "I believe in honesty."

"Interesting strategy."

Damon tapped his foot. "Tell me about it."

Tilting her head, she looked at him and raised her eyebrows. "Help me out."

Coming to stand by her side, he wrapped an arm around her shoulders and dropped his head. "I thought you didn't need my help."

Instead of arguing with his whispered rebuke, she leaned into his comforting weight and considered how much information the lieutenant needed before he understood her motives. Helping Damon recover his investment so she could drag him into bed would hardly win her sympathy points.

"Anna Claire's running a con," Damon said. "Vivian tried to help me untangle it."

She flinched, but hearing him speak the truth lightened her load. *Will he regret involving me?*

Sliding the papers out of the way, Lieutenant Jayne rested his chin in his hand. "What kind of scam?"

"A pyramid scheme," she said.

"A con," Damon said. "Hundreds of people could go broke."

Hearing the statements overlap, she smiled. "Investors benefit from spreading the word about Anna Claire's investment opportunity, but Anna Claire hasn't produced tangible returns. Have you heard about a cryptocurrency called ScanCoin?"

Lieutenant Jayne shook his head.

Standing, she slipped from Damon's warmth and paced the small room. "Damon invested in the digital currency, but he wants to withdraw his funds. Anna Claire won't let anyone divest. The office is closed for renovation, and movers are emptying her house." She swallowed. Damon's presence anchored her narrative. "I think she's on the run."

"So you scaled her wall?"

She raised her chin and stared at the ceiling. "Damon lost his drone."

"Come again?" the lieutenant asked. "You mumbled."

She straightened and looked at the police officer. "I don't mumble."

"But you do climb trees?"

She raised an eyebrow. "It was for a good cause."

Shaking his head, he stood and walked to the edge of the room. "I have better things to do than babysit you two."

"Are you sure?" Damon asked. "You could have booked us an hour ago."

Lieutenant Jayne stopped walking. "You're not worth my time."

She grinned. "So we're free to go?"

Lieutenant Jayne pursed his lips, but he nodded.

Stepping forward, she cocked her chin and stared. "What are you hiding?"

"Me?" He cocked his head. "I'm not the one who decided to spend the afternoon improvising an extreme fitness routine."

She rolled her eyes. "Like I would ever—"

"Sweat?" the lieutenant asked.

Damon snorted.

The officer held up his hand. "Answer one question. Why were you trespassing at Anna Claire's property? You could have invited yourself over for tea. Why the cloaks and daggers?"

"She's running a scam!" She slid her chair toward the desk, and it rattled on the linoleum before jamming on a desk leg. Wincing, she waited for the sound to die.

"And nobody else realizes that fact but you two?" Lieutenant Jayne soundlessly slid the second chair into place at the desk.

She bit her lip.

Damon put a hand at the small of her back. "Last week at the ScanCoin gala, Vivian gave the woman a piece of her mind. Vivi means well, but she and Anna Claire are not on friendly terms."

"So no tea and crumpets," Lieutenant Jayne said.

She looked back and forth between the two men. "Sorry, guys. We disbanded the secret club for female CEOs. Maybe I should save myself the pain of a sprained ankle and reopen the local chapter."

"You told the guard you and Anna Claire were friends," Lieutenant Jayne said.

The cramped room, and the threat of prison time, pushed her to her limit. "I lied!"

Damon laughed.

Lieutenant Jayne pulled out his phone. "If other people invested in ScanCoin, I doubt Mr. Clarke is the only individual who would like to recoup his investment."

His astute observation garnered her attention, and she leaned forward. "What do you know?"

He looked up from the screen. "I'm a police

officer."

"You're also playing nice," she said.

"Am I?" He swiped the phone screen and shrugged.

"Why are you letting me go?" Raising her eyebrows, she held out her hands for handcuffs. "Book me."

The officer pursed his lips. "That only happens in the movies."

Damon laughed. "Man, I kind of like you."

Lieutenant Jayne cleared his throat. "I think you're right about one thing. Anna Claire's on the move. After her last security detail died, she came to the Palo Alto police station and recruited a local officer to fill his position."

She put her hand over her mouth and replayed the university graduation ceremony that almost cost Johann and Hadley their lives. Lieutenant Jayne killed Horst Sakmann, but Horst served as the private security coordinator for a tech CEO. "Horst worked for Anna Claire!"

Lieutenant Jayne nodded. "Why is a technology CEO nervous enough to hire full-time security? Why is she so scared she's paying for full-time protection?"

Concentrating, she stared at the linoleum floor. *Damon and I aren't scary people.* She thought of the crowd of workers milling outside the warehouse, the harried restaurant owner, and the innocuous whiskered man walking his dog. *How do I judge whether someone is scary? What if someone at the gala had more to lose than Damon?* The woman wearing the lime-green dress came to mind. "I don't know why she's scared. Maybe someone else already tried to withdraw their investment."

"Or maybe she's not acting alone." The lieutenant cleared his throat. "The Atherton police force is charging you with trespassing."

She snapped up her head. "What? I thought we were free to go."

Holding up his palms, Lieutenant Jayne raised his eyebrows. "Hear me out."

"Like we have a choice," Damon said.

The lieutenant pointed. "If you'd stuck to the letter of the law, you wouldn't be here."

"Man, you saw those mutts and that beefy mall cop. I couldn't leave her."

"Fair enough." Turning to her, Lieutenant Jayne raised his eyebrows. "Trespassing is a minor offense, but Anna Claire might press charges."

Perspiration dampened her armpits, and her heart rate skyrocketed. "I can't have a criminal record!"

He raised his eyebrows. "I doubt Anna Claire will show up to file the paperwork."

"Oh! But if she does"—blinking, she focused on the next steps—"we could ask her about our investments in ScanCoin." She looked at Damon and swallowed. The scale of his investment and the associated stakes dwarfed her proof-of-concept deposit. "I mean, you could ask her about your investment."

"I think you're enjoying this hunt." He worked his jaw. "You might need a hobby."

She tilted her head and wondered how to tell him she viewed him as less of a hobby and more of a scintillating distraction. "I can think of other ways to enjoy our time together."

Lieutenant Jayne opened the door, held it, and

gestured to the hallway. "Think long and hard about whether you want to be the person asking Anna Claire questions." He met Damon's gaze. "Curiosity puts a target on a man's back. I understand Ms. Hoat's employee was the victim of a hit-and-run."

Gasping, she rearranged her understanding of Michael's injury. Instead of a distracted driver's haphazard mistake, had the driver targeted Michael? She glanced at the door handle and Lieutenant Jayne's polished gun.

"It's my money," Damon said. "I'm the only person with real involvement."

"To make a point, criminals often cast a wide net."

She swallowed and edged her back against the wall. "I work with computers."

The officer turned. "But you also know how to shoot a gun. Who else might have that skill?"

Chewing on her fingernail, she replayed Michael's accident. The driver, a man, looked nothing like Anna Claire, but the lieutenant's point hit home. She thought she could save Damon, but in doing so, she might endanger herself and the other people in her life. Her cuticle bled, and she tasted blood's sharp, metallic tang. Pulling away her hand, she watched a bead of blood swell.

"Nobody's getting shot, Vivi." Damon urged her through the doorway. "He's trying to scare you."

Passing by the officer, she looked over her shoulder and met his gaze. *It's working.*

Lieutenant Jayne raised his eyebrows.

She swallowed. *Before Damon returned, my life was cut and dry, but that doesn't mean it was better.*

****

Throughout the cab ride, Damon remained silent.

Shifting on the cab's ubiquitous, brown upholstery, she held her purse. Nestled inside the soft leather, the written summons Lieutenant Jayne issued her felt like it weighed as much as an anchor.

"This is the place?" the driver asked.

His belly made her think the driver spent too much time driving and not enough time exercising, but he obeyed traffic signs and abstained from running red lights. Given her experiences with local drivers, he already earned his tip. She pulled out her phone to finish the transaction and compensate him for his time. "Yep."

Damon climbed out, walked to her side of the cab, and waited by the passenger door.

She opened the door and stood on the sidewalk. "It could have been worse. They could have arrested us."

He looked at the wall surrounding Anna Claire's home. "There's still time."

She dropped her phone into her purse and rummaged for her keys. Success made Vivian a millionaire, but it made Anna Claire a billionaire. Differences in account balances defined their worlds, but their approaches toward people defined their lives. No matter how many times Vivian's palms sweated or her feet ached, she followed through on her promises and did her best to keep Hoat Analytics and her employees moving in the right direction. Anna Claire's walled estate, shaggy trees, and untended pool suggested the woman had other priorities, but her failure to step onto the stage at the ScanCoin gala condemned her leadership.

Vivian had to consider the possibility that

confronting Anna Claire in the museum bathroom had placed a target on her back, but she refused to play the woman's game.

"Do you want me to drive?" Damon asked. "You seem distracted."

Looking down, she realized she held the car key fob and stood beside the electric vehicle. How long had she stood there, thinking about Anna Claire while Damon and the cab driver waited? "No, I have it." She clicked the unlock button and stepped toward the vehicle.

Intense heat and a flash of light engulfed the car.

Thrown backward, she shielded her face.

"Vivian!" Damon rushed around the flaming vehicle, wrapped his arms around her torso, and dragged her away from the inferno. "Are you okay?"

His voice no longer sounded deep and playful. Reaching up a hand, she cupped his cheek and closed her eyes. "I'm fine." The wind surrounded them with acrid smoke, and she coughed. At the end of a quiet cul-de-sac, Anna Claire's slate-gray home hid behind a screen of mature, native oaks, but Vivian's electric vehicle went up in flames. She thought she could save Damon, but her involvement endangered everyone she knew. Closing her eyes, she weighed her choices, but abandoning her quest felt as cowardly as hiding behind a wall. She needed help, and she needed it fast. Opening her eyes, she swallowed and managed a weak smile. "Help me stand?"

Forehead furrowed, he offered a hand.

She held tight and used his strength to stand. "Thank you."

The cab driver gave the vehicle a wide berth. "Car

bomb. Lady, you must have pissed off someone big."

She watched a hundred thousand dollars go up in flames. She could replace the vehicle, but her sense of security remained shattered. Before the explosion, the car had no signs of external damage, and lithium-ion batteries needed time and heat to ignite. When the wreckage cooled, insurance investigators would find the chemical remnants of old-school chemicals. Nothing short of explosives could have made her car go boom, but the person who planted the device tied it to her key fob. They must have known she would never enter the vehicle. Squeezing Damon's hand, she met the cab driver's curious stare. "I think you're right. What an intimidation tactic."

First responders raced up the street. Their sirens wailed.

Homeowners peeked from their wrought iron gates.

She took a deep breath. "Can I buy out your day?"

Using a fingernail, the driver pried a piece of food from his teeth. "Lady, I'm with you all day. This is the most exciting thing that's happened in a week."

"A week?" she asked.

He flicked the recovered bit of food into the bushes. "You'd be surprised what kind of shenanigans I see from the driver's seat. You think the yahoos cruising San Mateo County like opera and tech hoodies?" He kicked a piece of smoking debris toward the inferno and shook his head. "The only quiet things on the Peninsula are the guns and the waves."

Blood drained from her head, and she felt lightheaded. Holding tight to Damon's hand, she drew a deep breath and looked at the smoking wreckage. "I hope we disappoint you."

****

Swallowing, Vivian unlocked her bungalow's front door and turned off the alarm. The cab driver brought her back to the office, waited for her and Damon to pick up coffee, and kept his conversational chatter to a minimum. She rewarded him with a large tip and promised to call him for her next ride. He seemed disappointed nothing eventful happened, but he shrugged and thanked for her for the generous tip.

As the sun began to set, a rental car sat in her driveway, and the entry code waited on her cell phone. With the code, she could access the rental vehicle and continue zipping around Palo Alto to attend to her interests. Damon's silence might be harder to manage. "Do you want to regroup? Go home? Recharge?"

"There is no regroup, Vivi." He prowled around the house and tested the lock on the new front window. "I'm all in. You need to call Johann. Get a security expert who has an eye for weaknesses to evaluate your house. Upgrade your system."

She agreed with his statements, but exhaustion sapped her strength. Ignoring Precious's whines from the crate, she dropped to the couch for a brief rest. "Anna Claire's in over her head."

"So are you."

Massaging her temples, she leaned her head against the couch. "I know."

"So, you need help."

"The police are on alert. They promised to increase patrols. I'm safe enough in my house, and I'll work from home tomorrow. Stay the night?" The question took more courage than climbing the wall.

He dropped into a chair and hung his head. "I'm

done with ScanCoin."

"Damon!" She straightened. "That's everything you have."

"Not everything." He raised his head and made eye contact.

At the intensity in his gaze, she swallowed. "Write down everything you know about the cryptocurrency. We'll give the police your information and let them assemble a case."

"And you'll call Johann for help?"

She frowned. "I don't need Johann."

He planted his hands on his knees and stood. "Vivian, I can't protect you from a crazy woman."

"She's not crazy. She's overwhelmed."

He paced the room.

She held her breath.

"Fine," he said. "Drop me off at Mama Clarke's house. Better yet, stay inside. I'll walk."

He remained at her side all afternoon, and she could no sooner let him walk home than she could expose her employees to additional threats. Watching him flex and roll his shoulders, she knew she could ease his frustration and protect him inside the bungalow. "Stay for dinner."

"Not hungry." He strode toward the front door, opened it, and slammed. Pivoting, he drew a deep breath and made eye contact "If you can't accept help, you're as lame as the teenagers smoking pot behind the convenience store."

She winced.

Precious howled.

Self-sufficiency helped her leave the Central Valley. Technology made her rich. If Anna Claire targeted her for her interference, pride and data would be of little use, but physical separation might save Damon. As much as she wanted to curl up on the couch with him and listen to the reassuring sound of night bugs, she stood, opened the front door, and gestured for him to go first. "I'll give you a ride home."

She put the rental car in Drive, but crossing San Francisquito Creek felt like a precipice. Once she dropped off Damon, the separation would stick. A quick U-turn brought her back to Palo Alto's old neighborhoods.

He drummed his fingers on the door panel.

Arriving in front of her bungalow, she exhaled. "I'm not done with you, yet. I want you to stay with me. We'll figure out an appropriate response over dinner."

He crossed his arms. "You're a terrible cook."

Offense seemed like the obvious choice. "I'm an excellent cook."

He raised his eyebrows.

She swallowed and risked a glance. "Silvia's niece keeps my freezer stocked."

He eyed the bungalow. "We're not going after Anna Claire. Enough is enough."

"Okay." She gripped the wheel. "We'll let the police handle it."

Turning, he placed a hand on her knee. "Honestly?"

"It's your money." She swallowed and savored the warmth of his contact. "You made the decision to invest it in ScanCoin."

"And?" he asked.

"And I'll call Johann for help." The commitment

192

left a bitter taste in her mouth. As Hoat Analytics grew, she valued Johann's friendship, but she secretly enjoyed her success outside his sphere. Each milestone felt like giving the handsome, arrogant, German asshole the finger. *I might have been your executive assistant, but look how far I came!* Of course, he helped her put together the initial financing for her company, but she believed she would have succeeded without his help. In case she was wrong, she kept her petty attitude to herself and tried to be a better person. Damon deserved the best person she could be, and if that meant she would eat humble pie and call Johann for help, she would do it.

Damon exhaled. "What's for dinner?"

"That's it?" She waited for more conditions. If they sat in the car any longer, a nosy neighbor would come outside under the pretense of watering plants.

"No, that's not it, but we'll talk after dinner." He pulled free his hand and released the seatbelt. It retracted into place with a smooth whir. "Preferably enchiladas."

Smiling, she climbed from the car and stared at the white house. Damp, chilly breezes blew off the bay. Somewhere in the Central Valley, heat radiated from the asphalt, but that place no longer felt like home. She craved the creaking, wooden floorboards and snug, craftsman security of her bungalow. The oaks groaned in the wind, but bright-green grass and emerging buds made her smile. *The house has withstood a hundred years of foggy winter mornings and scorching summer afternoons. It can withstand a few more decades, and I can withstand Anna Claire.* "What if I don't have enchiladas?"

He walked around the vehicle and slung an arm around her shoulders. "I'll settle for scrambled eggs."

"Classic." Leaning on his shoulder, she led him to the front door. A summons for trespassing required a strategy, and a burned-out car required an insurance report, but her ankle hurt, and Damon's gaze promised warmth. *I'll deal with the fallout later.*

Precious yawned from the couch.

"You're supposed to be in your kennel." She planted her hands on her hips. "How did you get out?"

Precious stretched and nuzzled under a pillow.

"Do you need to let her outside?" Damon asked.

She checked every lock in the house, but nothing looked amiss. Returning to the living room, she eyed Precious's floppy ears peeking from the linen pillow cover. White hairs threaded the dog's luxurious red fur, but when the animal moved from the slipcover, she would leave a warm impression. *She's guarded this house her entire life.* "Leave her be. She earned that spot."

"You're the boss," he said.

Pulling away from his shoulder, she turned. "What does that mean?"

He shrugged.

"I've never been your boss." Exhaling, she sat on a chair, slipped off her shoes, and rubbed her aching feet. "Even if I were your boss, I doubt you would listen. Johann trusted your discipline, but I think he also trusted you to make decisions. Do you trust yourself?"

"I used to." Walking into the kitchen, he opened the freezer. "Silvia hooked you up."

She hobbled after him and leaned against the doorframe. "Damon, I agreed. We're not going after

Anna Claire."

Tossing a casserole dish in the microwave, he closed the door and set the timer. "Good to know." Keeping his back to her, he braced his hands on the counter.

She walked across the kitchen and trailed a hand from his broad shoulders to the tight muscles of his lower back. Slipping an arm around his waist, she laid her head against his back. "What's bothering you?"

He turned in her arms. "This thing between us doesn't require discipline." Tipping up her chin, he lowered his head, brushed his lips across hers, and pulled back. "Walking away requires discipline. What if I don't have it?"

"No." She gripped his shirt. For a moment, she tasted relief in his arms, but circumstances overshadowed the teasing glimpse of pleasure. "You're doing the right thing."

He raised his eyebrows.

"What did EPA teach you? When the going gets tough, run away?"

"No, but that strategy served me well in prison." He slipped free and crossed his arms. "Maybe we can get matching jumpsuits. If we go to Vegas tonight, the guards might give us conjugal visits."

"I'm not going to prison!" She threw up her hands. "Someone's trying to intimidate me."

"The plan's working."

Turning, she jabbed his chest. "Did the dogs or the car bomb scare you? We agreed to spend the night on lockdown and regroup."

He raised his eyebrows. "We agreed to let the police handle the investigation and call Johann for

195

help."

Secure in her bungalow, she considered her inability to drive him home. She wanted him at her side, and she wanted to make him whole. If regrets weighed him down, he might lose the jovial optimism she cherished. Even if he never recovered his money, he had to try. "Are you walking away from your investment? The market value of all the world's cryptocurrencies surpassed one trillion dollars. You own a piece of that wealth."

He brushed off her finger. "The market will slide. Economists define money as a medium of exchange, widely used, which crypto isn't"—he swallowed—"yet."

"And if it picks up steam?" she asked. "If people buy more than drugs and pizzas?"

Running a hand over his face, he sighed. "Cryptocurrency mining activities require lots of electricity. Armies of quants occupy warehouses like Anna Claire's, wasting their lives trying to solve math problems and generate more coins." Reaching toward the back door, he flicked off a light switch. "Localized energy demand often exceeds local power capacity. That's why ScanCoin can't rent generic cloud servers. What happens when a regime cuts the power? Poof, the mining's gone. Both major currencies want to cut power consumption by switching from proof of work to proof of stake."

How about proof of lust? Standing in the dark, she heard the trees moan and exhaled. Instead of fighting, she could spend her time exploring his heated skin, and she had outfits more alluring than prisoner jumpsuits. "Maybe ScanCoin's algorithm doesn't require energy-intensive mining operations."

"It does require continued investment." He flipped on the lights. "If the US falls behind on blockchain technology, the US dollar might lose its status as the world's reserve currency, and ScanCoin might lose its momentum."

"B-banks and money transmitters could embrace cryptocurrency for international transactions." She mined her memory for articles and sales pitches she barely read. "I'd take a contract payment in crypto."

"And then?" he asked.

She swallowed. "I'd convert it into cash."

The microwave beeped.

He reached for the door and paused. "You trust the things you know, but what happens when the currency feels like someone else's problem? Prominent cryptocurrency firms have threatened to move their headquarters overseas. The senior executives cried foul about excessive regulation from the federal government."

"What?" She imagined rows of cubicle-dwelling office workers assigned to monitor emerging currencies. Innovation could be sexy, but it could also be a drag. The same people monitoring web traffic might be more useful at a place like Hoat Analytics. "Which part of the government?"

"The Securities and Exchange Commission concluded the most well-known currencies lack central control so they're exempt from securities laws. Other cryptocurrency companies maintain a hoard of currency that triggers SEC review and evaluation. Regulators care about the difference between a digital currency and security matters." He waved his hand. "It all feels nebulous. Stashing my cash in ScanCoin was a crap decision. Watching the value fluctuate makes me more nervous than a digital artist hawking nonfungible art. I should have bought gold."

She toyed with a button on his shirt. "I take it the prison library wasn't limited to economics textbooks on supply and demand."

He grasped her hand. "No, it wasn't. Amazing people donated their time."

She looked up. "Did you ask the volunteers about ScanCoin?"

He shook his head. "I didn't want to show my hand."

Or hear their laughter.

Raising her hand to his lips, he kissed her fingers and let her go. "I also spent a lot of time in therapy."

She frowned and reconciled his upbeat approach to life with the introspection required on a therapist's couch. "Therapy?"

A soft, sad smile wrinkled his cheek, but it failed to brighten his eyes.

"Talk therapy. Lots of feelings." He shook his head. "Shitty coffee."

Pulling back, she tilted her head. "Why?"

"Issues."

She rolled her eyes. *Playing Robin Hood isn't an issue. It's a feature. I said he's disciplined and decisive, but he's also generous.* The uncertainty nagged. "Will you tell me why?"

"Nothing scary. Just"—he cleared his throat—"working on my self-worth."

Keeping her reaction in check, she smiled and laid her head on his chest. "I think you're worth a lot. Keep going to the therapy. Everyone struggles with self-worth."

"Not like me."

"Okay." His skin felt as warm as a sunbaked window. She kissed his neck and wondered if he minded delaying the enchiladas. *I told him I would straddle him on the couch, but Precious claimed the couch. Maybe we can improvise.* Feeling his hands cup her ass, she wrapped her hands around his shoulders, leaned into his strength, and smiled. "If ScanCoin's off the table, we're no longer colleagues."

He rubbed her back. "We were never colleagues. You like to put people in neat boxes."

Realizing she was the only person thinking of sex, she blinked. "Boxes?"

"This thing between us requires finesse," he said. "I'm no good at finesse."

She pulled back. "You're good at making up excuses."

He dropped his hands. "Excuses?"

"I'm broke! I'm scared of dogs!" She made her way to the table and pulled out a chair. Exhaustion hit her, and she sighed. "Go after what you want! Isn't that what a therapist would say?"

He rubbed a hand over his hair. "I want you to stay safe. I want you to come to me without needing a shoulder for support."

"I've always had weak ankles," she said. "When I was a kid, I rolled them all the time."

He held up his hands. "Then why do you wear those ridiculous shoes?"

"Because I can!" Closing her eyes, she leaned her head against the chair's back. "Because I love how they make me feel. I love the balance and rhythm of walking across a room and knowing that if most men in the room donned a pair, they would look like fools." Raising her head, she met his gaze. "It's trivial, but I'm good at it, and you're not."

The microwave dinged, again.

Shaking his head, he walked to the appliance, reached for the handle, and paused. Meeting her gaze, he turned and walked toward the front door.

"Where are you going?" she asked.

He rolled his shoulders. "Home."

Sitting straight, she counted how many times he threatened to walk out the door. She could keep going after him, but unless he wanted to stay, she needed to preserve her pride and let him leave. "What about dinner?"

"Eat it. You could stand to gain a few pounds."

Sighing, she closed her eyes. "Everyone has an opinion."

"I'm not everyone. I'm your friend," he said.

She waved a hand in the air.

"And I want to be more than your friend—"

Something fluttered in her heart, and she raised her head.

"—but you have to trust me and listen. That drone?"

She laid a hand across her chest to calm her erratic heartbeat.

"It wasn't worth the cost of risking your life. I told you not to go over that wall." He walked back across the room and stood over her. "We're not choosing between friends and fuck buddies. You want this thing between us to work? Sometimes, you'll have to listen."

Opening her eyes, she stared. "Why did you take a knee?"

He pulled her to standing and scooped her into his arms. "Because you're a stubborn, hard-headed woman, Vivi. If I hadn't taken a knee, you'd probably have driven your car up to the wall and climbed onto the hood."

She raised a hand and cupped the side of his face. His emerging beard tickled her palm, and she smiled. "You know me well."

"Are you ever going to listen to me?"

She swallowed. "I don't want to come home and be the CEO."

"Good." He adjusted her in his arms. "I don't want to be your house bitch."

Laughing, she dropped her hand. "What does that leave us?"

"Room to negotiate." He strode toward the bedroom.

"Negotiate about what?" she asked.

"Whatever it's going to take to make you to listen to my advice."

"Oh, I'll heed your advice, all right." She hummed. The deep, appreciative sound rumbled in her chest and vibrated between them. "Your arguments have merit."

He tossed her on the bed.

Laughing, her ass hit the mattress, and she gasped.

"Strip," he said.

Raising an eyebrow, she rose to her knees and unclasped the small black button securing her pants. Feeling his gaze on her body, she parted the fabric and revealed red, lace hip-huggers. The fabric dipped low in the front, skimming the soft, freshly shaved skin above her sex. She admired the soft curve of her stomach, tilted her head to the side, and looked over. Standing at the bed's edge, hands on his hips, he looked tense and absorbed. Capitalizing on his rapt attention, she slipped a finger beneath the lace, stroked her sex, and raised the finger to her lips.

He looked up and watched her gloss her lips. "Did I say you could stop?"

She froze. "Excuse me?"

"I said, strip."

Dropping her chin, she let her hair fall forward, grabbed both sides of her blouse, and raised it over her head. The silk slid across her skin like a satin burn. Arching her back, she freed herself from the shirt, dropped the silk on the bedside, and faced him on her knees.

He raised his eyebrows.

She shimmied out of her pants, tossed the garment on the floor, and planted her hands on her hips.

"All of it." He twirled his finger and pantomimed tossing her sexy lingerie in the corner like a pair of discarded slippers.

She gasped. "The lace?"

"The lace," he said.

Looking down, she admired the swell of her breasts and rolled her eyes. *His loss.* Unclasping her bra, she dropped it on the bed and discarded the hip-huggers. Memories of their night together spiked her pulse. She wetted her lips. "You've overdressed."

He stripped off his clothes and stood three feet from the bed.

"Aren't you coming?" she asked.

He narrowed his gaze.

She watched the muscles in his thighs twitch. Whatever held him back, his jutting cock showed no reservations.

"One day I'm going to tie you up."

She wet her lips and leaned forward. "Yes."

"Slide my finger into your ass while you're riding my cock."

When did he get so dirty? When did my body decide I love it? She nodded, unable to form an appropriate response. Running Hoat Analytics gave her purpose, but Damon gave her relief. She struggled to find a balance between the extremes, but if he wanted to take the lead for the evening, she would go along for the ride.

"You need to ask for what you want."

"I will!" She breathed.

"Right now, I want you to suck my cock."

She chewed her bottom lip and tabled her fears. No matter how many vehicles Anna Claire blew up or how many times Vivian had to visit the police station, she would find the energy to answer Damon's demands. At the end of the day, cocooned in the bungalow, he reminded her life's pleasures gave her days meaning. "I'll suck you dry."

Stepping forward, he reached for her arm and pulled her against his chest. Dropping his head to her neck, he inhaled and used his teeth to graze the tender skin behind her ear. "Do you want it?"

The whispered question sent ripples of pleasure through her core. She pushed against his shoulders, creating space where she only wanted closeness. Cupping his balls, she smiled and slid to the bed's edge. He felt hot and heavy in her hands. She licked her lips and slid to the floor until she rested on her knees.

He cupped her shoulders.

The gentle pressure urged her to continue. She watched him as she teased and sucked his cock, feeling the pressure at the back of her mouth. He pulsed and grew beneath her touch, giving her a heady sense of power. *I didn't need the lace.* Smiling, she closed her eyes and hummed with him in her mouth.

"Vivi," he said.

Releasing him, she looked up.

"Deeper."

She raised her eyebrows, caught off guard by his request. "Deeper?"

Pulling her up, he positioned her on the bed's edge and stood before her.

He smelled like hot, salty sex, and she loved the challenge.

"Take it all," he said.

She swallowed and raised her eyebrows. Cupping his ass, she licked her lips and took him in her mouth, curving his penis into the depth of her throat.

He moaned and squeezed her shoulders.

Far from feeling out of control, she breathed through her nose and used her mouth and throat to set a pace that left him gasping for breath. His reaction sent a jolt through her system. Reveling in her ability to show off and take him, she squeezed his ass and urged him to finish.

"Vivian!"

Feeling his cock pulse, and his release fill her throat, she loosened her lips and smiled.

"Fuck," he said.

Grinning, she licked his taste from her lower lip.

Tracing the muscles on his chest and the thin line of hair below his belly button, she tilted her head and met his gaze. Upside down or not, she raised her eyebrows.

"Give me a minute."

Flopping back onto the bed, she looked at him and wondered how much recovery time he needed.

He squeezed a breast and thumbed a nipple. "I think you liked showing off."

"I think you liked my lips wrapped around your cock."

Laughing, he nodded.

She glanced at his member, confirming the growing evidence of their connection. *In bed.*

"Show me how you touch yourself," he said.

She smiled and knew exactly where the command would lead. "Aren't you ambitious?"

He rolled a nipple between his fingers. "We can do this the slow way or the fast way."

Tilting her head, she savored the pressure on her nipple. "Oh?"

"I can spend all night touching you."

Her pelvic muscles clenched in response. "Or?"

"Show me what you like. Show me how much you like to taste yourself."

She trailed a hand between her breasts, dipped two fingers into her folds, and rubbed her clit. The pressure and slide promised to satisfy her needs, but the look in his eyes egged her to prolong the experience. *I've done this a thousand times. Why does it feel so charged when he's watching me?* Moaning, she watched his pupils dilate. *He's watching every breath I take.* She closed her eyes, unable to bear the intensity of his gaze. "Don't you want to join me?"

"Do you want me?" he asked.

She raised a finger to her mouth, sucked her juices, and nodded.

"Say it, Vivi."

The pressure she built in her core demanded her attention, but she bit her lip. "Why?" Grinding out the response felt like punishment. *I don't want honesty. I want to feel him inside of me, and I want to ride him home. I should have kicked that dog off the couch.*

"Because I've dreamt of you saying it."

She stilled her hand and opened her eyes. "I want you to fuck me, Damon." Spreading her lips, she dared him to maintain eye contact.

His gaze held steady.

"I don't want to do this alone."

Reaching for her hand, he pulled her to his chest and held her tight around her waist.

His cock pressed into her thigh, and she shifted, eager to feel him replace her fingers. She raised her head and sucked his bottom lip. Releasing him, she shifted and straddled his leg, eager to rub her clit against something heated and warm. The skin-to-skin helped, but she needed more than friction. "You really thought about me."

Tearing open a condom, he shifted her hips and lowered her to the bed. "Every chance I had."

Her legs fell open, as greedy as her mouth to take him. "Was it enough?"

He braced his weight on the mattress, slid inside her, and gritted his teeth while he held the pose. "The thought of you would never be enough." Reaching between their bodies, his thumb found her clit and mimicked the pace she set.

She arched, abandoned her questions, and met him thrust for thrust. Feeling him move within her, the pressure he kept on her clit, and the steady resistance of his weight, she submitted to her suppressed release. Freed from an audience of one, pleasure washed through her body, and her cries reverberated against the bedroom walls.

Roaring, he followed her lead and moved off her body.

She turned her head, letting the cool night air refresh her skin. "Never enough," she whispered, feeling in awe of her body and what it could accomplish.

He raised his head from her shoulder. "What did you say?"

The microwave's lonely, clipped chirp called for attention. *I should have sprung for the silent model.* Crickets chirped in the trees. The owl called. Her heart rate wound down, and she sighed, trailing her hand along his side. "I said, dinner's ready."

He cocked his head.

She pushed his shoulder and rolled away. Standing on the hardwood floor, she admired his body sprawled across the bunched duvet. Her nerves hummed with the remnants of pleasure, but she scowled, searching for the triumph and accomplishment she experienced after sealing a deal. Turning, she pulled a robe from the armchair in the corner and bit her lip. Her limbs felt heavy, but Damon's jests and her bristling amusement would carry them through dinner and back to bed. *Then what?*

Chapter Eleven

Sober, morning light streamed through the white curtain panels. An unfamiliar alarm roused Vivian from her dreams. Shielding her eyes, she squinted. "Damon, is that your phone?"

Leaving one arm cradling her shoulders, he turned and fumbled toward the nightstand.

"It's on the floor." She followed his warmth and savored the pleasure of waking next to him. If she could start every day like this one, her productivity would lag, but her serotonin would soar. She yawned and nuzzled into his shoulder.

Picking up the phone, he silenced the alarm and dropped an arm over his eyes. "Pretend you didn't hear it."

She yawned and lifted her head. "You might as well get up."

"Work is overrated."

She smiled and scooted to the bed's edge. His muffled response sounded like a petulant teenager's protest, but his muscled body inspired delicious, adult thoughts. *Teenagers don't have glutes that look like conjoined bowling balls.* She second-guessed her practical response to the alarm. *Maybe I should stay.*

Reaching out a hand, he snagged her ankle. "Five more minutes."

Temptation beckoned, and she hesitated. "I have a

meeting."

"Five more minutes"—he yawned—"for me."

What about my responsibilities? The sex rocks my world, but he upended my life. Nobody makes a hangover remedy for a criminal summons. Taking a deep breath, she pulled free of his grasp and stood. "Aren't you supposed to be early for your first day of work?"

He rose and propped himself on one elbow. "You expect your employees to be early?"

"I do." She reached for her thin, cotton robe.

"What time do you get in?" he asked.

"Usually by eight."

He checked his phone. "It's five after eight. You're late for your double standard."

Missing the luxury of waking up in his arms, she put her hands on her hips. "Do you want a ride or not?"

Yawning, he stretched his jaw. "I can manage."

"Great." Despite the robe, she felt naked in the bright, morning light. She belted the fabric and walked toward the bedroom door. "I'll have more time to pow-wow with my lawyer."

"About what?"

Turning, she stared. "The summons?"

He flopped onto the sheets. "Don't worry about it, Vivi. You climbed a tree."

The push and pull between their lives could never reach equilibrium. Agreeing to help meant extra resources, not absolution. "I climbed a tree, and I ended up with a trespassing charge! I'm the face of Hoat Analytics. People depend on me."

"Unlike me." He stared out the window. "You think a felony conviction is a speed bump on my life's long, rocky road—"

She opened her mouth to reassure him.

"—but a misdemeanor is the end of your career."

She inhaled, caught in a snare of her design. She sat on the bed, but she hesitated to touch him. "I have to be proactive, Damon. Someone else can spin the facts and set a trap."

"They're not catching an opossum." He sat and swung his legs over the bed's side. Dropping his forehead to his palms, he sighed. "How bad can it get for you? No invitations to be the keynote speaker?"

She brushed her knuckles along his side. Beneath the tight muscles, she felt the strength of his ribs. *We're both people, aren't we?* "Have you heard of the wheel of pain? It's a media strategy. Dodge and repeat the facts until the story shifts to meet your narrative. I'm already fighting lawyers on IP concerns. A summons for trespassing won't inspire confidence in my leadership. Credibility matters."

He shifted and raised his eyebrows. "Only your credibility matters."

The motion dislodged her hand, and she cradled it in her lap.

"Spin the whole thing into a misunderstanding or a wild night gone awry," he said. "Pull the same shit you tried on the security guard. 'We're friends.' " An escaped down feather rested on his thigh. He picked up the feather and flicked it into the air. "La-te-da."

She stood and rubbed her eyes. "Indeed. My reputation matters."

"Then you shouldn't have gone over the wall."

I did it for you. The thought of saying the words aloud felt too raw. "You matter, too."

He stood. "You shouldn't have to choose between your reputation and my life."

"That's not what this is about!" Frustration raised the volume of her response. She clapped a hand over her mouth. "I'm sorry for yelling."

"Scream as much as you want, Vivian."

Hearing her full name felt like a rebuke. "Are you upset with me?"

He shrugged. "The *Prince and the Pauper* isn't life. I don't believe in fairy tales."

She stared and wondered when he found the time to read Mark Twain's critique of social inequality. *How much library time do they give a man in prison?* "You keep surprising me."

He shrugged. "Cable television."

The glib, unashamed response made her laugh. *I don't care which one of us is the prince or the pauper. I care about him.* She shook her head and ran a hand through her hair, wondering if she had time left to tame it. "Damon, it's not only about me versus you. I'm thinking about my employees and my company. If someone drags my name through the mud, they also harm my business." She thought of the Outcomes Foundation and her expansion ideas for Hoat Analytics. "I want to do something good with my life."

"So do I." Pulling his shirt over his head, he rolled his shoulders. "I get it."

"You do?"

"You're signing contracts, and I'm sending kids to school. I'm glad I don't have your constraints, Princess."

"I liked Vivi better."

He dropped a soft kiss on her lips. "I do, too."

Stepping into his pants, he slid his phone into his back pocket and walked from the room.

"That's it?" She raised her voice to carry down the hall.

"You're a busy woman."

She poked her head into the hallway. "And if someone asks you for a comment?"

He turned and made eye contact. "Vivi, how would they reach me? I'm nobody."

A woman couldn't dream of a nobody. He was a big-hearted, jocular man with a knack for making money—legally and illegally. Generosity ran in his veins, and he fired her passions. She could no sooner prove his worth to him than she could prove Anne Claire ripped off his investment, but she would keep trying. "That's not true!"

He patted his pocket. "Nobody on this side of town has my number, except you." He stared at her chest and shook his head. "You're a busy woman."

Her nipples hardened. Wishing she had time to explore the invitation in his gaze, she cleared her throat. "I'm meeting my lawyer at nine."

Saluting her, he turned and walked down the hall. "Great. Give me a call when you're done."

Precious barked.

"I hear you, mutt," he said.

The backdoor opened, and Precious's claws clicked and skittered across the floor. *I should make plans to meet up with Damon for dinner. We can rehash the day and solidify our story about retrieving the drone. Or we can spend the evening in bed.* She turned on the shower and padded down the hallway. "Damon?"

Precious barked from the backyard.

Frowning, she scanned the kitchen and the inactive coffeepot. "Damon?" She paused and listened. The oaks swayed. Precious scratched at the door. Letting her shoulders sag, she closed her eyes and leaned against the wall. *This is my house. Why do I feel so alone?*

****

Vivian's phone rang at four o'clock. Pausing in the hallway between two meetings, she swiped the screen and nestled the device against her shoulder without looking at it. "Hello, this is Vivian."

"You were right about being proactive," Damon said.

She smiled.

"Mama Clarke scanned the crime map. When she put two and two together, she ripped me a new one."

"She's a clever woman. The summons barely made the police log, and Atherton's finest used our initials for the write-up. Lieutenant Jayne must have pulled strings."

"Must be good to have friends in high places," he said.

She swallowed and wondered how often the connections she made in the business world enabled Hoat Analytics' success. Fast-tracked permit applications, client referrals, and media write-ups gave her momentum, but a criminal record would be hard to live down.

"Proactive worked at the restaurant, too." He cleared his throat. "I told my new boss about doing time. He thanked me for saving him the cost of a background report."

"And?" she asked.

"And we got on with it."

213

A sense of relief rushed through her system, and she relaxed her shoulders. "That's great!"

"The restaurant is a mess."

Biting her lip, she lowered her phone to check the time. *I want to hear about his day, but I can't miss the next meeting.* "Damon, let's get dinner"—she frowned, wondering if he wanted to go anywhere near another restaurant—"or grab takeout."

"What did your lawyer say?"

"He told me to stay out of trees, and he would take care of the rest."

Damon laughed. "I have a better idea than takeout. Meet me on the corner of Bryant and Hamilton."

"Why?" She pictured the street corner and tried to imagine Damon haunting roll-up doors and white-wall galleries. If the area housed a hidden gem restaurant, she would know about it.

"Hot Art Cool Nights starts at seven."

"Oh, perfect." The immersive art and community festival happened on the first Friday of each month. The leaders of Palo Alto's eclectic art district distributed a monthly map that led enthusiasts through a maze of galleries, artist collectives, street artists, culinary favorites, and staged musicians. Unlike the annual Festival of the Arts, participants skipped the city's tree-lined University Avenue and sought pockets of activity on windy side streets. "I haven't been in months."

"Why not?"

"No time." She saw Michael round the corner and waved.

He tapped his watch.

She focused on saying goodbye to Damon. "I have to go."

"Seven," he said.

Her email account might run out of storage, she had two client proposals to review, and she scheduled a check-in with Michael, but she would make time for everything. Spending time with Damon helped her balance the load. "I'll be there."

****

Standing on the sidewalk, Vivian shifted, conspicuous and isolated. Small groups moved around her. She toyed with her phone and watched a couple stroll down the sidewalk holding hands. The setting sun illuminated the narrow space between their bodies. Each step created a peeking prism of light, and she wondered what kind of history held them together. *I thought love happened in a flash. I didn't think you had to fight for it.*

A warm hand touched her arm.

Recognizing the ginger undertones of Damon's cologne, she turned to face him, but she caught sight of Shani near the curb.

The woman sat in the driver's seat of a pink sedan. She met Vivian's gaze, flipped the bird, and merged into traffic.

Vivian worked her jaw. Shani's bright-pink nail color amplified the rude gesture, but frustrated by her inability to respond, she cleared her throat and turned to Damon. "What was she doing here?"

He took her hand. "Jealous?"

She met his gaze. "Should I be jealous?"

"I don't know. Do you want a monopoly on giving me rides?"

That depends on what kinds of rides we're discussing. She imagined herself in his shoes and ignored Shani's rude goodbye. *Of course, he called his friend. I would have done the same thing.* She squeezed his hand. "I'm surprised you went home after work."

"I needed a shower."

"You could have showered at my place."

"Could I?" He cocked his head.

She thought about his question. *Do I want Damon to come in and out of my life at his leisure?* She imagined waking up next to him every morning. *I like him and trust him. I could put up with an extra toothbrush, but how much more?* "Yeah, you could."

Raising a hand, he kissed her knuckles. "That's good to know."

The warmth of his touch anchored her awareness, but the man had a habit of walking away. The wind piggybacked his gallant gesture and raised gooseflesh on her skin. Feeling more exposed than when she stood alone, she pulled free, rubbed her arms, and turned. "Are you hungry?"

"I ate at the restaurant."

She scanned a line of food trucks idling along Bryant Street. *Been there. Done that.* "Lucky man."

"What do you want to eat?" he asked.

"I feel like steak."

He swung an arm around her shoulders. "Maybe I could eat again."

"Good to know." She smiled, told herself to relax, and fell into step. Watching the people in the crowd, she thought some seemed more interesting than the art. The shivering people holding up their phones to follow First Friday maps looked like tourists. They stopped to check street names and consult dashed lines. *Locals know to bring sweaters for the evening chill.* A group of people peered in a gallery window and idled on the street corner to chat. Their layered clothing and casual obliviousness looked familiar. *Residents.*

For a city with seventy thousand residents, Palo Alto felt remarkably like the small town where she grew up. Families who traced their roots to the agricultural community maintained a tightknit circle. Investors and technology workers moved through public spaces, dropping cash and enthusiasm in their wake. She existed at the edge of the new wave. Hoat Analytics maintained a respectable client list, but the editors at *Time Magazine* had no interest in making her Person of the Year. *Do I even want that type of success?*

"You're quiet," Damon said.

"It was a long day." She yawned. "You must be tired after your day, too."

"Not really." He paused and looked at a large canvas hanging in the window of an art gallery.

The General displayed a proud rooster standing against a black background. Stippled and splatted with colorful paint, the animal held high its head. *So, that's what happens when Jackson Pollock meets farmhouse chic.* She read the description just below the work of art. *"Silence is golden until you have something to say."* Straightening, she looked at Damon. "I could spend days imagining what that animal has to say."

He grinned. "'Don't eat me' is probably at the top of his list."

She laughed at his practical response. "True."

"What were you thinking?" he asked.

She looked at the rooster and cocked her head. "How did I get into this mess?"

He laughed.

The sound surrounded her like a warm embrace. "Where are my troops?"

"Back at the henhouse."

She watched the shadows settle against the eastern hills. "Farmers cull male chicks soon after they've hatched. If the general wants troops, he'll have to rally them before the farmer turns them into chicken meal."

He shuddered. "That's rough."

Pulling him away from the gallery, she shrugged. "Eat or be eaten. That's life."

Raising his eyebrows, he sighed. "Is it?"

She exhaled and walked along the sidewalk, thinking of his ad-hoc scholarship program. Despite a limited education, his mind worked like a steel trap. Instead of quoting Shakespeare, he relied on the accumulation of practical knowledge. *If he spent his teens buried in textbooks, would he be a different person?* She thought of the time she spent watching old movies, reading classics, and surfing chat rooms for companionship. *If chance switched our upbringings, would I be laid back?* She thought of him supporting EPA's youth. "Is that why you funnel all your money into scholarships?"

"Close. I'm giving those kids a chance to make a difference."

She wondered if he would have stayed in northern California or left the university for a fancy job in another state. Giving his close relationship with his mother, she assumed he would have stayed. "What did you want to be when you grew up?"

He laughed. "Not a teacher."

She exhaled. "It was an idea."

"I don't know. Secure? Rich?" He shrugged. "Something to take the burden off Mama Clarke."

"Those aren't really jobs."

"I know, but what's the point of a job? It's a means to an end. If one of my neighborhood kids has a dream or a passion, I'll find a way to fund their education. I don't think traditional higher education is the only path to success."

"Like you."

He shoved his hands in his pockets. "Yeah. I'm feeling real successful right now."

She tugged free a hand and squeezed it. "I could see you as a banker or a loan officer."

He laughed. "The paperwork would kill me. Sometimes kids need three months of rent or a week's worth of professional clothes. I've cut checks for internship programs, science education, job shadowing, and apprenticeships. My goal is to help those kids obtain their first job and establish a career."

She thought of his mentoring. "But you've sent kids to college."

"If that's where they wanted to go." He cleared his throat. "I also helped Shani set up her salon."

She stopped walking and stared.

He made eye contact. "What? She runs a good shop and employs people."

Jealousy sat on her shoulder like a heavy weight she struggled to dislodge. *I'm not sure what to do with the man, but I want him.* Biting her lip, she inhaled and lived in the moment. *He's here with me, not her.*

Scanning the crowd, she looked for relatable couples. The movies she grew up watching failed her. None of the couples promenading along the twilight street matched the dapper, Caucasian ideals of old Hollywood. Age, gender, and ethnic background twisted through a funhouse maze of experience and wealth. Disoriented by the permutations, she blinked and zeroed in on the first couple she saw. No longer backlit by sunlight, they looked like ordinary, middle-class tech workers.

A third figure approached and embraced the older woman.

She squealed and returned the kiss.

Vivian turned her head to give the threesome privacy.

"And Shani hires other people from the neighborhood," Damon said.

She blinked. "What?"

"Shani's salon?"

Swallowing, she accepted nobody's life experiences overlapped. From an early age, she felt she walked a tightrope. Her family, congregation, and education expected her to replicate their styles. She conformed, but the straightjacket pulled too tight. Life on a pedestal left little room for individual freedoms. "Shani seems loyal. That kind of friendship says a lot about a man."

He wiggled his eyebrows. "Such as?"

She rolled her eyes. "Damon, not everything has to be about sex."

He cocked his head.

"I mean, don't get me wrong…"

Laughing, he pulled her close.

His teasing kiss coaxed her into parting her lips. No longer soft and searching, he wrapped his arms around her with the assurance of someone who knew what he expected to find. She tilted her head, eager to deepen the kiss and erase her misgivings about opening up her life.

A bagpipe wailed.

"What the hell?" He jerked back and scanned the street.

She spotted the sound's source. Boulder stood on the street corner. Instead of a three-piece suit, the kilt and the bright tartan sash of the Clan MacIntyre hovered above his pale knees. His cheeks, often ruddy from booze, swelled with the force required to inflate the bagpipes. Next to him, a drummer kept time on a side drum, and a tip jar swelled with donations for the Caledonian Society. "Somebody likes the way he sounds."

"Or they're hoping he'll collect his tribute and disappear."

Rubbing her ear, she smiled. "It's not that bad."

Boulder hit a high note and held it.

She winced.

"Kill me," Damon said.

"Let's turn the corner." She headed toward a gallery she loved. "I want to show you something."

He gripped her arm. "Wait." Releasing her, he marched across the street.

She watched him grab two young adults by the back of the neck. The first twenty-year-old sported a beard that looked like a moth-eaten sweater. *I hope he hasn't been growing it very long.* The second—she swallowed—was Ricky.

Damon dragged them away from the musicians and pushed them against a storefront's brick wall. His muscles bulged, but he held the men steady and used his gaze as much as his strength.

Strolling participants stopped to watch.

The men flailed for a minute, looked at each other, and went limp.

"Why'd you have to be here?" Ricky asked.

"I'm everywhere," Damon said. "If it wasn't me, it was your mama, your teacher, or the cops. In this town, anonymity isn't an option. Stop risking your future for a quick score." He jerked his head toward the piper. "What're you going to buy with a tip jar? You're worth more than that shit."

Tears ran down Ricky's cheeks.

She debated an intervention but wondered what she would say. *He doesn't need my help, and I don't think he's going to hurt those guys. Look what he did for Ricky.* She swallowed. Ricky's resume sat on the top of the stack. *Look what we're doing for that kid.* Glancing across the street, she confirmed neither Damon nor his quarry shed blood, and then she smiled at Boulder as if he had lyricized *Highland Cathedral*.

The older man made eye contact. Veins popped on his cheeks, but he continued to blow.

She raised her eyebrow. *How does it feel to earn pity tips?*

A man walked past on the sidewalk and bumped her shoulder.

Startled, she grabbed the purse at her side and stared at his back. "Hey!"

He looked over his shoulder and kept walking.

Dropping a hand, she wondered why his whiskered face looked familiar. She stepped into the road to stand guard near Damon. Before she could step onto the curb, she saw him release the pair and send them stumbling down the sidewalk. "What was that about?" She kept her voice low.

"Sticky fingers."

She eyed the cash peeking from the jar at Boulder's feet. "What did you say?"

"I told them to keep playin' and see what happens. A hard head makes a soft behind."

Turning, she tilted her head. "What?"

"Mama Clarke used to say that before she got the belt."

She struggled to close her mouth. "She beat you?"

"Maybe once." He ran his hand over his head and shrugged. "Kids in my neighborhood are used to tough love. Ricky knows I won't beat him on the street corner, but I'm sure as hell going to tell his father what I saw. He'll decide what to do. If he keeps playin', he's gonna see what happens, and it's not gonna be pretty."

His voice deepened, taking on the cadence and rhythm she heard at his party. "How do you do that?"

"What?" He scratched the base of his skull.

"Talk to me like we're at work and then talk to those kids like you're one of their crew?"

He laughed and pulled her away from the bagpiper. "It's called Code Switching, Vivi. Every Black person in America knows how to pick their words."

She looked at his profile and wondered if he chose his words with her. *I don't want him to change who he is to please me. I want laughing, energetic Damon.* Her confidence faltered, and she felt conspicuous again. *I don't want to change who I am, either.* "At your party, Shani said she's had enough colorism to last a lifetime."

"I'm surprised you remember anything."

She remembered feeling out of place and

gravitating toward his presence. No longer interested in the galleries, she wondered if she and Damon had become the art. From the other side of the street, a pair of senior citizens stared. "What happens if we stay together? I don't want your friends and family to resent me."

"Why would they resent you?" He wrinkled his forehead.

She stared at the sidewalk. "I don't want to take you away from your family." Looking up, she met his gaze. "And I don't know how comfortable I would be in your mama's home."

He caressed her cheek. "Your care matters."

His touch lingered long enough to make her crave the privacy of a room.

He dropped his hand.

She blinked and reached for him, but she came up short.

"You're going to have to trust me and my ability to make decisions," he said.

Like ScanCoin? "But"—she cleared her throat— "Shani and all that stuff about colorism and how I don't belong."

"I can handle Shani's opinions on life."

She wondered what other damage Shani's bright-pink nails could accomplish, and she exhaled.

"The question is, can I handle you?"

The tenor of his voice sent a thrill through her core. "Am I a challenge?"

"The best kind I know."

His whispered response heated her cheeks. "I feel like everyone is watching us."

He laughed and put a hand at the small of her back.

"Vivi, your friend with the pipes is about to have a heart attack. The only way we would be the center of attention is if you stripped naked and took advantage of me." His hand dropped to her ass. "Which I fully support."

"When we get home." Trusting his observation, she wiggled against his touch.

Glancing at her, he smiled.

"Food." She scanned the street. "I think I need food."

"Good, it's my turn to feed you."

She stalled, remembering Silvia's comment about her weight loss. "You don't need to feed me, Damon."

"I like you the way you are, Vivi, but food is a love language. Let me take care of you."

Concerns about her diminished curves slid to second place. *Who said anything about love?*

He squeezed her ass and dropped the hand. "I know a little Greek place you might like."

She knew which restaurant he had in mind and grinned. Before his arrest, he picked up shifts at the Greek restaurant on University Avenue. Johann liked to conduct his business on a secluded patio, but she had not been there in a long time. "Returning to an old haunt?"

"Who do you think gets better service?" he asked. "The people paying full price, or the people who know the back of the house?"

"You haven't worked there in years," she said.

"Georgios vouched for me this morning."

Unsurprised, she gave thanks for the restaurant owner's big heart.

Damon led her toward the restaurant.

The stained wood and plaster exterior looked warm and welcoming. Through the windows, she spied a healthy crowd filling the yellow dining room's round tables.

Reaching for the door, he froze.

She stumbled and grabbed his arm. "What's wrong?" She followed his gaze and realized his stumble made perfect sense.

Near the pizza oven, Anna Claire sat at a table for two.

Hanging copper pots and a roaring, wood-burning fireplace evoked decades of grease, but Georgios and his wife were meticulous. "I think I lost my appetite."

"It's now or never."

He shifted his weight, jumping in place like someone psyching themselves up before a sports game. Swallowing, she thought of her stocked refrigerator. "Have you heard of movie night?"

He raised an eyebrow.

"Fishnet stockings?"

"You can stay outside," he said.

She glanced at Anna Claire sipping white wine. Butting heads in the restroom was one thing, but protecting Damon trumped her impulses. "This place is too public for a confrontation."

"She's a thief." He leaned toward the table.

"Leave her crimes to the police. As soon as she figures out what you want, she'll leave the restaurant. She won't let you make a scene."

He rubbed his hand over his face and nodded. "She's never met me. I'll be clever."

"Clever?" She rolled her eyes. "Why didn't I think of that?"

Chapter Twelve

"Wait!" Vivian grabbed Damon's arm.

"What?" Turning, he stared.

Scanning the restaurant, she looked for an excuse to keep him from marching up to Anna Claire's table. *I like to watch movies; I don't like to be in them.* The rich aroma of savory meats and pungent charred herbs made her stomach rumble. "I'm really hungry." She leaned on his arm. "Maybe I'm about to faint."

"Maybe you should choose more practical shoes."

She blinked. *Does he know anything?*

He raised his eyebrows.

She sighed. His confidence appealed to her, but an enhanced security system and increased patrols did little to protect them from public violence. Meeting Anna Claire in person might be the smartest or the stupidest thing she had ever done, but she would do it for Damon.

The greeter opened the door and tilted her head. "Hi, do you have a reservation?" She looked at Damon. "We're really full tonight."

She considered stomping on the woman's foot, but she opened her mouth for a scathing rebuke.

"Ahh! Damon! You came!" Arms wide, Georgios walked from the restaurant, embraced Damon, and slapped his back.

The silver hair at his temples shone against black

hair and tanned skin.

"It's so good to see you, my friend."

The two men exchanged a series of shoulder claps and braced expressions of pleasure. *I'm never going to understand men.* Risking a glance at the greeter, she smiled.

The woman swallowed. "I'm sure we have a wonderful table for you and your guest."

She struggled not to laugh. "It's okay"—she glanced at the woman's nametag—"Maria. We all make mistakes." She wondered what happened to Cynthia and the succession of undergraduates Georgios and his wife took under their wings. *Does he welcome them home like he welcomed Damon?*

"Come sit on the patio where we can have privacy." Georgios leaned over and kissed her cheek. "It's good to see you, too, Vivian."

"How's your wife?" she asked.

"As fat as ever!"

She laughed, knowing the man plied his wife with *loukoumades.* He deep-fried the balls of dough, bathed them in honeyed syrup, and added a flower. Once, he told her ancient Olympians ate the dessert, but she doubted the Greek diet fads included extra-glazed donuts. *Times change, but food is still the language of love.*

"And my wife," he had said, "she's worth more than any gold medal."

She smiled at the older man. Surprisingly pleased to visit the restaurant, she almost forgot about Anna Claire, but the woman sat near the ovens like a cream-cloaked serpent.

Maria carried two menus toward an unmarked

door.

Georgios signaled a server wearing a crisp, white jacket uniform. "Bring us *mydia*." He turned back to the table. "You like mussels, don't you?"

She swallowed her revulsion. "I'm developing a taste for seafood."

"Oh, you will love it!" He pinched his fingers toward the sky. "We steam fresh mussels in herbed red wine. How can you go wrong?"

Her gag reflex begged to differ, but the restaurant's food always pleased her palate. *Why should tonight be any different?* Looking over her shoulder, she saw half the dinner crowd watching their progress. Meeting Anna Claire's gaze, she smiled like the president of the local volunteer squad. "Sounds delicious."

The woman cocked her head.

Placing a hand on the small of Damon's back, she smiled.

"Are you sure?" he asked. "You've never been a big fan of seafood."

His observation warmed her heart, but her protective radar hovered near the red zone. "I'm willing to try new things."

Georgios clapped his hands.

"Can we eat in the main dining room?" she asked.

"Are you sure?" The owner paused. "You always loved the patio."

Damon raised his eyebrows.

She glanced toward Anna Claire's table and hoped he received the message.

He shrugged. "Whatever the lady wants."

Sitting at the small table in the room's middle, she waited for the server to place a napkin in her lap, scooted her chair toward the white tablecloth, and beamed at Damon. "After the mussels…"

He nodded. "Steak."

"You're so clever."

"I try." He winked.

Georgios consulted with Maria, waved at them, and returned to making the rounds among his guests.

Sipping her water, she rubbed condensation from the glass between her fingers. "Your English teacher said you were a straight-A student."

He laughed. "And you believed her?"

She rolled her eyes. "This was your idea. Work with me."

He glanced over his shoulder toward Anna Claire's table.

"Don't be obvious." She sipped her water. "She'll bolt."

"Obvious would be a friendly shakedown."

Choking, she glared.

"Can you see them?" He fidgeted with the silverware.

She set down the glass and picked up a paper menu, thankful the Greek Restaurant used large cardstock. *Good taste never goes out of style.* For quick service restaurants, scanning a QRC code felt appropriate, but Georgios drilled his staff on service. She examined Anna Claire over the menu. Her loose, glossy black curls and flawless, light-brown skin glowed in the flickering firelight. Seated, strangers would not recognize her height or her penchant for heels. *Why doesn't she look panicked? We could have been friends.* She considered the man seated at the table.

Dressed in a gray crewneck sweater, he let Anna Claire do most of the talking.

"I think I recognize her guest."

"Who is he?" Damon asked.

"A venture capitalist named Sanjeev Padney. He's a fast follower."

He shifted in his seat. "What does that mean?"

She picked up a napkin and dabbed at the edges of her mouth. "It means he doesn't like to take risks or stick out his neck."

He let his knife clatter on the table. "It's still going to get chopped."

She cringed. "Not if we can help it."

"If Anna Claire's skipping town, she's not leaving until she has every last dime." Damon rolled his shoulders. "I'll tell her I'm thinking about giving my story to the press."

"Where's your proof?" Recalling the sight of Ricky slammed against the brick wall, she looked at the diners and shook her head. "I don't think a direct confrontation will work."

Anne Claire put her napkin on the table and stood holding a wine glass. She walked across the room.

Few diners looked up, but she watched the woman glide. *I assume she hasn't been staying at a local motel.* "Clever better happen fast," she said. "Anna Claire's coming this way."

He straightened in the chair. "What?"

"Stay cool." Smiling, she met Anna Claire's gaze and gave Damon time to settle. "Here to sell more bits and bobs?"

Anna Claire swirled her wine. "I heard you paid me a visit. Shouldn't you be in jail?"

"A mistake, to be sure." She chose her words with caution, making sure she erred on the side of honesty. "There were a million places I would rather be than in your unpruned bush."

Damon choked back a laugh.

She cleared her throat. *That did sound a little dirty.* Meeting Anna Claire's gaze, she blinked.

"My security detail told me of the incident. I instructed him to press charges, but here you are. Perhaps they lost the paperwork."

She winked at Damon. "I have friends in high places."

He widened his gaze.

"Such as?" Anna Claire sipped her wine and angled her body.

Her stance gave her a better view of Damon, and Vivian hoped he was ready.

He turned his chair, stood, and offered a hand. "I'm Mathew Peterffy. And you are?"

Anna Claire tapped her chin. "Peterffy. Where have I heard that name?"

Vivian accepted a glass of wine from the server and smiled her thanks.

"Perhaps you've seen my name in the papers." Damon dropped the hand.

"Perhaps." The businesswoman smiled. "I'm Anna Claire."

Damon frowned. "Is Claire your family name? Wait, are you from the South? I've heard double names are common down there." He tilted his head. "If you ask me, two names are a bit excessive. Nobody calls me Mathew Louis."

Vivian glanced at the floor to hide her smile. *I*

wonder if Louis is his actual middle name.

"I'm from California." Anna Claire cleared her throat. "From the Mammoth Lakes area."

He covered a yawn. "When I'm stateside, I prefer Aspen."

Code switching is the least of my worries. He's getting in too deep. She considered intervening, but she trusted him to extract himself from his clever pretenses. *Wait, maybe he has been to Aspen.*

"Georgios seems very fond of you." Anna Claire glanced at the server hovering near the wall. "How do you know my friend, Vivian?"

Damon looked over. "You two are friends?"

She swallowed. "Acquaintances. It's a small town."

"Well! La-te-dah! Pull up a chair, Anna." He turned his chair and gestured for her to sit. "Join us."

"It's Anna Claire, and I have a dinner guest."

He shrugged. "I don't mind. Bring your date with you."

"Sanjeev Padney is not my date. He's an investor."

"Oh, what do you sell?" Damon asked.

Vivian snorted. "Worthless tokens."

Anna Claire looked up and narrowed her gaze.

Sipping her wine, she winked. "I pay attention."

The woman tossed her head and sent her hair falling over her shoulder. "Vivian doesn't believe in the future of cryptocurrency, but people like Sanjeev believe. They're open-minded and poised to prosper."

"Imagine that." She bit her lip.

"Since the last financial pandemic in India, the world's best-known cryptocurrency outperformed gold and generated remarkable returns."

"I already own that currency." Damon scratched a spot on the tablecloth. "I mined it myself."

Anna Claire squared her shoulders. "Sanjeev told me his Hindu family members consider *Dhanteras* and *Diwali* the most auspicious occasions to buy gold." She lowered her voice and stepped closer to Damon. "Last festival season, Sanjeev didn't shop for gold. He shopped for cryptocurrencies."

Vivian sighed. "You're not selling the world's best-known cryptocurrency."

Narrowing her gaze, Anna Claire wet her lips and set down her wine. "She's right. I'm selling something better." She held up her phone. "Mathew Louis Peterffy, let me tell you how ScanCoin is faster, better, and smarter than the currency that gets all the press."

He tapped his fingers on the edge of the chair. "I don't do phones. After the pandemic"—he shuddered—"the thought of all those germs gives me the creeps. I've gone back to a sterile laptop."

The businesswoman lowered her phone and stared. "Really?"

He rubbed his fingers together. "Microchip implant for access and payments. It's more common in Sweden."

Anna Claire tilted her head and picked up her wine. "We should do lunch."

He winked at Vivian. "I'm already taken."

She raised her glass. Losing a million dollars to ScanCoin could not have erased the smile from her face.

The server arrived bearing a steaming plate of mussels. He hovered at the edge of the table.

"If you want lunch, Anna Claire, I want to see the

full lifecycle. Show me the happy customers who've invested, profited, and pocketed their windfall." Damon raised his eyebrows. "Until then, if you'll excuse us."

Anna Claire exhaled. "Mathew, I like the way you think. I'd be happy to have my assistant set up a business lunch. Something casual." She glanced over her shoulder. "Customer experience counts."

Sanjeev motioned to his watch.

"Something discreet."

Damon relayed his email to Anna Claire. "I'll give you an hour."

Vivian stared at the steaming seafood. *He should have given her his mamma's number. She would make one hell of a personal assistant.* Imagining Shani answering the phone at the salon, she smiled. *At least Mama Clarke would deliver the message.* Hearing Anna Claire's heels on the tile floor, she looked up and met Damon's gaze. "You are clever."

He leaned forward in his chair. "I'm sweating like an all-star player."

Picking up her fork, she tapped the shell of a mussel.

He shook his head. "Don't eat that."

Her innate suspicion of seafood kicked in, and she froze, her fork suspended in midair. "Why not?"

"You don't like seafood."

She set down her fork and exhaled. "I'm polite."

Reaching for a hand, he held it on top of the white tablecloth. "You don't have to be polite."

"Really?"

He leaned across the table. "Is Anna Claire watching us?"

She glanced over his shoulder. "Yes."

Raising her hand to his lips, he kissed her fingers and winked. "I'll eat all the mussels."

"Is that a joke?" Her stomach rumbled. "I don't get it."

His laughter drew the attention of the surrounding diners.

Georgios walked up and slapped his back. "Good?"

Dropping her hand, he gave the man a warm smile. "I'm loving it, but Vivi really wants a piece of meat."

"Lamb?" Georgios angled toward her.

Unwilling to spoil the unexpected charm of the evening, she looked at Damon and gauged her feelings. She appreciated his advocacy, but hunger clawed at her stomach. *Drinking one glass of white wine and pulling the wool over Anna Claire's eyes won't make up for the possibility of offending Georgios.*

Damon raised his eyebrows.

I play hardball at Hoat Analytics. Why can't I play hardball at home? Thinking of all the times she ordered salads and cold vegetable noodles, she exhaled and looked at the restaurant owner. "Cow. Beef. Honestly, I could eat an entire steer."

The man grabbed his belly and laughed. "I will bring you *brizoles*, fried potatoes, salad, and *sadziki*. Tonight, you eat like an Athenian on a holiday weekend."

"And tomorrow?" she asked.

"You do what is good for you." He winked.

She swallowed, trying to live in the moment. The combination of Damon's smile, tender steak, and candlelit wine might turn into a treasured memory. His quest to reclaim his money might succeed, but his enthusiasm for sharing her bed might fade. *Happy endings only last until the credits roll.* She smiled at Georgios. "That would be delightful."

The man rested his hand on Damon's shoulder. "And you, my man? It's on the house."

Damon eyed the mussels. "Surprise me, Georgios. You've never steered me wrong."

Georgios called over the server. "Bring my friend *ourounopoulo.*"

"What is it?" Damon asked her.

The Greek walked toward a commotion in the corner of the restaurant.

Damon angled his head. "Do you know?"

She smiled. "Roast suckling pig."

He coughed and slapped his chest.

"Think of it as ribs." Raising her wine glass, she saluted him. "Or take your own advice, Damon. Ask for what you want."

"I don't want to eat a damn baby pig." He pushed back his chair and headed toward the kitchen.

Watching him go, she sighed and looked at the plate of cooling seafood. Dipping her finger in the red wine sauce, she raised her finger to her lips. Herbs and garlic mingled with wine. A savory, unexpected flavor she attributed to the mussels lingered on her tongue. She considered trying a morsel, but afraid of disappointment, she resisted.

Damon's laughter rang from the kitchen.

Looking toward the bustle of smoke and steam, she smiled at the camaraderie of men. *He always makes friends, doesn't he? That trait says something about him, but I'm sitting alone at a table.* She looked at Anna Claire.

The woman raised her glass.

What does that say about me?
****

Streetlights illuminated the roadway. Stopping at a red light, Vivian turned and looked at Damon. "Why won't you come back to my place?"

He smiled. "Because Mama Clarke misses me."

The streetlight softened the edges of his jaw. Combined with the wine's effects, he looked as sleepy and content as she wanted to feel. Instead of matching him glass for glass, she had abstained, kept her gaze on Anna Claire's table, and savored the pleasure of his company. Beneath the table, his leg pressed against her skin, felt like a warm anchor. Patrons' gazes lingered on his sprawled power, and she had smiled, content to let them admire the scene. "You're walking a tightrope."

He nodded. "I've done it my entire life."

"The effort must exhaust you."

Closing his eyes, he smiled. "You're worth it."

"It's not all about me." Words tumbled from her mouth. "You're trying to get Anna Claire to return your investment. You're sending kids to school, Robin Hood."

"I missed my chance," he said.

"That's not true!"

"Isn't it?"

The light changed, and she resisted her urge to put the vehicle in Park. Easing away from the intersection, she gripped the steering wheel. Sex pulled them together, but uncertainty and practicality threatened to pull them apart. "As soon as you reclaim your investment, formalize your scholarship program and solicit donors."

"I know, Vivi. You said the same thing before I went to jail."

"Then why haven't you done it?" Frustration sharpened her retort. "I mean, why aren't you sharing what you're doing with the rest of the world? People are good, and they want to help."

"For a tax write-off," he said.

"Most people…"

He stroked her thigh. "I don't want rules and board members, Vivi. I want to help the kids in my neighborhood and trust my instincts." He squeezed her hand. "In the past, they never let me down."

"Anna Claire thinks you're a hot shot."

He laughed. "At least someone does."

She slowed for a stop sign and glanced over. "What does that mean?"

"Anna Claire is fishing." He shifted in the seat. "She'll believe what she wants to believe."

"So do you."

He shook his head. "I'm not selling a con."

"No, but you used fake credentials to grab her attention. High net-worth individuals speak a language of private and public companies, real estate"—she sighed—"options and leverage."

"I told you, I can do finance."

A driver honked their horn.

Hitting the gas pedal, she sighed. "Name-dropping Aspen won't be enough to fool that woman. Anna Claire will listen for buzzwords. Can you talk smack about art, airplanes, and cars?"

"Can you?"

She eased off the accelerator. Caught between two worlds, she wondered if she should apply her advice to herself. Coaching Damon made her feel like an imposter and a shade. "I lived in the country." She gripped the wheel. "Now, I focus on data."

"Well, here's a data point: Anna Claire has eight hundred thousand dollars of my dollars."

"What's going to make her give it back?"

He hummed. "The risk of losing eight million. Eighty million. Whatever she took from her investors."

Drumming her fingers on the steering wheel, she slowed for his mother's house. "We tried honesty and surprise." The car came to a stop, and she shifted in the seat. "What's next?"

He made eye contact.

His features hardened and obscured his easy affection. "Three strikes and you're out, Damon. Do you want to swing and miss on a lie?"

Putting his hand on the passenger door, he gripped the handle. "I know I'm not rich, Vivi."

"You don't have to be rich."

He raised his eyebrows. "I can't force Anna Claire to surrender my investment."

She exhaled and watched him engage the door handle. The rush of traffic noises and cool night air flooded the car cabin. Rubbing her arms, she considered getting out.

Hands braced on the doorframe, he leaned into the car and cocked his head. "Only one trap can catch Anna Claire."

"What's that?"

"The same one that caught me." Straightening, he turned and walked toward the front door. "Goodnight, Vivi."

Watching him walk away tore at her heart. She

wanted to bolster his confidence and help him succeed. Instead of spending time baiting Anna Claire, she wanted to try cooking a recipe with him and take Precious for a long walk in her neighborhood.

A car backfired in the distance.

Shaking off surprise, she grabbed her purse, locked the car, and raced after him. "Damon, wait!"

He turned and cocked his head. His hand lingered on the front doorknob. "Did I forget something?"

Clearing her throat, she smiled. "Me?"

He straightened his head. "What?"

She rubbed her arms. "Aren't you going to invite me in?"

He raised his eyebrows. "To do what?"

Exhaling, she spied the blue glow of a television. "Watch a movie."

"With Mama Clarke?" he asked.

She missed the quiet simplicity of sitting with her family and watching movies. Her mind never stayed quiet, but the comfortable peace between thoughts felt a lot like meditation. "Sure."

"Oh, this will be rich." He opened the door and held it wide, sweeping his hand toward a television's blue glow. "After you."

Breezing past him, she smiled. "Aren't you gallant?"

"Hardly."

She swallowed and preceded him into the dark living room.

Mama Clarke sat in a recliner. The blue light from the television reflected off her sleek, gray hair. Instead of gold jewelry, she wore a faded, floral housedress.

"That you, Damon?" she asked.

He walked across the room and leaned down to kiss the woman's cheek. "Hey, Mama."

"How was work? You were gone too long."

"I had dinner with Vivi. She came over to watch a movie."

The woman jerked up her head, and she narrowed her gaze.

Stranded in front of the door, Vivian lifted a hand and waved, too afraid to unpin her elbow from her waist. *She's a woman, and this is a house.* She swallowed. *Damon's house.* Squaring her shoulders, she walked toward the recliner and paused three feet away from the woman's protective glare. "Mind if I join you?"

Mama Clarke turned back to the television. "Suit yourself."

Damon dropped onto the oversized microfiber couch and draped his arm over the back. "What're you watching?"

"*The Main Event*," Mama Clarke said. "That subscription service done it again."

Vivian cocked her head and stared at the screen. A kid in a mask took down a male wrestler who had muscles so defined he could have starred in a superhero film. She sat on the couch.

The sweaty male hit the mat.

She flinched and eased back.

Mama Clarke cheered. "That's it, boy! Black don't crack!"

Why don't I have a slogan? Charmed by Mama Clark's appreciation, she settled into the crook of Damon's arm. "This is nice."

He dropped his head close to her ear. "You want

242

popcorn?"

The whispered question tickled her skin. Guessing he did it on purpose, she slapped his thigh.

Mama Clarke kept her gaze on the screen. "No necking on the couch."

Damon laughed and rolled his head. "Yes, ma'am."

The deference in his voice impressed her. Focusing on the screen, she saw a middle-aged woman with purple lipstick whistle at the good-looking male wrestlers. Fanning herself, the character told her grandson which wrestler she would pick for herself. Then she touted her profile on social media. Vivian shook her head, wondering if her grandmother had ever seen a wrestling match. *It's no different from watching James Bond in short shorts.*

"You tell them, Sister." Mama Clarke leaned forward. "Me, I'd take the one with the mohawk."

Resting her head on Damon's shoulder, she smiled. "Your mom's kind of funny."

"She's actually my grandma," Damon said.

Vivian straightened and stared. "What?" Aware of her volume, she clapped a hand over her mouth.

"Shh!" Mama Clarke said.

"How did I not know that?" Her whispered question sounded harsh, but perfectly reasonable. "I mean, you never mentioned it."

He shrugged. "Genetics don't matter. She always treated me like her son."

A million thoughts raced through her head. *I can't ask him about his mom and dad. I can't turn this revelation into a big deal in Mama Clarke's home.* She bit her lip and sank against the back of the couch, wishing she consumed more wine. *What else am I*

243

going to find out? Damon's a Kung Fu Ninja? She stared at him, unable to watch the movie. Mama Clarke looked nothing liked her apron-clad grandmother, but the therapy made more sense. "What other secrets are you keeping?"

"I like sweet potato pie."

She rolled her eyes and watched the movie. At times corny and predictable, the sequences filled the living room with sound and overpowered her ability to analyze the data. *I'm living in the moment*—she yawned—*even if I'd rather be living out my fantasies in bed.*

"You can go," Damon said.

Shaking her head, she stayed planted on the couch.

Mama Clarke snored.

She turned to him, resting her elbow on the back of the couch and supporting her head. "Twenty years ago, did you watch *Like Mike* and dream of making it big in the NBA? NASA? Don't tell me you never played make-believe with Shani and the other neighborhood kids."

"I told you I didn't spend a lot of time on sports." He cleared his throat. "Shani reminds me too much of my mother."

His soft-spoken confession startled her. She shifted and stroked the back of his neck. "Is that why you like me? I'm the polar opposite of your mother?"

Shaking his head, he tucked a strand of hair behind her ear. "When I'm with you, I don't think of my mother. I think about being a good person, working hard, and running circles around my peers."

Smiling in the semi-darkness, she felt her cheeks warm.

"I also think of peeling off your prim dresses and kissing you until you scream my name."

"Damon…" Mama Clarke told them to keep their hands to themselves, but words could be a more powerful aphrodisiac. She shifted, aware of her arousal. The absolute inappropriateness of the conversation heightened her response. "We could go back to my house."

He shook his head.

The music changed, and she turned, glancing at the rolling credits.

Mama Clarke shifted.

Unfolding her legs, she stood. "I should go."

"I'll walk you out." He rose and offered a hand.

She glanced at Mama Clarke and met her stare. Swallowing, she smiled and looked at Damon. "We should talk about all this."

"All what?" he asked. "It's my past."

"The past matters!"

He put his hand on the small of her back and pushed her into motion. "I'm more interested in the future."

Outside, moths buzzed around a yellow porch light casting shadows on the concrete steps. "I feel like I should have known." She rubbed her arms. "Is it a sad story?"

Pulling her close, he rested his chin on her head. "It's not a sad story. I'm here, aren't I?"

"But…"

He silenced her protest with a kiss.

His rhythm buried her questions and erased the locale. For a moment, she forgot the uncertainties sucking the joy from her recent days. Business intelligence and big data analytics had nothing on the sweet taste of Damon's lips, or the hungry pressure of his hands holding her close. She broke the kiss, turned her head, and sneezed. "Sorry."

He laughed.

"I believe you can do it," she said.

"Not on the front porch. What would Mama Clarke say?"

She slapped his chest. "I mean, Anna Claire. I think you can play her like she played everyone else."

He rubbed together his hands. "I'll get the confession. Lieutenant Jayne or Atherton's finest will take the next steps."

"What if you never get back your money?" she asked.

"What if I do?" He raised his eyebrows.

"Either way." She brushed a speck of lint from his chest. "It doesn't change how I feel about you."

He captured her hand. "And how's that?"

Swallowing, she struggled to articulate her feelings. *I like him so much it scares me. I don't know if naming my feelings changes the dynamics between us. Does a definition matter to him?* "Spending time with you is the highlight of my week."

He sighed and dropped her hand. "You love a good puzzle, don't you?" Stepping back, he ran his hand over his head. "I'll see you at the baby shower, Vivi."

"Goodnight, Damon."

He opened the front door and leaned against the jamb. "Goodnight, Vivi."

Standing in the yellow porch light, she bit her lip and weighed her choices. *He's not a puzzle. He's kind, generous, and loving.* She raised a hand, prepared to draw him close. *But what am I?* Unable to answer the question, she lowered the hand and nodded.

"Goodnight, Vivi."

She smiled. "Goodnight, Damon." Walking to her car, she unlocked it and slid into the driver's seat. The cold leather sent a shiver up her legs. *I need more time to figure out how I feel.*

Starting the car, she punched the accelerator and ripped down the Bayshore Freeway. *I shouldn't have to define my feelings to enjoy spending my days with a man.* Warning lights flashed on the console. *What happened to living in the moment?*

A state trooper passed in the opposite direction.

Easing off the pedal, she took the off-ramp toward downtown Palo Alto. Behind midlevel office buildings, her illuminated bungalow waited in a tree-lined neighborhood. Precious snoozed on the couch and emails filled her inbox. She stopped for a red light and rested her arms against the steering wheel. *How can I have so much and feel like it's not enough?*

Chapter Thirteen

That weekend, Vivian smiled at the otherworldly twilight she created in her backyard for Hadley and Johann. Huge, white balloons hovered below the oak trees like a cluster of moons. Dark-green ivy wrapped their cotton strings like ladders to the stars. Candles glowed on polished, wood trestle tables, mingling with the landscape lighting to imbue the backyard with a romantic, fairy mood. In front of each metal bistro chair, a folded white napkin held a copy of the menu and a delicate pink peony bloom. *Well, if I didn't create the decorations myself, at least I paid for them.* She fixed a strap on her elaborate gold sandal. *And the food.*

"The backyard looks beautiful." Silvia stood at Vivian's side with her hands on her hips.

Absently rubbing her arm, she looked at the romantic setting and second-guessed her choices. "Maybe I should have gone with pastels."

Silvia shushed her. "Soft pastels are traditional, but Johann will appreciate the neutral decor."

Biting her lip, she made eye contact with Silvia and thought of the endless lunches and phone calls she fielded in Johann's hillside compound. "You're right. His house is a study in muted hues."

The woman laughed and plucked a glass of sparkling water imbued with lemon and rosemary from a passing server. "Hadley added touches of color and brightened the palette." She crossed her arms. "You should visit."

"Maybe." She looked at Hadley standing beneath a glowing white balloon. A pink-and-white floral, maxi dress cupped her breasts and draped her stomach. The mommy-to-be scratched her stomach and smiled at Buffy, her former graduate assistant. Sipping her water, Vivian felt thankful for Silvia's anchoring presence. "She looks happy."

"I'm glad you invited the men."

Raising her eyebrows, she turned away from Hadley's and Buffy's intimate laughter. "Are you?"

"Johann gives Hadley everything she asks for, but he spends too much time in his home office."

"Running you ragged?"

Silvia rolled her eyes. "He's nervous about the birth. A moment of celebration might calm his nerves."

She looked at the other side of the backyard where Johann and his father stood side by side. Rudolf's gray hair distinguished him, but both men wore dark suits, and their confident stances guaranteed they booked private jets to attend business meetings. *Once upon a time, I thought I wanted that arrogance.*

The back door opened, and Damon's laughter rang from the house. He followed a member of the catering crew down the back steps and slapped the man's back.

Stumbling, the man held onto the silver tray in his hands.

"Try not to get in the way," she yelled over the soft chatter of mingling guests. "It's not your party."

He grabbed a skewer from the server and strolled across the grass.

His easy swagger and the dark, stormy blue of his

button-down shirt projected easy confidence. Defined muscles rippled beneath his skin. The subdued strength made her smile. *Sometimes the biggest prize is a hidden gem.*

"Your crew spends too much time arranging skewers and not enough time circulating them," Damon said.

She frowned. "Hadley might be hungry."

He pulled a small, marinated mozzarella ball from the skewer and popped it into her mouth.

Eyes wide, she chewed the soft delicacy.

"I took care of it," he said.

Silvia toasted him. "Smart man."

"I couldn't do anything about the two grandmas bickering over the cake."

Vivian laughed. Hadley's mother and Johann's mother had met at the Kona-Kohala Coast wedding when they had unknowingly both worn ivory dresses. Thwarted, the women took one look at each other, exchanged pleasantries, and retreated to their sides of the flower-strewn aisle. Vivian remained sitting in the last row. She accepted Johann's invite to the wedding, but she felt self-conscious sitting on his verdant lawn. *Doesn't everyone here know we were once intimate?*

Grinning, she sipped her water and wondered what the attendees thought about her lawn—she smiled at Damon—and her date. *Actually, I don't care.* Placing a hand on the small of his back, she leaned close. "I'm glad you came."

He winked. "Last-minute additions make the best party guests."

"After everyone leaves, will you stay?"

Lifting her chin, he lowered his head but stopped.

"Self-conscious?" she asked.

He tilted his head toward her ear. "Afraid I won't stop."

The baby shower could have gone up in flames. She grinned and claimed the kiss he denied her. His lips tasted sweet with the juice of roasted bell peppers. Pulling back, she licked her lips. "Stay after the party. It'll do you good."

He raised his eyebrows.

"Boxes of lingerie," she said.

His smile faltered. "What an offer."

Frowning, she struggled to reconcile his easy affection with the intensity she felt. She told him spending time with him was the highlight of her week, but she sensed he wanted more. *I'm not sure I have anything more to give.*

"Did you receive my email?" a woman asked from inside the kitchen.

"I did. Why would I read a German book on childrearing? I raised two American children!"

She recognized the voices of the future grandmothers and rubbed her ear, praying they confined their arguments to the cake. "Charming ladies."

Damon laughed.

"Since you haven't read the book"—Johann's mother stressed the last word—"I suppose it would be otiose to inquire what you thought of our methods."

Rolling her eyes at the archaic phase, Vivian grabbed Damon's hand and headed toward the garden gate.

Car doors slammed and well-dressed couples walked through the portal. A server handed each guest glasses of infused water or cold champagne. She greeted every person, while Damon stood beside her. A few introduced themselves to him, but she struggled to articulate his presence.

One after another, the guests headed toward Johann or peeled off toward Hadley.

"Nice crowd," Damon said.

Watching Buffy head toward the house, she felt like bolstering Hadley's numbers. She traced the waistband of Damon's jeans through his midnight-blue shirt and dropped the hand. "Give me a minute?"

"Sure." He pulled out his phone.

Walking away from his warmth, she headed toward Hadley. "How are you feeling?"

Hadley rubbed her stomach. "The girls are kicking."

"Did you consider keeping the gender a surprise?"

Laughing, Hadley shook her head. "Vivian, I'm a scientist. The minute the doctor drew blood, I wanted to know everything about these girls!"

She smiled. "I get that impulse."

Hadley scanned the yard. "Where's your dog? I expected her to claim a spot under the table."

"Too much excitement for an old dog." She imagined the servers bringing out the main course. Precious's rear end would quiver with excitement, only to be denied. "I kenneled her for the night."

"Your house looks amazing," she said. "Thank you so much for hosting the shower."

Smiling, she focused on the fresh, spring grass. "No problem."

"Are we finally friends?"

Looking up, she met the woman's gaze. "Silvia told us we would be formidable allies."

Hadley offered a hand. "Allies."

Taking the woman's hand, she shook it. "Allies don't throw parties."

Hadley raised her eyebrows. "They don't?"

She smiled. "Friends do."

Laughing, Hadley bit her lip. She widened her gaze and grasped her stomach.

"What's wrong?" She rushed toward the woman, ready to catch her. "Contractions? Do you need help?"

Hadley blushed. "Sometimes, when I laugh too hard, I pee."

Clapping a hand over her mouth, she grinned and wondered what quirks of life Hadley discovered outside the lab. "Your secret's safe with me."

"I'm so ready to meet these girls."

She eyed the swell of her friend's stomach. "How far along are you?"

"Thirty-four weeks."

"Six more weeks to go."

Hadley shook her head. "Most twins come early."

Her pulse spiked, and she scanned the growing crowd, wondering if any of the guests made their fortunes delivering babies. "Not this early!"

Gripping her arm, Hadley squeezed. "Don't worry, Vivian. It'll be okay."

She nodded. *I once told her to toughen up or release Johann. Now, who's the weak one?*

More couples streamed past the servers. The newest partygoers looked more eclectic and academic than Johann's cohorts. Judging by their flowered skirts and chinos, she pegged them as Hadley's friends and colleagues.

Waving, Hadley walked toward a couple wearing

white linen. She turned and looked over her shoulder. "Vivian?"

"Yes?"

The woman grinned. "We need to talk about you and Damon."

"We do?" She crossed her arms. *Maybe friends are overrated.*

"You told me you preferred to work alone."

She swallowed. "I did. The responsibility stops at my door."

"But you have employees."

Her employees ran her company, but Damon occupied her thoughts and warmed her bed. "Damon's not an employee."

Hadley wiggled her eyebrows. "And I heard he hasn't stopped at your door."

She laughed. "Wouldn't that be a show for the neighbors?"

After a light dinner, laughter and champagne chased away the nighttime chill. She sat at the end of the polished wood table, a hand nestled in Damon's grasp. Holding court at the opposite end of the table, Hadley and Johann unwrapped the beautifully wrapped packages Silvia handed them.

The couple "ohh'd" and "ahh'd" over each outfit.

"He could buy the entire baby store," Damon said.

She swirled a glass of champagne and made a noncommittal sound. "The thought counts more than the adorable outfits."

Hadley's mom stood and clinked a fork against her stemware.

Wincing, Vivian maintained a smile.

"I am so excited to become a grandmother. I might

not have been there every minute Hadley needed me, but I plan to spoil these baby girls." She sipped her champagne. "I wish Jecca was alive to see her nieces. You all would have loved my Jecca."

Vivian glanced at Hadley and saw her wipe away a tear. *She loved her sister, but I don't think that's a tear of joy.* Releasing Damon's hand, she rose and cleared her throat. "What a lovely thought, Ms. Heron." She signaled the servers. "Who's ready for cake?"

A server rushed inside the bungalow.

Mentally scrambling to fill the silence, she considered the adventures she and Hadley shared. *I don't think gunmen and feuding brothers make for good speeches.* "Some of you probably think the Outcomes Foundation refers to makeup."

A woman in a black sheath dress laughed.

Her partner frowned and leaned close.

"The Outcomes Foundation grew out of Hadley"— she pointed toward Buffy—"and her research assistant's investigation into the pain-relieving properties of cannabidiol. Based on data from preliminary studies, the derivatives Hadley and Buffy extracted from CBD are more than a cannabis craze."

Several of the guests put down their phones and looked up.

She winked at Hadley. "Unfortunately for you, Hadley's both a romantic and a shrewd negotiator. She has the intellectual property locked up tighter than Fort Knox."

A man in a five-piece suit picked up his phone.

"But you can support Hadley's research from the goodness of your heart." She set down her glass. "If that incentive isn't enough, consider the ailments of old age. You might need the hippie medicine she's brewing in her lab." She scanned the crowd.

Several guests laughed, but multiple stared.

"When the babies turn one, skip the college savings account," she said. "Johann can afford their tuition."

Guests raised their glasses.

She took a deep breath. "Consider donating to the Outcomes Foundation. Acknowledge Hadley's contributions to pain management and teach the girls to be proud."

The server who rushed inside the bungalow returned with a tray of cake slices. The white, Chantilly icing and red, glazed berries drew admiring glances from the crowd. He set a piece of cake in front of Hadley.

Hadley met her glance across the table. *Thank you*, she mouthed.

Raising her glass, she smiled. "You're welcome." As the guests added their support, she sat and exhaled.

Damon squeezed her thigh. "Impressive speech."

Shrugging, she reached for her water. "Public relations training."

He smiled. "It sounded like it came from the heart."

Feeling her cheeks warm, she placed a hand over his and scanned the guests seated around the polished tables. The men and woman chatted and leaned back in their chairs, their smiles and conversation assuring her of a job well done. She looked at the mismatch of cultures and envied the little girls who would grow up with two loving parents. "I'm glad everything worked out."

"You're a good friend." He lifted a fork of cake to

his mouth. "Remind me to put my birthday on your calendar."

"September twenty-seventh," she said. "I called you."

He set down the fork and kissed her bare shoulder. "You gave me hope."

His lips left the slightest hint of moisture, and she shivered, blaming her reaction on the soft, spring wind. *Or maybe it's his presence. What kind of community would Damon and I make for a couple of kids?* She imagined the awkwardness of her technology-focused employees organizing a baby shower or the steely stare of Mama Clarke presiding over her living room. *We could make it work.* She sipped her champagne and filed that imagery for another day. "Thanks for sorting out the kitchen."

Popping a raspberry in his mouth, he winked. "I thought about shooting the whipped cream in your fridge."

"You didn't!"

He laughed and settled an arm around her shoulders. "Nobody sent me to charm school to learn manners. You'll have to take me as I am."

She relaxed into the warmth. The evening was going well, but they sat among friends. Did Johann and Hadley seem surprised by their closeness, or had everyone accepted their casual intimacy? The shadowed garden obscured her ability to gauge the partygoers, and most of the crowd's attention went to the expecting parents. Age and experience should keep her apart from Damon, but he fit at her side like a missing puzzle piece. As long as he kept his hands off the whipped cream, she could mellow and avoid angering friends like Shani. "Some manners are innate."

He laughed and pressed a kiss to her shoulder.

She sighed.

"Hadley, dear, don't eat too much cake," Hadley's mother said. "You don't want to get too big."

Vivian straightened in her chair.

Heads turned, and conversation stalled.

Hadley's father bit his lip.

The man's wavy brown hair sported streaks of gray, but his tan skin suggested he led a healthy and robust lifestyle. *Is he going to intervene with his wife?*

Hadley put down her fork and leaned against Johann's shoulder.

He turned from his conversation and raised his eyebrows.

"I'm too tired to deal." Hadley jerked her head toward her mother. "Can you help?"

How many times have they had that conversation? Vivian suppressed a smile. Mothers could drive people crazy, but she assumed they did the best they could. Thinking of her mother and grandmother, she watched Hadley's mother fidget beneath the lit balloons. Her puffed cheeks made her look like a confused child. She considered offering Hadley a comforting word to cover her mother's *faux pas*, but she feared stirring deep waters.

"Ms. Heron, why don't we bring the gifts to the car?" Johann asked. "If they don't all fit, we can put the rest in your car."

Ms. Heron settled her napkin on the table. "If you get too big, you won't fit behind the wheel of your car." She held up her hands. "I'm just saying!"

Hearing crickets chirp, Vivian took a deep breath

and prepared to intervene.

Buffy knocked over a glass of water and gasped.

The focus of the table shifted.

"Oops! My bad." Buffy dabbed at the water and pushed some into Ms. Heron's lap. "I'm so sorry!"

Shrieking, the older woman rose and brushed at her skirt.

Buffy's freckled cheeks reddened, and her hazel eyes widened.

Vivian wondered if Buffy honed her skills on a stage. She bit her tongue and settled back to watch the show.

"I'm so clumsy." Buffy handed the woman a napkin and twirled her long ponytail. "It's getting late, Ms. Heron. I'll help Johann load the gifts. You have a long drive back to Marin."

Grinning, Vivian appreciated the subtle eviction. *Maybe I should poach Buffy.*

Hadley's mother frowned and elbowed her husband. "Are you going to sit there?"

He stood and put his arm around his wife's shoulders. "Buffy's right. We should let the kids enjoy themselves."

She flicked water from her fingertips. "But I'm the grandma!"

Johann's mother raised a delicately arched eyebrow.

Hadley's parents left.

The servers bought out steaming cups of coffee. Scooping up dirty dishes, they ferried the plates and stemware back to the kitchen.

Silvia rose from her spot at the table and headed into the house.

Hadley reached out a hand. "You don't have to do that." She swallowed. "Please, sit and enjoy the party."

Rolling her eyes, Silvia patted her hand. "They'll never do it right."

She shook her head. "No wonder you and Damon get along."

He laughed.

After a few minutes, Buffy rose and headed toward the house.

She frowned. *The party is dissolving before my eyes.* "And where are *you* going?"

"To get more champagne."

"Oh." She settled back into the warmth of Damon's side. Glancing at him, she saw him texting beneath the table and wondered if the party's ease was all in her head. "Who's that?"

"Anna Claire."

She straightened and gripped his thigh. "You told her you don't do phones, and you have a microchip implant."

He snorted and kept his gaze on the phone screen. "We're using a messaging app. She doesn't know the difference."

But I do. Sighing, she rubbed the condensation from her water glass. "I don't like the dishonesty."

He looked up and made eye contact. "Vivi, she stole my cash. Dishonesty is the tip of the iceberg."

"So now it's your cash?" She rose and placed her napkin on the table. "I thought it was for the kids."

"It is!"

Walking away from the dinner party, she sighed and retreated to the swarm of workers occupying her kitchen. Silvia and Buffy stood in the corner near the table, sipping glasses of champagne and chattering in Spanish like magpies. *Does Mexico even have magpies? How much do I really know about Silvia?*

Since moving into the executive assistant position, Silvia seemed happier with the world around her. Instead of flipping through her favorite magazines and watching Spanish language channels, she volunteered at Catholic Charities and fostered connections in the Latinx community. A few weeks ago, Vivian had remarked on the change during lunch.

Silvia raised a piece of salmon to her mouth and paused. "I was hiding, but I don't want to hide anymore."

"Hiding from what?" she asked.

Silvia averted her gaze. "History."

"Everyone has history."

Putting down her fork, Silvia raised her eyebrows. "I've seen you shoot a gun."

"Farm girl." She shrugged. "I can also drive a stick shift."

"Who taught you those things?" Silvia asked.

"My grandfather."

"Well, my grandfather didn't have time for lessons. He worked in the field until the day he died." She shook her head. "And he didn't die an old man."

She wanted Silvia to reveal more, but she had felt better knowing Silvia found happiness in Palo Alto, even if it came to her late in life. Stepping inside the kitchen, she slipped off her sandals. "You two look cozy. Buffy, I didn't know you spoke Spanish."

"When you grow up in a Novato apartment complex, you either learn Spanish or you have no friends. I like to practice, and Silvia likes to gossip."

Silvia tipped her glass. "*Salud*."

Buffy gestured toward the back door. "Need anyone else bounced?"

Her frustration with Damon's texts and Hadley's parents waned. "You did a great job, thanks."

Picking at her cuticles, Buffy averted her gaze. "I, uh, poked around your house."

"Of course you did."

"What's with the shoe system?" Buffy asked.

She straightened her shoulders. Most people stayed in the living room like polite guests, and the ones who ventured into her room knew her well enough to appreciate her quirks. "I like shoes."

"But why are they in numbered cubbies? It's, like, a waste of space. Dump them on the floor."

"Aren't you a scientist?" she asked.

Buffy stared over the rim of her glass. "I work for a foundation."

"That's noble."

She sighed. "It's life. Maybe I'm too scared to risk everything like Hadley. Your shoes make me think you're scared, too. Trash your closet every once in a while. Cleaning house can be cathartic."

Thinking about the amount of money she invested in her shoes, she considered the suggestion, but she could find other ways to take risks. "Different priorities."

Shrugging, Buffy placed her glass by the sink and hip checked the dish washer.

The washer rinsed the glass and dropped it in a large, gray plastic rack.

"Maybe you're afraid of chaos. Maybe you're afraid to be vulnerable." At the backdoor threshold,

Buffy turned. "Hadley told me you were a little uptight."

"That's rude." She frowned and wondered how far she would have come without her defensive sensibilities. "I'm sure she made the comment in confidence. Don't betray her trust."

"What's the difference between rude and honest? I appreciated the warning." The woman tightened her ponytail and let the door slam behind her.

Instead of spitting out a line about manners and civility, she considered Buffy's observation. Her shoes, her closet, and her life provided the predictability and the armor she needed to face an uncertain world. What her defenses did to her remained unknown. Maybe her polish had veered so far off course that she held herself to an impossible standard. She turned to Silvia for affirmation. "Am I that uptight?"

Silvia shrugged. "Who cares? You both work."

"You would." Sighing, she picked up her sandals and walked from the kitchen. The shelves lining her closet held rows of court shoes, espadrilles, wedges, and flats. *This room's like a trophy case, but where is the rest of the team?* She placed her gold sandals in spot forty-eight. Eying a pair of beaded flats on the top shelf, she stood on one foot, reached for the flats, and missed. A wooden stepstool waited in the corner. *I don't need all this stuff in my house.* Gauging the strength of the shelves, she placed her foot on the lowest shelf.

"When you pull the whole thing down on yourself, I'm going to laugh," Damon said.

Ignoring his warning, she reached for the flats a second time but came up short.

He walked up beside her and lifted down the shoes.

Placing her foot on the ground, she clutched the flats to her chest. "Thanks."

"You could have asked for help," he said.

"I didn't know you were there."

"Where else would I be?" He turned toward the door.

"I'm glad you're there," she said.

He paused and looked over his shoulder. "Are you?"

The hesitation in his voice hit home. She spent the last twenty-four hours worrying about menu choices and decorating schemes, but nobody lingered for the last sip of wine. *I can't hold onto him because I'm lonely.* Balancing on one foot, she slid her foot into a flat. "You should be with someone who values you."

Congratulating herself on a level tone, she switched feet and kept her gaze averted. Tender from the sprains, she hopped, struggling to bear the weight. "You need someone who applauds what you're doing for those kids and knows when to tell you to pull back. You're fighting so hard to improve the next generation that you're forgetting about yourself."

"I know who I am," he said.

Looking up, she met his gaze. "Do you? Flirting and texting with Anna Claire to lure her into an admission? Neither one of you deserves that guilt. You'll hate yourself for doing it, and she'll hate herself for falling for you."

"Falling for me?" He crossed his arms.

"Your ruse!"

Shaking his head, he left the room.

Hating the abandonment, she marched down the hallway and snagged his shirt.

He froze.

The shift in momentum upset her equilibrium, and she slammed into his back. Instead of letting go, she tightened her grip. "I'm sorry I yelled. Anna Claire's a grown woman. I know you're working for the kids."

Inhaling, he turned and tipped up her chin. "After changing a kid's life, they look at you in a different way. I don't care if the kid is eight or eighteen. They know someone cares."

She settled a hand over his heart and felt the rhythmic pulse within his chest. "I'm proud of Hoat Analytics, but I worry I lost a decade of my life. I don't want the same thing to happen to you."

"I remember every day I spent in jail. It haunts me."

The quiet confirmation comforted her. Pulling him close, she rose on her toes and brushed his lips. He tasted like their herb-drenched meal, but the taste felt light, like a reminder of shared happiness.

He stepped into her and wrapped his hands around her waist.

The hard warmth of his skin anchored her senses. She forgot about the servers scrubbing the kitchen and the business titans trading jabs in the backyard. She forgot about the years of toil and the sleepless nights she spent building Hoat Analytics. She even forgot about the what-might-have-beens. In that moment, the handsome man in her hallway kissed her back, and nothing else mattered.

Then he stopped.

Blinking, she searched for an explanation.

He smoothed his thumb across her lip and sighed. "You can't end arguments with sex and lingerie. I have standards."

She tilted her head. Beyond the bungalow's confines, they worked to define their relationship, but in the bedroom, their attraction took charge. "What about sex toys?"

He growled.

Splaying her fingers across his chest, she met his gaze. "I was jealous."

He covered her hand and stilled it. "I know, but you don't have…"

She shook her head, cutting off his statement before he could counter the argument. *I'll admit my flaws, but I won't be the only person doing it.* Rolling her lips, she tasted the lingering sweetness of champagne. *If he stays over, we can spend all night doing it.*

"Is this how you treat your employees?" he asked. "A moment of suspicion and they're locked out?"

She planted her hands on her hips. "I'm not locking you out. I'm tabling the life coaching."

"For sex." He threw up his arms. "Now, who's the distraction?"

Swallowing her medicine left a bitter aftertaste. "That's not what I meant, and my employees don't second-guess my decisions. They trust my instincts."

He narrowed his gaze. "What does that mean?"

"The people who work for me can read a trend line." Crossing her arms in the intimate hallway, she thought of the crowd lingering on the flood-lit lawn and dropped her voice to a whisper. "Let go of the money."

"Vivi, you haven't lived my life." He shook his head. "You never could."

His sad, bittersweet smile almost broke her heart.

"Whatever drama you had growing up"—he sighed—"worked out fine for you."

"I worked hard for what I have," she said. "I earned scholarships."

He covered a yawn. "I bet you also aced your standardized tests and submitted a pile of glowing recommendations. What's a kid supposed to do with a subsidized lunch and a sharpened pencil?"

"Work hard? I didn't realize you were a socialist."

Laughing, he shook his head. "The kids I sponsor, they don't know that term. They know insecurity, frustration, and envy." Turning, he slammed a hand against the wall. "Who the fuck cares if I text Anna Claire? She took the money that belongs to those kids."

The vibrations traveled through the old bungalow, and she winced. "Damon, I'm sorry."

He exhaled and hung his head.

"I want to help you."

"As long as helping me doesn't inconvenience you." Raising his head, he made eye contact. "What happens when the fun wears off?"

Unable to answer his question, she stared. Success made her a millionaire, but she remembered her roots. If he thought she was shallow, she should consider whether Hoat Analytics was an achievement or a glorified currency mill. The soft taps of heels shattered the tension in the dark hallway. Turning, she saw Silvia standing in the pool of light spilling from the kitchen. The light shadowed her features, but her eyes looked bright and alert.

"You've been gone too long," Silvia said. "Your guests are leaving."

She looked at Damon.

He straightened and exhaled. "Go."

I need more time to unravel my emotions, but I can't do it when I'm standing beside him. She turned toward the kitchen, hating the way her dress fabric brushed against his pants. Head high, she walked through the busy kitchen and stepped onto the back steps.

From the grass, Hadley looked up. "Oh! I wondered where you went."

"Bad choice of shoes." She pointed her toe.

Laughing, Hadley climbed the steps, squeezed her forearm, and smiled. "Thank you for a lovely evening."

She nodded. "I'm sorry about your mom's comments. You're beautiful, and you'll make a wonderful mother."

Hadley's smile faltered. "Thanks. I needed to hear someone beside Johann say those things." She shook her head. "The hormones make me extra emotional."

Grasping Hadley's shoulder, she dropped her chin and raised her eyebrows. "But you didn't cry."

Hadley grinned. "I know! Dry cheeks all around. Win-win!"

Looking over her shoulder, she saw Damon walk out the front door. *Can relationships be win-win?* Hearing the door close, she listened to the house creak beneath the towering oaks. Without Precious, hours of wakeful contemplation promised to lengthen the night. *Maybe exhaustion and a martini will push me into oblivion.* She plastered a smile on her face and turned back to Hadley. "Let me help you carry your gifts to the car."

Chapter Fourteen

The Monday after the baby shower, Damon called Vivian. "Guess who wants to see me."

Disappointment stole her breath. She stood outside a client's building and let the mid-afternoon sun warm her back. Even though she wanted to talk to him and assess where she stood, a conference room full of people waited for her presentation. "Anna Claire."

"I'm going to invite her to lunch."

"What?" A warning noise rose in the back of her throat. She swallowed the unladylike sound and breathed. *What's stopping him from swapping his affections from me to her? Are women so fungible? She can give him more than a good fuck and stray dog fur.* Remembering the disappointment in his hallway gaze, she tabled the thought of sexual favors and swallowed. "I mean, that's what you wanted."

Valentina tapped her watch.

She focused on the call. "How will Lieutenant Jayne hear her confession?"

"Is he a priest?"

She shifted her weight and rubbed her insole against her shin. "The woman's committing fraud."

"Exactly." He chuckled. "Digital eavesdropping is illegal in California, but when people dine out at a restaurant, they can't expect privacy. Eavesdropping got me into this mess, and eavesdropping will get me out of it."

"I thought it was stolen cell phones." She scraped her shoe over a discarded wrapper. When it moved without revealing a mess, she dipped, picked up the waste, and tossed it in the nearest trash can.

He cleared his throat. "Will you focus on the future?"

"I'm trying." She cleared her throat. "I want to be there."

"You can't come. She knows you're against ScanCoin."

"Maybe you value my opinion. Maybe we're exclusive." The possibility elicited a smile, but she recognized the wistfulness of her suggestions.

"My reclusive wallflower of a wife."

His voice softened with the wishful comment, and she snorted. Nobody in town would believe she was a wallflower. *I already overstepped friends with benefits.* She ran a hand through her hair and waved at an acquaintance. Success made her wealthy, but it also made her well-known. "You're right. I can't be there."

"I'll find a way," he said.

She hesitated. "Will you?"

Holding the door to the client's building, Valentina tapped her watch.

"I'll call you later." Ending the call, she dropped the phone in her purse and strode toward the building. "What?"

"That wasn't a client, was it?" Valentina asked.

Shaking her head, she wished fishnet stockings and liquid eyeliner were the biggest problems in her life. *Why didn't life cast me as a dumb blonde?* She breezed past Valentina and hoped her guests retained their patience and interest in her analytics. "It wasn't a client."

"Interesting," she said.

She looked over her shoulder. "What?"

"The last time I heard you lose your cool, someone parked on a tree root."

Remembering the incident, she widened her gaze. "Jumping curbs is a terrible, selfish practice. Those trees will outlive all of us!"

"I get that." She caught up and made eye contact. "But do you?"

"I do." Life came in waves, and managing the tide led to success. Brushing pollen from her sleeve, she squared her shoulders. "After we nail this presentation, we're taking the team out to dinner to celebrate the contract. You all deserve the reward."

"How big is the contract?" she asked.

She smiled. "Big enough to pay for you and Michael to splurge on a fancy dinner and call it a business expense."

Valentina pumped her fist.

Vivian strode past and entered the building, determined to represent the work her employees did on behalf of Hoat Analytics. The team might be nimble, but they were detail-oriented, and they made waves.

Two hours later, they won the contract.

After the lengthy dinner, Damon showed up at her house with a brunette wig. "Can you be inconspicuous?"

Taking the thing from his hands, she stepped back and hoped he came inside. Between her buzz, his acquiescence, and his lips, she could tout midnight affairs as her new favorite way to unwind. The other C-suite tech geeks would have to find their own handsome men. "I own tennis shoes and jeans."

He sat on the arm of the couch. "Shani said you'll give yourself away."

Stroking the fine, smooth hairs, she smiled and looked up. "Anna Claire won't know I'm there."

He raised his eyebrows.

"Stay awhile?" she asked.

Shaking his head, he stood and kissed her cheek. "I have to brush up on my Johann impression."

She rolled her eyes. "I prefer you."

He made eye contact. "Good."

Rising, Precious ambled to her side and sniffed the wig. The dog sneezed.

Looking down, she laughed. "Don't worry. The wig's not for you." By the time she looked up, Damon was gone, and her lonely bed beckoned.

The next morning, she stood in the bustling, stainless steel kitchen of the West Coast Fish House. Anxious to do a good job, and self-conscious of jeopardizing Damon's plans, she repeated Samuel's instructions like a student cramming for a test.

The waiter scrunched his nose.

She tried not to flinch. The kitchen offered minimal opportunities for social distancing, but the acne-speckled server looked like he might sneeze. Reaching up, she shifted the brunette wig. Crashing Damon's welcome-home party was not supposed to upend her life, but here she was, playing server, while he luxuriated on the patio. *I wanted to be on standby in case he needs help, but what will I do? Rip off my wig and accuse Anna Claire of fraud? Damon doesn't need me to make that accusation.*

"Taking orders isn't hard," Samuel said. "Repeat the order in your head until you get back to the kitchen."

She stared at the menu resting on the stainless-steel preparation counter. "Shouldn't the restaurant specialize in fewer dishes? That strategy has to be more cost effective."

He snorted and turned toward the swinging doors. "Tell that to the next gluten-free vegan who wants 'everything to taste so good.'"

She followed him onto the floor. "Why would they come here?"

He shrugged and handed her an apron. "Beats me. They want to eat with their friends?"

She glanced at the patio where Damon sat at a two-top table. His black sunglasses and gray shirt looked crisp in the bright, afternoon light. Nearby patrons lingered over late lunches, but he lounged in his chair, idly rubbing together his thumb and pointer finger. *He could have been an actor.* Closing her eyes, she thought about his expression when he came, eyes closed and straining for release. *I can't go back to being friends with that man.*

"Will she show?" Samuel asked.

She blinked and focused. "What?"

"Anna Claire? The chick who you're trying to catch?" Samuel picked his fingernail. "What'd she do, anyway? I thought she was rich."

"So did I." She checked her phone. Damon's quarry was already ten minutes late. "I don't know if she'll show."

Directly behind the empty chair at Damon's table, Lieutenant Jayne shared a table with a sallow, bleach-blonde colleague. Fine lines spanned the woman's forehead, but she kept her gaze trained on Damon as if she trusted neither him nor the circumstances that brought them together. *At least it's a sunny day.* "Lieutenant Jayne and Captain Wilson won't wait much longer, will they?"

"Your order's up," Samuel said.

"Huh?" She stared.

He dropped his chin and pointed to the pass-through between the kitchen and the bar area. "Table nineteen's fish tacos. On your way to the table, pick up a few extra napkins. Those chicks look like they're worried about their appearances."

"Can we stop saying chicks?"

"Broads."

She rolled her eyes. "You're a hoot."

He winked. "I get off at eight."

Looking at Damon, she shook her head. "No, thanks. The tacos."

"If you stall much longer, the plates will get cold," Samuel said.

She exhaled. "You know, I earned a full ride through school."

He handed her a stack of napkins. "No coffee shop lattes?"

She swallowed. "I didn't make them."

Laughing, he slapped her back.

The force of the gesture sent her stumbling. She grabbed the edge of the bar, glad the tacos waited safely on the counter. "Easy, dude."

"Your tips are going to be shit," he said. "Hurry up!"

Rolling her eyes, she picked up the plates and

balanced one in each hand. Despite her tennis shoes, her hands shook, and the plates wobbled. *Thank goodness, the owner didn't assign me a four-top.* Advancing on the teenage girls who ordered the tacos, she lowered a plate on each side of the table.

The couple held hands and stared into each other's eyes. Neither looked up.

She chewed the inside of her cheek. The first girl sported a diamond tragus piercing that looked suspiciously real. Her companion's dark shades eclipsed half her face. "Can I get you two anything else?" She waited. "A glass of water? A margarita?"

The girl with the earring perked up.

They're definitely underage. "I'll need to see your ID." She waited for a response, heard nothing, and walked away. *My tip from that couple was already going to be shit.* Leaning her hip against the bar, she covertly examined the pair. Despite cooling tacos, they continued to hold hands and gaze at each other like star-crossed lovers. She sighed. *Make out or eat your food, already.*

"You working or taking a vacation?" Samuel asked.

She tilted her head.

He brushed a lock of hair out of his eyes. "What?"

"Working," she said.

"Well, a new customer walked in."

Straightening, she scanned the patio and saw Anna Claire stride toward Damon. The woman's sleek cream pantsuit made Vivian's apron and jeans motif look like thrift store rejects. She brushed crumbs from her jeans. *I wish we had met under different circumstances.* She pursed her lips. *Also, it would be nice if she wasn't a crook.*

Damon stood and gestured for Anna Claire to take the open chair.

At least he didn't kiss her cheek.

The woman shrugged out of her jacket and revealed a leopard print camisole. Clanging, gold bracelets lined her arms. She draped the jacket over the chair's back and slid into the offered chair, tucking her feet and matching leopard print heels beneath her seat.

Good call. The waitstaff here is terrible, but silk spots, and cleavage won't be enough to distract Damon. Trust me, I've tried. Tightening her apron strings, she picked up a pitcher of water from the bussing station and walked toward Lieutenant Jayne and Captain Wilson.

The blonde officer looked up. "That her?"

She nodded and filled the woman's water glass. Based on the positioning of the tables and the direction of the wind, she could hear Damon and Anna Claire exchange pleasantries. *Their conversation might be audible, but it's not admissible to court.*

"I was surprised at your choice of venue," Anna Claire said.

Damon laughed. "Don't tell me you ate like a queen in Mammoth Lakes?"

Anna Claire moved her chair closer to the table. The heavy metal rubbed on the concrete. "No, but I appreciate the finer things in life."

Vivian rolled her eyes. *I bet you do.* She met Captain Wilson's gaze.

The woman offered a brief smile.

Taking empathy where she found it, she turned and walked back to the bar.

"All good?" Samuel asked.

She shrugged.

He handed her a stack of promotional flyers and a permanent marker.

"What's this?"

"We're sending postcards to the local neighbors. Damon said inked signatures look better than a printed ones."

She swallowed. "How many flyers are in this stack?"

He smiled. "Three hundred."

I can do three hundred. She uncapped the marker and readied a hand. "What name should I sign?"

"Chef Caesar. If you run out, I have another two thousand postcards behind the bar."

Slapping her chest, she coughed and looked at the server. Data analytics left her with atrocious handwriting. Any scribble with capital "C"s would work. "Right."

"Or you can have one of my tables."

She considered the teenagers and their untouched tacos. *At least crab cakes taste good when they're cold.* Turning back to Samuel, she smiled and pulled the first postcard from the stack. "I'm good."

After thirty postcards, she paused. Damon said he planned to press Anne Claire on ScanCoin, but she heard the woman's laughter clear across the patio. It clattered against her nerves like the sound of too many bracelets. Putting down the marker, she watched Anna Claire uncurl her legs and slide them closer to Damon. *They're not touching, and I'm not jealous.* She swallowed. *Why do they have to look so good together?* Reaching behind the bar, she snagged a lemon wedge and placed it on a plate. Thankful she only had one table, she ferried the lemon to Lieutenant Jayne's table and offered the wedge like a plated gift.

"ScanCoin isn't a scam," Anna Claire said.

"Why am I the last one to hear about it?" Damon asked. "Even Vivi knew about the tokens before I did."

"Vivi? You mean Vivian Hoat? How serious are you two?"

Grinning, Vivian kept her face averted from their table.

"She's fun from time to time," he said. "Nothing more."

The plate slipped from her hands and clattered onto the table.

Captain Wilson stilled it.

She met the officer's gaze. "I'm so sorry!"

The woman cleared her throat and jerked her head toward the bar area. "Not a problem."

Ignoring the cue, she lingered and dabbed at a water spot on the tablecloth.

"The exchange works, but I need more than your financial expertise," Anna Claire said. "I'm in over my head."

"How so?" Damon asked.

"Heavy investors"—she cleared her throat, clutching a hand around her water glass—"won't let me end this phase of the investment."

"What investors?"

"Men from the Baltics. Men who like to make threats. If I open the exchange, and there's a run on the currency, they have too much to lose."

"So, it's a pyramid scheme," he said.

She maintained eye contact and slowly sipped her

water. "It's not a pyramid scheme."

He crossed his arms. "Speculation and gossip drive up the value, and early investors take the windfall. Who's running the company, you or the Baltic investors?"

Anne Claire straightened. "I am."

"Then you don't need my help. I don't bounce people or hire hit men. I make money. Open the exchange and let the market determine ScanCoin's valuation. Once the dust settles, I'll judge whether I want to invest." He rubbed his fingers together. "Or not."

She leaned on her elbows. "Some things are more valuable than money. Some things can't be bought."

"Like what?" He looked past Anna Claire's shoulder and made eye contact.

For a moment, Vivian froze, transfixed by the warmth of his expression.

Captain Wilson kicked her ankle.

"Ouch!" She shook off the rebuke and wondered if Damon and the officers believed Anna Claire's claims. *I wouldn't put it past the woman to hire an actor to threaten her life.* She looked around the patio, but the only people she saw were horny teenagers and sated diners. *Men are so easy. The lieutenant's concerns about private security are a symptom of systemic patronization. Did I call the police every time I heard something go bump in the night? No, I installed lights.*

Busying herself with rolled silverware on a side, she remembered the night Damon slept over and sighed. *I've never slept that well in my entire life.*

"I made mistakes with my first company," Anna Claire said. "I'm not ashamed to admit it, but I won't end up broke. I never intended ScanCoin to get this big, but I'm not about to lose it."

Rolled silverware fell from Vivian's hand and landed with a thud. She looked over her shoulder to see if anyone marked her ineptitude.

"Few mistakes are permanent," Damon said. "Make it right."

"How?" Anna Claire asked.

"Open the exchange. Let people reclaim the money they invested."

Anna Claire leaned back in her chair. "You've already invested, haven't you?"

He raised an eyebrow.

Can he keep his cool? She hurried to the bar for another piece of lemon. Pivoting, she feared the lemon would slide off the plate and cupped her hand around the plate while she ferried the second slice to the officers' table. She kept her gaze trained on Damon's table and hoped she kept her footing, as well.

Damon and Anna Claire stared at each other.

"I'll give you back your money," Anna Claire said.

Vivian tried not to clap.

Damon steepled his fingers. "That's not enough," he said. "This feels like a shakedown. Open the exchange, or I'll take my suspicions to the police."

Anna Claire shook the ice in her empty water glass. "I have everything to lose."

He leaned forward. "Make the right choice."

Anna Claire frowned. "Why?"

The restaurant noise swallowed his soft-spoken response.

Vivian edged toward their table to hear the conversation.

"Server!" Wannabe Juliet turned in her chair and beckoned her to the table. "Can you come here a moment?"

Adjusting her wig, she exhaled and headed for the teenage couple. "Can I get you two a check?"

The girl with the diamond stud nodded.

"Separate or together?" she asked.

Removing her sunglasses, the second girl looked up. "Actually, you can get us the manager. You're like, the worst server we've ever had."

That's probably true. She glanced at Damon's table, unable to gauge if he needed her help. *What could I do? Lieutenant Jayne and Captain Wilson are close. If there's anything I need to know, he'll tell me, won't he?*

"Are you even paying attention?" the blinged-out teenager asked.

"What?"

"Get the manger." She enunciated the syllables in each word.

Vivian blinked and looked at the girl. "Why?"

"Because these tacos are awful. You're awful. I can't believe we even came here."

"Tacos are on the house," she said.

The girl laughed. "You can't decide to give away food."

"I'll buy them"—she tightened her cheeks and forced a smile—"because I'm such a terrible server."

"Whatever. You can't even afford a good colorist."

Picking up a strand of the wig, she exhaled. "Can you two go? Leave. I'll clean up the mess."

The girl with the piercing stood. "Do you know who I am?"

"A brat?" Vivian ran her tongue across her teeth.

The taste of the world felt foreign, but it had escaped, and she liked the sound. *She is a brat. Politeness doesn't always win.* Smothering a smirk, she waited for the girls' retort. *Can she play games like an adult?*

The girl with the shades pulled out her phone.

She focused on Miss Incognito. "What are you doing?"

"Putting this disaster on my channel."

"What? A bad taco review?" She crossed her arms. "You didn't even eat them."

The girl tossed her hair over her shoulder. "Ready?"

"Ready," her companion said.

Standing against the backdrop of the Fish House, the girl pulled in her chin and gasped. Grabbing her stomach, she doubled over and hacked.

Is she seizing? She hesitantly tapped the girl's back. "Are you okay?" Scanning the patio, she looked for Samuel. The sounds of the girl's retching intensified. "Do I need to call a doctor?"

A dining patron stood and headed toward her.

"Quick! Get a trashcan," Vivian said. "She's going to be sick!"

The heaving girl looked up and winked. "Isn't that your job?"

Vivian withdrew her hand. A few weeks on a farm would temper the teenager's entitlement. "What?"

Seconds later, a glob of green, slimy lettuce, and pale, watery food flew from the teenager's mouth and landed on her shoe.

Shaking her hands in revulsion, she worried the girl's bulimic projectile had landed on more than her shoe. "You vomited on me!" The word disgusted her as much as the slime seeping past her laces. "What is going on?"

Crossing her arms over her stomach and leaning forward, the girl peered at her partner's phone. "The Fish House is the worst seafood restaurant in California. I ordered the clams, and as soon as I put a clam in my mouth, I felt ill. Like, really ill."

Vivian put her hands on her hips. "You had tacos."

"The food here made me ill," the girl said.

Her friend circled her finger in the air.

She coughed. "I wish you could have seen the clam ooze on the side of the plate. The dish should never have left the kitchen! Our crap server offered to comp the dish, but who's going to comp my clothes?"

The girl holding the phone panned to Vivian.

Oh, so now I get screen time. She wanted to throw up her hands, but she lifted her chin and stared at the girl giving the monologue. *I'm not a server. I run a multimillion-dollar company, and I should have seen you coming a mile away.*

"Nobody should come to the Fish House." The girl gagged. "You'll regret it."

Samuel came hurrying toward her and the pair of teenagers. "What can I do to help?"

"Get the manager," said the girl with the phone.

Vivian held up her hand. "Don't listen. She only wants more drama for her followers. I already offered to pay for her food. The rest of this"—she shook the limp lettuce from her shoe—"drama is a show."

"I thought the customer was always right," the girl said.

Not when the customer's an adolescent bitch. She smiled through her teeth. "You learn something new every day." *Like the value of having quality people in your life.* Turning the live stream audience on the girls suddenly held a lot of appeal. *If I can make a million dollars, I can probably make a couple of teenagers regret their decision to mess with me.* "You know, on second thought…"

Samuel pulled her away from the table and his head. "Not worth it."

Looking over her shoulder, she considered sticking out her tongue, but she straightened her spine and looked at Damon's table. *Why didn't I spot the trap?* She bit her lip and glanced at Damon. *Do I put too much faith in people?*

He raised his eyebrows.

Instead of a tête-à-tête, she saw censure in his frown. *I'm good at handling people who understand the rules of the world. What happens when people don't play by the rules?* Swinging her gaze toward Lieutenant Jayne and Captain Wilson's table, she found the couple staring. Blinking, she recognized the empty chair across from Damon. "What happened to Anna Claire?"

Samuel released his hold on her elbow. "She split."

"Did Lieutenant Jayne get what he needed?"

The server shrugged.

Walking up from the street, the restaurant owner carried two paper bags.

The teenager girls left their table and teetered toward the patio gate.

"Get out of my way." The girl with the piercing brushed past the man.

Stepping back, he watched the pair leave and looked over.

What? He knew I would be here, but I don't think

he anticipated how much damage I could accomplish. Instead of explaining the situation, she looked at Damon. *I should have let him handle this mess. He had a plan.* Torn between explanations and the need to exonerate him, she exhaled and glanced at Samuel. "How many people are going to see that video?"

Keeping his expression neutral, he arranged bottles of hot sauce and cleared his throat. "We'll need more than postcards."

Meeting Damon's gaze, she swallowed. *I should have stuck to data and the things I understand.*

He stood, walked toward her, and cupped her elbow. "Are you okay?"

"A little high school drama." She swallowed. "I'm sorry for causing a scene."

He tugged the side of her wig. "Your hair's about to fall off."

An indignant laugh escaped her lips. "Sorry."

"For what?" He cupped her cheek.

"Distracting you, scaring off Anna Claire, and ruining the reputation of the Fish House." The moment of tenderness felt good, but failure dulled her ability to enjoy it. Turning her face, she pried out the bobby pins, pulled off the wig, and ran her finger under the wig cap's edge to dislodge it. Her hair probably looked like a matted mess, but she could care less. "I should have stuck to chat rooms, PowerPoint slides, and rented office space. That's where I thrive, isn't it?"

"Vivi," he said. "I'm no worse off than when we started."

She looked at Samuel and Caesar deep in conversation.

Caesar's shoulders slumped.

"You're about to lose your job." Bile seared her throat, and she hoped the fish house stocked antacids in the break room.

Damon looped an arm around her shoulders. "I don't care. I'll find another one."

She shrugged off the embrace. "How many times can you fall down, Damon?"

"As many times as it takes," he said. "I'm a strong man."

Shaking her head, she sighed. "I don't want to be the one to hold you down."

"What does that mean?" He cocked his head.

"It's been fun." Handing him the wig, she walked away from the patio. Every fiber of her being compelled her to turn and look over her shoulder, but she felt like a character actress who reached for stardom but fell flat on her face.

"Vivi!"

Damon's voice cut through the wind and the chatter of the patrons. Shaking her head, she walked toward her car. *He's always the one to leave, and I'm the one who never chased him down.* Stopping at the crosswalk, she closed her eyes and bit her lip. *I didn't give him enough credit; the distance hurts.*

Chapter Fifteen

Sunning her legs in the shady backyard felt like a useless endeavor, but Vivian wanted to take her mind off the disaster at the Fish House. She donned a pair of shorts, her favorite feathered mules, and a halter top she could never wear at work.

Precious whined at the back door and asked to come inside.

"What? Did you find a squirrel with a particularly tasty tail and find out you have indigestion?" She eyed the treetops, wondering if a wounded tree rat stood sentry for its peers. The vulnerability and wobbling uncertainty of stepping out on a limb never felt so real. "You guys are made for an aerial life. I'm not." She adjusted her seat on the teak, Adirondack chair. "Maybe I should have stayed in the Central Valley."

Scratching at the root of a tree, Precious shoved her nose into a hole.

"Watch out for snakes. Sticking your nose where it doesn't belong can land you in trouble."

The dog kept digging.

"Suit yourself." *She made it this long without me. Why do I think she needs my advice?* The afternoon wind whistled through the oak trees. Longing for the heat of summer in the valley, she stretched out her arms and felt the rays filtering through the leaves. Inside the bungalow, work, wine, and womenswear offered cold comfort. *I have Wi-Fi, seltzer water, and the hint of a summer breeze. I've earned the right to spend my afternoon as a woman of leisure.* Dropping her head on the chair's back, she rolled her eyes. *Boredom sucks—* she eyed a chattering squirrel—*nuts.*

Precious raced to the side gate and barked.

"No," she said. "It's the mail carrier. Don't you know he brings your dog food?"

"Well, I'm not into role play," Damon said, "but I'm willing to give it a shot."

Straightening, she reached for her sunglasses and slid them to the top of her hair. He looked tastier than a freezer pop. "What are you doing here?"

He closed the gate, scratched Precious behind the ears, and strolled into the backyard.

"How did you know I was back here?" She watched him pull out the second chair and settle into the wooden frame. *I shouldn't be so happy to see him. I'm supposed to play it cool—s*he cleared her throat— *for his good.* "I could be at work."

He spread his legs, leaned back, and closed his eyes. "You didn't answer the front door."

"Most people would have gone home."

"Your car's out front."

She sighed and dropped the shades over her eyes.

"Why'd you run off like that?"

Turning her head to the side, she stared at his profile. Through hard work and perseverance, success improved her life so much that failure felt like an impersonal outcome she would rather forget. "I didn't run off."

"You ran like a teenage girl getting her first period."

"Well, aren't you blunt?"

He smiled. "You like blunt."

"No, I don't."

"If you tried it, you would. What do you and Hadley do at the Outcomes Foundation?"

She rolled her eyes. "Go home, Damon."

He laughed. "You can't run me off that easily."

Straightening her head, she looked at the shifting canopies. *I don't want to run him off, but I don't want to ruin his life, either. How much resentment would build while he played second fiddle?* She cleared her throat. "How's your job?"

"Fired."

"And your money?" she asked.

"Still gone."

She closed her eyes and bit her lip. *I made everything worse. Before he and I came together, he had hope and the potential for a new beginning. I screwed up both those things.* "I want to make it up to you."

"Like I said, I'm not much into role playing, but you can wear the wig to bed."

She exhaled and faced him. "I'm not talking about sex."

He raised his eyebrows. "What are you talking about?"

Fearing his response, she decided to throw out an offer and see where it landed. "I want to help fund the scholarship program."

Sighing, he stood and picked her up. "No."

Arms flailing, she gripped his neck for purchase. "What do you mean, no? You're trying to help people!"

"Not with your money." Cradling her like a kicking

toddler, he sank back into his chair. "What's wrong with you, Vivi?"

She snorted and wriggled out of his arms. "Good question."

He tightened his hold.

"You could open your own restaurant." She expected the suggestion to land with the wet slap of a dead fish.

"Well, that sounds like more fun than teaching," he said.

She stiffened. "Teaching is a noble profession!"

Laughing, he loosened his grasp. "Why do you feel the need to fix my life?"

"I take care of things." She thought about the data-driven solutions she presented to businesses and non-profits. Her trees, her dog, and her shoes were spotless. "That's what I do."

"Do I need to take care of you?"

She rolled her eyes.

He tucked her head against his chest.

Wiggling got her nowhere. His arms felt like bands of steel, and the heat of his body felt better than the filtered sunlight. Adjusting her position, she gave in to the position and sighed. "Your negotiation tactics need work."

"I'm a grown-ass man, Vivi. I can take care of myself."

"Fine." His heat beat against her ear. *I sleep so well when he's here.* "Suit yourself."

He cleared his throat. "Anna Claire shut down the entire ScanCoin website."

Raising her head, she knocked his jaw.

"Ouch." He rubbed his chin and laughed. "Maybe I

should have left you in your chair."

Scrambling out of his lap, she turned and felt her ankle wobble in the grass.

"Those shoes are ridiculous," he said. "What's the point?"

Eyeing her feathered mules, she frowned. "Foot fatigue is a real thing. Before dancers put on a show, they go through grueling hours of rehearsals. Ask a dancer if they think good shoes are ridiculous."

He stood and smoothed the lines at the corner of her eye. "You're not a dancer."

She bit her lip, knowing she would never have succeeded in that skill, either. Whether she could tap or not, she was too smart and too stubborn to conform to studio contracts. *I'm no Hedy Lamarr.* She grinned. *The lady was smart, but could she code in Python?*

"And you don't need shoes to help you feel beautiful." He cupped her cheek. "That's my job."

She wanted to lean into his touch. She wanted to sink back into the chair, soak up his warmth like a cat in the sun, and trust they could reign over different worlds. *Only one world exists.* She ruled corporate slide decks. He sized up situations and took action. When alone with her, his energy contracted and enveloped her with pleasure and banter. *But what's in it for him?* She pulled away from his touch. *Nothing.*

"Why did you run?" he asked.

She pivoted and waved a hand in the air. "Those girls! They made me feel like an idiot. The whole livestream was…"

"I think the word you're looking for is 'bullshit'."

Throwing up a hand, she sighed. "The tacos were fine!"

He rubbed his jaw. "Fine? You looked like you wanted to slap the one with the earring."

"I did!" Meeting his gaze, she exhaled and let the admission soothe her outrage. "I mean, I should have."

Capturing her hand, he turned it in his grasp and rubbed her palm. "But you stayed cool."

Her shoulders drooped. "Not cool enough to stop their shit propaganda."

"People can say whatever they want about you, me, and the tacos. A long time ago, Mama Clarke taught me something I've never forgotten. *Make sure your reaction scales with the consequences*. How much harm can those girls do?"

"I'm sure they have followers." Before she reinvented herself in Silicon Valley, she watched the popular girls wield their power in the Central Valley. Returning to the bottom of the social hierarchy was never an option, but the Fish House encounter left her feeling powerless, and she would rather forget the glimpse of her past.

Extending his arms, he cupped her shoulders. "Do their followers spend a lot of money at the Fish House?"

She closed her eyes. "Why did the Fish House fire you?"

Skimming her arms, he threaded their fingers and raised her hand to his lips.

The warmth of his kiss anchored her senses. Opening her eyes, she blinked.

He lowered her hands. "The owner said he wants his customers to focus on the food's quality."

She snorted. "Maybe he should cull his menu."

Clearing his throat, he crossed his feet at the

ankles. "I made that suggestion."

She pulled free a hand and absently rubbed her arm, considering whether to hold back or cave to the comfort she wanted. *But what does he need?*

"I also suggested firing Samuel, changing produce suppliers, and reorganizing the prep space."

She looked up. "That's what you do, isn't it? You see needs, and you address them. I see patterns. You see…"

"I see you."

She frowned. "I would say gaps."

He pulled her into his arms. "Turns out Samuel is the boss' nephew."

His teasing smile tabled her concerns. "No wonder he was so chill about his job."

"By chill, you mean lazy."

She laughed. "But you need that job." He nuzzled the tender spot behind her ear. Bending her neck to give him better access, she closed her eyes and savored the contact.

"I also need you," he said. "You don't have gaps, Vivi. You're a force, and I love watching you roll."

Need blossomed in her core, but she tamped it down. "When did Anna Claire flee?"

He nibbled her ear. "When your wig shifted."

Gasping, she pushed against his chest.

He tightened his hold.

"Although, the game was already up," he said. "I had already invested. Well, Mathew had invested."

Slowly raising her chin, she met his gaze. "Is Louis your middle name?"

He nodded.

"What happened to your parents?"

"Long story." His teasing smile faltered.

She swallowed. "Did the police get what they needed?"

"I think so, but what good does it do? Anna Claire's probably halfway to"—he made a pensive sound—"Liberia by now."

She frowned. "What do you know about Liberia?"

He looked up. "It's in West Africa. Land of the free? Home of the Black?"

Rolling her eyes, she pulled away.

"Anna Claire's not dumb," he said.

"That's a matter of opinion." She crossed her arms.

"Some countries offer more favorable regulatory climates than the US. Moving ScanCoin's headquarters to the U.K. or to Singapore wouldn't end all US jurisdiction, but those countries would become ScanCoin's chief regulators." He scratched his head. "I'm sure she's gone."

But you're here. She tilted her head. "You might be right. Liberia's laws are more secretive than Panama's laws, and it's a definite tax haven. For a few hundred dollars, anyone in the world can set up a tax-free Liberian company and secure total anonymity."

He furrowed his brow. "How do you know these things?"

"A former life." She thought about the days she spent in the management consulting company. "I learned to judge people and identify red flags." She smiled. "After hearing my advice, some clients fired me. Their insults were very creative."

He tipped up her chin. "Tell me who they are. I'll beat them up."

She smiled. "They're long gone."

"So, Liberia's not out. Maybe she went to Switzerland?"

Releasing the tension in her back, she leaned against him and tucked her head beneath his chin. "Maybe."

Kneading her muscles, he held her close. "I didn't like watching you walk away."

"My ass looks better in heels."

Laughing, he squeezed her butt.

She smiled. "I should have let you handle the whole thing. You didn't need me there."

"I need you," he said. "You're hilarious and good in bed."

Rolling her eyes, she pulled free and smoothed her halter top. "That's not enough for a relationship."

"Who said anything about a relationship?" He stroked her arm.

She tapped his chest. "You did! You care about me."

He let his mouth hang open. "When did I say that?"

"When we were naked!"

"Fucking?" He pulled back the hand and scratched the back of his head. "You can't hold a man to the things he says in bed."

I might lose my hair over this man. Why are people so complicated? She spun and marched toward the back door. Pausing, she turned and pointed. "You asked if sex would ruin our friendship. You asked me if I cared!"

Crossing his arms, he stood in the sun-dappled backyard. "Don't you?"

She narrowed her gaze. "Yes."

He flung wide his arms. "Then what's the problem,

Vivi? Come back."

I don't need a man in my life to feel fulfilled. Then he returned from prison, and I realized I wanted him. Not in my bed, but in my life. What does that makes me? A hypocrite. Biting her lip, she swallowed her words and walked toward the house.

"Vivi!"

The nickname sounded so poignant she hurt.

"Why are you walking away? You're a damned CEO, woman. Buck up!"

She reached for the backdoor. "You're the one who taught me to walk away." Pausing, she waited for an apology or an admission. *You're right, Vivi. I shouldn't have walked away when you bailed me out of jail. I shouldn't have slipped from your house like a paid escort.* Hearing nothing, she looked over her shoulder and prepared herself to say goodbye.

"I had to take care of business," he said.

She dropped a hand from the doorknob. "What?"

"After my arrest, my grandmother hadn't heard from me in days. I called Johann to bail me out of jail, but I had no way of reaching Mama Clarke."

She faced him.

"After we hooked up, I left to give you space and to piece together my life."

"I didn't want space." She rubbed her arms.

He walked toward her. "I worried you did." Climbing the steps, he closed the distance between them. "What do you want?"

"I don't know." The whispered admission hurt. "I pushed and pushed to build Hoat Analytics, but I'm afraid the only thing left of the person I am is a closet of shoes. My friends need things. My employees need things. What do I need?"

He tipped up her chin. "Your friends love you for who you are, not what you can give them."

She raised her eyebrows.

"Me and Silvia," he said. "Hadley."

She snorted. "I'm not inviting Silvia over for a threesome."

Laughing, he joined her on the step. "Vivi, this is Silicon Valley. Boring ass computer jobs are a dime a dozen."

Working her jaw, she conceded the point.

He winked. "You must be a good boss."

"I pay those people," she said. "Pretending to like me is in their best interest."

"Is that what you're afraid of?" He cocked his head. "That I'm pretending to like you?"

She looked away, searching for an anchor. "No."

"That I want something from you?"

She swallowed.

He wrapped a hand around her waist. "Vivi, the only thing I want from you is your smile. Maybe scream my name so loud the neighbors complain. I don't want your money. I don't want you to dress me like Black Cary Grant."

Biting her lip, she hung her head, afraid to meet his gaze and confirm her daydream. *But he looked so hot at the gala!*

"I definitely don't want to be your PR monkey," he said.

Looking up, she opened her mouth to object to his phrasing.

He shook his head. "I want to rev you up and watch you fall. I want front row seats when you handle people and put them in their place. It's sexy as hell."

"What kind of person do you think I am?" She thought of the teenage drama queens and wondered if her reputation landed her closer to their roles than she knew. She left the Central Valley to find success, but losing herself along the way was never part of the goal.

"A strong one," he said. "Strong to hang with my shit." He stroked her cheek. "I want to tease you and test your resolve. I want to wonder whether you'll laugh at a shared joke or hold steady and maintain your composure."

She rolled her eyes. "Remind me not to invite you to board of directors' meetings."

"You don't have a board of directors."

"Advisory board." She rolled her eyes. "When you said you followed my work, I thought you cut out a newspaper article and used it as a bookmark."

"You don't think much of my affections," he said.

She ran a hand along his back. Her uncertainty magnified the sensation, and the soft cotton of his T-shirt bunched beneath her fingertips. *How can one man give so much?* "Come inside and show me these affections."

He widened his gaze, but he cocked his head and stared.

"You came here for a reason, Damon. I'll tell you what I want. Go inside and get naked."

He turned her chin. "I didn't make myself clear."

The hesitation threw her off guard. "You d-don't want to come inside?"

"I do."

So, what's the problem? "Are you hungry?"

He lowered his head, grazing his five o'clock

shadow against her neck. "No."

"You want to talk about ScanCoin?"

He nipped the soft curve of her neck.

The surprising gesture made her smile.

His lips traveled north.

She felt the scrape of his teeth, this time tugging at her earlobe. His hot breath tickled the fine hairs on her skin. "Again." Her faltering plea masked the emotions roiling her system. His entrance brought relief and excitement. Lust, resistance, and confusion followed her up the steps.

Pulling back, he made eye contact. "Admit you care about me."

She pulled away. "Of course, I care about you."

He tightened his hold. "Admit we're more than friends."

Feeling his hand flex against her hip, she swallowed. She could walk inside the bungalow and leave him standing on the back step. Months might pass, but the friendship would endure. She tilted her head. Beneath the shadows of the oak trees, his warm brown eyes intensified into determined black. Letting a hand drift farther down his back, she traced the dip where his muscles tightened before the powerful swell of his glutes. "I care about you. I want you to be happy." *With me.* She swallowed and flexed her fingers, releasing the stress of the conversation without revealing her need.

"I am happy," he said.

She accepted the admission. "Quit stalling." He held her gaze long enough to make her wonder if he guessed her thoughts. *Can I be enough for him? Will he grow bored and move onto someone else?*

Shifting from her grasp, he leaned past her and opened the door.

Precious raced past him, surging toward her sun-soaked sheepskin.

Walking into the kitchen, he kicked off his shoes, crossed his arms, and pulled his shirt over his head.

She followed his movements, watching his muscles flex. *I'd say anything right now to make him stay.* "Damon…"

Turning, he made eye contact and raised his eyebrows.

She swallowed.

Unbuttoning his pants, he let them fall, stepped out of his boxers, and left the pile of clothes on the wooden floor.

She forced herself to look him in the eyes. "Damon, I care. I want you here. I don't know what that means, but I want more than sex."

He bent down. "Okay, I'll get dressed."

"Wait! I meant, after the sex."

He laughed and straightened.

Intent on proving her point, she smiled and led him toward the kitchen table.

He followed her lead. "You're overdressed."

"I'm aware." With little effort, she pushed him against the wooden surface, his warm, brown eyes widening, waiting for her to make the next move. The trust in his gaze erased her uncertainties. She pressed her body against him and centered her hips against his arousal, claiming his lips for a kiss.

One hand anchored her hip, but his other hand rose and fiddled with the closure on her halter top. Picking up the pace of the kiss, he slid his tongue against hers and angled his head. Then he pulled back and swore. "How the hell do I get this thing off you?"

She flicked the strap and released the fabric. Her shirt dropped and exposed her breasts. "Satisfied?"

"Not even close." Cupping her breast, he pulled her flush and hummed in the back of his throat. Fingers splayed along her skin, he kneaded and teased her nipple. "Bras are overvalued."

Grabbing his head with both hands, she pulled his mouth to hers and resumed the kiss. His cock twitched and drew her attention. She inhaled, thinking his skin tasted of sunlight and warm beaches. Stepping back, she shimmied out of her shorts. "Clothes are overrated."

Scanning her from the top of her head to her feathered mules, he grinned. "Your thong matches your shoes."

The observation pleased and amused her. Leaning forward, she kissed his neck. "We have one problem."

He stilled. "You're out of condoms."

She swatted his chest. "Don't be ridiculous."

Laughing, he raised an eyebrow.

"If I grab one, will you bolt?" Her voice faltered.

"I'm not going anywhere, Vivi." He pressed a kiss to her shoulder.

The tender reassurance calmed her uncertainties. She walked down the hall, hoping he watched the sway and dip of her hips. *Who says shoes aren't important?* Hearing his whistle, she grinned. Pulling the foil packet from her bedside table, she strode into the kitchen and tossed him the condom.

Catching it, he placed it on the kitchen table. "You promised to tell me what you want."

She shimmied out of her thong but left on her

shoes. "I'm hungry."

"Are you?"

Opening the refrigerator, she withdrew the can of whipped cream and checked the expiration date. Relief flooded her system, clashing with the need and playfulness that kept her smiling through her uncertainty. A muscled man with a jutting cock stared as if she were the main course. His confidence and assurance encouraged play. Uncapping the whipped cream, she took a hit and grinned. "It'll taste better on your skin."

He grabbed her and pulled her close.

His lazy kiss told her he was up for the game, but the divot between his chest muscles fascinated her. Grinning, she laid a line of cream from his collarbone to his belly button. Within seconds, the cream melted and slid down his skin. "Oh, no!" She licked the path, laughing and doing her best to capture the slide. Feeling him inhale, she grinned and wondered if her miscalculation might be a win. *I'm not sure how much patience I have.* Exploring his body with her tongue, she let the cold cream sliding over heated skin captivate her. *I could spend all evening teasing him.* Pulling back, she met his gaze. *But I don't think he'll let me.*

He grabbed the can and placed two swirls on the curves of her breasts. Picking her up, he licked the cream and drew her nipple into his mouth. Sucking and teasing the sensitive peak, he used his hands to support her weight.

She wrapped her legs around his chest, rubbing her heat against his skin for the friction she needed.

Pinning her hips with one hand, he released her breast and trailed a hand along her side. His thumb traced her hipbone and stroked her clit. "How much cream do we have left?"

"Not enough." She closed her eyes and let the firm pressure of his touch tease and heighten her arousal. Anchoring one hand over his shoulder, she shifted and wiggled out of his grasp. Wrapping her fingers around his length, she found his slippery head and stroked him.

He sucked in his breath.

The reaction emboldened her. She braced her weight on his shoulder and met his gaze. "Are you still worried about whether I care?"

He shifted his grip and slid the soft pressure of his thumb past her folds.

She closed her eyes and forgot her question. The gap between their needs meant something, but the heat of skin pressing against skin felt real.

Pulling up, he amplified the pressure.

"Damon." Her breathy exhalation ended with a moan.

Drawing out her moisture, he found her clit with his thumb.

The rhythm consumed her attention. Dropping his length, she let her needs lead her response. Safe in his arms, she dropped her head, closed her eyes, and felt every stroke.

He increased the pressure.

Gasping, she arched into his touch. "Take me to bed."

He maintained the pace. "What's wrong with the kitchen table?"

She was glad she never went in for china and placemats. "I love that table."

Turning, he set her down on the cool, wooden

surface.

The table rocked. Her arms flailed for purchase, and she heard the whipped cream can clatter to the floor. She winced, but the pressure in her core chained her to the promise of her pleasure. Bracing her arms on his shoulders, she smiled. "As soon as we get dressed, I'm buying a sturdier table."

He laughed and withdrew his thumb. "Lie back."

His soft command pushed her higher. She lowered her back to the polished surface and scooted her bottom to the edge of the table.

Narrowing his gaze, he grinned, pumped his sex, and reached for the condom. "You look good enough to eat."

"No more stalling!"

He laughed and lifted her right leg in the air, trailing a hand between her breasts until he claimed her second leg and settled himself between her thighs.

She watched him, intent on savoring the first thrust. *Damon's generous. He'll let me come first.*

He shucked her mules, crossed her legs like an X, and raised his eyebrows.

She felt the pressing heat of his cock poised against her entrance. Rising on her elbows, she stared, waiting to see how he would make this happen.

He held her ankles and pressed into her. "Tell me if it feels good."

The first thrust felt like an iron brand.

She collapsed back onto the table. The added friction of her crossed legs rubbed her clit. His length felt heavy and deep. Tilting her hips, she gasped. "It feels good."

He grinned and thrust again.

Pleasure and restraint strained his features. His hips set the pace she needed, and her breath quickened. Skin slapping against skin, she received him and focused on the pressure building in her core.

"You feel so tight." He ground out the words.

The pressure flashed into a furious rush, and she submitted to her release. The searing pleasure left her gasping for breath. Feeling his body shudder within her, she dropped her head against the wood and breathed deeply as he loosened his hold on her legs. His thrusts slowed to contentment.

He leaned forward and pressed a kiss against her breast. "I've always cared."

Lifting her head, she blinked away the warm afterglow of sex. "The whole time I was with Johann?"

"Every damn minute." He pulled out, slipped off the condom, and tossed it in the trashcan. Bracing his arms on the edge of the table, he looked at the floor, and then he raised his head and made eye contact.

She frowned, struggling to reconcile the time she spent bantering with Damon like a good friend. "You said nothing."

"Why would you pick me over him?"

She pulled her ass away from the edge of the table and crossed her legs, finding herself square in the middle of the space where she ate her meals and sorted her paper mail. *I'm never getting rid of this table.* Trailing her thumb across his pec, she smiled. "Johann never let me paint his chest with whipped cream. He never let me go undercover and involve myself with his business."

Damon laughed.

"And I never asked him to do those things."

Tipping up his chin, she rose to her knees and pressed his face to her abdomen. "People like you, but more importantly, you like me."

"You have no idea."

His whispered response thrilled and confused her.

He cleared his throat and rested his chin against her bellybutton. "When you let down your guard, you're playful and sweet." He wrapped an arm beneath her butt and picked her up. "You're also good in bed and on tables." Striding toward the living room, he dumped her on the couch cushions. "You look fine sprawled on your ass."

She laughed and scrambled to her knees. The curtains were open. If her geriatric neighbors caught sight of them, they might have a heart attack. She would take the risk. *Let the geezers have a thrill.*

Sitting beside her, he leaned against the cushions, splayed his legs, and closed his eyes. "The day has me beat."

"After I catch my breath, I'll close the curtains and order dinner."

"Thanks."

No longer considering space for his toothbrush, she settled beside him, stroked his arm, and wondered if he would stay the night. *ScanCoin is behind us; the only thing I need is a hot shower, a bottle of wine, and Damon in my bed.* Smiling, she closed her eyes. *Life is good.*

Chapter Sixteen

"Alarm." Vivian pulled the duvet over her shoulder.

"Yours."

Raising her head in the early morning light, she blinked. *Damon's right.* She fumbled with her phone, shut off the alarm, and stared at him sprawled on his back. *He's right for me.* The scattered pockmarks on his face might bother him, but she saw a man who teased her into a good mood, helped kids, and befriended a half-blind dog. She laid her head against his chest, content to linger amid the tumble of bedclothes.

"I can hear you thinking," he said.

"I wonder if I have more whipped cream."

He lifted his head.

She trailed her fingers along his chest. Her past relationships felt so transactional that she reveled in their easy intimacy. "I enjoy messing around with you."

"I noticed."

His morning erection stiffened beneath the sheets, and she grinned. "I usually make Irish Coffees with the whipped cream. I've never played with it. I'll have to stock up."

His dick twitched, and he turned to his side. "Why not?"

"I hardly see people past a date or two." She pushed him onto his back and straddled him. "I wonder

if homemade whipped cream would hold up better."
Shifting her hips, she let the warm sheets separate their
sexes. "Maybe I'll learn how to cook something."

He anchored her hips. "I've never tried homemade
whipped cream."

She gasped and met his gaze. "You haven't?"

"Mama Clarke isn't the type to make things from
scratch."

"She did the best she could." *What happened to his
mother? Will he tell me when he's ready?* She sat back
on her haunches and stared. "My grandmother made it
for Sunday pies. Some memories stick."

He splayed his hands atop her thighs. "If Anna
Claire's leaving the country, I bet she went to say
goodbye to her mom."

"Let's go back to the whipped cream."

He laughed, grabbed her wrist, and yanked her
onto his chest. "We can do both."

She struggled to sit up and planted a hand in the
middle of his chest. "She stole millions of dollars. I
doubt she cares whether she's in her mother's good
graces."

"I bet she cares," he said. "She'll say goodbye
before she flees."

Thrusting forward her breasts, she shifted her
shoulders and captured his attention. "You can find the
woman's phone number and call for a heart-to-heart,
but right now, you're in my bed." She rose and sat on
his chest. "I have plans for this day."

Laughing, he flipped their positions and braced his
hands on either side of her head.

"Much better," she said.

He pressed a kiss to her forehead and swung his

legs over the bed's side. "Vivi, I'm serious."

"So am I. Get in bed." Biting her lip, she considered whether to beg. *If lace and whipped cream aren't enough, what else do I have?* She watched him plant his hands on his hips. He stood in her room with his legs braced and his thighs corded with muscles. His jutting cock stood at attention. Her gaze followed the contours of his chest and the thin line of hair running from his bellybutton. *Screw being a tease. I'll break out the sex toys.*

He rubbed his brow. "She said she's from Mammoth Lakes."

Blinking, she realized batteries and vibrations would not save her morning. "Huh?"

"Anna Claire is from Mammoth Lakes. How long would it take to drive there?"

She frowned. "Airlines have direct flights from Palo Alto."

"You have a rental car," he said.

Sighing, she stood, slipped into her robe, and tightened the belt. "Would you do it again, Damon? Would you invest in ScanCoin?"

He smiled and wrapped an arm around her waist. "No, I would pick a more established currency."

"Then let it go," she said.

"Would you?" He made eye contact. "Would you walk away from a three-million-dollar contract you thought you could win?"

Even though she felt his cock pressing against her thigh, and could definitely reshuffle her meetings, she exhaled and stepped back. "No, I wouldn't."

"Good, I wouldn't expect you to give up."

Precious padded into the room.

She leaned over, scratched the dog's ears, and kept her gaze averted. "You're a capable man, Damon. You want to follow Anna Claire and have a frank chat with her mother? You take the car."

He walked past her and slapped her butt. "I'd rather you came with me. You need a vacation."

Straightening, she rubbed her backside. "I spent last night wrapped in your arms. That was a vacation."

Rolling his eyes, he walked from the room. "You want more."

Her employees at Hoat Analytics depended on her. She couldn't keep rearranging her responsibilities because Damon had new schemes to chase down Anna Claire. "I can't bail on work and jet out of town for the weekend." She glanced at Precious. "I have a dog!"

"And a dog walker!"

His laughter echoed in the hallway, mocking her protestations. She swallowed and wondered if disrupting her evening routine would alter her entire life. She walked into the hallway. Unsure of his location in the house, she raised her voice. "Precious will be lonely without me."

"Put her in the car," he said from the kitchen.

She imagined picking fur from the leather upholstery. "She might get car sick."

Damon peered around the corner. "How do you take her to the vet?"

Raising her chin, she met his gaze. "The vet comes to my house."

Laughing, he went back to the kitchen and turned on the coffeemaker. "Get dressed, Vivi. We're going to Mammoth Lakes. Asking her, surprising her, and tricking her haven't worked. Shame might be the only tool I have left."

His voice trailed off, and she wondered if his strength could resist another letdown. She walked into the kitchen and admired his cheeky pose. Standing in the room's middle, he looked as confident as a warrior, but without a stitch of clothes to warm his skin. *If I'm willing to reorganize my schedule for sex, why can't I do it to spend real time with him? Who cares whether we retrieve his money or not?* She swallowed. *He cares.* "What if she's not there?"

Looking over his shoulder, he smiled. "Then you can spend the weekend licking me from head to toe."

She grinned and gave her staff the props they deserved. A quick jaunt to Mammoth Lakes would be worth the hassle of rescheduling her meetings, even if she did have to de-fur the car. "I'll get my snow boots." Tossing off a grin, she headed toward her closet. *What could go wrong?*

****

Tossing him the keys, Vivian walked around the car and opened the passenger door.

"You want me to drive?"

"If you don't mind." She let Precious into the backseat, secured her with a harness, and eased closed the door. Before it latched, she considered admonishing the dog to be good. *Like that will work. She'll bark at every cow she sees.* Shaking her head, she slid into the passenger seat, buckled her seatbelt, and opened her computer. She could take a few calls and use her phone as a hotspot, but she hoped serious work could wait.

Shrugging, he settled into the driver's seat, started the car, and backed from the driveway.

The slow, warning beep made her smile. Cruising

down the street, he hit the gas, and she felt the car lurch forward. Instead of apologizing, he did it again. She cleared her throat. "The car's very reactive."

"Suits you."

She grinned.

He followed the navigation system and left the city.

Trusting his smooth handling skills, she let calls and emails consumed her attention. Looking up, she spied Sacramento's office towers. "I can't believe we have to drive south from Lake Tahoe to maintain a hot spot."

"The Central Valley's in the way," he said. "This route made sense, but if you want to save an hour, you can close your laptop and wind around hilly, two-lane roads."

She looked at the river running through the capital city and thought about the irrigation canals in the valley. On some level, she missed them, but she made her choice. *Homemade pies and black-and-white movies might be rarer than I thought.* "I'd rather stick to the highways."

"I figured."

She adjusted the laptop to keep it from overheating. "Did you learn all that stuff in the chat rooms?"

She glanced at the screen and wondered what he recognized. The program on her screen looked like a glorified spreadsheet. As the numbers updated, code scrolled through a pop-up window. "I learned the beginnings in the chat rooms. At first, I wanted help with my homework. People had too many solutions, and I realized a thousand approaches led to the same solution." She watched the code advance. "Some approaches were more elegant and more efficient than the others."

He tapped the steering wheel. "Do you keep in touch with those people?"

"They're not my friends," she said.

"Why not?"

"Everyone hid behind aliases and screen names. I didn't throw up a profile pic and tell everyone I looked good in a polka dot bikini."

"I'm sure you do."

She rolled her eyes and glanced over. "That's a surefire way to end up with reams of dick picks."

"The only dick pick you should be looking at is mine." He reached for his belt buckle.

She swatted his hand. "Two hands on the wheel."

"You're no fun."

"I know." The whispered admission felt heavy on a sunny day. "I mean, not right now." The highway climbed into the mountains, and she sighed. "The questions I asked online were so basic and fundamental people must have known I was a kid. But I could have been a kid anywhere in the world, boy or girl. People didn't care; they wanted to help me."

"They could have been smart kids, too."

She shook her head. "These guys"—she sighed, hating the reality of early computer programming— "weren't using macro recorders to automate their spreadsheets. They tossed out VBA script without blinking."

"VBA?" he asked.

"Visual Basic for Applications. It was a programming language Excel used to create macros throughout the 1990s." She deleted an email she had no interest in reading. "Big Tech mothballed it in 2008."

"Ancient history," he said.

She smiled. "VBA came from BASIC, a family of programming languages started in the 1960s. Some of these guys were the first university students to use computers. Sharing's a tradition in this community. They wanted to share what they knew."

"But they didn't know you."

She exhaled. "Does that matter?"

He shrugged, keeping two hands on the wheel. "What name did you use?"

"Lovelace1815," she said.

Making eye contact, he smiled. "Sounds dirty."

She looked away. "Not in my world."

"I think you lied to those geeks," he said. "They didn't know you were a kid. They didn't know you wanted to cheat on your homework."

"I wasn't cheating!"

He switched lanes and settled against the backrest. "Do you want kids?"

She stared. The code occupying her thoughts vanished from her mind. "What?"

"It's an easy enough question."

Tucking her chin, she stared at the laptop. Pines and fir trees lined the highway. Beneath their shadows, the flicker of the screen seemed harsh. "I'm not sure I would be an exemplary mother."

"Why?"

She swallowed. "My grandmother said something that stuck. She said she couldn't see me with kids."

He snorted. "That's ridiculous. Your grandparents should have spent more time loving on you and less time teaching you about eyeliner and guns."

"Maybe." She stared out the window. Eyeliner and

314

guns could be a heady combination, but she lived in a rational world. Tiny humans seemed like the antithesis of rationality. "I might not be cut out for dirty diapers and messy fingers."

"That's a phase," he said. "They grow out of those years fast."

"And then what?"

"Then you try to turn them into decent human beings."

She smiled. "Like I said, I might not be cut out for the task. I'm hard to love."

"Not true. You're"—he scratched his jaw—"quirky. You so smart you have a head start on most people."

Turning her knees, she closed her laptop and slid it into her messenger bag. "Maybe. What about you?"

"An army." He grinned.

She widened her gaze. "Of kids?"

Dropping his hand, he gripped his thigh. "But probably kids in foster care. Kids who need a home they can count on. I can't wait to be Mr. Mom."

Reaching for him, she slid a hand beneath his hand and felt his thigh muscles flex. "That's lovely." She thought of the transitivity of kids coming in and out of a foster care home. Courts prioritized reuniting kids with biological family members. The kids deserved that chance of reunification. She struggled to imagine herself amid so much unpredictability, but she trusted Damon to handle it. "What happened to your parents?"

Staring ahead, he drove.

"Damon?"

"I don't want to talk about it," he said.

Withdrawing her hand, she clasped it and held it in

her lap. *For a moment, I forgot it was easier to be seen and not heard.* She sighed. "I hope you'll tell me."

"Nobody likes sad stories."

She thought of the kids he mentored and sent to school. *Stories with happy endings take longer to tell.*

Fifty-two emails, seven hours, two sandwiches, and a brisk walk with Precious consumed the drive. As the Eastern Sierra peaks towered over the highway, Mammoth Lakes came into view. Single-story cabins and shingled driveway signs announced the old part of town. Looking toward the snowline, she spied ski lifts running up Mammoth Mountain. *Yesterday's storm might have been the last of this season's snow.*

She booked a room in the newest development, but she wondered if engineered nightlife, après-ski treats, and shopping venues obscured the area's character. *The town bleeds into Yosemite, Devils Postpile, and Bodie.* A hint of the old west lingered. *Where would Anna Claire's mother live?*

Using the laptop and the hot spot, she researched leads while Damon drove. Anna Claire didn't use her last name, but it had to be in early press releases or newspaper articles. How many women could plot their identities from an early age? She thought of the days she spent daydreaming about her future. High school pep rallies held little appeal, and she doubted Anna Claire attended them. Maybe she had shaped her identity from an early age. Women could be beautiful and strategic.

He cleared his throat. "Maybe her family moved around a lot."

A highway road sign proclaimed the area's population.

"The town has eight thousand residents. How often do you think families move houses?"

"Extended family?"

She rolled her eyes. "We'll have to get lucky."

"I was planning on it."

Smiling, she dismissed the awkward silence filling the car after she asked about his parents. *Maybe he feels like he's being disloyal to Mama Clarke.* She fished a knit hat out of her overnight bag. Snow season lasted until June, and the forecast said the temperature would fall to a chilly twenty-six degrees. "Did you bring warm clothes?"

He put the vehicle in Park. "I brought what I have."

"We'll make it work." Opening the door, she stepped onto the cobblestone street and inhaled the crisp, clean air. The uneven ground would be hell on her ankle, but Damon offered an arm, and she gladly leveraged his support.

Shingle-clad towers and alpine-inspired shops lined the streets of the new development. Visitors wearing rainbow-colored puff jackets looked like throwbacks from the golden age of après-ski, but she doubted any of the guests wearing a Fair Isle sweater, or a color-blocked beanie with a pom-pom hit the slopes in 1972. Doubting her choice of the upscale development, she thought of the low buildings she saw in the old town. *If I have to choose between brown siding and economical shingle roofs, I choose color.*

A valet from the hotel approached the vehicle. His black shirt bore the hotel's emblem, and he smiled with the warmth of a person who never met a stranger. "Checking in?"

Damon tossed him the keys. "Thanks, man."

"Does it need a charge?"

"Yes," he said.

She opened the back door for Precious to jump out, scratched the dog's head, and tucked her hair behind her ear. "The reservation is under Hoat." The passive-aggressive statement sounded weak, but asserting herself felt like the right move. *If Damon's keeping secrets, then he's not all in.* She swallowed. *What a vacation.*

The valet slid behind the wheel of the vehicle.

Handing Damon her messenger bag, she held Precious's leash and stared at the entrance to the lodge. "Let's shower before we go door to door."

He slung the bag over his shoulder. "I didn't think there would be so many possibilities."

"We'll either get lucky, or someone will warn Anna Claire before we get too close. Then we'll have to spend the night in bed."

He scrunched his face. "You make failure sound good."

She tried not to laugh. "We'll do our best."

Precious barked.

He rubbed the dog's head.

The lobby of the lodge bustled with late-afternoon guests. Children clutched chocolate chip cookies and adults congregated with cocktails. Piles of luggage waited near the bell stand. *I guess our stuff will find its way to our room.* She grinned and let the energy of the lodge settle her uneasiness. *I don't care if this is a fool's errand. Damon was right. It feels good to get away from Palo Alto.*

"Hello, Ms. Hoat." The receptionist came around the front desk and crouched in front of Precious, holding out a hand. "Aren't you a beauty?"

Precious sniffed the woman's hand and wagged her tail.

Looking up, the receptionist withdrew a dog treat from her jacket. "Can she have this treat?"

Vivian nodded.

"Is she coming to day camp today?"

She scanned the counter for a service menu. "Day camp?"

"It's a safe, supervised, slobbery camp for our favorite canine guests. Do you have her shot records?"

"They're on my phone." She saw Precious nuzzle the woman's leg. *Traitor.* "I can email them to the"— she bit her lip—"camp director."

"Perfect!" The receptionist clapped and led Precious toward a pair of double doors.

Watching the pair disappear, she wondered if she should be jealous of her dog's leisure. *I'm sure she'll have more fun at camp than she would in the hotel room.*

Damon placed a hand on the small of her back. "She still loves you."

"Does she?"

He cleared his throat and led her toward the lobby. "Let's get a beer."

"Irish Whiskey," she said.

Laughing, he mumbled something about whipped cream.

The sound eased the tension from her shoulders. Watching him walk up to the polished wooden bar and lean across the surface, she inventoried ways to spend the evening. *Hot tub. Private hot tub. Naked hot tub.* She grinned. The noise of the great room might swallow polite requests, but Damon's deep voice could cut through the chatter.

The bartender set down his rag and walked right up.

I should learn that trick. Settling onto a stuffed couch, she admired Damon's butt. Within minutes, he and the bartender looked like old friends, while impatient guests waved credit cards at the opposite end of the bar.

Scanning the room, she looked at the pink-cheeked families and groups of adults sprawled around the lounge, tapping phones, or consulting maps. In a place like the lodge, their carefree smiles made sense. She smoothed her pants and caught her reflection in a large mirror. The grin on her face startled her. *Damon makes life feel fun. Even when he's on the other side of the room, I feel connected. I have so much room in my life, why shouldn't I love him?* She gaped at her reflection, closed her mouth, and crossed her ankles. *Take a deep breath.*

He returned carrying two drinks.

Looking up, she accepted a steaming glass mug and sipped the fortified coffee. "Thanks. I want to check on Precious. She's not a puppy anymore."

He sat on the couch and spread an arm over the back. "No problem. I'll scout out statuesque Black women. How many can I hit on before neighbors report me to the police?"

"Funny." She licked the whipped cream from her lip. "Maybe we'll get lucky."

The side of his mouth tipped up in a small smile. "Maybe."

Standing, she carried her drink across the lobby

and waved at the receptionist. "Hi, can I check on my dog?"

"Sure!" The woman swiveled her computer monitor.

A grid of camera feeds showed dogs lounging in a fenced yard. Wrought iron tree guards surrounded aspen trees and cold-hardy annuals. Precious sat in the corner, ears flopped on the ground, while a pack of Pomeranians yipped. She sighed. "Maybe I should bring her up to my room."

"She'll make friends," the receptionist said. "If it makes you feel better, we can give her another treat."

She followed the woman through the swinging double doors. Past the barrier, the lobby's tasteful décor ended, and the rubber skid-marked efficiency of sheetrock and vinyl began. Framed posters proclaimed the hallmarks of customer service, wooden plaques broadcast tenure awards, and yellowed newspaper clippings commemorated notable events. She sighed, wondering if her visit to doggy day camp was a waste of time. Glancing from the corner of her eye, she stopped in her tracks. Anna Claire's confident smile beamed from a magazine cover.

The receptionist looked over her shoulder and stopped. "Anna Claire's our local celebrity."

Trying not to reach across the counter and pull the woman back to the desk, she swallowed. "Oh, do you know her?"

"She used to babysit me. You know that viral challenge to identify the most famous person from high school? I totally posted yearbook photos of Anna Claire, but her real name's Anita."

Forcing a smile, she abandoned her idea for a cover

story. "What's her, um, last name?"

"Agrawal. When I started skiing, her mom snuck me hot chocolate at The Pineapple Pinnacle. They were just the sweetest pair."

She traced the name's letters into her palm and held onto the sensation. Anna Claire transitioned from Anita Agrawal into a crypto deviant, and Vivian would hold onto that fact without letting the receptionist or the lobby crowd discover her interest. "The pinnacle of what?"

"Um, the mountain." The receptionist tilted her head. "Mrs. Agrawal runs the interpretive center and the tiki bar at the top of the mountain. Lulu's Oasis is the place's real name, but we all call it the Pineapple Pinnacle. If you don't ski, take the gondola and enjoy the mountain views. Nothing beats a concoction of fresh juices and strong rum."

"I can ski." She bit her lip, trying not to reveal her excitement. *But the only coconut I want is Damon. If we can start Operation Shame and sic Anna Claire's mom on her, we can retire to the hotel suite before dinner.*

The receptionist brushed a speck of lint off the picture of Anna Claire. "That's good. It's beautiful weather, but stay off the backside of the mountain. Accidentally skiing into the wilderness area is too easy."

She fluffed her hair and remained calm. "I'll check it out."

"Do you want to see your dog?" The receptionist jerked her chin toward the end of the service hallway.

She weighed her options and shrugged. "You know, I think you're right. Precious is an expert judge of character. She'll make friends."

"You are so right!"

Am I? She met the woman's gaze and grinned.

The woman raised her eyebrows. "Is there's anything else?"

"No, I'm good. On second thought, send up a bottle of red wine to decant. Make it good." She could care less if the lodge charged her three hundred dollars for the pleasure. Pivoting, she strode across the lobby and schooled her progress to a reasonable gait. "Damon, her real name's Anita Claire Agrawal. I found her mother."

He scanned the crowded lobby. "Where?"

"She works on the mountain!" Excitement made her want to jump in place, but she made fists at her sides. "In a tiki bar!"

Standing, he stretched. "I wouldn't have pinned that family for kitsch."

She tugged the beer from his hand and pulled him toward the front doors. "Didn't you see Anna Claire's leopard print camisole? Pure kitsch." The prospect of ending the ScanCoin hunt and exposing Anna Claire's schemes put a bounce in her step. "We'll take the gondola."

"Vivi, I hate gondolas." He resisted her pull.

She faltered and looked over her shoulder. "Why?"

"Too exposed."

She waved a hand at the papier-mâché antlers lining the lobby's walls. "This place is like a theme park. What could go wrong?"

"Did you forget Tahoe?"

The sobering reminder of their mountaintop adventures with Johann and Hadley moderated her enthusiasm. Damon warned them a gondola ride left them exposed, but their slope-side adventures landed them in real trouble. "It won't be like that again. Anna Claire isn't a trained killer."

Standing, he sighed. "And to look at you, I wouldn't think you knew how to fire a gun."

She swallowed.

"All right, let's do it," he said. "We came this far, didn't we?"

She squeezed his hand.

The shuttle to the gondola base was nearly empty. "As far as I'm concerned, we're having a civilized conversation with a small business owner." She scooted into the seat near the window. "Mrs. Agrawal either has no clue we're after her daughter, or she'll take one look at us and bolt down the mountainside. Either way, we'll be done by dinnertime."

Crossing his arms, he filled the aisle seat and stared out the window. "I hope you're right."

She rested a hand on his thigh, tapping her fingers as the driver neared the base station. A few jean-clad day-trippers stood at the front of the line, but twenty dollars procured two tickets and an empty pod. She climbed into the pod and made room for Damon.

Resting his elbows on his knees, he tapped a foot. "The last time we climbed a mountain, Horst took a pot shot at Hadley's vehicle. We're sitting ducks up here."

Exhaling, she looked at the scar above his eye. The mark faded, but Horst and Hadley's pseudo-brother, Gary, rotted six feet below ground. "That man wanted to kill Hadley. We want to reclaim your money." She swallowed. "We can go back to the lodge."

He sighed and leaned back. "Did you tell Lieutenant Jayne we're here?"

The gondola swayed in the afternoon wind, and the motion emphasized their vulnerability. "No. Did you?"

He shook his head.

She chewed her cuticle and stared out the window. "We should have taken everything to the police and booked one-way tickets to Hawaii."

Laughing, he pulled her hand form her mouth. "I did tell the police." He cradled her hand in his lap. "Lieutenant Jayne didn't camp out at the Fish House to humor me."

She admired the tangle of their fingers. *We complement each other.*

"Even if the police catch and convict Anna Claire, the courts will tie up the money for years. Investors like me might never recoup our funds."

She looked up. "Investors like you?"

He traced the tendons on the back of her hand. "In Silicon Valley, eight hundred thousand dollars is chump change."

Hearing the weariness in his voice, she squeezed his hand. "You're not a chump."

"Thanks."

Climbing into his lap seemed like the appropriate response. Instead, she looked out the glass lining the swaying pod. Wan sunlight bathed the lodge in pink light. Within a few hours, the sun would set behind the mountain, the shops would close, and the twinkling lights strung through the trees would illuminate the winding paths leading to overpriced restaurants. *I don't care about his money or mine. I care about his happiness.* She turned on the polished plastic seat and faced him. "And you have me."

Looking up, he made eye contact. "I do?"

She smiled and pulled his hand to her lips. "Damon, I want you to know…"

A man in a black parka climbed into the pod at the base station a hundred feet below their gondola car.

Dropping Damon's hand, she stood and stared at the showy form. Amid the cheerful, color-blocked skiers, his dour expression and cropped beard stood out like a mourner at a cocktail party. She gripped the metal grab bar. *I don't believe in coincidences.*

Damon pulled her back from the window. "Vivi?"

She held tight to the bar. "That's the man from the Fish House. The man with the dog outside Anna Claire's house!"

Damon stood and peered through the glass. "You might work too hard."

Shaking her head, she closed her eyes and struggled to count the number of times she saw the man with the beard. "I saw him at the art festival, too." Horrified, she opened her mouth. "What if he's following us?"

Tucking her body behind his, he narrowed his gaze and stared at the lower pod rising into the air. "Anna Claire mentioned heavy investors from the Baltics won't let her end this phase of the investment."

Her pulse skyrocketed. She gasped and covered her mouth. "We're exposing her."

"Fuck." He scanned the small pod.

An emergency lever hung from the ceiling, but stopping the gondola would leave them hanging from a wire like a bobbing holiday ornament.

"We won't get off the gondola," he said.

Pulling out her cell phone, she cursed the lack of reception. "We have to warn Anna Claire. What if he's coming for her and her mother?"

He rubbed a hand over his face. "What's she going to do? Short-change his mojito?"

She gaped. "I'm serious. We're leading him right to her!"

"So am I." He pulled her to the seat and dropped an arm across her shoulders. "The crowd is our friend. Hang tight."

The weight of his arm felt like a manacle. She shifted beneath the pressure, aware of his strength and his reluctance to use it. *Neither of us has a gun to defend ourselves. He was right. We are sitting ducks.* She exhaled and bit the edge of her sunglasses. "I was so eager to lure you into bed that I forgot common sense."

He kissed her hair. "That excuse will get you out of anything."

She smiled, but the strain belied her nerves. "Would you leave your grandmother exposed at the top of a mountain?"

He furrowed his brow. "Nobody messes with Mama Clarke."

"Does Serge know that?"

He raised an eyebrow. "Serge?"

She exhaled. "I made up the name."

The gondola rose up the side of the mountain. Somewhere below, Precious chased fluffy dogs, and a bottle of wine breathed in a decanter in their hotel room. "You're right," she said. "We'll ride the pod back down the mountain and play it cool. Nobody has a problem."

Near the summit, the cable slowed, and the gondola eased into the landing house. A sign proclaimed the eleven thousand foot elevation and offered arrows pointing toward the mountain's amenities. Gusts of wind swung the pod, and she gripped the handrail, feeling seasick.

A uniformed attendant swung open the door. "You guys getting out?"

Biting her lip, she looked at Damon.

He shook his head. "No, man. We're good. Along for the ride."

The attendant stepped back.

A tall woman wearing an ivory snowsuit stepped into the pod and shook out her hair.

Vivian recognized Anna Claire and gasped. She thought she would pull information from Mrs. Agrawal, but finding Anna Claire was one hundred times better. She reached toward the crypto queen and intended to pull her to the seat. They could ride the gondola in perpetuity until Anna Claire fessed up.

Anna Claire ripped off her sunglasses. "You!"

Chapter Seventeen

Vivian clambered to her feet and surged from the gondola car. "Wait!"

Turning her back, Anna Claire marched toward the tiki bar and flipped her the bird.

She propelled herself from the pod, stumbled, and grabbed Damon's hand.

Lulu's Oasis looked like a thatched-roof cabana waiting for an orgy to happen. Sunset frescos graced the walls, coconut palms shielded round, shellacked tables, and pineapple chandeliers hung from the ceiling. A pile of leis waited by the lava rock fireplace, where a bevy of skiers had stripped off their outwear, shucked their boots, and pushed their wool-clad feet as close to the fire as they dared. Their fruity drinks rested on rum barrels, and an iron suckling pig rotated in the flames. Vivian stared at the pig. *How did they get everything up the mountain?*

Anna Claire blew past the empty greeter stand.

The woman standing behind the bar put down the glassware and the polishing rag she held. "What's going on?"

"Nothing, Mom. A few friends."

The woman raised her head and her hands to the sky. "*Guédé*, what has she done now?"

Vivian cocked her head and looked for similarities between the two women. Anna Claire's mother had the same high cheekbones and regal air, but her skin sagged beneath her chin. Despite the cold, she wore a white blouse and skirt and a purple neck scarf. *I thought tiki ran its course in the 1970s, but I bet she makes a killer Mai Tai.*

Anna Claire shoved her phone and her wallet in the pockets of her snowsuit. "Go back to making drinks."

Eyes lined with kohl, Anna Claire's mother narrowed her gaze. "Papa *Guédé*, my Father, take care of me, my home, and my family. Guard my headstrong daughter!"

"Enough!" Anna Claire yelled.

Snapping her head toward her daughter, Mrs. Agrawal pointed her finger. "Anita Claire, you watch your mouth. I am still your mother!"

The skiers by the fire turned their heads.

Anna Claire, nee Anita, flipped her hair over her shoulder. "Like I could forget. Everyone in town calls me Tallulah's daughter. Lulu's Oasis. The Pineapple Pinnacle. I had to reinvent myself to get out of your shadow!"

Ms. Agrawal pulled a worn bead necklace from behind the bar. Closing her eyes, she silently counted the beads and rubbed each talisman with a devoted practitioner's familiarity.

Choosing an adversary, Vivian walked up to the bar. *How many times has she gone up against her headstrong daughter and lost? I wish I had been brave enough to rebel when I was a kid.* She thought of the chat rooms and the late nights when she turned off the desk lamp and dimmed the monitor. *Maybe I was brave.* She laid her hands on the bar. "We're not here to cause problems, Ms. Agrawal."

Ms. Agrawal opened her eyes. "The *Loa* sent you. He will not take a life before its time. He will protect the little ones."

She tilted her head and struggled to make sense of the woman's statements. Behind Ms. Agrawal, a candle illuminated a miniature coffin, sequined bottles, and a skeletal figure wearing a top hat and cane. Cigarettes and a small bottle of white rum stood like offerings to the grinning figure. "I don't understand…"

"Leave her alone." Anna Claire swung her jacket over her shoulders and opened the tiki bar's back door. "She's crazier than you." Walking into the snowy outdoors, she left the open door swinging in the wind.

A gust blew through the establishment and fanned the fireplace flames.

A patron turned from his cocktail. "Shut the door!"

Caught between her desire to soothe the older woman and defend her presence in the bar, Vivian cleared her throat and turned her back to Ms. Agrawal. Calculating the rate of the gondolas, she figured she had ten minutes before Serge-Or-Whoever departed his pod. She looked for Damon.

He stood by the entrance, arms crossed.

He could handle Ms. Agrawal. Biting her lip, she followed Anna Claire out the back door and closed it.

A small window separated her from warmth and the protection of Damon's smile.

Anna Claire stepped into her ski boots. "You don't give up."

Skewing her chin, she stared. "Why would I?"

"Congratulations! You've won. You're at the top of the food chain, and you've come out on top again. Fuck off and go cozy up with your boyfriend while you mock me."

"I don't want to mock you. I want you to honor the terms of your business agreement. I want you to give Damon back the money he invested."

"How much did he invest?" Anna Claire gestured toward the building, shook her head, and yanked a cord from around her neck. "It doesn't matter." She tossed a lanyard holding a USB drive to the ground. "The drive holds a key associated with half a million dollars. Take it."

Picking up the gadget, she rubbed the plastic box between her fingers. In the span of her lifetime, data moved from disk to drives to chips. How could such a short span of time change so much about their lives? Looking through the window, she made eye contact with Damon. *Will this money make him happy?*

He pulled away from the bar and headed toward the exit.

Ms. Agrawal scowled.

She sighed. *One more mama who doesn't like me.* She turned back to Anna Claire. "It was never about the money."

Anna Claire laughed. "Of course, it was about the money."

Handing back the USB drive felt like the wrong move, but she saw a woman in distress and wanted to comfort her peer. "Why did you change your name?"

"People see what they want to see. My father was from the *Vaishyas* Indian caste. They're the farmers, traders, and merchants. Nobody expects those families to handle money. My mother? She fancies herself a Haitian voodoo priestess. Me? I'm Black. I'm Indian. I'm nobody. Anita Agrawal triggers expectations. Anna

Claire fades into the noise and leaves behind the memory of a successful woman. Anna Claire can be whoever you want her to be."

She gripped the drive and stared at the snow. Expectations mattered as much as results. Without the right combination, technical innovations floundered in obscurity. Anna Claire had the chance to reshape the conversation. Instead, she took the money and fled. Vivian vowed to make a different choice.

Damon opened the door and stepped into the mountaintop air. A snowflake drifted on the wind and landed against his cheek.

For a moment, she envied the snowflake, but it melted and left a trail as faint as dried tears. *I never wanted to put him in danger.* She looked up. Accumulated snow bulged over the eave of the roof. The tiki bar's nostalgic décor warmed weary skiers, but the architecture endangered them. "Watch out for the eaves."

He looked up and stepped away from the overhang.

She tossed him the drive and jerked her head toward Anna Claire prepping her skis. "Our friend reconsidered her decisions and decided to give you back some of your money."

The drive dangled from his fingers. "That easy?"

Grinning, she winked. "I'm persuasive."

Anna Claire's quick bark of laughter interrupted the moment.

She frowned and faced the woman. "Do you have something to add?"

Boots in her skis, Anna Claire held two ski poles and shook out her lustrous, black hair. "You're not persuasive, Vivian. You're lucky."

She snorted. "Lucky? You grew up in a winter wonderland. Does your mom know you're a fraud? Does she know her baby girl is on the run?"

"Her name is Tallulah." Anna Claire exhaled and stomped her feet in the compressed snow near the doorway. "And no, she has no idea she's about to lose me."

She stepped forward. Her interest in Anna Claire waxed and waned, but old advice stayed true. *Look for friends who will drink beer with you and watch your dog. I wouldn't trust Anna Claire to do either, but I respect Tallulah's authenticity.* "Tell her goodbye."

Anna Claire held up her hand. "Keep your saccharine advice. If you'd been one gondola pod later, I'd be on my way to Antigua without your prim, condescending advice."

She snapped her fingers. "Antigua! I put my money on Switzerland."

Damon cleared his throat. "You said Liberia."

Looking over her shoulder, she found him leaning against the building. *He always has my back.* She glanced at the overhang.

He rolled his eyes, but he straightened and walked into the sunlight.

She looked past him and scanned the mountaintop homage to colonial nostalgia. A pile of ski boots dripped melted snow onto the carpet. *The skiers don't care if this bar dishonors indigenous people, misuses island iconography, and exploits religious traditions. They want a buzz and warm toes to carry them down the mountain. What does Anna Claire want? A tax haven.* She snorted and turned. "I guess Antigua will feel like home. You'll just be a number there."

Anna Claire slipped the pole straps over her wrists. "Cute."

Struggling for a hook, she estimated she had five more minutes to recoup Damon's cash before the Baltic Bouncer arrived. "Antigua is a tax haven, but it's a small island! No corporate tax, no income tax, no capital gains tax, no withholding taxes"—she lowered her voice—"and no place to hide! You stand out, Anna Claire. You can't disappear into the island crowd."

Turning, Anna Claire stared. "Are you planning to visit and out me?"

Instead of cool confidence, she saw fear in the woman's nervous glances. She jerked her thumb over her shoulder. "Your friend from the Baltics is behind us. I recommend calling the police."

"For the love of..." Anna Claire staked her poles and propelled herself toward the run.

"Are you trying to lose him, too?"

Anna Claire lifted her ski pole and flipped her the bird.

She was beginning to hate that gesture.

Damon whistled. "The two of you should rent a boxing ring."

"Good call. I'd be in bed instead of standing on the top of a freezing mountain. As soon as the sun goes down, we're in trouble. Neither of us is dressed for this kind of adventure." She exhaled and thought about the silk underwear and down vests waiting in her bungalow. "I'd rather be warm."

Torn between abandoning the quest and chasing Anna Claire down an icy hill, she thought about the blue and white tiles in her bathroom. The movie heroines immortalized on the walls danced backwards and in high heels, but their characters waited for their leading men to rescue them. *Times have changed.*

She examined the scatter of equipment lodged in the trampled snow and reached for the smallest pair of ski boots. The wet lining stank of sweat, mildew, and melted snow. Dropping her shoes, she slipped her foot into the first boot, winced, and clicked the line of clasps. "Anna Claire doesn't need shame. She needs help. I don't have a crowd, but two people are better than one."

He grasped her arm. "I have what I need. Don't race down a mountain to rescue a woman you barely know. Stay with me."

The promise of warmth and rum failed to erase the memory of fear in Anna Claire's eyes. "I'll meet you back at the lodge. Call Lieutenant Jayne. He'll find someone local to help her."

"Vivi," he said. "I can't let you put yourself between that woman and a sinister man."

"You're not *letting* me do anything." She pulled free and chose a pair of skis. "I love you, Damon, but you have to let me go."

He widened his gaze. "Now? Now you toss out those words? Right before you leave me behind."

"I'm not leaving you." She winked. "I'm challenging you to keep up." Grinning at his wide-eyed expression, she turned, bent her knees, and chased the figure in the ivory snowsuit. Late afternoon light hindered visibility and cast a pink glow, but she focused on the set of tracks leading from Lulu's Oasis, adjusted her stance, and leaned into the wind.

Anna Claire looked back over her shoulder.

Picking up her right pole, she offered the woman a

cheeky wave and lowered her center of gravity. As she gained speed, the wind blew her hair into her face. *I'm gaining ground.* She shook the cold from her cheeks. *And frostbite.*

Jerking her hips and coming to a stop, Anna Claire sent a spray of snow into the air. Using a pole, she pivoted and headed toward the wilderness area.

Vivian skidded to a stop. The receptionist's warning echoed in her mind. *What if Anna wants to get lost in the wilderness area?* Too far from the summit of the mountain to identify faces, she exhaled and weighed her options. *What's the difference between loneliness and isolation? I can spend the rest of my life organizing my shoes and other people's data, but Damon's the breath of fresh air I didn't know I needed. Whom does Anna Claire have?* She planted her poles and headed for the trees. *As far as I know, it's Tallulah and me.*

Fir needles snagged her clothes. She longed for the puffy insulation of a coat, but she made progress. As she snaked through the trees, whip-like tentacles scored her arms and pulled tears from her eyes. The wind intensified and stung her cheeks. She gritted her teeth and followed tracks cutting across the falling slope. *I should have grabbed a helmet, but sunglasses will have to do.* The evergreens thinned, and late afternoon sunlight cast shadows beneath the cold, rotten corpses of dead trees. Frowning, Vivian focused on her target.

Anna Claire dodged the silver trunks. Glancing over her shoulder, she changed her angle of descent and headed toward a treeless bowl.

The bowl's untouched snow sparkled in the late afternoon light. Vivian angled her skis, came to a stop, and looked for a way to cut off Anna Claire's path.

Should I bomb down the mountain? She scanned the pristine, white field. The skeletal trees glowed, and their eerie, ice-caked branches tinged with light.

Anna Claire's scream ricocheted off the tree trunks surrounding the bowl.

Snapping her head to follow the sound, Vivian listened for a second scream. *Where did she go?*

The windswept, crackling landscape swallowed Anna Claire's echoes.

Scanning the icy bowl, she looked for the sprawled figure of a wipeout, but the wind erased the woman's tracks. Easing forward on the icy field, she strained to hear a voice. "Anna Claire?"

A stinging gust carried away her question.

She raised one ski and tapped the snowpack. The ground felt hollow underfoot, and she swore. *I didn't come down here to lose my life to an avalanche.* Inching forward, she listened for the *whumping* sound of settling snow. "Anna Claire?" The wind slackened, and a faint rotten-egg smell teased her senses. Wrinkling her nose, she eyed the narrow cracks forming around her skis. *I have to return.*

The wind stilled, and a woman's sobs rose above the icy field.

Releasing the borrowed skis, Vivian dropped to her knees and eased forward. "Where are you?"

"In the fumarole!"

Anna Claire's voice sounded closer than she expected. She eased over a small rise, no bigger than a mogul, and gasped.

On the other side of the accumulation, Anna Claire clung to the side of a gaping hole.

The pristine snowpack had collapsed beneath the

woman's weight, but she gripped a protruding tree root like a hanging squirrel holding onto its nut. The smell of rotten eggs intensified, and Vivian pinched the bridge of her nose. "What happened?"

"Pull me up," Anna Claire said.

She considered the situation. *I don't know anything about a fumarole, but she looks good and trapped. Start the countdown until our Baltic shadow appears.* She sat on her haunches. "In a minute."

"What?"

Rubbing her arms, she watched the erratic wind skate over the snow. "The temperature's dropping. Will you last the night? You shouldn't have gone off the trails, Anna Claire. For a woman who grew up on the mountain, you have terrible common sense."

"Pull me up!"

At the urgency in the command, she grinned. "What did you give Damon?"

"Pull me the fuck up! Do you know what this thing is? It's a volcanic vent. If you don't stop pussyfooting around and do your job, I'm going to asphyxiate."

"Language! Are we all animals?"

"If I could reach you, I would slap you upside the head. For the love of God, pull me up."

She rolled her eyes. "I'm not the fucking ski patrol."

"Damn you!"

Maybe. She grinned and looked over her right shoulder. The silver trunks of dead trees suddenly made sense. Mammoth Mountain sat on the edge of a volcanic chain extending to Mono Lake. An earthquake in the late 1980s killed more than a hundred acres of trees, but she figured the ground had never stopped moving. *No wonder the resort roped off this area. Anna Claire's been gone too long.* "I wonder who will get to you first. Serge or the ski patrol?"

Anna Claire screeched.

The frustrated sound could have shattered glass. She frowned and rubbed her ear. "My money's on Serge."

"His name is Patrikas," Anna Claire said.

She grabbed the discarded skis, sat on the waxed plastic, crossed her legs, and gave thanks she chose jeans. "Let's call him Pat."

"Pull me up!"

"What did you give Damon?"

Silence.

"Okay, I'll head down the mountain and report your disappearance somewhere in the vicinity of"—she tapped her lip—"where are we?"

"I gave him a million dollars," Anna Claire said.

Tilting her chin, she considered her advantage. "Why? He only invested eight hundred thousand. Are you in the habit of wearing your wealth?" She peered over the edge of the fumarole. "What else is hanging around your neck?"

"For the love of God! It's money."

She narrowed her gaze. *God won't pull you out of that hole.* "Exactly. How much do you have?"

"Zero dollars."

Using the skis to distribute her weight, she inched to the edge of the precipice and assessed the situation. Anna Claire held onto a buried tree root, but without purchase for her clanking skis, she lacked the ability to climb from the vent. Grinning, she rolled a snowball and tossed it to the left of the woman. "Try again. How much money?"

The woman flexed her fingers. "The ScanCoin website funneled investments into a legitimate cryptocurrency. The value fluctuates with the market. I don't know how much I have."

"How much money does ol' Pat want?"

Anna Claire made eye contact. "All of it."

She whistled. "You picked a mean bedfellow."

"I'm not sleeping with him!"

She kept her expression neutral. "Good call, but how did you get in so deep?"

"It started with an email," Anna Claire said. "He needed help with a real estate transaction. We met for lunch, and he said he wanted to invest without leaving a paper trail."

She thought of the modest ranch house on Bishop Street. "You laundered money through ScanCoin, too? How stupid are you?"

Anna Claire's eyebrows pinched together.

She shrugged. "Give the money back to the original investors."

"I can't."

Vivian formed another snowball.

"The legit currency's blockchain prevents me from knowing who made the investments. I have a lump sum account. It's all or nothing."

With enough resources, Anna Claire could reconstruct an investment roster from client records. She narrowed her gaze. "You never intended to open the exchange."

Anna Claire closed her eyes. "I made mistakes setting up ScanCoin. I gave away too much, too soon." Opening her eyes, she met Vivian's gaze. "I never meant ScanCoin to affect people like Damon."

"People like Damon?"

"Poor people! The help! This was my way of wringing proceeds from the greedy investment community. People who did their research put their money elsewhere. People who feared missing the next rush gave me their money."

She snorted. "Damon's not your pool boy, Anna Claire. He's the most generous person I know. If you spent more time enjoying your life, you'd realize what you had before ScanCoin was more than enough. The leafy, green estate? The thriving payment company? People would kill for those achievements."

Anna Claire closed her eyes. "You should learn to dream bigger."

She looked across the snowy landscape. "Pat would kill for those dreams."

"I know." Anna Claire hung her head.

She thought of Precious, the bungalow, and the flexibility of running Hoat Analytics. Damon's presence in her life balanced the demands of working long hours. As soon as she left the mountain, she would make sure he understood her admission of love. "I understand wanting more, but I won't commit fraud to achieve it."

Anna Claire looked up. "Are you going to pull me up?"

Realizing how much she pitied Anna Claire's decisions, she shook her head. "You got yourself into this hole. You can get yourself out."

Anna Claire rolled her eyes.

Kicking snow into the woman's face felt too much like a schoolyard squabble. *But damn, it would feel good.* "I know Tallulah taught you to believe in yourself."

The woman sighed. "Teaching me to read a contract would have been more helpful."

She smiled. *The right lawyer would have helped, but you pay for what you get.*

The heavy whir of a motor swelled above the crackling, wind-whipped field. Looking up, she saw a lone snowmobiler crest the opposite side of the bowl and cut across the surface. Terrified of avalanches, she waved both hands and signaled the rider to stop.

The figure slowed, changed course, and wove through the tree line.

I hope that isn't Pat. Almost sure Damon drove the machine, she focused on Anna Claire. "Here comes your savior. He's the kind of person who makes life worthwhile. Not money or prestige"—she bit her lip and exhaled—"but kind people, like Damon."

Slowing the snowmobile fifty yards from their location, he hopped off, shook his head, and cupped his hands around his mouth. "Are you two having a damn tea party?"

Brushing the snow from her hands, she sat on her haunches and shrugged. "A little chat. Anna Claire has a few things she'd like to tell you."

"Pull me up!" Anna Claire kicked against the packed snow.

The wall's edge crumbled.

Vivian wanted to reach for Anna Claire's arm and give her purchase, but she would lose her advantage. Swallowing, she looked at Anna Claire and shook her head. "Careful."

"Don't pander to me!" Shifting her weight, Anna

Claire kicked her skis and tried digging them into the walls of the chute. The bindings released, and her skis clattered into the fumarole.

Vivian watched her struggle.

Snow rained over Anna Claire's face. Her sleeves pulled away from her wrist.

Spying a small, inflamed incision on the underside of Anna Claire's wrist, Vivian frowned. She replayed their last encounters and searched for an explanation. Somewhere between the gala and the patio lunch, Anna Claire endured an elective procedure. A sheath of bangles hid the evidence in a casual setting, but against the white backdrop, the swollen, raised mark marred Anna Claire's wrist. *Interesting.*

Swearing, Anna Claire pulled another lanyard from her neck. She swung it up to ground level and looked at Damon.

"How many of those things do you have?" he asked.

"That's the last one! Get me out of here before Patrikas arrives."

He met Vivian's gaze. "Who's Patrikas?"

She grinned and crossed her arms. "Serge."

"Oh." He reached for Anna Claire's arm.

"Not so fast," Vivian said. "Give Damon the rest of the money."

The tree root shifted, and Anna Claire screamed. "I told you that's all I have!"

She shook her head, picked up her ski pole, and poked the woman's exposed wrist.

Anna Claire winced and squeezed shut her eyes.

"Still a little tender?" Looking at Damon, Vivian held out her hand. "Give me your knife."

He narrowed his gaze and reached toward his pocket.

Anna Claire opened her eyes. "You wouldn't."

"Yeah, I would." The snow amplified her whisper. She took the pocketknife, asked Damon to hold her legs, and leaned over the edge of the fumarole. The smell of rotten eggs intensified, and she wondered how Anna Claire withstood the fumes. *Like she has a choice.*

Anna Claire grunted, let go of the root, and swung away from Vivian.

Looking over her right shoulder, Vivian met Damon's gaze and jerked her head toward the direction Anna Claire hung.

He rolled his eyes but angled his body.

Turning back toward Anna Claire, Vivian inched along the opening, repositioned her arms, and trusted Damon's hold. "Hold on tight, Anna Claire."

"This is assault." Anna Claire swatted her arm and slipped farther down the root. Gaze wide, she anchored both hands on her wooden lifeline. Her chin trembled.

"I'll be happy to see you in court, but I doubt you'll make it." Vivian brandished the knife. "Which would you prefer? Die rich or live poor?"

"Neither! I didn't stick a RFID transponder into my arm so I could give it to you."

"Why did you do it?"

Anna Claire squared her jaw. "You wouldn't understand."

Vivian feared she might. Losing everything she worked for could make a woman desperate, but so could love and determination. She considered Anna Claire's position and unleashed Damon's snap blade.

No matter how much empathy she had for Anna Claire's predicament, drawing out the encounter would lead to tragedy. She reached down, grasped Anna Claire's wrist, and endured her slapping protests.

"Let go of me!"

Gritting her teeth, she scored the underside of Anna Claire's arm. Like a ripe avocado, the skin held firm before the knife tip sank into flesh and gave beneath the blade's pressure.

Blood welled and ran down Anna Claire's sleeve.

Vivian's stomach roiled. The woman's bright-crimson liquid dripped into the snowy, white chute. It ran down the fumarole wall like the tears streaming down Anna Claire's face. The wind and biting cold slowed her motions, but she met her opponent's agonized gaze. "I know it hurts." She dropped her voice. "I didn't want our pursuit to come to this point, but I love him."

Anna Claire squeezed shut her eyes.

"Hurry!"

The wind carried away Damon's command.

Dipping the tip of the blade beneath a glass case, Vivian liberated the transponder and trusted blood to adhere it to the blade. Her hand shook, but she raised the knife to the surface, tossed the tool onto the snow, and exhaled. Releasing Anna Claire's arm, she looked over her shoulder and met Damon's gaze. "There's the rest of the money. Now, pull her up."

He tugged her away from the unstable opening and released his hold on her legs.

Spreading her hands wide on solid ground, she cleared her throat. "Please, be quick."

Crawling to the edge of the opening, he grasped

Anna Claire's forearm with one hand and hauled her to the surface.

She scrambled away from Vivian. Blood stained the snow and coated her hand. With tears staining her cheeks, she faced Damon. "We could have been good together."

He picked up the bloody glass case holding the transponder and pocketed it. "I'm willing to bend the rules, but I can't stand cheaters." Rising, he pulled Vivian to her feet and wrapped an arm around her waist.

She leaned into the heat and protection from the wind. The snow shifted, and she grimaced. "We need to go."

Anna Claire clutched her arm.

"Your Baltic friend is coming for you, Anna Claire. He'll kill you for giving us the cash, or he'll kill you for hiding it. Either way, I suggest you run." She unclipped her boots and tossed them at the woman's feet. Ski bindings had to meet industry standards for quality and dimensions, but she refused to be the reason Anna Claire found herself unable to clip into Vivian's borrowed skis. "If you're going to survive, you'll have to work with what you have."

Damon pulled her toward the snowmobile. "You're shivering."

She rubbed her arms and hoped the movement loosened her numbing fingers. "Let's get warm."

Anna Claire twisted her lips and jammed her ski boot into Vivian's skis. "This is cute."

"Cute?" She raised an eyebrow.

"You had a little Nancy Drew adventure, but when the hot chocolate gets cold, what's keeping you two together?"

She laughed. "You spent too much time grooming your image, Anna Claire. Can't you recognize happiness?"

The woman eyed the snowmobile.

"Don't even think about it." Damon shifted his weight.

"Fine." Anna Claire swapped her boots for Vivian's borrowed pair. She gripped the edges and swore. "You have tiny, chicken feet."

She looked to Damon, hoping for a translation.

He shrugged.

Anna Claire snapped the bindings on the boots. She glanced at Damon, shook her head, and rose. "Chicken feet are a charm for a powerful protection. You have more protection than you need. You're greedy."

"That's rich, coming from you." She met Damon's gaze and raised her eyebrows. *Should I do more to help her?*

He patted the pocket containing the implant. "Your call."

Turning to Anna Claire, Vivian sighed. "After you leave this mountain, who will protect you?"

"I don't need protection." She brushed snow from her hair. "Tallulah's not putting on a show. Haitians have made sacrifices to the *Loa* for hundreds of years. In our family, most people ask for health. She asks for money. She taught me how to survive."

Vivian frowned. The tiki bar seemed less contrived. "You can't blame ScanCoin on a voodoo ritual."

"The *Loa* are tired and worn down, like my mother. I won't become her." Anna Claire flipped her hair over her shoulder. "Killing the animal isn't the point of the ritual. Blood transfers the life energy of the sacrifice back to the *Loa*." She pointed a finger at Vivian and Damon.

Anna Claire's teeth, once the proud work of a cosmetic dentist, protruded like a skeleton's maw.

"You are the sacrifice, Vivian Hoat. I won't worry about Patrikas coming after me. He wants the money. I'll send him straight back to you."

She shuddered, glad Damon had her back. "So be it."

Anna Claire staked the borrowed poles. "I deserved ScanCoin." She stepped into the skis and shook out her hair. "One way or another, I'll rise again." With a thrust, she pushed away from the fumarole.

What will Patrikas do when he finds Damon and me? She glanced at Damon. *To save a life, I'll give back every bit of cash.*

Damon walked toward her.

The snow shifted and cracked.

Widening his gaze, he sank to his knees.

Turning she head, she watched Anna Claire traverse the bowl. "Wait!" she shouted above the shifting wind.

Anna Claire's borrowed skis cut a path into the heavy snowpack.

The cracks at Vivian's feet widened, and she heard the resonant sound of snow releasing from the pack. Eyes wide, she sank to her knees and backed into Damon's embrace. He held her close, his arms banded across her chest.

Within seconds, the snowbank in front of her shifted and slid down the bowl. A cloud of powder rose in the sky, being carried up the mountain by the whipping wind. The avalanche grew in size, pulling snow from the rim of the bowl and tugging masses from rooted trees.

She closed her eyes, steady and sure in Damon's arms. The jocular, handsome man she knew had a soft spot for the kids in his neighborhood, but she loved his Robin Hood ways and gave thanks the pursuit of ScanCoin brought them together. *It doesn't matter what's on the USB drives or the bloody chip. We did everything we could to recover his investment.* "She didn't have to go."

He tightened his grip. "You were fierce, Vivi."

"But?"

Turning her in his arms, he lowered his head to her neck and inhaled. A shudder wracked his body.

She felt the tremor and smiled. *I know he cares.*

"Don't do it again," he said.

"Do what? Fight for you? Follow your lead? You led me to this tiki-infested mountain." She expected a laughing release from him.

He shook his head and exhaled against her skin. "Don't leave me without a way to follow you. Don't leave me stranded, wondering if you'll die or live. Don't leave me at the top of a damn mountain in a button-down shirt and a thin-ass sweater."

Storing away the promise of his words, she watched the mountainside collapse. Below the wave of snow, Anna Claire must be skiing for her life. Her muscles tightened, but she had nothing to offer the local businesswoman who made it big and then made life-altering mistakes. Exhaling, she wondered if Anna Claire ever looked back.

Chapter Eighteen

Clinging to Damon's back, Vivian shielded her face and second-guessed her decisions as he navigated trees and drove the snowmobile to the base of the mountain.

Before Damon left the fumarole, he explained Tallulah's silent acceptance.

After listening to a summary of Anna Claire's antics, she wordlessly passed her snowmobile keys across the polished bar.

A ski patroller rushed to the vehicle. "Where's Tallulah?"

"She's fine." Damon tossed the man the key. "She wanted to take the gondola down the mountain."

The patroller shook his head. "Hell of a night for a joy ride."

Vivian pressed together her lips.

Beneath the floodlights, wide-eyed guests stared at the mountain. Teenagers swapped clips and hailed friends. A man clutched two young boys to his body, shaking his head and conversing with his spouse.

Unable to say anything conclusive, she cleared her throat and looked at the patroller. "Anna Claire might be caught in that avalanche."

The man widened his gaze, and he scanned the base station crowd.

"I saw her disappear into the wilderness area and

chased her. The dead trees?"

He turned.

"She skied into that big bowl."

"And you didn't stop her?" the patroller asked.

Rubbing her arm, she sighed. "She's a grown woman."

The man radioed the information to a dispatcher and sighed. "I always admired her."

She shivered and hoped Anna Claire would have a chance to rebuild his admiration. "I expect she made it down the mountain."

He raised his eyebrows.

She swallowed.

Throwing an arm over her shoulder, Damon leaned close. "Do you want to call Lieutenant Jayne?"

She borrowed the patroller's phone, dialed the officer's number, and cupped a hand over her mouth. "It's Vivian Hoat. You were right. Anna Claire's on the run from someone named Patrikas."

The lieutenant sighed. "Did she say anything else?"

Looking at Damon, she swallowed. "She said, 'One way or another, I'll rise again.' "

"So, she's a woman on the run."

Or she's buried beneath the run. A rhythmic tapping came through the earpiece. Like a pencil tapping wood, a soft, swinging pause followed every beat. She imagined a metronome, marking the time, and she wondered if Anna Claire heard the roar of the falling snow. Swallowing, she met Damon's gaze. "I hope so."

The RFID transponder waited in his pocket, as reality-bending as gravity. What once seemed heavy and false now held unknown potential. *But I've never been upright and true.* The wind-whipped ride down the mountain prevented her from discussing her uncertainties. *How much does he have? Does it matter?* She swallowed. The press of base station crowd erased the possibility of privacy.

Putting down the phone, she led him to the idling shuttle bus. She and Damon were the only passengers on the shuttle, but he claimed the seat beside her. "Should we have gone after her?"

"I have too much life left to spend it buried under a pile of snow." Squeezing her hand, he held it fast. "You offered a chance. That's more than she ever gave me."

Looking out the window, she watched clouds gather above the ridgeline and obscure the moon. *We need more than fairy lights to illuminate this night.*

The bus rocked on the plowed roads, but the driver kept two hands on the steering wheel.

Her phone rang.

"Ms. Hoat? This is the receptionist from the lodge. I called you earlier, but the resort's avalanche response jammed the cell towers."

She plugged her ear opposite the cell phone. "Again, please."

"I said, I'm calling about Precious, your dog."

Apprehension coursed through her system. Unprepared bad news, she closed her eyes and gripped Damon's hand. Words failed her. Her lips ached from the pressure of her teeth, and her struggle to contain her fear.

Damon squeezed her hand.

She swallowed. "What's wrong with Precious?"

"She's laconic," the receptionist said.

"Laconic, that's it?" Exhaling, she dropped her

shoulders. *She's an old dog. The lodge is a new place. Minus the eyesight and pancreatic lesions, her vet said she's the epitome of health.*

"I think you should come pick her up from camp."

The woman dropped the cadence of a hospitality worker, and her voice wavered. *Laconic might be a euphemism for barely breathing.* She swallowed. "We're coming."

Damon squeezed her hand and matched her pace from the shuttle bus to the hotel lobby.

Inside the imposing hotel, guests stood in clusters around the fireplace and spoke in whispers. First responders and media occupied an emergency response center created from bar tables and clustered couches. Medical professionals cleaned abrasions and sent serious injuries to the local hospital.

A nurse turned the bloodied leg of a patient. "We're a critical access hospital. Our facility is designed to keep essential services in the rural community."

Moaning, the patient squeezed shut her eyes. "This is critical. I'm about to pass out!"

"It's three stiches," the nurse said.

"Call my mother!"

"We're small and mighty, but we only have seventeen beds. You'll have to take the next flight."

A helicopter whirred overhead, and the lights flicked.

The patient wailed and threw a hand over her eyes. "But I'm afraid of heights!"

Patting the woman's shoulder, the nurse checked her heartbeat and called for a gurney. "You'll live."

Vivian swallowed. "The snowpack traveled farther

than I thought."

Damon scanned the assembly. "The resort missed the brunt of the impact. On a busy winter day, the injuries could have been much worse."

The possibilities of widespread damage made her shudder, but if ScanCoin grew out of her control, community members would need more than stitches. *How many uncles and aunts might have risked their retirement funds for a chance to catch the next big wave?* "I didn't mean to kill her."

He squared her shoulders and dropped his chin. "She triggered the avalanche, Vivi. All she had to do was ask for help."

Asking for help could be a monumental task. She looked over his shoulder. A child sat on a pile of luggage waiting near the bell stand. She wondered where the child's parents were, but then a man walked by the pile and swung the child to his shoulders. She then accepted how simple and fulfilling life could be. "I'm going to find Precious."

"I'll come with you," he said.

"Thanks." She smiled.

The receptionist put down a phone and leaned her hands on the desk, her eyes closed while she drew deep breaths. Fallen mascara collected beneath her eyes.

Vivian wanted to offer the woman a tissue. Instead, she cleared her throat.

The receptionist's eyes sprang open. She blinked and stared. "Yes, can I help you?"

Compared to her late-afternoon cheer, the woman's voice sounded artificial and mechanical. She looked at the woman's name badge. "Hi, Abby. I'm here for Precious."

Abby turned to the pair of double doors. "Don't worry, amid all this chaos, we kept her safe."

"You've had a long shift," she said.

Pausing, Abby made eye contact. "The longest."

Damon held open the swinging double door and allowed her and Abby to pass.

Beyond the barrier, the chaos of the lobby ended, and the solitude of serviceable sheetrock began. A light shone at the end of the hallway. Past more doors, cooks in white hats bustled through a kitchen lined with stainless steel bakers' racks. *I know I don't belong there.* She looked for the gateway to doggy day camp.

The receptionist's radio crackled to life. "Abby, come back to the desk. Abby? Abby, we need you!"

Sighing, Abby raised the radio to her lips.

Vivian shook her head. "Go take care of the other guests. We'll find Precious and bring her up to the room."

"Are you sure?" Abby asked.

She nodded.

Sighing, the receptionist turned and sprinted back to the lobby.

"She's going to be okay." Damon cupped her elbow. "Let's get her upstairs."

The lights flickered. An expletive-laced shout emanated from the kitchen, and she cringed. "I'll follow you."

The doors to the kitchen swung open, and a whiskered man strode down the hallway.

She froze. *Patrikas.*

Following her gaze, Damon stepped in front of her. "Keep your distance."

The man sneered. "I don't believe in coincidences.

356

Anna Claire disappeared, but here you are."

He spoke with the measured precision of someone who learned English late in life. She judged the distance to the lobby and wondered if a scream would permeate the bustle of the lobby.

Damon walked forward. "I don't believe in coincidences, either."

The lights flickered and failed.

Caught in the dark, echoing hallway, she gasped for breath. Reaching for Damon's strength, she caught his shirt and focused on his familiar scent.

He grasped her hand behind his back, squeezed it, and yanked her to the floor.

Breathless, she debated whether to stay crouched against the plastic-streaked vinyl or rise and stand beside him.

"You strike me as a man who likes to make threats," Damon said.

Patrikas laughed.

The hollow sound echoed in the dark hallway. Fear crept up her spine, colder than the mountain wind. The icy apprehension compelled her to run for the visibility of the crowd. *I'll call for help. I believe in help.*

"In my line of work, I don't make threats. I take action," Patrikas said.

The lights flicked, and she saw the two men standing ten feet apart.

Braced for action, Patrikas lunged and threw forward his weight, crashing into Damon's steady strength.

Damon pivoted, caught Patrikas's arm, and slammed him against the wall. "Take your actions back to whatever frozen tundra you call home." He pushed the man to the floor, raised his fist, and snapped his head to the side. "Whatever shit threats you spouted to Anna Claire don't faze me. I don't hide behind rent-a-cops." Hauling Patrikas to his feet, he rammed him against the sheetrock. "If I see you again, you're dead."

Blood dripping from his mouth, Patrikas sneered. "You're one man. Where I come from…"

Damon's fist slammed into the man's stomach. "We both have friends."

The lights failed again, and she heard the heavy breathing of two men. Rising, she inched her way toward the lobby, prepared to call for help.

"And my friends have nothing to lose," Damon said.

A heavy thud and the shriek of skidding plastic paralyzed her. An object clattered to the floor and glass shattered.

Patrikas grunted and swore, his accent thick and unintelligible.

Footsteps retreated down the hall.

She breathed, senses alert, wondering which man remained.

"Vivi," Damon said.

Her heart soared. The lights flickered on, and she ran toward him, throwing her arms around his neck. "Are you okay?"

He cupped her face.

As he caught his breath, his chest rose and fell.

The heavy rhythm felt as steady and powerful as the motors on the mountain. Repulsed and drawn to his strength, she leaned into his touch and swallowed. "You're always careful with me. The kids."

He closed his eyes. "I'm careful when I need to be.

Without a reputation, you don't survive in EPA."

Pulling back, she met his gaze. "You're working to change that fact."

He pulled away and braced his hands on his knees. Breathing hard, he swallowed. "I am."

"Damon." She looked at the floor. Anna Claire's confident smile beamed from a magazine cover. Shattered glass surrounded the plaque, and a smear of blood marred the picture. "You're doing a good job."

He shook his head and sighed. "Let's get Precious."

"But Patrikas…" She gestured toward the doorway.

"Won't come back." He walked to the set of doors leading to the courtyard. Throwing open the door, he scanned the courtyard and whistled.

Precious raised her head and whimpered.

Striding to the dog, he lifted her in his arms and returned to the hallway.

Her steady companion lacked her usual enthusiasm, but she burrowed her head into Damon's armpit. "Let me have her."

He shook his head.

Walking up to the pair, she stroked the dog's head and pressed her face into Precious's fur. The sweet, heady scent calmed her breathing. "I didn't plan to leave you so long."

Wriggling in Damon's grasp, Precious shoved her white snout against Vivian's face.

Pulling back, she smiled. Precious's strong eye twitched. With her thumbs, she stroked the animal's ashen mask.

Precious raised her head and pressed against the gesture.

She smiled. "Does that feel good?"

The animal whimpered.

"Let's get you upstairs," she said.

Damon shifted the dog's weight. "She's probably lonesome."

Precious closed her eyes.

She felt the animal's rising chest and smiled. "I guess the Pomeranians weren't any fun. That's okay, girl. We'll take care of you."

Nobody in the lobby blinked as she, Damon, and the dog walked toward the elevator bank.

The lights flickered again.

"Can somebody fix the damn generator?" a man shouted.

His wife pulled him back to the couch. "Get Larry a drink."

She smiled and thought of her grandparents. The old movie posters in her bathroom charmed visitors, but she wanted to replace them with portraits of the people who raised her. *They may not have been perfect, but they taught me to recognize a hero when I found one.*

The suite she rented on the fourth floor boasted a spacious wood and stone-clad bedroom with a king-sized bed, a sitting room with a roaring fire, and a gleaming marble bathroom with a soaking tub. *It's not my bungalow, but I admit the lodge's architect deserves her awards.*

Damon lowered Precious to a loveseat near the fireplace.

Settling on the cushions, she guided the dog's head to her lap.

Precious exhaled.

After a few minutes of petting the dog and

whispering reassurances, she rose. "I think she's okay."

Damon wrapped his arms around her waist. "Are you?"

She turned in his embrace and sighed. "Maybe." Resting her head against his chest, she gave into the doubt and anxiety shadowing her decisions. "I wouldn't have left Anna Claire at the fumarole."

He nuzzled her hair. "I know."

Looking up, she met his gaze. "Do you?"

"You're generous and loyal, Vivian. Even to a woman who you barely know."

She frowned. "I took all her money."

He laughed. "It wasn't really her money. Remember the kids."

"I valued honesty." She sighed. "Now I'm a thief, an imposter, and a trespasser."

"Was it for a good cause?" he asked.

She swallowed. *It was for love.* "Can you respect someone who's inconsistent?"

"Vivi, you teased me with clothes and underwear. I respect the hell out of that. Your willingness to climb a tree and retrieve a drone?" He exhaled. "That isn't the type of lie that matters in a life."

"But it's a slippery slope. The next thing you know…"

He sighed and pulled back. "You're selling stolen goods."

She gasped and grabbed his arm. "It's not like that."

"Because I had no other options?"

She straightened. "Because you were trying to do something good!"

Shaking his head, he tipped up her chin. "That

terrible wig? You were trying to protect me."

"I wanted to be there."

He cupped her cheek. "I know."

The tenderness of his gaze unnerved her. *Loving him erodes my principles. How far will I slip to keep him by my side?* Pulling back from his grasp, she reached into his pocket and retrieved the blood-caked hardware. The USB drives and the transponder felt too light for the weight of their decision. "Anna Claire's greed erased the identities of the investors. Who doesn't keep records?" She sighed. "We don't even know how much currency you have."

He closed her fingers over the hardware. "How much we have."

She placed the drives and the transponder on a smooth, wooden table. "It's your money, Damon. Whatever is on that hardware is yours. The next decisions are yours."

Separating the drives from the chip, he pulled them close and left the glass-encased transponder in the middle of the table. "You put together the pieces."

Wincing, she remembered scoring Anna Claire's skin and the give of her flesh. "How much did she collect?"

"Millions."

She met his gaze. "How many millions?"

"Does it matter?" He braced his hands on his hips.

She considered her mental calluses. Anonymous data insulated her from the pain of ten dollars and the pleasure of ten billion. *Zeros are numbers on a screen. Until you have a goal in mind, a few extra zeros hardly matter.* "I thought you had a poet's heart, but I didn't realize how much strength poetry requires. You keep putting yourself out there and trying to do something good. The little decisions. The value judgments." She sighed and met his gaze. "I want you to keep pursuing your dreams, Damon. I love your optimism."

He released her hand. "I thought you loved me."

"I do!" Spinning away from the table, she sat next to Precious and anchored a hand in the dog's silky fur. The animal's pants sounded louder and raspier than usual. She stroked the dog's ears. "Are you too hot?"

Precious lolled her head.

She frowned. "Something's wrong."

"I know. The minute I feel like I have you, you pivot and pull back."

She frowned. "Something's wrong with Precious."

Lifting her head, Precious edged off the loveseat. Her hind legs trembled.

It's old age.

The dog collapsed to the floor and fell to the side. Her body jerked and stiffened.

"Precious!" Vivian dropped to the floor and spread her fingers over the dog's heaving side. Muscles beneath the animal's skin twitched, and drool pooled below her mouth. "Come on, old girl! I'm right here."

Damon crouched beside her. "Do you want me to call her vet in Palo Alto or the local one?"

"Call Palo Alto." She stroked Precious's ears and hoped the seizure passed before serious injury occurred. The sweet, old dog came into her life without warning and taught her to take open-ended risks. Analytics yielded financial success, but her life was empty until she learned to make room for Precious's affectionate kisses.

Whining, Precious went limp.

Amy Craig

"I'm here." Monitoring Precious's racing heartbeat, she waited until it stabilized before she rose for a bowl of cool water and wet a towel. Returning to her pet's side, she rubbed Precious's paws to cool her down and whispered all the things waiting back home. "The squirrels and the dog walker will both miss you." She closed her eyes and fought tears. "I'll miss you. I didn't know how much I needed a companion until you leapt onto the couch and cracked open my stubborn heart."

Precious closed her eyes, and the shaking subsided.

Laying a hand on her chest, she waited for Precious's breathing to calm. "That's it, my lovely. Ride it out."

Damon ended his call and rubbed the short, soft furs on Precious's nose. "The vet said one seizure might be old age. If she has another one tonight, bring her to the local emergency vet. If she stabilizes, he'll see her on Monday morning at your house."

Releasing her breath, she laid her head against Damon's shoulder. "Thank you. I couldn't leave her to make the call." She swallowed. "What if she died at doggy day camp without me?" The thought broke her heart in two. "No wonder you don't want kids. I'm falling apart over a dog. I'm not sure I can handle anything more."

He settled against the base of the loveseat and pulled her between his legs.

Cradled within his arms, she kept one hand on Precious, but she let her body relax against his chest.

"It's not that I don't want kids," he said. "It's that I'm not sure I'd be a good father."

She rolled her eyes. "Don't be ridiculous. The scholarship fund? The neighborhood kids? They love

364

you."

He kissed her temple. "They love what I do for them."

Tilting her face up, she watched the firelight cast shadows on his features. "Do you think they're using you?"

Smiling, he shook his head. "No more than any other kid would do. I learned to wheedle candy out of Mama Clarke before I was two. Kids play adults; it's what they do."

She sighed. "The army of foster children?"

He rested his chin on top of her head. "Hmm."

"You're scared." She closed her eyes, blocking out Precious's easy breathing and the flickering light that could soften every sin. "You don't want to love your own kids."

"Parenting doesn't require love," he said.

He's wrong, but love comes in many forms. She thought of the hours spent watching movies with her grandmother and the trips to the rifle range with her grandfather. Every Friday, her exhausted mother put down the groceries and asked about her day. "Yes, it does."

He sighed and dropped his head to the upholstered seat.

The loss of contact created a void. She held her posture and tried not to break into a million pieces.

"Mama Clarke is my daddy's mother," he said. "When I was eighteen months old, he died of a heart abnormality."

She shifted, turning between his legs so she could monitor Precious, but she focused her attention on him.

"The abnormality's called hypertrophic

cardiomyopathy." He cleared his throat. "The walls of his heart thickened until they disrupted his heart's electrical system. The coroner called it Sudden Cardiac Death. It's an inherited condition, but nobody knew he had it. Every year, Mama Clarke reminded my pediatrician to check my heart."

"I'm sorry." The threat of losing him worried her, but Mama Clarke's awareness ensured the care he needed. Faced with life's brevity, she wondered how much the diagnosis encouraged him to bend society's rules.

"I kind of remember him. Pictures and stuff fill in the gaps." He smiled. "He was a boxer."

She swallowed. "And your mom?"

Sighing, he bit his lip. "She was a bartender at the club where my daddy boxed. She skimmed cash off every few transactions. Or, instead of putting cash into the register, she voided transactions and put the cash in her pocket. I guess she figured the manager would never check the register tapes."

"The manager caught her?"

He shook his head. "When the bills for her hair and nails never added up to what she brought home, my daddy confronted her. The next day, she ran off with another boxer." He sighed. "What's the value of an infant and a man who loved her?"

She swallowed and imagined a woman in a hot-pink eighties dress holding an infant. Damon shied away from the physical similarities between Shani and his mother, but he still gave his childhood friend the money she needed. *I don't know how many people would be strong enough to make that distinction. Playing Robin Hood doesn't make him the town sheriff, but it gives him the opportunity to see the good in people and reward them.* She stroked his cheek. "Her mistakes don't reflect on you."

Cupping her hand, he smiled. "Don't they? My heart's broken. My DNA's wired for mistakes. So many kids in the world need help. Why would I have my own?"

Rising to her knees, she cradled his face and fought the dejection in his voice. "Because you're an optimist."

The corner of his mouth ticked up. "I'm trying to be predictable."

She snorted. "I'm predictable."

"We'll be a matched set."

"Don't be ridiculous. If I wanted predictability, I would date Michael."

He straightened and furrowed his brow. "Who the hell is Michael?"

"Nobody. I don't want a cardboard copy of myself. I want the generosity and spontaneity you bring to my life."

"Does the court jester get an allowance?"

She stared. *Why won't he admit he loves me? Predictable men don't squirrel away every cent they have to help neighborhood kids go to school. They don't choose people over the mindless hum of the television.* "Sometimes predictable isn't enough."

He closed his eyes. "I'll never be enough, will I?"

The weight of the world might subdue his optimism, but she could help him carry the load. She jabbed her finger into the middle of his chest. "I told you I love you."

He remained motionless.

Cocking her head, she jabbed him again.

He captured her hand and pressed it flat against his chest.

His heart beat beneath her palm, and she focused on the steady rhythm.

"I heard you," he said. "You love a pockmarked high school graduate with a dubious heart."

Pulling a hand free, she sat between his legs. "You don't believe me."

He smiled and exhaled. "You didn't love the man you knew before my arrest. What makes you love me now? Bigger muscles and a loaded wallet."

She glanced at his crotch and arched an eyebrow. "I've never heard it called that before, but sure, it helps."

He worked his jaw but remained silent.

Crossing her arms, she sighed. "Three years ago, if we got drunk and indulged in a one-night stand, I might have developed a thing for you."

He lifted his head and worked his jaw. "A thing?"

"A thing. Except I was dating someone else, and you were selling stolen goods out of a convenience store. Neither of us was ready to love one another."

"I've never needed alcohol to be with you."

"But you did need me to fall for you." Rising, she walked across the room and turned off the fireplace. "Why didn't you tell me how you felt three years ago?"

He sighed.

"You know what I love most about you, Damon? Your hopefulness, your smile, and your ability to see the best in people. But what about yourself? What the hell is your plan? Congratulations!" She threw up her hands. "You won the prize. What next?"

Precious lifted her head.

Damon frowned.

"Do you know what you want, or do you close your eyes and fade to black?"

He rubbed a hand over his face. "Vivi, I never thought we'd get this far."

"When are you going to believe in yourself?" A lump grew in her throat, and she dropped her voice to a whisper. "I believe in you."

Gazes locked, Damon blinked.

Precious whined.

Walking to Precious's side, she bent her knees to lift the old dog.

Damon rose to his feet. "Here, let me help you."

Shaking her head, she lifted the animal in her arms and stared. "I don't need your help, Damon. I need your love." Cradling the dog like an infant, she carried her to the bedroom and laid her on the bed.

Stopping at the doorway, he braced his arms on the frame. "We had a good thing going, Vivi."

"We had different goals in mind. I opened my life, and you claimed a trophy."

Gripping the frame, he flexed his muscles. "That's not how it is."

Walked toward him, she steeled herself for action. Damon's scent and the comfort of his presence called to her, but she refused to change her life for someone too afraid to change his. "You can't trade your life for the lives of those kids, for me, or for anyone else." She scanned his body, torn between her need to feel his arms wrapped around her and her need to protect her feelings. "I don't need your wallet or your dick, Damon. I need your heart."

Biting his lip, he closed his eyes. "My heart is broken. I can't give you everything you need."

"That's not true," she said. "Your heart's the most valuable thing you have, but I need you to take a risk."

He stared. His right eye twitched.

She waited for two beats, then three. "On me."

With one foot in each room, he weathered her silence.

Shaking her head, she turned her back on him and walked into the bathroom. *I thought he had hope, but the hope was for everyone else.*

Precious whined.

"I don't know if I can do it," he called from the front room.

Standing in front of the bathroom mirror, she braced her hands on the vanity and closed her eyes.

He cleared his throat. "Love isn't the ultimate goal."

It is for me. She waited. *Why else would we do anything at all? Children. Careers. Hobbies. People love the things in their lives that bring them joy. They hold up their achievements and shoulder their burdens for the promise of a brighter day. Until I was an adult, I didn't realize I wanted a happy ending.* She met Damon's gaze in the mirror. *Now it might be too late.* "Some of us get fewer years than others," she said. "Make them count."

He turned and walked from the room.

She staggered to the bed and turned toward Precious. *I need someone who can return my love.* Rubbing the dog's silky ears, she sighed. *What's better? Loving a man I can't have or living alone?*

Precious raised her head and nosed her hand.

Running her hand through the dog's silky fur, she shuddered and buried her face against Precious's ruff. "Thanks for pulling through, my lovely. Few people can stand losing everything at once."

Chapter Nineteen

Vivian woke up in the suite and found Precious breathing easily, but Damon had gone. A note by the phone said he would be in touch. She called him, but his line went to voice mail. *He's always the one to leave, but what if that's the right move? What if he can't do it?* She scanned the empty hotel room. *The isolation still hurts.*

She drove home, clutching the wheel and trusting autopilot to keep the car in the lane. She pulled up in front of the bungalow and heard Precious whimper. "We're home." Opening the door to the backseat, she lifted the geriatric dog in her arms and toddled toward the front door. Thankful for the keypad entry, she shifted Precious, punched in the code, and carried the dog to the couch. White slipcovers protected her oversized furniture, but she wondered if indelible marks and silky dog fur were the hallmarks of a happy, well-lived life.

She scanned the weathered wood and the cool leather pieces in the room. Damon's bright colors and affable grin shone brighter than the muted color palate she picked out. *I shouldn't invest in art. I should invest in the people who I love.* The bungalow never looked so empty.

A day later, Precious burrowed her snout under new throw pillows.

She stroked the dog's back, grateful to feel her steady breaths. *Damon won't call.* Closing her eyes, she dropped her head to the back of the couch.

A stiff wind blew a twig against the windowpane.

Precious raised her head and barked.

Staring at the front door, she opened her senses and listened for menace, but she failed to find a threat.

The next day, she reprogrammed the landscape lighting, fired the dog walker, and blocked out a month of afternoons. Spending warm evenings in the state parks felt like an indulgence, but Precious needed exercise, and she needed space. *I need time away from a computer screen and the pull of data. I need generosity and spontaneity.* She tried not to think about Damon. *I need to get on with enjoying my life.*

The next day, she put on a dress.

Lieutenant Jayne called her and asked for a meeting at new Palo Alto police station.

His clipped request hardened her resolve. Prepared to face the consequences of her actions, she pulled out her favorite heels and freshened her lipstick. Leaving Precious dozing on the couch, she left the bungalow.

The boxy, new public safety building on Sherman Avenue looked like a throwback to Nor-Cal Mod, but she appreciated the city's efforts to enhance the street canopy and co-locate public services. Smiling for the receptionist, she stopped. "I'm Vivian Hoat. Can you provide directions to the elevators?"

"Around the corner," the man said. "Go through the metal detectors, get a sticker, and head on up."

"That's it?" she asked.

He put down his newspaper. "Did you want to visit the jail cells?"

"I'm good." Smiling, she recalled the day she fell out of Anna Claire's tree. A trespassing charge lingered at the end of her worry list, but she had a hard time caring about the threat. *I doubt Anna Claire will show up to my court date.*

Following the receptionist's instructions, she rounded the corner and joined the line of people waiting for security clearance. Pushing down her cuticles, she sighed and checked her phone for missed calls and texts. Shoulders back, she pressed her lips together and looked toward the front of the line.

Damon's broad shoulders passed through the metal detectors.

Every fiber of her being compelled her to push aside the people in line and wrap her arms around his waist. *We're headed to the same place.* She drew a deep breath. *Patience. I only need patience.*

The line moved slower than geriatrics at a buffet.

Throwing her purse into the plastic bin, she stood before the detector. Stepping in place, she felt torn between her visceral need to comply and her urgency to chase down Damon. Catching sight of him eroded her defenses and exposed her raw, vulnerable regrets about the way they ended their time together.

The portal officer waved her through the detector.

She snatched her purse from the screening officer. "Thank you."

He held up his palms. "You look like your tail is on fire and your ass is catchin'. Best be gettin' on with it."

His twang came straight from the Central Valley. She stumbled, searching for her grandfather's kind, blue eyes. "Excuse me?"

He dipped his head. "Must be something important.

If I were you, I wouldn't dawdle."

"Dawdle." *We're probably related.* Shaking off her confusion, she hurried after Damon. Her heels clicked on the polished terrazzo. Rushing to the elevator bank, she stuck a hand between the closing doors.

Damon grabbed the door, and the elevator shuddered. He made eye contact and widened his eyes. "You shouldn't do that."

"I don't mind the risk." She slid into the chamber and stood beside him.

He crossed his arms in front of his chest. "You should."

The other people in the elevator shifted and made room for her presence.

"Where are you going?" She resisted the urge to lean close and savor his proximity.

He kept his gaze trained on the door. "Second floor."

"What? Lieutenant Jayne's on the third floor."

Shifting his stance, he looked over and frowned. "Are you in trouble? Again?"

She stepped closer, closing the allotted space. "I assumed he wanted to talk about Mammoth Lakes." Inhaling his scent, she promised to offer the *Loa* an entire family of goats or chickens. She remembered Anna Claire's threat and shuddered. *Maybe not chickens.* She put a hand on the small of his back.

He flinched.

The gesture seared her raw, vulnerable nerves. Dropping her hand, she clasped both hands in front of her heart. "I'm sorry."

"I know…" He closed his mouth and pressed together his lips.

The door opened.

Stepping forward, he paused. A deep inhalation raised his shoulders, but he kept his gaze fixed on the second floor foyer. "Not yet, Vivi."

Maybe never. Numbed from the encounter, she rode the elevator to the third floor and kept her appointment with Lieutenant Jayne.

"You're late," he said.

She tried not to think of Damon. *Why would he be here? Why would he shy away?* She sighed. *I wasn't ready to see him; I should have ignored the call and gone hiking.*

"Have you heard anything?" he asked.

Looking up from the polished concrete, she met Lieutenant Jayne's gaze. "Pardon?"

He crossed his arms. "Anna Claire disappeared in Mammoth Lakes."

"In the avalanche." She watched the news like a retiree afraid to leave the couch.

Picking up a sheath of papers, he raised an eyebrow. "No bodies were recovered."

"Check the crevasses. She could be anywhere."

"Her mother isn't worried."

"Tallulah," she whispered the name like an incantation.

He nodded. "Do you think Anna Claire made contact?"

Staring out the window, she considered the question and the downtown buildings. *So much innovation and ingenuity calls this city home, but Anna Claire never settled here.* "Follow her belongings. The day I fell from the tree, she had packers assembling her household goods. Where did they go?"

"She didn't say?"

She shrugged and turned away from the window. "Antigua."

He wrote down the name. "It's a small island."

"I know."

He cleared his throat. "You don't seem like yourself, Ms. Hoat."

"Why is Damon here?" She made eye contact. "Did you know he would be here?"

"Something about unclaimed property." He raised his eyebrows. "If he found money or other valuable property, he can turn it in to the police. If the true owner has not claimed the object in ninety days, it's his to keep."

She marveled that a microchip loaded with computer code could shape so many lives, but Damon's adherence to the rulebook intrigued her more than the chip's crypto cache. "Ninety days is a lifetime."

Lieutenant Jayne flicked something from his finger. "Lifetimes count."

She smoothed her dress. *I don't care if Damon loses the money. I told him how I felt. The rest is his call.* Looking up, she met the lieutenant's gaze. "Do you need anything else from me?"

He worked his jaw. "If Anna Claire makes contact, I want you to come to me first. Not Damon. Not Johann. Whatever threat prompted that woman to hire security and flee the country is too dangerous for civilian resolution. Chances are, you won't come out ahead."

"And you told Damon the same thing?" she asked.

"Damon isn't the person who took off down the mountain like she had something to prove." He cleared his throat. "His words, not mine."

The only thing I want to prove is how much I love him. She remembered his flinch in the elevator. *He might never be capable of loving me back, and that has to be okay.* She left the police station, went home, and collapsed on the couch next to Precious.

The dog nuzzled her side.

Raising her head, she looked at her pet. "No news."

Precious laid down her head.

"We'll be okay." Looking out the window at the shifting oak canopies, she sighed. *Won't we?*

****

A month later, the barista at the fair-trade coffee shop set down a mug of boiling water and a wrapped tea bag.

Vivian took the items. "The first week I started coming here, you learned my order."

Blushing, the barista nodded.

She glanced at the woman's nametag. "Thanks, Emily."

"Anytime, Ms. Hoat. I heard you're buying the building."

She nodded and dunked the tea bag. In this town, word traveled fast, and fortunes rose and fell on whispered tips. "I hope it's a fruitful investment."

"And the coffee shop?"

"Completely necessary," she said.

Emily pumped a fist in the air.

Purchasing the office space provided workspaces and meeting rooms, but daily collaboration was the real draw. Revamping the kitchen into an open-concept lounge space would add cost, but she wanted staff to chat over coffee and build community connections.

Work should be about more than trend lines and endnotes. When they needed a change of scene, the downstairs coffee shop would beckon.

She dropped the tea bag into the hot water and surveyed the bustling coffee shop. People hunched over laptops, hands pressed to earpieces to keep track of a call. *VPN lets people work from home, but every employee at Hoat Analytics claimed a desk. Availability is charming, until you're trying to focus and accomplish intensive work.* She thought about the weeks she and Damon spent chasing Anna Claire. *It wasn't meant to be. Work can be enough.*

Outside the coffee shop, contractors drilled anchor points for a small park. The owner of the shop loved her suggestion, and he threw his small business weight behind her finances. The city's standard designs allowed for trees in planters, bistro tables, and shade umbrellas. She would miss the parking spaces adjacent to the building, but she recognized the value of roots. If her discussions with the city played out, she would replace the lost parking spaces, plant the trees, and make the small park permanent. The contractor's jackhammers shook the foundation of the building, but it held strong. She sipped her tea. *It had better hold. Do people appreciate the cost of seismic retrofits?*

Accomplishments and a practiced smile kept her moving through the day, but at night, she broke down and mourned what she had with Damon. The screech owl returned with a mate, taking up residence in a cavity near the top of an oak. Each night, the pair's even-pitched trills brought tears to her eyes. She wiped away the dampness, sighed, and rooted for the pair.

A white satin dress and a bouquet felt like the

wrong end goal, but she missed him. She wanted his teasing laughter, his steady hand, and his attention to detail in her life. Closing her eyes, she cupped the hot mug of tea. *I want his steady hands on me. What will I do if I run into him again?* She sighed. *I'll either turn away or win an acting ward. I'm fine. We're fine.* Her stomach clenched, and heartburn seared her throat. *Everything's fine.*

The Steadman lawyer met her in the main conference room. His white linen shirt and golden tan looked like a summer advertisement. "I want to move forward. How do we reach an agreement that satisfies both parties?" She raised a hand. "Without revisiting IP."

Terry checked his notes. "A partnership."

"Every contract is a partnership."

She thought of Damon. Instead of worrying what she could do for him, she should have focused on what she could do *with* him. "The Steadman Group developed a mobile-centric Carbon Management Platform for small-scale farms, but the product could help a number of small businesses improve efficiency and sustainability. If my team can capture the data, your team can present it in a user-friendly format. We're stronger together, but we can't cannibalize each other."

"The Steadman Group isn't at risk."

She played with an earring. "Then why have three of your competitors booked time on my calendar?"

Terry paled and scooted his chair from the table. "I'll bring your offer back to my client."

"And the lawsuit for breach of contract?"

He paled. "A misunderstanding, I'm sure."

She narrowed her gaze.

He raised his palms. "He'll withdraw it."

"Good." She waved down Michael passing in the hallway. He walked with a slight limp, but as the swelling receded, his swagger returned.

Michael popped his head into the room. "You ready?"

She aimed a closed-mouth smile at the lawyer gathering his papers. He had known her long enough to recognize a dismissal. She recalled the last time she booted him from the conference room and hoped today's conversation would stave off a third occurrence.

Terry departed.

Michael claimed the man's spot. He wriggled in the seat.

"Toasty?"

"Like a furnace!"

Valentina and Isaac entered the room and chose seats at the conference table.

Based on their proposals, she promoted the employees and sketched out divisions within Hoat Analytics. Michael led Machine Learning, Valentina carried Data Monetization, and Isaac headed Predictive Analytics. Of the three divisions, his held the most ambiguity, but she trusted him to stay abreast of emerging technologies. "Tell me what you need, and we'll be done for the day."

Thirty minutes later, her assistant opened the door. "You have one more appointment."

She checked her calendar and frowned at the unscheduled interruption. Work-life balance mattered more to her than ever. "It's almost four o'clock."

"This appointment's waiting downstairs."

Rising, she walked to the window, parted the

blinds, and saw Damon standing on the sidewalk with Precious's leash in his hand. Her pulse skyrocketed. Taking a deep breath, she looked at the dog. *Traitor.*

Precious barked and head-butted Damon.

Focusing on him, she let a smile warm her face. Friendship and affection matured into love, but she spent weeks stitching together her reserve, and he showed up with her damn dog. *He's playing dirty.*

Michael ushered his colleagues from the room.

Turning from the window, she resumed her professional demeanor. "Thank you for everything you've done."

His cheeks colored, and he walked toward the door. Turning, he looked over his shoulder. "Can Precious come up to visit?"

She smoothed her dress. "Why not? I own the building."

Michael grinned.

Alone in the conference room, she paced, closed her eyes, and exhaled. *One final chance.*

Her assistant opened the door and admitted Damon and Precious to the conference room.

Meeting his gaze, she smiled with the politeness and professionalism that enabled her to build Hoat Analytics into a trusted firm. *We offer the right tools, the right metrics, and the right applications to understand small business data.* She repeated the mantra in her head and straightened her shoulders. *My team and I built something that makes us proud.*

He released the leash and leaned against the closed door.

"Hello, my lovely," she said.

Precious bolted past her and sniffed every corner of

the room.

You're definitely sleeping on the floor tonight. Out of excuses, she focused on Damon. The lines at the corners of his eyes looked deeper, but his skin shone beneath the overhead lights. He sported jeans and the nascent shadow of a bead. "You forgot to shave."

He offered her a faint smile and rubbed his jaw. "You know me. I like to keep things fresh."

Would it be unprofessional if I jumped into his arms and wrapped my legs around his waist? She eyed the frosted glass partitions, took a calming breath, and gestured toward the table. "Have a seat."

Pulling out a chair, he settled his frame onto the black leather and steepled his fingers. "I have a proposition."

She raised an eyebrow and reclaimed her chair. The table's expanse gleamed like the Pacific. Unable to see the other side, she shifted and hoped happiness waited over the horizon. *I'm a hell of a first mate, but Damon has to build the ship.*

"Do you know how much money Anna Claire had on that chip?" he asked.

She tossed and turned, trying to answer that question. *If half a million dollars merited a USB drive, what amount of money earned a place under Anna Claire's skin? Does the amount matter?* She met Damon's gaze. "More than a million dollars."

He nodded. "You suggested a nonprofit."

"Nonprofits come with several advantages…"

He held up a hand. "I'm suggesting a bank and a trust."

Leaning back, she crossed her arms and considered his suggestion. "A bank."

"A bank that reins in overhead and makes low-interest loans to qualified community members."

She snorted at the rose-colored proposition. "Good luck finding a board of directors."

He grinned. "I have a few people in mind."

She uncrossed her arms and gripped the armrests. "Who?"

"The people who understand what I'm trying to do. The people I trust with the lawful, informed, efficient, and able administration of a nonprofit institution."

"Nonprofit banks don't exist," she said.

He tapped his temple. "I did some research."

"Is that what you do? You go off for a while and formulate plans?" The ache in her heart tripped her control. "Maybe I should open a library."

He spread his fingers on the table. "I won't disappear again."

Sighing, she stood and turned away. "Anna Claire's stash wasn't enough, was it? You need north of fifty million dollars to sustain a bank's overhead."

He laughed. "It was enough."

Biting her lip, she wondered if he was in over his head.

Laying a hand on her shoulder, he turned her and held her at arm's length.

She struggled not to collapse in his arms.

"I hope community members become depositors," he said, "but the bank will invest the money from Anna Claire."

To help him, I endangered that woman's life. Was I really trying to help myself? The guilt gnawed her stomach. Her first, indignant impression of Anna Claire evolved into a curious appreciation. She sorted the woman's actions into columns of rights and wrongs, but shied away from her gray position. Looking up, she met Damon's gaze. "You'll have to tell everyone what happened."

He dropped her arms and shrugged. "Why get the lawyers involved? Without proof of investment, nobody can redistribute ScanCoin's money back to the investors. What's keeping every person in California from making a claim? Anna Claire funneled the money into a black hole. Her website was like a magnet; the closer you got, the stronger the pull, but she always intended to run."

She cleared her throat. "Toward the end, I wanted to be friends with her."

"Send your Christmas cards to Antigua."

Looking out the window, she sighed. "I wonder if she made it. I wonder if she's still alive."

"Me, too."

The silence in the room felt like it belonged to the past. She chose a chair. "Tell me about the trust."

He dropped into an opposing chair, settled his hands over his stomach, and grinned. "The trust will own the bank and receive the dividends. It will also fund scholarships, make grants, and invest in local communities. Instead of playing Robin Hood, I'll use these resources to improve the community."

"It will be legitimate." She leaned forward, and hope flared in her chest. "You won't have to hide."

He dropped his hands and straightened his posture. "Are we still friends?"

She wanted to be more than friends, but his safety mattered more than her feelings. Swallowing, she lowered her shoulders and released some of the tension keeping her up at night. "Of course, we're friends. It's us against Silvia."

"Vivi…"

She held up her hand. The table gave her coverage, but the nickname chipped away at her defenses. "Don't call me that."

He rounded the table and pulled out the next chair. "I don't want to be friends."

Swiveling away, she shielded the tears in her eyes. She wouldn't interfere with his plans.

He turned her chair to face him. "I want to love you."

"Wanting something isn't enough." She choked back her desire for commitment and focused on his possibilities. "You have so much good left to do."

He took her hand. "If I let myself love you, I won't hold back. Too many people disappeared from my life. What if I hold you too tightly? What if I disappoint you? You don't need me to take care of you. I've always loved that about you and feared it at the same time."

Cupping his cheeks, she brushed her thumbs against his short beard. The roughness felt as familiar as the warmth of his lips, but she refused to rush the moment. "What if you spend the rest of your life second-guessing what might have been?"

He smiled and leaned into her touch. "What if you spend your life regretting what you jumped into?"

"I won't." Her confidence in Damon imbued the words with truth.

"I haven't said these words in a long time." He cleared his throat. "I love you."

For the first time since leaving the mountains, she

caught her breath. The sweet smell of coconut, ginger, and mandarin flooded her senses. Instead of fighting his presence, she laughed and rested her forehead against his forehead. "I love you, too, but this is still my company." She dropped her voice to a whisper. "I want to rip off your shirt and show you how much I missed you, but I have to set a good example."

He raised his head and looked past her shoulder. "So no sex on the conference table?"

Making a mental note to access the security team's video feed, she laughed and wondered what other kinks she might discover in a lifetime. "Not until after hours."

He pulled back and checked his watch. "I can wait."

Precious barked from a sunlit corner.

A knock sounded on the door.

She wet her lips and sighed. "So can I."

Michael opened the door. He held a plastic container of dog treats shaped like squirrels and shook the snacks. "Come see your favorite person."

The dog made a beeline toward the man and followed him from the room.

She smiled at Damon. "So who is on your board of directors?"

"I thought about serving as the president."

She raised an eyebrow. "You'd draw a salary?"

He shrugged. "Man's gotta eat."

"What happened to the USB dollars?"

He shrugged. "It's Silicon Valley. How long can a million last?"

"I'll float you."

He raised an eyebrow. "Will you, now?"

She thought of her account balance. Between

acquiring the office building and donating to an urban forest nonprofit, she felt broke, but she wanted to acknowledge the things bringing meaning to her life. Damon's presence in the room felt like the brass ring she never hoped to grab. She grinned. "Too bad you're a crap investor."

Leaning back, he shook his head. "I was about to offer you a seat on the board."

She reveled in the pleasure of bantering with him. "I'd rather serve the trust."

"I thought you would say that." He held up a thumb. "The board will include a few banking professionals, but I trust Johann, Hadley, Silvia, Shani, Georgios, and Mama Clarke."

"Keeping it in the family." She imagined the crew convening over financial reports and wondered if she could sell tickets to the show.

"Who else would you add?"

When ScanCoin officially collapsed, people would suffer and rage. Already, indignant investors huddled with their lawyers, waved their gala invitations, and demanded Anna Claire's presence. Bank statements and IP addresses piled up in an investigator's office, but nobody could find the woman capable of untangling the web. *The investors took a risk, but Anna Claire's mother will hurt the most.* "Offer Tallulah Agrawal a spot. Let her help shape her daughter's legacy."

Looking out the sunlit windows, he exhaled. "Some problems require complicated solutions. I'm doing the best I can."

Taking his hand, she squeezed it. "I think you're doing really well, Damon."

"Not everyone agrees."

"Silvia gave you lip?"

He shook his head. "Mama Clarke."

Sighing, she stood and pulled him up. "Let's go see her."

"Now?" He glanced at the frosted windows. A silhouetted crowd clustered around Precious. "I thought we could go for a walk and grab dinner."

She stepped closer. "I recommend a clean slate."

"A clean slate?" He frowned.

"Before you see my underwear."

Wrapping his arms around her waist, he dropped his head to her neck and inhaled. "Well, if you're offering."

Tilting her head, she considered giving her employees a show that rivaled trend lines and artificial intelligence. "I am, but I want you to be all in, and I don't think you can do that without Mama Clarke."

He grinned.

She walked from the conference room and grabbed her purse from her office. Precious basked in the attention of her over-paid and over-degreed employees. "Office mascot?"

Micheal tossed the dog another treat.

"Not too many," she said. "I'm getting my car. Bring her down in a few minutes."

Employee number one, lead Machine Leaning expert, and lover of dogs, nodded.

The elevator doors opened. Walking past Damon, she entered the stainless-steel cage, faced the doors, and gripped the handrail with both hands. The chain on her purse swung and clanked against the wall.

He pressed the button for the ground floor.

Reaching past him, she hit the stop button.

He raised his eyebrows. "Is there a problem?"

"You're dressed."

He grinned.

Needing no further encouragement, she unbuttoned her sheath dress and let it pool on the ground. Standing in heels and black lace underwear, she gripped the handrails and thrust out her chest. *Three, Two, One...*

He swore, shucked his shirt, and closed the distance. "I like it when you don't play fair." Gripping her hips, his thumbs rubbed her skin through the lace. "You have no idea how many times I've thought about you like this." Pausing, he looked at the camera in the corner. "What about the security feed?"

Wrapping her arms around his neck, she shrugged. "Being the boss has its rewards."

He pulled her flush against his erection. "Exhibitionist."

She shifted her hips, loving the feel of him growing beneath her touch. "I want what I want." She ran her hands up his sides. "And what I want is you."

Releasing her, he dropped his jeans and stepped out of his underwear.

She pulled off her thong and added it to the clothes scattered on the floor.

"I don't have a condom," he said.

"I really don't care." She imagined a plucky little boy with curls jabbing Damon's thigh. "Having your kid would be a blast, but I get your concerns." She opened her purse, grabbed the foil packet, and dropped the rest of the contents onto the floor. "You're lucky one of us is optimistic enough to come prepared." Winking, she tossed him the packet.

He caught the condom, laughed, and lifted her.

"You say the sweetest things."

Bracing her hands on his shoulders, she met his gaze. "Are you sure? About everything?"

Claiming her lips, he pulled her flush against his chest.

Letting his mouth convince her, she tightened her hold. Her body responded like a racehorse allowed to run. She rubbed against him, desperate to feel him inside her. Breaking the kiss, she tightened her legs around his waist and met his gaze. "Are you sure?"

"I love you, Vivi." He closed his eyes. "I'm still learning what that means"—shifting her, he made eye contact—"but damn, it feels good."

Chapter Twenty

Vivian parked her car on the street in front of Mama Clarke's convenience store. Faded advertisements plastered the windows, but workers stirred cans of paint by the front door. She turned to Damon. "Your grandmother is upgrading?"

He smiled. "People breaking into the store and stealing packs of cigarettes don't worry her. Technology and neighborhood pride protect her better than thick metal bars."

"The trust's first investment?"

He shrugged. "The trust doesn't exist yet. I have to claim the transponder from the police department."

"But it will exist," she said. "What will you call it?"

"All Hail Damon."

She slapped his thigh.

Rubbing his leg, he grinned. "I don't know, Vivi. I'll pick something catchy and approachable. Maybe the neighborhood kids can help me come up with a name."

She rolled her eyes. "They'll come up with a combination of superheroes and bathroom humor."

He reached for the door handle. "I'll limit the naming competition to the high school students and recent graduates. They'll understand what's on the line."

His dedication to the kids inspired pride. "The

futures they imagine are on the line."

He nodded. "Exactly."

She climbed from the car and examined the nondescript buildings on the block. "You should open the bank's headquarters in East Palo Alto."

"On this block?"

"We need a third person to help run the trust." She eyed Mama Clarke's store. "You and I can't serve as the only trustees."

"I know." He scratched his head. "Who do you recommend?"

Grinning, she thought of a pain-in-the-ass woman whose freckles and sandy blonde hair hid a quick wit. "What about Buffy?"

Frowning, he cocked his head. "Hadley's sidekick?"

"She's less sidekick, more menace. After she blew the air horn at Hadley's graduation ceremony, I thought I lost my hearing for good."

He shoved his hands in his jeans pockets. "Why her?"

Thinking about the baby shower and her diplomatic gestures, she grinned. "Buffy doesn't take lip from anyone."

"Even you?"

She fell in step. "Even me."

He pushed open the glass door and held it. A bell chimed. "Maybe she could give me a few tips."

Slapping his butt seemed inappropriate, but she narrowed her gaze and thought about the satisfaction of making contact. *I can wait until we get home.* Walking inside the store, she grinned. Advertisements for wire transfers and lottery tickets hung from the ceiling, but the interior smelled like a county fair. Cinnamon, grease, and tobacco mingled with a heavy dose of cleaning products. *I bet Mama Clarke makes a mean churro.* She eyed the leaning bags of corn chips, Mexican snack foods, and fried chicken. *When does she have time to cook this food?*

Mama Clarke stood behind the counter. Arms crossed, she raised an eyebrow and dropped her chin.

Self-conscious, Vivian wished she added jewelry to her workday ensemble. Glancing at her unblemished white, leather sneakers, she grinned and looked up. *Women show their strength in different ways.*

Mama Clarke shook her head and glared at her grandson. "You come to admit your mistakes?"

"Nope," he said. "Still starting a bank"—he took her hand—"but I won't have to do it on my own."

Mama Clarke braced her hands on the counter. "You shouldn't risk what you have."

Releasing her hand, he spun and held wide his arms, encompassing the store. "You took a risk to start the convenience store. Look at the returns."

Mama Clark's gaze softened. "I'm looking at them."

He walked up to the counter, leaned over acrylic-shielded lottery tickets, and kissed his grandmother's cheek.

Vivian smiled. The loud, smacking sound announced his loyalty, but she wondered what Mama Clarke would think about what she and her precious grandson did in the elevator. "Hah."

Pivoting, Mama Clarke stared. "You got something to say, girl?"

She cleared her throat and smiled. "Thank you for

sending Damon to see me."

"I didn't have anything to do with it."

"Oh?"

The older woman cracked a smile. "His ass woulda grown roots at the library."

She doubted Damon's time at the library would be endless. He had too many ideas and too much enthusiasm for a life among the stacks. "Like, I said, thanks."

He winked and looked at his grandmother. "Vivi's onboard with the bank and the trust. You going to make this difficult, Mama Clarke?"

"I only had one son." She braced her hands on the counter. "Your daddy loved you more than anyone else in the world. How could I do less?"

Vivian's heart opened even wider. She loved Damon and respected her family, but Mama Clarke changed her life to meet her grandson's needs. From welfare recipient to small business owner, she took risks and crafted a life for herself and for Damon. She wondered what happened to the woman's husband, but she tabled that question, smiled, and wrapped an arm around Damon's waist. "You did good."

Mama Clarke dropped her chin. "I know I did. Make sure you deserve him."

She swallowed. "Why do you say that?"

The older woman wrinkled her nose. "I'm guessing you spend all your time at the office. How much time you got left for Damon? Or my grandbabies?"

"Grandbabies." She laughed and met Damon's gaze. "I like her."

"An army of foster children." He crossed his arms over his chest.

She raised an eyebrow.

He swallowed. "And a few of our own."

Mama Clarke whistled. "Well, I'll be damned."

"Are you sure?" Her whispered question meant more than the piles of lace waiting at home. She wanted a little boy just like Damon, but her heart could grow to love multiple children. Compromise meant success, and if she and Damon could meet halfway, they could solve any problems.

Damon dropped his hands. "If that's what we decide, I'm all in."

She grinned and resisted throwing her arms around him.

The bell chimed.

Looking over her shoulder, she saw Shani walk into the store carrying a white paper bag. The woman's jeans hugged every inch of her hips, and her knitted crop top teased a wide expanse of skin. Even though she felt secure in Damon's love, she stood straighter and raised her chin.

The woman paused, made eye contact, and sauntered to the counter. She placed the bag on the scratched acrylic. "Mama Clarke, I brought you the things you needed from the drugstore."

"What did you need?" Damon asked. "I could have picked them up."

Mama Clarke brushed aside the gesture, lifted the bag, and stored it out of sight. "Shush, boy. Some things are none of your concern."

He frowned and stepped closer. "You sick?"

"No."

"You need something for the house?"

Shani laughed. "She has a date."

He crossed his arms. "A date. Who?"

"None of your damn business!" Mama Clarke slapped the counter.

Vivian choked back her laughter.

He jabbed the counter with a stiff finger. "I want to meet him."

"Don't you have plans, boy?" Mama Clarke glanced over. "I won't live forever. Go open a bottle of wine and get busy. Hell, that one she brought to the party's still on top of the fridge."

Shani coughed.

She rolled her eyes. "Next time, I'll bring flowers."

Mama Clarke laughed. "Whatever you're doing, keep doing it. Don't let go of him."

She smiled at Damon and felt warm inside. "I won't."

He considered the three women and backed up. "Um. Are there, like, deliveries out back?"

Mama Clarke slapped the countertop and laughed, grasping her chest. "You always was a softie."

Vivian cocked her head and considered the woman. *I should put her in charge of contract negotiations.*

"You don't have time to be opening boxes of chips," Mama Clarke said. "Go put together your bank and trust."

Shani cocked her hip. "You going legit?"

He shrugged. "I recouped some of my cash."

Vivian rolled her eyes. *Some of it.*

"Doll, I planned to ask you to be on the board of directors for a bank."

"Damon, I run a salon." She flicked a piece of dirt from her nail. "How can I help run a bank?"

"You're a good boss, and you're in the black." He

397

looked around the store and whistled. "I know how hard you work. You're two steps ahead of most business owners."

Shani flipped her hair over her shoulder. "True." She narrowed her gaze. "Does it pay?"

Vivian stepped forward. "Most small banks pay their directors an annual retainer of about ten thousand dollars."

Shani narrowed her gaze. "Aren't you gone yet?"

Tilting her head, she smiled. "They also pay per-meeting fees and equity compensation, but we hoped you would do it for less."

She narrowed her gaze. "How much less?"

"Much less." She dropped her chin. "Consider it volunteer work."

Damon cleared his throat. "It's not that bad. You'd basically help manage my money."

"Amen," Shani said.

He laughed. "But you won't spend it."

Shani pulled out her lip gloss and reapplied the shine. "I have money of my own. I'm sure I could pick up a few investment tricks."

"That's probably a conflict of interest," Vivian said.

Shani glared.

She held up her hands. "What do I know?"

"You must know something, girl." Shani popped her gloss back into her jeans. "You landed my man."

Hearing a concession, she grinned.

The bell chimed, and Johann walked into the store.

His face looked sallow, and his blood rimmed his eyes. She rushed to his side. "Are you okay?"

"So much blood," he said.

Biting her lip, she looked at Damon.

He cocked his head and walked up to Johann. "What's up, Boss?"

"Two girls. Amalie and Adela." He shook his head. "They're fine. Hadley's fine, but she wants cigars for the staff. I offered my Cubans, but she wants something specific." He pulled a piece of paper from his pocket and looked at Mama Clarke. "What in the world is a sweet cigarillo?"

She laughed at the cheap souvenir. *Hadley might have all the money in the world, but I'm glad she still has a sense of humor. What else goes in the gift bags? Cans of beer?* She snorted. *The twins might be half-German, but the swag bag is all Americana.*

Mama Clarke took the paper from Johann and pulled down a box from the shelf behind her. She slid the box across the countertop and crossed her arms. "That company is the largest cigar maker in the world."

Johann took the box, frowned, and shook his head. "Not in my world."

Laughing, Damon slapped him on the back. "Congratulations, Boss. They're on the house."

Turning, Johann inclined his head. "Thanks." He looked up from the box and took a deep breath. "I heard you came into money."

Damon worked his jaw. "Word travels fast."

Johann paused and made eye contact. "Vivian didn't tell me."

That bond broke a long time ago.

"Who did?" Damon asked.

Johann pivoted. "The police department knows what's on the transponder."

Damon shrugged. "I'll handle it."

Johann narrowed his gaze. "How did you get that key?"

"A side investment." Damon took her hand. "It paid off big."

She squeezed his hand and looked at the two men. Feeling no tension between her past and her present, she thought about the future. "Damon picked up a few investment tips at the Greek Restaurant. He's funneling the windfall into a structured arrangement."

Johann shifted the box of cigars to his hip. "Really?"

"Damon and I would appreciate your help," she said.

"For the foreseeable future, my expertise is confined to diapers." Clearing his throat, he headed for the door but paused and looked over his right shoulder. "As soon as I come up for air, I'm available to help you two."

She trusted his commitment and grinned. With Johann's expertise and credibility, Damon would have an easier time establishing his credibility. A diverse set of skills and assets would set him up for success.

Johann stopped and scratched his head. "I hear stories about old hard drives and first-generation cryptocurrency investments. Those drives must be worth a fortune by now." He shrugged. "When you ran your side business, I'm sure you never came across that kind of junk."

"Mostly cell phones, knives, and cans of pepper spray." Damon shrugged. "A few unidentifiable electronics. Maybe a hard drive."

"Just an idea." Johann rubbed his eyebrows. "In the meantime, I can't think straight on so little sleep." He left the store.

In his wake, the bell over the door chimed.

"Who was that? He's hot," Shani asked.

Vivian shook her head. "Taken."

The woman sighed and headed for the door. "All the good ones are gone."

She looped her arm through Damon's arm. "No, but you'll find them where you least expect them."

"If you say so. You were certainly a surprise."

Vivian gasped.

Damon coughed and slapped his chest, but his laughter escaped.

Squaring her shoulders, Shani set her hips in motion, and let the door slam in her wake.

Watching her leave, Vivian smiled and appreciated the depth lurking beneath Shani's lacquered, pink exterior. As much as she empathized with Anna Claire, she knew the billionaire had one objective, and that shallow pursuit of wealth would have limited their acquaintance to friendly cocktails. *I'll take Shani's honesty any day of the week.* She watched Shani strut toward her car. *However, I'm not putting her in charge of my wardrobe.*

"You going to stand around all day, or you going to do work?" Mama Clarke asked.

Damon laughed and walked through a pair of swinging double doors.

Alone with the older woman, Vivian turned and faced Mama Clarke.

"I took the belt to that boy when he needed it." She crossed her arms. "I still have that belt."

She smiled. "Message received." *Although I'm more likely to tie him up than whip him.*

Mama Clarke snorted, pulled out a rag, and wiped down the acrylic.

Wait, was she threatening to take a belt to me?

Returning through the doors, Damon pushed a dolly loaded with cardboard boxes. He stacked the boxes by a display stand and tossed her his pocketknife.

Catching it in the air, she flipped open the blade and grinned.

"You know how to use that thing?" Mama Clarke asked.

Thinking about the cut she made to Anna Claire's arm, she sliced the packing tape and dug into the box. "When it counts, I learn fast." Expecting laughter from Damon, she looked up and made eye contact.

He softened his gaze and leaned against the doorjamb. "You can do anything you set your mind to, and I'm so proud of you."

Reveling in his easy love, she considered abandoning the box, but he shared her interests and her heart. They had plenty of time to merge their lives and iron out the details. In the meantime, she would stock the store's shelves and while away an afternoon listening to Mama Clarke's stories. She winked. "I love you, too."

A word about the author...

Amy Craig lives in Baton Rouge, Louisiana, with her family and a small menagerie of pets. She writes contemporary romances and women's fiction with intelligent and empathetic heroines. She can't always vouch for the men. She has worked as an engineer, project manager, and incompetent waitress. In her spare time, she plays tennis and expands her husband's honey-do list.

https://www.amy-craig.com/

Other Titles by this Author
A Winter Rose
The Peninsula, tie-in to *The Crevasse*

www.ingramcontent.com/pod-product-compliance
Lightning Source LLC
Chambersburg PA
CBHW072259020726
47501CB00002B/314